To All

OPTICAL ILLUSION

PAINT #1
An M/M Romance

by

EMMA JAYE

Amazon Bestseller

Great to finally
meet you !

Emma Jaye
xx

First Published Sept: Aug 2016
Purindoors Publications

Editing
SublimeNovels.com

Follow Emma Jaye via the following platforms for exclusive teasers, giveaways, and more:
FACEBOOK

NEWSLETTER

emmajayeauthor.com

GOODREADS

TRIGGER WARNING:

Not suitable for readers under 18.

Contains scenes of drug taking, violence, mental health issues and adult scenes.

This book is dedicated to all the people who have played a huge role in turning my words into stories.

Nero, who is my go to cover designer, who still manages to shock me, love you!

Renee, promotor extraordinaire, an unsung heroine who deserves to be recognized for all the work she does for her kidnapped authors.

Trish, Anita, Layla, Neil, E.G. and all my other author buddies and beta readers.

To my family, for putting up with 'hmm, what?' when they've been taking to me.

And lastly, for the guys of Years and Years, who songs provided the inspiration for Chris.

CONTENTS

CHAPTER 1

Jase

"You sure this is what you want?" Matt asked quietly, eyes on the ground in front of them as they walked back from the school. Even though they could negotiate the shortcut around the back of the church blindfolded, where his feet were going was suddenly incredibly interesting to Jase's best friend.

He'd been putting off telling Matt he wanted to leave home and had been planning this conversation for months. His parents had been sworn to secrecy so it wouldn't disturb Matt's GCSE revision. They had just got their results and time had finally crept up on him. It was time to bite the bullet time to make sure, once and for all, that Matt didn't consider him anything more than a friend. Because if he didn't, all bets, and all plans to leave, were off.

It was a gorgeous summer evening, grasshoppers sang in the grass and stars shone down between the trees as the pair made their way back to their parents' homes in the sleepy Sussex village of Stepthorne. It didn't seem right that everything was so normal, so calm, when he was in turmoil.

The pair of only children had grown up next door to each other in almost identical houses. Their mothers, despite the twenty-year age gap between them, had shared their care. Matt's mum worked in the office of their family haulage firm. Jase's mum was a teacher at the village primary school; his father was an ex-army Captain turned high-court bailiff. Both their fathers worked long hours and were often away from home, so the next-door neighbours spent a lot of time together to stave off the loneliness.

It hadn't been an exciting childhood for either of them. But while Matt had been content to play with his toy lorries, Jase's imagination had roamed the world, being a hero. Even though they preferred different toys, they seldom argued. Jase made room in his games for vehicles and

Matt suffered 'end of the world' scenarios as long as they escaped in cars. The only type of toy they both possessed were Transformers.

People who didn't know better often assumed they were related even though Matt was dark-haired and slightly shorter than his blond and green-eyed best friend. They'd gone through school together getting in trouble for smoking behind the bike sheds, climbing trees, making the village girls squeal by putting frogs in their bags, and playing kiss chase. Although Jase usually did the catching and Matt did all the kissing.

Their idyllic existence hit a major bump seven months ago. Matt's mother, Auntie Gwen as Jase had always called her, suffered a stroke. The family employed an au pair to help. Matt started working after school and on weekends at the family firm to fill the void his mother had left.

The time Matt had for Jase decreased even more when he started going out with Sarah, a short, curvy, sarcastic blonde girl that Jase couldn't help liking. She made Matt smile, something that hadn't happened a lot over the last few months. The fact that it wasn't him putting that expression on Matt's face gnawed at his insides, but he kept his own smile on his face, because that was what his friend needed.

The last few months, coping with his mum's illness, his dad's frantic efforts to keep home and business going had taken its toll on Matt and his father even though Jase and his parents had tried to help out as much as possible.

The end of year public exams had come at exactly the wrong time for Matt. It hadn't helped that Sarah had achieved straight A's. Jase had done ok, but he almost wished he hadn't as Matt had barely scraped a crop of D's.

When they'd opened their brown results envelopes, having been camped out with their friends on the school's front lawn that morning, Matt congratulated both of them.

"How d'you do?" Jase asked after he and Sarah had shared their news.

Matt showed him his paper and shrugged. "Grades don't matter when you're the boss of the company."

Sarah had almost pushed Jase out the way to embrace Matt, and they'd stayed locked together while Jase had tried, and failed, to pretend it didn't bother him that Matt preferred Sarah. That was the moment Jase's decision about signing his army application solidified, but he'd pussyfooted around telling Matt until after they'd walked Sarah home. She'd made numerous hints all evening that she wanted Matt to herself, but Matt told her they had plenty of alone time coming over the holidays before she went to sixth form.

"But the army?" Matt asked. "Surely there's something else you can do instead of getting shot at? With your grades, you could go to sixth form. If it's action you're after, I'm sure your dad would find you something in the bailiff business."

Jase shoved his hands in the pockets of his jeans and hunched his shoulders; this was as hard as he'd thought it'd be.

"I've listened to Dad all my life about what he got up to in the army. It sounds interesting, and I can make a real difference. You know what a wannabe hero complex I've got. You're all set up, career, girlfriend, but I haven't found my place yet. All I know is that my life... isn't here."

Matt stiffened at the implied insult. "Too good for us 'boring people' are you?"

Jase let out a bark of wry laughter and shook his head. "You'll be too busy working and getting laid to even realise I'm gone."

Matt turned towards him as he paused to open the churchyard gate.

"Is that what this is about? You're running off to join the army because I'm busy with the firm and Sarah? I know you felt a bit like a third wheel tonight and you're not great at the social stuff, but mate, Stephanie's been making eyes at you for months. She's up for it, I promise you. Sarah's her best friend, they tell each other everything. My old man will give you a job even if your dad can't sort you out with something because of your age. We could double date, work together, and hang out all the time. It'll be great."

Matt's enthusiasm for his plan was painful, even more so because it would work, or at least it would have done, except for one tiny fact.

"Let it go will you? You know haulage is never going to be my thing. I'd get bored, muck it up and it'd cause a problem between us. The army doesn't just swallow you up for years. I'll be back every now and again, my parents still live next door, remember? But I can't stay here for the rest of my life."

Personally, Jase thought his little speech, which he'd practiced in his head hundreds of times, had been damn good, but Matt clearly didn't think so.

"Why the hell not? If you want to travel, take a gap year, see the world, then come back where you belong, with me."

Matt had never uttered a truer word, and that was the problem in a nutshell. Jase looked into the eyes that had occupied every thought, every fantasy, for years. He hoped he saw sorrow and longing in those dark depths. Matt had always done everything people expected of him, perhaps Sarah was just another one of the 'expected' things Matt thought he had to do.

A spark of hope that he'd been wrong all these years, blossomed. He was planning to leave anyway, but if he didn't find out, didn't make sure, he knew he'd spend his life regretting this moment. Plucking up every ounce of courage he possessed, he stepped forward and closed the gap between them. With a dry mouth and heart pounding, he lifted his hand to cup Matt's face and stroked his cheek with his thumb. His resolve strengthened with the hint of Matt's spicy body spray that he hadn't been able to smell until he was this close.

"This is why I have to leave."

Matt opened his mouth to speak, but Jase put his thumb on his lips. "I need you to know that I've loved you since we were kids."

Matt took hold of Jase's wrist, eyes glassy with tears. "I know mate, it's always been you and me against the world, we're the terrible twins right? So why are you fucking off to God knows where and leaving me? I know your dad's been pressurising you to join up, but you don't have to. It's not too late to change your mind; you haven't signed anything yet, have you?"

Matt's eyes widened as Jase traced his lips with his thumb. Convincing himself that Matt was shocked in a good way, rather than frozen in horror, he plunged on.

"You've never noticed what was right in front of you unless it had an engine in it, have you? Did you ever wonder why I'm never with a girl unless we're double dating? Or why I'm always around whenever you're getting changed?"

Matt shoved at his chest, forcing Jase to step back. "Ha ha, very funny. Where's the camera?"

Jase dropped his hand as his heart cracked, even though this was exactly what he'd expected, what he'd known deep down. Matt was straight, through and through; wishing he wasn't, wouldn't change the truth. But now the floodgates were open, he couldn't shut up. He needed his best friend to understand the part of him that he'd kept hidden for so long. Looking down at the grass, he gathered himself, then looked back up into Matt's red and confused face, tears stinging his eyes.

"It's not a joke, I wish it were. Seeing you with Sarah tears me up inside. I love you, Mathew Kemp, and not just as a brother. I want to touch and kiss you, I want to see your face, hear you gasp, when I make you–"

Matt shoved him so hard he stumbled backward to keep from ending up on his arse on the grass.

"What the fuck? When have I ever given you the idea I'm into blokes? And since when the fuck were you?" Matt whispered harshly as he pushed his hand through his thick, almost black hair and turned to check they were alone.

Jase half-expected Matt to run off, or punch him, instead he blew out a breath and looked up at the clear August night sky for inspiration. Then he turned back to Jase who was wishing some stray sniper would take him out. A quick clean death would be preferable to this.

"No one saw, so let's just forget that ever happened, ok?"

Jase sighed and rubbed the tear that was threatening to escape away with the back of his hand. Although he'd hoped he wouldn't, Matt rejecting his advances wasn't unexpected. The dismissal of his feelings as something that could be forgotten as easily as a petty argument, hurt even more. Leaving and getting a fresh start was the only thing left to do.

"If I could forget what I feel for you, don't you think I would have done it by now?" Jase said quietly as the crack his heart became a chasm.

"Bye Matt," he said to his shoes, hunched his shoulders and walked away, knowing he'd just destroyed the best friendship he'd ever had.

When he got home, he signed the final paperwork for the army. His dad beam with pride.

CHAPTER 2

Jase

Writing that first letter to Matt from basic training a month later was one of the hardest things he'd ever done. To his joy, he received a reply within days.

We all do stupid things sometimes; I've already forgotten it.

Yeah, he'd been stupid, naive even, but he was grateful that his personal issues hadn't completely fucked up their friendship. If Matt wanted to forget that his best friend loved him, he'd take it, because the alternative was far too painful.

That line was the only time Matt ever referred to the incident. The rest of the letter mentioned the business, his mother's health, how his dad seemed a lot happier now that the au pair, Marietta, had taken up residence in the spare room to look after his mum full-time.

The added, *Thinking of you and all those hot squaddies, wish I was there, luv Sarah xx* in purple ink was like a kick to the balls. He imagined them lying together on Matt's bed as they wrote it, laughing about him and cuddling.

* * *

Over the next decade, Jason Rosewood travelled to, and worked in, some of the most godforsaken, troubled and often starkly beautiful places in the world. There had been letters, phone calls and the occasional visit home. Neither Matt nor Jase mentioned what had happened on results day again.

Jase could almost believe Matt had genuinely forgotten about his stupid confession of undying love until he brushed up against him unintentionally in the pub a year later. Matt shifted deliberately away.

It hurt, but at least their friendship survived, even if it had been awkward for a couple of years. And right now a friendly voice was exactly what he needed.

"Matt Kemp speaking."

The pang of loss was sharp as the voice on the other end of the phone no longer gave him shivers of desire. Even his subconscious had moved Matt entirely into 'friend' category. Over the years, he'd tried to convince himself that it had just been a childhood crush, but he'd never stopped comparing other guys to Matt. Nobody ever matched up, probably nobody ever would. He'd come to terms with a lonely existence, peppered with short, friendly, and ultimately meaningless, hook-ups to relieve the tension and boredom of army life.

He schooled his voice into what he hoped was a 'normal' tone despite the fact that he shouldn't be out of bed and his limbs trembled. "So formal these days, Mr Kemp. Anyone would think you were the owner of a million pound company."

Kemp International Haulage had gone from six vehicles to twenty in the eight years since Matt had taken over. He still lived in his parents' old three bedroomed home, even though his mum had passed and his dad was in a nursing home due to dementia. When Jase had joked that he really should use some of his 'millions' to buy a bigger house, he'd always given the excuse that his dad would get confused if the house wasn't the same when he visited.

Jase didn't own anything apart from the clothes on his back and a few odds and ends in his boyhood bedroom. His achievements weren't in material objects. Rising to the rank of sergeant in the military police, he'd been offered a commission a month ago if he signed up for another three years. With a little more time, he could reach the rank his father had and perhaps even higher. Nothing would please his dad more, although his mum probably wanted him to settle down and produce grandchildren. He'd never 'come out' to them, although they might simply assume he was a career soldier, rather than gay; both resulted in him being single with no intention of changing things.

He had intended to sign on the dotted line and accept the commission after his shift that day. It was the afternoon a teenage boy decided that becoming a martyr was an excellent way to spend his Tuesday.

Jase had been dealing with identifying a soldier accused by an Afghani man of pursuing his daughter. Keeping the peace between horny, lonely squaddies and the local population was one of his main roles. A glance at a girl that was considered completely normal at home could cause problems here.

Pausing to gather the Farsi words he needed in his mind, he started slowly. "Mr Marwat, I can assure you that we will investigate this matter fully. The British army does not tolerate–"

He hadn't even seen the boy who blew himself up on the doorstep of the military police station. His female colleague, who had stepped around the counter to try and calm Mr Marwat as she spoke far better Farsi than Jase, died instantly, as had the irate parent.

The counter saved Jase's life, but not his ankle; if he hadn't been standing half way across the gap in the counter, he might have gotten away with only one hell of a headache and punctured eardrums. Everyone kept telling him what a lucky bastard he'd been, but two weeks later, his leg still hurt like a bitch.

Unfortunately, the army thought it would be difficult to be an effective officer with a smashed ankle. Something about being unable to chase suspects with a walking stick. When he'd woken up in the medical wing of Camp Bastion, the offer of a commission had changed to either an honourable discharge with a disability pension or a permanent desk job at the Military Corrective Training Centre in Colchester. Working in a prison office was probably almost as bad as being an inmate. Plus, his sentence would last far longer than the maximum two years that prisoners were allowed to spend there.

He'd been shipped home a week ago and had immediately undergone four hours of reconstructive surgery. This was the first time he'd been out of bed without a wheelchair or a physio hovering over him.

"Jase! How the bloody hell are you? Where are you? Stupid question, you probably can't say. More importantly are you coming back for a visit soon?"

"I'm coming home, for good." He smiled slightly at the pause on the other end of the phone.

"Did you just say..." The hope in Matt's voice made him grin as he pictured the look on his face.

"I did. I'm officially out in a month."

The next part would not be so easy and he'd spent the last twenty-four hours considering what to say. As his injuries hadn't been life threatening, and he'd only been unconscious for less than an hour, his next of kin hadn't been informed. It was up to him what he told them, and if he had anything to do with it, it would be lies all the way. It was done and dusted now, and telling them what a lucky escape he'd had would just distress them unnecessarily.

"Got any jobs for an ex-military copper with a limp?"

"What d'you mean, a limp? Have you been hurt? Fuck, did you get shot? How many times did I tell you joining the army was a stupid idea?" The immediate, genuine concern in Matt's voice as he talked a mile a minute caused a grin.

No one at home had any idea where he'd been stationed or even that he was back in the country. Workwise, he'd always played his cards close to his chest. As an experienced officer, he went where and when he was told, sometimes with very little notice. To avoid disappointment, and his mother's embarrassing 'welcome home' parties, he'd never give them set dates about when he'd be visiting until he was almost on the doorstep.

"Thousands. I've got your dulcet tones whinging about it as my ringtone. I plan on telling people I got shot in Afghanistan saving sick, disabled orphans from a fate worse than death. It'll

7

definitely get me more free booze and sympathy than admitting I shattered my ankle falling over a penguin when I was pissed after a night out on the Falklands."

Matt let out a bark of laughter. "Only you could survive more than a decade in some of the world's worst war zones and then get felled by a bird. Although thinking about it, they never were your strong point were they?"

Jase shifted position to ease his throbbing ankle as he leaned up against the wall in the corridor of the military wing of the Queen Elizabeth Hospital in Birmingham.

"Laugh it up, home boy. At least I've been further than Bognor Regis."

He could almost see Matt's hurt expression at the denigration of his family's traditional holiday spot. Jase had accompanied them on many occasions, just as Matt had joined his family on holiday, except the Rosewoods went abroad. Spain and Portugal had seemed so exotic when they'd been kids.

"What's wrong with Bognor? You've got to admit, there aren't any flocks of roaming killer penguins. Still, I bet all the gay blokes in the world will be mortified that you won't be chasing them for a while, or have you got someone special these days?"

Even though they usually skirted the issue of Matt's love life, Matt always asked after his. Jase always pretended his sex life was fantastic to ease Matt's mind about not being the person he'd wanted him to be all those years ago.

"No one special, but you know me, I'm never lonely. You?"

Matt had broken up with Sarah; or rather, she'd broken up with him, a few months after Jase left for basic training. She'd wanted to concentrate on her studies, and it had paid off. She'd been a GP in Stepthorne for the past three years. Matt had dated girls for six or seven months on several occasions, but a workaholic who, up until recently, shared a home with his bad tempered, increasingly senile father, apparently wasn't conducive to a long-term, romantic relationship.

The long pause on the other end of the phone had his attention. "You still there? Matt? Talk to me."

"I'm getting married. You were going to be the first person I told after Dad. But it's a bit of a last minute thing, we only decided last night and the ceremony's next Thursday."

'Impulsive' was not in Matt's emotional repertoire. "She's pregnant?"

"Yeah, but that's not the only reason. I love her...and her son, he's five. It'd mean a lot to have my family beside me. Dad isn't with it most of the time and although I've known some of the drivers for years, they're not family; not like you and your folks. I know they'll be there but... I know this is a long shot, especially as you're on the other side of the world, is there any chance you can get here? The reception's at the social club."

Army wheels could work painfully slowly. Sorting out a discharge from hospital in his current condition in less than a week wasn't going to be easy. It would have been impossible if he actually been in Port Stanley but it wouldn't be as difficult as standing beside the love of his life as he married someone he could never compete with.

"I'll be there. You know I'll always be there for you." He said automatically. "But if she ever hurts you, I'll have her guts for garters."

"Knowing Kate, she'd have yours," Matt chuckled. "Do you remember Sarah's little sister?"

The image of a diminutive, fiery redhead popped into his mind. Good God, Matt's goose was well and truly cooked. Sarah had been possessive, but her little sister had performed sneak attacks on them at school and on the way home. One minute you'd be walking along, minding your own business, the next you had a little sister hanging off your neck. The grin faded from his face as he remembered what else Matt had said. Kate had a son. Other people's lives had moved on to the next stage, and he was still pretty much the same as he'd been a decade ago, except for a few scars.

He looked up as Yvonne, or Captain Craig as he was meant to call the doctor in charge of his ward, strode down the corridor in her horribly shiny, creaking black lace-up shoes. If Kate gave him the shivers, Captain Craig gave him full on palpitations.

"Sergeant Rosewood," she barked. "You're meant to be in physio."

"Crap, I've got to go. The wicked witch has found me, see you next week." Putting the phone down without waiting for Matt's reply, he turned his best smile on the middle-aged nurse.

"Just phoning home, my best mate's getting married next week, seems he's erm, got a girl in the family way. Any chance I can be there? Apparently I'm the best man."

Her eyebrows rose an inch "Lord help us if you're the best we've got in the man department. He'd be better off with a spaniel. Far more reliable."

"Please?"

Yvonne narrowed her eyes, but he held his ground. Facing insurgents was easier than this.

She gave an exasperated sigh, hands on her hips. "Oh all right, I'll see what I can do to get you to the ceremony, if only for that poor girl." She wagged a finger at him. "But I'll only talk to the doctor if you obey my instructions to the letter for the next six days. You will be using crutches when you do stand-up, which I expect you to keep to a minimum. There will be no stag night, no alcohol with your medication and no women for you, my boy," she said firmly. "And if you destroy the surgeon's handiwork, I'll make sure every single medication you receive when you're back here will be given by injection or suppository. Have I made myself clear?"

Even though he felt a little sick at her diabolical threat, he gave her his best winning smile. "Yes, Ma'am. You can trust me."

Her raised eyebrows and pursed lips told him just how much she bought his act, but then she moved in beside him to help him back to the ward.

CHAPTER 3

Jase

"For God's sake, stop sweating, you'll look like you've been in a sauna by the time we get to the reception," Jase murmured as he adjusted Matt's lavender tie. All his weight was balanced on his good leg with one crutch tucked under his armpit.

They were standing in a side room in Stepthorne's tiny church. The flint building echoed with five hundred years of christenings, weddings, and funerals, as well as the memories of two little boys poking each other and giggling their way through nativity plays and harvest festivals.

Matt's mother, and both their grandparents and great-grandparents were buried in the churchyard. They had both been christened here and their parents had been married here, although Matt's parents had married fifteen years before Jase's.

"And you're so tough that you wouldn't be sweating if you were getting married in a few minutes?" Matt raised a dark eyebrow.

Jase snorted. "Like that's ever going to happen."

"Gays get married too. You never know, you could meet the love of your life in the next few hours."

The twinkle in Matt's eye reminded Jase exactly how much he loved him, although his passion and fierce hurt had mellowed over the years. Being his friend, having him in his life in whatever capacity Matt would accept, was a hundred times better than nothing.

It had been nearly ten o'clock at night when Jase's dad had finally pulled back onto their driveway. When he'd told his parents where he was, his dad had insisted on coming to get him. The hard look his dad had given him when he'd trotted out the penguin story told him that the old soldier didn't believe a word. It was also clear that his father would respect his decision to keep things to himself. Getting his own head around what had happened before dealing with the emotions of his loved ones was his priority.

Distracted by the memories of the smell of blood, choking dust and evacuated bowels, he answered Matt's question about the possibility of getting married himself one day without thinking.

"Never going to happen. My personal happy ever after sailed a long time ago."

Matt shifted uncomfortably. Cursing himself for a fool, Jase hopped back as step as he patted Matt on the upper arm.

"Don't worry about it; these painkillers are buggering with my head."

"Listen Jase, maybe you coming today was a bad idea, if it's going to be too difficult for you..."

Pulling a smile up from his single highly polished boot, he said, "I wouldn't miss this for all the money in the world. You're family, and you always will be. My feelings are my problem, not yours. Besides, seeing this today will be good for me. Turn a mental page, so to speak."

"Yeah?"

The hope in those dark eyes still hurt. This was clearly what Matt wanted to hear, and today, he'd do everything possible to make his day as perfect as possible. Dealing with his mother's death at seventeen, his father's early onset Alzheimer's a few years later, and having to take over the family haulage firm at eighteen had been incredibly hard for Matt.

Guilt still gnawed at him for not being here to help his best friend through those tough times. He'd managed to get special dispensation to attend Gwen's funeral, but he'd had to be back at his barracks by nightfall. Now he was here, he'd do his best to make up for the years he'd been away. Taking on a ready-made family wouldn't be the easiest thing for a somewhat emotionally repressed guy like Matt, and he was determined to help. It was the nearest he'd probably ever get to having a family of his own.

Forcing a grin, he gave Matt's silver-grey clad shoulder a gentle punch. "You bet. Now let's get out there before the bride turns up. Having her pissed off at you on your wedding night would not be good. She'll be hormonal enough with a bun in the oven."

"Know a lot about pregnant women do you?" Matt grinned.

Jase did his best to look affronted. "I'm gay. Being in touch with our emotions goes with the rainbow badge."

Matt burst out laughing, relieving the tension which was what Jase had intended. "You have got to be the least 'touchy-feely' bloke I know. But don't worry, Kate's not a crier, and Ryan's more likely to kick you in the shin if you upset him than turn on the water works. Remember what she was like as a kid? Well he's worse."

Dread, worse than when he was about to storm into a bar full of plastered, fighting squaddies, gripped Jase. Babysitting wasn't part of 'best man' duties was it? Kids terrified him; you never knew what they were going to do next. And using handcuffs on them was probably frowned upon. One minute they were high as a kite, the next they were having a tantrum or grizzling on your shirt. Give him a six foot four legless corporal every time.

11

Keeping his mental fingers firmly crossed, he asked nonchalantly, "Who's looking after the kid tonight then?"

"Sarah and Crispy Bacon."

Jase blinked. Matt's drivers tended to give each other odd nicknames, but he hadn't heard that one before.

Matt grinned his million watt, bright white smile and reached for the door. "You'll see. You're not the only one who has secrets. Did you really think the penguin story would work? You've got a tan and its winter in the Falklands."

The sunlight streaming through the stained glass windows picked up the dust circulating in a packed church as he made his way slowly up the aisle. All eyes were on him, and that wasn't how this should be; Matt and Kate were the important ones, not him. Although he had to admit, he did look damn good in his uniform. Shame about the crutches.

It wasn't difficult to pick out Matt's employees, for some reason all the drivers looked similar, but with slightly different dimensions. Perhaps the guy with the hideous fake tan was 'Crispy Bacon'. Close-cropped hair, even shorter than his own Army cut, was the unifying theme although waistlines expanded with age.

He had a sudden vision of being back here over the next few years, christening the next member of an ever-expanding brood of little Matts. Hopefully they'd be a bunch of cheeky little shits who would keep Matt on his mental and physical toes for life. Matt developing dementia in his early sixties like his father, or having a stroke at fifty like his mother, didn't bear thinking about. The fact that his own parents were hale and hearty only seemed to emphasize just how unlucky Matt had been.

Conflicting scents of furniture polish, flowers, powerful aftershaves, and perfumes hit his nose as they made slow progress down the aisle. Matt nodded to his guests, although Jase only recognised half of them. His own parents were near the front, his mother in a pink and cream floral dress with a wide brimmed hat to rival any in the church. He couldn't help smiling at the way they were still chatting like best friends after thirty years of marriage. It was a shame their only child was never going to make them grandparents; they'd be so damn good at it.

Judging from the number of programs being used as fans, Matt wasn't the only one feeling warm on this late May day. It was nothing compared to the dry heat of an Iraqi summer.

As they approached the front of the church, they saw the vicar talking to Matt's father who sat in a wheelchair next to the front pew. Jase hoped the man he remembered as large, vigorous and with a forceful personality was lucid today. From what Matt said, some days were better than others.

"Who's that?" The quarrelsome, reedy voice was overly loud in the background murmur of quiet conversations.

Matt crouched down by his father's chair. "It's Jason, Dad. You remember Jason, David and Susan's boy; he used to live next door."

Watering eyes squinted up at him without a hint of recognition. The thin lips pressed together firmly in annoyance at he turned back to his son.

"Don't lie to me, Mathew, just because you think you're all grown up it doesn't give you the right to treat me like I'm stupid. That's not Jason Rosewood; Jason's only a boy. Where's my Bacon? He said he was going to be here."

Matt patted his dad's hand awkwardly. Losing his wife had started a mental and physical decline, that appeared to be picking up speed with every passing day. Matt had taken the heart-breaking decision to put his dad in a home with specialist care a year ago after he'd nearly caused a house fire when he'd forgotten he'd left a pan on the stove. Jase's parents had raised the alarm and Richard had spent ten days in the hospital suffering from smoke inhalation and minor burns.

"Don't worry Dad; your Bacon will be along in a minute. Remember I told you Kate doesn't have any adult male relatives? He's going to give her away."

The old man shook his head. " 'Tisn't right, he should be your best man, not this soldier. We don't know any soldiers. Who is he anyway?"

Jase shifted his balance a little to ease his throbbing ankle. 'Awkward' didn't really cover this.

The vicar, who didn't look old enough to be out of short trousers, let alone be an ordained minister, cleared his throat.

"Would you mind taking your positions gentlemen? I think the bride has arrived."

Matt stood up and showed Jase where he was meant to stand. The thought that 'Bacon' had probably done all the things a real best man should have done, organising the stag do and being Matt's advocate in what was a traditionally female orientated event, irritated the hell out of him. He probably would have stepped into his shoes as best man today if Jase hadn't shown up. Sarah, or even her little boy could have walked Kate up the aisle.

It was daft, but he felt as if his place as Matt's best friend had been usurped by a complete stranger, one who all these people knew and were clearly enamoured with. Being a stranger in the place he'd grown up was probably the price he had to pay for leaving them all behind. Matt kept fidgeting, glancing behind them towards the front of the church.

Jase nudged him with his elbow. "Calm down. If anyone is going to make a tit out of themselves and fall flat on their face it's going to be me, not you or her. In fact, I think I can arrange that if it'd make you more comfortable."

Matt turned to him. "I'm doing the right thing here, right?"

What am I meant to say? 'No, run away with me and leave your unborn kid in the lurch?'

"Yes, you're doing the right thing. I've never seen you this happy." Then he grinned. "Besides, there's always divorce and coming over to the dark side."

Matt's mouth dropped open briefly in shock before his jaw snapped shut. "I hate you," he growled.

"Nah, you don't, but I think I hate this Bacon character. What's he got over everyone anyway?"

At that moment, the old lady on the organ hit the first notes of the Wedding March. The congregation got to their feet and a couple appeared at the end of the aisle. The bride was as petite and red-haired as he remembered and beaming from ear to ear. Nevertheless, Jase couldn't stop staring at the person beside her. Matt nudged his arm, causing him to make a grab for his crutch before it hit the floor.

"Roll that tongue back in, soldier. I take it I forgot to mention that I have a long lost half-brother? Who, in case your gaydar is even worse than mine, which is bloody impossible given my track record, is most definitely playing on your team."

Apart from the fact he had longer, curlier hair that was cropped short at the side, and was significantly shorter and skinnier, the young man dressed in a pearl grey suit with a painfully bright lavender shirt was his best friend's spitting image. If the clock had been rolled back fifteen years.

The youngster raised his eyebrows and smirked as he caught Jase staring at him, then whispered in the bride's ear. Who blushed. A lot.

CHAPTER 4

Chris

"Do you think we can change the tradition of the best man sleeping with the bridesmaid, just this once? Because he is fucking ed-di-ble. Actually, that's what I'm going to call him, Eddie Bull. 'Jason Rosewood' is much too soft a name for that. That uniform is fucking hot. Officer and a gentleman eat your heart out. Quick, give me your bouquet, I've got something more important to hide than an invisible baby bump."

Kate giggled as she went an adorable shade of deep pink. Being a natural redhead must really suck.

"We're in church, behave yourself for once."

"I think I'm going off the idea of giving you away for free. Do you think Matt would consider a swap for Eddie instead?"

Glancing back up at the guy with the crutches standing beside his brother in an immaculate olive green army uniform with a red cap, Chris decided, not for the first time, that he'd really landed on his feet. Looking back over the last seven weeks, he couldn't believe how hard he'd tried to avoid the man Kate was about to marry. It wasn't the stupidest thing he'd done, but it was bloody close.

Seven weeks before...

What made him look up at that exact moment, he'd never know, but the sight that met his eyes froze him briefly. Kate, the feisty red-haired nurse, who let him hang out at the nursing home whenever he wanted, was talking to his half-brother in the doorway of the retirement home's dayroom. He'd never spoken to Mathew Kemp, but he'd seen him, and spied on his house and business to see what sort of person shared his genes.

Straight-laced, industrious and traditional had been his conclusion. Certainly not a person who would accept someone like him. His cover story for Kate and the rest of the nursing home staff was that he was the old man's nephew, but that he didn't get on with his cousin. So far the nurses had alerted him when Mathew came to visit his father. Each time, he'd left swiftly by a back door.

Kate had been trying to get him to talk to Mathew since he'd first arrived and she was also becoming increasingly insistent that he visit her sister, a local GP. Doctors kept records, and the last thing he wanted was for someone to put two and two together and track him down. He was fine, sure he had a bit of a cough and wasn't as bouncy as usual, but sleeping rough, if you could call what he did sleeping, was bound to put anyone off their game.

"Sorry Pa, got to go. I'll be back later though, its cottage pie on Wednesdays right?"

"But you haven't finished the picture..." Richard indicated the drawing he'd been working on with a shaking gnarled finger. It was a colourful fantasy piece with a mostly 'grey' Richard, touching the hand of a multi-coloured young man. The rainbow colours crept up Richard's arm. He'd said he wanted some of Chris's energy. Chris had tried to portray the sentiment, although he wasn't sure the old man would appreciate the 'rainbow' if he realised what it signified.

The old man could get argumentative, but he always settled when he watched him draw. Kate had presented him with a packet of coloured pencils from the craft room yesterday, and this was the first time he'd tried them out. It was certainly an improvement on drawing with a biro on waste paper and cardboard, which was what he'd been often reduced to over the last twelve months. The freedom to do as he pleased more than made up for it.

There were only two exits from the day room. Matt and Kate were standing in the entrance to the rest of the building. His only way out, without a confrontation, was the patio door lead onto the terrace. If he opened it, the alarm would go off scaring the shit out of most of the residents, but he didn't have a choice. Keeping his head down he walked towards it.

"Come back, you need to finish me, I've only got one arm." Richard's strident call and his attempt to stand took his brother's attention. Chris moved a little faster.

He thanked his lucky stars as Richard started to kick up a bigger fuss.

"What are you doing here? I don't want you, I want my crispy bacon. I always have crispy bacon with breakfast. It's your fault, go away, go away now."

"Nurse? Why hasn't my father had the breakfast he wanted?"

Chris hit the exit bar, wincing at the clanging alarm and the panicked shrieks of the residents as he scooted out the door. Nurses and care assistants were dashing towards the day room from all over the building as he made himself scarce. Once outside the nursing home, he found himself one of the many benches around the grounds. This one overlooked the driveway, so he could see when his brother left. This early in April, it was still bloody cold. The sooner he got back inside, the better.

It wasn't as if he had anywhere else to go until later, except for his tent in the woods at the back of the converted country house. The two person tent fitted into his backpack along with the rest of his few possessions, but it was becoming more of a prison than a haven. Besides, it was starting to hum, big time. Still, he didn't use it unless an alternative place to spend the night failed to present itself. Being on his own during the day had always been ok, the nights? Not so much.

The only gay club in town, 'The Toolbox' didn't open till eight, so he had eleven or so hours to kill. The perk of hanging around the nursing home was that if he helped out with feeding some of the more disagreeable residents, they let him sneak a meal too. The owner of The Toolbox paid him for dragging people onto the dance floor when it was quiet and podium dancing when it was busy. Dancing made people thirsty, which increased the revenue at the bar. It also gave him access to lonely blokes who sometimes let him sleep over, let him have a hot shower and give his clothes a wash.

An hour later, Matthew Kemp still hadn't emerged and Chris's shivering had turned into full body shakes. He couldn't have missed the guy's bright blue pick-up heading down the drive, so this was going to be one of the few and far between long visits. His brother usually only stayed for twenty minutes but he did visit virtually every other day. Several of the other residents hadn't had a single visitor since he'd arrived a month ago. He always tried to give those ones a little attention too.

Stomach rumbling, he decided that he might as well go sit in his sleeping bag and munch some of the crisps he'd liberated from the club last night. Sitting still had never been easy, but he was losing weight he couldn't afford and being cold burnt up even more calories.

He made his way through the undergrowth, after making sure nobody was around to see his hiding place. He told anyone that asked that he had a bedsit in town, although he suspected Kate was slowly putting two and two together. Finding his mysterious, absentee father had been on his radar for years and now he'd done it, he was at a loss about what to do next.

After crawling into the dark green tent, he climbed into the sleeping bag and reached for the rather squashed packet of ready salted crisps. He'd given up on nicking cheese and onion ones because they stank the tent out even worse.

He hadn't got back from the club till four-thirty this morning and it was only nine now. The guy he'd been banking on to provide a bed for the night and a temporary cure for his insomnia, hadn't played out. After spending all night flirting and then sucking him off in his car, the guy's phone had rung and the bastard had scuttled back to his girlfriend. He'd had a pathetic skinny dick too.

Snuggling down, Chris decided the crisps could wait. He didn't actually feel hungry and the headache that had been clouding his thinking for the last couple of days throbbed like a motherfucker. Even if he couldn't sleep, closing his eyes for a while was a good idea. No one wanted to watch a baggy-eyed, lethargic go-go dancer.

* * *

The ground shook, but he tried to ignore it as he continued to draw the person sitting in his street art chair. The shaking continued and he pulled himself out of the chaotic, feverish dream.

Opening bleary eyes that felt as if they were filled with sand, he blinked.

Shit. His brother glared at him through the flap of the tent and he had hold of his leg. That rotten grass Kate was next to him. Neither of them looked happy. Kate wore a 'social worker' worried expression. Mathew just looked pissed off, his black eyebrows almost meeting in the middle.

"Why are you hanging around my father? You told this nurse you were my cousin. I don't have a cousin, especially not one called Bacon."

Kate shot the man beside her an exasperated look. "We're not angry with you, we're just curious, and a little worried. Are you living in this tent? Don't you have anywhere else to go?"

"Don't worry, I'm going, sorry to be a problem," he said quickly and started gathering his stuff. Unfortunately, the biggest thing, the tent, had to go into the pack first. The pair stepped back as he climbed out. Matt put his hand on his arm as he bent to pull up the first of the pegs that secured the structure to the ground.

"How old are you?" Matt asked, his voice losing the aggressive edge.

Chris huffed but didn't look at him. Great, two more do-gooders. The one time he'd been able to sleep in days and this pair had woken him up. Bastards.

"Old enough. Do you mind moving your hand?"

"And where are you going to go now?" Kate said, waving her hand in the air. "Another patch of rough ground? Are you even eating anything apart from scraps from the nursing home? I've been on leave, but I've been asking around, you've been here for nearly a month."

"We had an au pair called Marietta Bacon about twenty years ago, is that how you know my Dad? She didn't have any kids as far as I know but knowing my father he probably said she could come to him if she was in trouble."

Chris looked down at the hand holding his arm. "Let me go, or so help me I'll start yelling rape, murder and any other shit I can think of. I don't want money or anything else from him, I just wanted to meet him. I've done that now, so this is me, fucking off out of your lives."

Matt's questions and accusations started coming thick and fast. His face was close enough that if Chris had been inclined, he could have counted the pores on his nose.

"What do you mean, you don't want money? Does that mean your mother does? I bet she's been leeching off him and half a dozen other poor old sods for years. I bet she's passed his details onto you because he stopped paying so you could come and work him over personally. People like you make me sick. So how does it work, suck some poor lonely, desperate sod in, then blackmail him? I have you know that my father loved my mother very much, there is no way he—"

Kate tugged at the arm that had hold of him. "Matt? I hate to say this, and forgive me if I'm wrong, but he looks a lot like you. I noticed the resemblance straight away, which is why I believed the cousin story. Could it be—"

Taking advantage of his distraction, Chris pulled his arm free and broke into a run. This was just what he'd imagined happening. The disgust on Matt's face, and the pity on Kate's, were expressions he'd seen many times in his life and he wasn't going to stand around and take it again. Lust or hate were easy, but not fake concern, pity or disgust. He had no idea where he was going, but staying here wasn't an option.

He'd made it halfway across the lawn, before the grass decided to hit him in the face. He struggled immediately, kicking and twisting.

"Stay down you fucking rabbit and tell me what the hell is going on before I call the police." The next moment there was a knee on his arse and a hand on the back of his neck, effectively pinning him to the cold damp grass.

"You let him up this minute, Mathew Kemp. I've known you since you were a child and I won't stand for you bullying him. All he's ever done is be nice to your father and the other residents."

The weight moved off him a little, but the firm grip on his neck told him Matt wasn't going to let him go any time soon. Besides, the bastard had already proved he was faster, which was a bloody shock. No one had ever been able to catch him before, not on their own anyway.

"Well, Crispy Bacon or whoever the hell you are, what's your story?"

"If you let me spit out this mouthful of grass, you arsehole, I'll..." He was released so he rolled over and looked up into eyes that were exactly the same as his. It wasn't fair. Just because of an accident of birth, this man had a home, a business and a fucking nice car.

"Your saintly father, fucked the au pair senseless while your mother was—"

"Liar!" The volume of Matt's shout from only a foot away was a physical blow. Chris closed his eyes and braced for pain. *Why the fuck can't I keep my mouth shut?*

"So help me Mathew Kemp, if you touch one hair on that boy's head I will make sure you are prosecuted to the full extent of the law."

Chris had to admit, even from his position on the grass, given a choice he'd rather have Matt angry at him than Kate. Matt's face might be red, but Kate's eyes were shooting sparks. He might get an immediate punch from Matt, but he bet Kate could think up some unusual, long-winded and constraining punishments.

"What do you think I am? I wasn't going to hit him, just scare him into telling the truth. This is clearly some sort of extortion racket."

"Nice to know," Chris interrupted the couple that were glaring at each other as he rolled to a sitting position. "But I'm only repeating what I've worked out myself. If you can explain why your dear old Dad has had a standing order going into my Mum's account since I was born some other way, and the fact we're two peas in a pod, be my fucking guest. I didn't exactly feel wonderful finding out I'm the dirty fucking secret of some hairy-arsed, cheating lorry driver from the back of beyond and a maid who opened her legs for the boss."

19

Matt's jaw clenched at his 'cheating' comment but he let it lie, instead he said, "So you don't actually know who your father is? Haven't you ever asked your mother?"

Chris rolled his eyes. "Now wait, why didn't I ever think of that? Of course I fucking asked her. She always said, 'it doesn't matter, he doesn't want you anyway,' which is a fucking kick in the teeth if you ask me, " he said as he rubbed his elbow where it had hit the ground. Christ, his brother tackled hard.

"Get her on the phone, ask her now." Matt said as he stepped back and hauled Chris to his feet by his upper arm.

"I haven't got a phone."

Two phones were immediately proffered. He scowled.

"I haven't got her number and I haven't seen her for ages, don't want to either. I found the bank statements, came down here, seduced a clerk from the bank and found out where your father was. I just wanted to see what sort of man abandons his kid for thirty quid a month."

Chris stumbled back a step as Matt shoved his chest. "He. Is. Not. Your. Father."

"Yeah, yeah I get it. You don't want a nasty little shit like me rocking the squeaky clean family boat. I haven't told him who I am, but you could always ask him about my mum."

Matt scratched the back of his neck. "If you've been with him as much as Kate says, you'll know he can't even remember what day of the week it is sometimes, let alone anything that happened twenty years ago."

Keeping quiet about the date and having his brother think he was older than he was, wasn't a bad thing.

"Do a DNA test if it bothers you that much. I don't want your money, I just wanted..." he trailed off, not willing to open himself up to yet another emotional battering when he was so damn tired. *What's up with that anyway? I'm never bloody tired.*

"You wanted what?"

Sticking his hands in his pockets, he shrugged, looking down.

"When was the last time you had a proper meal, a bed to sleep in, or a shower?" Kate asked.

He paused, not quite sure whether to tell the truth or go with his normal bullshit. If this guy was his brother, surely family should stick together? At least that was what he'd heard.

"Sausage and mash, last night."

"You mean left-overs from the home."

He shrugged again. He could literally feel the pair of them sharing pity looks so he didn't bother looking up.

"And the bed and shower?" Matt prompted.

That had happened two nights ago when he'd gone home with some pushy top from the club. He was damn sure he wasn't going to tell them about that night. The git had marked him so badly he hadn't been able to wear his normal trunks and cut off vest at the club last night because of the bruises on his thighs, back and stomach. A bit of erotic spanking was one thing, but that cane had been bloody brutal.

"I'm booked into the fucking Hilton, what the hell do you think?"

"He's not here in the evenings," Kate said, "but he's been around at breakfast time for the last ten days."

Matt leaned in and gave him a sniff.

"Gerroff you perv. What are you, a fucking bloodhound?" Chris tried to shove him off but didn't succeed.

"He doesn't stink too bad, but he's a bit warm. You don't think he's been washing in the home, do you?" Matt asked Kate as if Chris wasn't even there.

"I run hot, it's not a big deal, and no, I bloody well haven't been sneaking into old people's showers without them knowing. What do you think I am?"

Two sets of eyes turned back to him. "Where are you washing then?" Matt asked.

"Does it matter?"

"It does if you want me to trust you," Matt said, folding his arms.

"Oh just tell him, Chris, what's the big deal?"

"It's not a big deal, not to me anyway." He looked between the two 'good Samaritans' as he spoke. Their expressions were about to go from pity to disgust and then he'd be free to get his stuff and get out of here.

"Last night I came back to the tent, because my hook-up went back to his wife. The three nights before that, I went to the places of the guys I picked up in the gay club in Cawton. Some of them let me wash my stuff as well as take a shower. Of course, I have to put out, but–" He shrugged.

Kate had her hand over her mouth, her eyes were glassy with pity. Matt looked as if he'd just trodden in something horrible. He'd been half-right. He'd seen both expressions a hundred times and both pissed him off.

"What? You think you've got the right to judge me with your perfect little lives? Well you can both fuck the hell off. I'm outta here."

"Right, you're coming home with me," Kate announced as if he'd just fall into place. "You can wait in the day room till the end of my shift, then we'll pick up Ryan from the babysitter. We can drop round to my sister's surgery afterwards. Come on then, chop chop the pair of you. I've got thirty frightened geriatrics to sort out."

"I'll take him. I live on my own; I haven't got a partner or child to think about."

"I haven't got a partner either. He buggered off when I found out I was pregnant. Seems to be a bit of a theme today, doesn't it?"

Before Matt could start defending his father's virtue again, Chris spoke up. "All this domestic bliss is bloody wonderful, but I haven't said I'll go anywh–."

"Shut up," the pair said at the same time, then grinned at each other.

"I can take him now. I'll get Sarah to check him out," Matt told her and gave Chris a glare, "do that DNA test and get him cleaned up."

"Hey, I am clean, I'm not some hobo," he protested as Matt took his arm and led him towards where he'd parked his monstrous pick-up.

"You either sleep in a tent in the woods or with strangers to get a shower. I think that classifies you as homeless, don't you?"

"What about my stuff?"

"It's crap. You can borrow some old stuff of mine."

"It might be crap, but it's my crap, and I'm not going anywhere without it. Some bastard could nick it while I'm gone."

Matt's expression told him how unlikely that was, but he still about-faced and walked back to Chris's camp site. Ten minutes later, all his worldly possessions were on the back seat of the crew cab pick-up. Matt waited while he climbed in the front seat. Then he locked the door with Chris inside while he walked around to the driver's side.

When he got in all he said was, "Belt up."

"What's with the door locking routine, you think I'm going to make a run for it?"

Keeping his eyes on the road as the truck rumbled to life, Matt replied, "I don't know, would you?"

Chris turned to the window and folded his arms. *Fucking smart arse.*

Electronic beeps indicated Matt was making a phone call. "Mary? It's Matt Kemp. Is Sarah around? Yeah, I'd appreciate it, it's a bit of a delicate one... no it's not me. I'll be there in twenty."

"Who was that, another one of your girlfriends? I hope you have a thing for girls in nurses uniforms, cos I think Kate fancies you."

"I'm going to pretend I didn't hear that. You are going to get a thorough check up. When was the last time you saw a doctor?"

"A week ago, or at least he said he was a doctor. Still if he wasn't, he was bloody kinky, he wanted me to..."

"Never mind."

He grinned at the slightly sick expression on Matt's face. It seemed his initial assumption that his shiny new brother was exceptionally straight in all manner of ways had been spot on. Teasing him might prove very entertaining. It might even get him out of this situation.

"How about your last address, date of birth, full name, that sort of thing. The receptionist will need your details."

"Didn't Daddy tell you my name?"

"He said he wanted his Crispy Bacon back. I had a right go at Kate for not giving him time to eat his breakfast."

Chris laughed at the sulky tone in his voice. "Yeah, Kate's a feisty one. You'd better watch yourself around her, I saw her checking out your arse. Then again, if we weren't family, and you weren't straight, I'd..."

"Give it a rest will you? So you're gay, big deal. So's my best friend. Your sexuality doesn't shock me, I just don't want to hear about all the ins and outs."

"What about the outs and ins? Both ways can be fun, although it depends on the guy. What's your friend, a take it, give it, or both sort?" Matt's hands tightened on the wheel as his jaw flexed. *Score one for Bacon.*

22

"Enough with the endless crap. What do I call you? Crispy Bacon is a crisp flavour, not a name. I'm not calling you that any more than I'd call you Ready Salted, Roast Chicken or Prawn Cocktail." His voice was so serious that Chris let out a bark of laughter.

"I don't know about prawns, unless they're the jumbo variety, but cocktail might be appropriate. Talking of prawns, is that why you drive such a big car? Is my big brother a little worried about the size of his prawn? Cos you know, if everyone had an identical tiger prawn sized cock, my mouth and arse would get bored."

"I've never had any complaints. I drive a lorry for a living; getting in a normal size car feels like I'm on the ground. And I don't give a shit about what you say as long as it's in appropriate company, and no, the doctor's surgery we are going to, even if I know them, is not the right place."

Chris was more than a little disappointed that Matt seemed to have cottoned on to his game. Perhaps it was time to up the ante. If he pissed him off enough, he might throw him out and he could be on his way and put the subject of his parentage behind him.

What did it matter who fucked who some random night years ago? Hell, he couldn't remember all the guys he'd slept with so why should anyone else, let alone his own parents, be any different.

"I've heard about you lorry drivers. A different shag at every stop. That sort of thing runs in the family does it? Cos it sort of explains why I..."

Chris was glad he had obeyed and belted up as Matt hit the brakes, hard. He shrank back against his window as Matt jabbed a finger in his direction.

"Dad loved my mum, and if anything did go on between him and your mother, which I highly doubt, it would have happened when he was at an all-time low after mum had a stroke. Your mother was employed to clean the house and if she and my Dad ever... it was because your mother must have...Shit." He banged his fist on the steering wheel making the horn blare.

"None of this is your fault is it?" Matt finished quietly as he checked his rear-view mirror and started the vehicle moving again.

For the first time, Chris felt sorry for the man next to him, instead of being jealous of his stable upbringing.

"Chris, you can call me Chris. I told your dad my name was Chris Bacon but the deaf old bugger misheard me. He started calling me Crispy Bacon so the rest did too."

"So your name's Christopher?"

"Did I say my name was Christopher?"

"Now you're just being pig-headed," Matt said as he turned into a car park that looked suspiciously like a doctor's surgery.

"About right for a bloke called Bacon don't you think?"

Matt parked the car and turned in his seat to face him. "Are you in trouble with the law or something? Is that why you're being so evasive? Or are you just lying about my dad and trying not to get caught out?"

Being told your happy family memories weren't what you thought they were must be like having your world turned on its head. He's got every right to be upset, and yet he's trying to help even though I've been a complete arse. Perhaps I should cut him some slack.

"Truthfully, I don't know if what I found out is right. I haven't got anything more to go on than a few letters where he asked about me and if the money he was sending was enough. I guess I wanted it to be true, about him being my Dad. It's a connection I've never had. Mum wasn't exactly consistent. We moved around a lot, and even then I was left with various friends, strangers really, while she was off doing whatever it was she did when she wasn't with me."

Chris could hear the ticking of the dashboard clock as they sat in silence. He only had to wait five clicks before Matt asked the question he'd been waiting for.

"Did they abuse you, these friends?"

Anger flooded him. "Why does everyone think a promiscuous gay kid from a single parent family must have been kiddie fiddled?"

"What you said about sleeping with random guys is true then? Do you know how dangerous that is?"

Rain started to pitter patter on the windscreen and Chris's head abruptly felt too heavy for his shoulders. He dropped it back against the headrest for a moment before turning to the man who could be, probably was, his brother. A man he'd known for less than an hour and was now acting like the parent he'd never had, but had always needed.

"I'm single and rather gorgeous, even if I do say so myself, and I always use protection. What's the problem?"

"How old are you?"

"Old enough to make my own decisions. Now are we going in or not, because it's going to be a bloody long, wet walk back to the club carrying that lot from here, and to be honest, I actually feel pretty shitty."

CHAPTER 5

Matt

What the hell had he got himself into? He had to admit that the sulky, belligerent, skinny youngster, who didn't look any older than eighteen, did resemble him as a teenager, apart from the mop of curly hair. And unless he'd done a hell of a lot of research, how did he know that his family had employed an au pair with the surname Bacon? He'd only been a teenager at the time himself, but he remembered the young, vibrantly energetic Mediterranean looking woman with the Italian/American accent exceptionally well because he'd had a crush on her himself. She'd been exotic, kind and physically demonstrative.

In the space of an hour, he'd gone from wanting to strangle this mouthy little shit, to wanting to save him and back again, several times. They were now sitting in Sarah's waiting room, or rather he was sitting and flicking through a magazine; Chris was slouched, picking at his nails, huffing every now and again as his knee constantly bobbed up and down.

The surgery door opened, and the girl he'd gone steady with for a year opened the door and gave him a smile that reminded him of Kate.

"Nice to see you, Matt. I take it this is the young man from the nursing home Kate has been telling me about?"

Chris shot to his feet. "Nice to meet you Doc. You can call me Chris. I'm his little brother, well half-brother anyway, or at least I think I am. Can you do DNA tests here?"

Sarah blinked and looked from Chris to him and back again. "Is this true?"

He stood up. "To be honest, I've got no idea. But it could be. Thanks for seeing him on such short notice, but whatever the case, he needs a check-up. He's been sleeping rough, and erm..." He paused, not exactly sure how to approach the subject.

Sarah saved him by saying, "Shall we go into my office? If you're alright with having Matt in there with you Chris?"

"I'd rather he wasn't."

"Listen here you little..." was as far as he got before Sarah interrupted him.

"Sorry Matt, doctor-patient confidentiality applies as he's clearly over sixteen. You are over sixteen right?" she asked Chris.

He gave her a sunny smile. "Oh yeah, I'm ancient. I'm actually his great grandad. I've been at the fountain of youth and I don't want this blabber mouth getting all my secrets. I've got a map tattooed on my—"

"Just go will you?" Matt groaned.

"Could you give the receptionist his details?" Sarah asked.

"What details? He said his name was Crispy Bacon of Under-An-Oak-Tree, Belleview Care Home."

She just stared at him, so he walked back towards the reception desk.

"That's it, trot along like a good boy, Mathew," Chris called out behind him. Then he heard, "Ow, what was that for? I thought you lot took an oath to so no harm," just before the surgery door clicked shut. It was nice to know he wasn't the only one Chris incited to violence.

He ended up giving his own address, and the name 'Chris Bacon' but the lack of a date of birth and previous doctor details were a problem for the receptionist. By the time the surgery door opened again, patients for the afternoon session had started to arrive.

Chris was subdued as he came out holding a green prescription form. Sarah mimed holding a phone to her ear as she mouthed the words 'I'll call you'.

He mouthed 'thank you' back and followed Chris out. He found him waiting by the pick-up.

Pointing at the prescription Matt said, "Pharmacy's over there," then nodded toward the tiny booth-like chemist's beside the surgery.

"Nah, don't worry about it. It's only for some vitamins. Apparently I haven't been eating my greens."

"Give." Matt held his hand out.

With a theatrical eye roll, Chris handed the form over. Matt unlocked the car, told Chris to, "Sit and stay," before locking him in and going over to the pharmacy.

The male chemist took the form and looked it over before starting to gather several different boxes from around the counter.

"Is it for you?" he asked.

"No, he's waiting in the car."

"Does he pay prescription charges?"

"Erm..."

The pharmacist blew out a breath in exasperation at the ignorance of yet another patient. "Is he under eighteen, or under nineteen in full time education? Does he have an exemption certificate or is he in receipt of a means tested benefit?"

"I guess I'll need to pay."

"That'll be thirty two pounds."

"How much? Are you sure?"

He checked the list again. "Yep. Two different antibiotics, iron pills and multivitamins both of which I can take off the list, they're only a pound, there's no point in paying the eight quid prescription charge for those, and not forgetting the sleeping pills. Do you want them or not?"

"Yeah, of course. The doctor wouldn't have prescribed them otherwise. But erm, none of that stuff is for anything infectious is it?"

He felt himself shrivel under the woman's gaze. "I think you'd better ask the patient that, don't you Sir?"

Suitably chastised, he nodded, handed over his credit card and took the white paper bag.

As he got back into his truck, he asked as casually as he could, "What did Sarah say?"

"Wouldn't you like to know?"

"Has anyone ever told you you're an annoying little shit?"

"Not for...," he leaned forward to check the clock on the dash, "about eight hours. She said she's got a form for the DNA test. Took a sample from me, but it's a private fee. Once you've got a sample from your Dad, it'll take five days for a normal speed, or a day for a rush job. Thanks for the pills. What sort of m and m's have I got?"

"Antibiotics, vitamins, iron pills and sleeping pills."

Chris screwed up the bag and put it beside him. "You can keep the sleeping pills."

"Sarah wouldn't have prescribed them if you didn't need them."

"I don't do uppers or downers, end of."

"These aren't street drugs, Sarah prescribed them for you, so you clearly–"

"Nope, not going to happen. You might need them though. I don't sleep much, wouldn't want to keep you awake."

Matt changed the subject, as he turned into the road where he'd grown up, where he still lived. "You hungry?"

"What you got? I don't eat any old shit you know. I've got a refined palate."

Matt glanced over at his passenger who still had that grin on his face. He could see the bumps of his breast bone through his thin t-shirt, his sharp cheek bones and the dark circles under his eyes. His clothes were rumpled, a little smelly and his neck was grubby.

Even if Chris wasn't his half-brother, he clearly needed looking after. And that meant more than a couple of good meals, somewhere safe to sleep for a night or two, clean clothes and a damn good soak in a tub. But he was probably too damn proud to accept charity.

"So, I saw that drawing you were doing for Dad. Pretty damn impressive."

"No big deal. He likes to watch me draw and it keeps my fingers busy."

"It is a big deal, you're really good."

Glancing over, for a moment Matt thought Chris was going to accept the praise like a normal person, then the genuine smile turned into a sarcastic one.

"Why Mathew, are you trying to get into my jock-strap, because until we know whether we are related or not, that's just weird."

Matt turned onto his driveway and turned the car off, trying not to grit his teeth at Chris' patented distraction technique, being a complete twat.

"Actually smart-arse, I was going to offer you a job. I want the lorries brightened up. I've got a guy who does vinyl wraps, but all he does is typography, he's not an artist. If you came up with a decent design, he could do all of them."

Matt didn't miss the way Chris's eyes lit up, even though he shrugged.

"Could fill a few hours I suppose."

CHAPTER 6

Jase

Jase took another sip of his coke, mindful of his doctor's instruction about no alcohol with his medication. The wedding reception was going well, although the drivers were putting away the free beer faster than a platoon just off tour. Music from the ancient music centre in the old hall filled the air with a typical multigenerational wedding theme from the sixties to the nineties and everything in between. Wooden tables heaved with platters that had clearly been supplied by the guests. The air of unprofessional, loving chaos was perfect. It felt like home, their home. Maybe, one day, it would feel like he belonged here again.

"So that was that," Matt said. "The results came back positive. He's my brother. Kate kept phoning to ask about him, Dad wouldn't stop going on about missing his Crispy Bacon, so I ended up driving him back to the nursing home on a daily basis. If I don't, he runs there and back. Kid's got some serious energy issues even with taking antibiotics for a chronic lung infection. While he entertained Dad and everyone else within a three mile radius, I chatted to Kate, and it went from there.

"To be honest, it feels like I've been hit by a bus. In less than seven weeks, I've gained an annoying shit of a brother, a wife, a stepson and a baby on the way. Kate and Ryan are the easy parts."

Jase shifted the position of his throbbing ankle, even though he was off it now, he'd done too much today. Watching the young man who looked so much like Matt help move tables to make room for the traditional wedding disco, he understood his friend's emotional dilemma. He just didn't share it.

"So he's healthy now?"

Matt grimaced. "He's getting there. His chest infection has almost cleared up and his iron levels are up a bit. Sarah said he's probably small because he didn't get proper food as a kid. He won't say a word about his childhood though. He's also a chronic insomniac, never stops moving unless he's taken a sleeping pill. He won't take them voluntarily, says they 'dull his edge' but I sneak one into his food when he really looks like death warmed up. When he does sleep he's much calmer for a couple of days but it's a running battle.

"How he keeps up the pace when he's still fighting an infection I don't know. Sarah said that when she first saw him, if she'd thought he would stay in hospital, she would have admitted him, stuck him on an antibiotic drip and given him a blood transfusion."

They watched as Chris and his mini-me Ryan, both dressed in black shirts and trousers went to stand in the middle of the dance floor. The noise gradually died down and 'The men in Black' theme tune from the movie started to play.

Christ that boy can move, Jase thought as Chris slid, stepped and gyrated his way through the routine he and Ryan had clearly practiced for hours. Most eyes in the room were on the very cute red-haired five-year-old, but Jase couldn't take his eyes off Matt's brother. He might look like Matt, but that was where the similarities ended.

"You know you were asking about a job?"

Jase tore his eyes away from Chris as the number ended. Kate, still wearing her elegant satin cream wedding dress, stepped forward to have her first dance with her son. Matt was notoriously dance floor phobic, so nobody kicked up a fuss that the traditional 'first dance' was between mother and son.

"I'm not desperate. I've got an army pension and some savings, but I'm happy to help out while I figure out what I'm going to do permanently. I suppose Dad expects me to be a bailiff, but I'm not convinced it's for me. This is going to take a while to heal anyway." He indicated his ankle, but didn't voice the doctor's opinion that it'd probably never be the same again. Pain was going to be his almost constant companion for the rest of his days, but at least he had 'days' to look forward to, unlike the others that had been caught in the blast.

"How are your investigative skills?"

Now that piqued his curiosity. "Does this involve him?" He nodded towards Chris who was currently whirling a laughing Sarah around the dance floor.

"Why, are you interested in my little brother?" The gleam in Matt's eye told him that he wasn't averse to the idea of him making a move on the puzzle that was Crispy Bacon.

"He's erm..." Jase paused, not sure of what to say. Sexy, vibrant, an enigma he wanted to unwrap, layer by layer? None of the options running through his mind were particularly appropriate to mention in his present company.

"That he is. I also have no more information about him than I told you. I don't know his full name, where he grew up, or even his date of birth. I checked Dad's bank records, I've got full power of attorney because of the Alzheimer's, and the payments go back as far as the records do, ten years. But they stopped four years ago, not because Dad changed anything, but because the account they were going into closed. All they had was an account number and the sort code of an internet bank, so not even an address."

Matt took a swallow of his beer and shook his head. "He's been living in my home for seven weeks, and I've only ever seen him asleep twice and that was when I slipped a crushed sleeping pill into his dinner. And he stayed still long enough to eat it.

"Even though I've tried to convince him to stop, he still works at the Toolbox on Friday and Saturday nights. Sometimes he comes home, sometimes he doesn't. He can disappear for days without explanation. All he does, when I ask where he's been, is grin and says something stupid about it being cute that I'm worried, and I am, I really am." Matt's lips thinned as he watched his brother. "But he's a grown man, or at least he says he is, and I'm not his father. I've got no right to tell him what he can or can't do. And if I do start laying down the law, I'm scared shitless he'll take off again and end up god knows where."

It sounded as if Chris was leading Matt in a merry dance, but Jase kept that to himself. Neither of them had ever been a parent, or a sibling, but he knew Matt wouldn't take this shit from any of his drivers, and he treated them almost like family.

"Does he contribute in any way?"

Matt scowled. " I know he sounds like a complete leech, but he's given me money every weekend, not a lot I grant you, but he's trying. He also valets the lorries, sweeps the yard, cleans the office, cuts the grass, does the windows, here, and at your mum and dad's. All without being asked. In fact, getting him to stop doing stuff is the problem. It's what he gets up to when he's not here that I'm worried about."

They watched Chris drag some of the drivers who were becoming rapidly inebriated away from the hired bar. He lined them up and started to teach them a few of the dance steps he'd used in the 'men in black' number. He'd definitely bitten off more than he could chew though as their co-ordination was shot to pieces due to the amount of free alcohol they'd poured down their throats. A chuckle broke from his chest as one guy freestyled what looked like an epically failing moonwalk. However, it was nice to see Chris, as a flamboyant gay man, being accepted in this not so modern village.

Maybe he'd been overly cautious about coming out here himself. Of course some people knew, and if anyone asked he never denied it, but he wasn't like Chris. To be honest, he'd never met anyone quite like Chris in his sphere of existence. Over the top twinks didn't tend to join the army.

"The little idiot is probably still hooking up with random guys from the club. He's certainly never mentioned anyone specific, but I've seen bruises on his wrists and sometimes on his neck and we're not talking hickies." Matt took another drink, then turned to Jase, frown lines etched on his forehead. His face should have been nothing but happy on his wedding day.

"It's his business, I know it is, but Kate and Ryan are moving in when we get back from honeymoon. It's a three bed house, and when the new baby gets a bit older it's going to be a problem. I don't want to chuck him out, he's family, and as far as I know he's got nowhere and no-one else to turn to, but with a little kid around and another on the way…"

"You want me to find out if he poses a risk?"

Matt shifted so his elbows rested on the cream tablecloth. He hung his head briefly before looking up at Jase again. "That sounds so bloody wrong. He's my brother for Christ's sake. More than anyone in the world, he should be able to count on me to trust him."

"But you don't," Jase stated.

Matt pulled at his tie, before undoing it. "I don't know, I really don't know. He's like a camp Duracell bunny that never runs out of power. The drivers call him Tigger cos he's always bouncing around. That first night, when I asked him about doing some designs for the lorries, I came down the next morning to find him still scribbling. He hadn't slept a wink and he'd done twenty-two different drawings. Some were designs, bloody good ones too, but there were also portraits of me, Dad and Kate."

"Do you think he's on something?"

"If he is, I haven't got a clue what it is, who supplies him, or where he keeps it. I find nothing when I searched his stuff, and he's totally paranoid about taking the sleeping pills Sarah prescribed. I've found them in the bin twice, so now I keep them."

"Just because you didn't find anything, it doesn't mean he's not using, just that he's good at hiding it." Jase concluded aloud as he watched Chris lead all the youngsters, and disturbingly, a few of adults, in a vigorous 'gangnam style' dance. He bet Chris did everything with enthusiasm and energy. Jase shifted in his seat as another part of his anatomy found that idea interesting.

"He's certainly good with kids," Jase said.

"And old folks. Everyone loves him, which makes me feel even crappier for not trusting him."

As the music ended, they watched Chris grab a pint of lemonade from the bar then come over, his face bright with excitement.

"Don't tell me, once I'm over thirty, I'm going to turn into a boring old fart too. Come on you two, Eddie here has got an excuse, but you've got two good feet. Go dance with your wife. I'll teach the squaddie how to hand jive so he's got something else to do with his hands instead of—"

"You do know my name's Jason, don't you?"

Chris took another quick swig as if he didn't have time to have a proper drink, then flashed a million watt smile.

" 'Course I do. I just think Eddie, as in 'Eddie Bull' suits you better."

Matt spluttered into his pint, only just avoiding spraying it across the table.

"Christ Chris, warn a guy before you say something like that, it puts images into my mind that I really don't want in there on my wedding night. Kate's fine with me not dancing with her, she knows I don't like it."

Chris scowled at his brother. "Why are straight guys always so dense about shit like this? Believe me, if you don't dance with her tonight, at least once, and without her coming over to moan about it, it'll haunt you for years. She'll bring it up again and again, probably at every anniversary and party till you both drop off the perch. Nip it in the bud."

"But—"

"Go slow dance with your wife, Mathew, or I'm stripping to 'I'm holding out for a hero,' right in the middle of the dance floor."

He held up a finger and put an exaggerated thoughtful expression on his face. "Actually, that's not a bad idea. It'll exhaust all the old folks, the parents will take their kids away, which will leave us to have some proper fun. I think it's about time I taught you provincial types how to go-go dance. This place would be seriously improved with some extra bump and grind." He started to get up.

Matt got to his feet rapidly, using Chris's shoulder to lever himself up. "Sit and stay."

Chris grinned, then stuck his tongue out, moved his hands into a sit up and beg position and panted.

"Would you behave?" Matt growled but Chris's grin only got wider.

"You'd better hurry up before I start humping your leg." Then he looked over at Jase. "Actually, his leg looks far more interesting, well one of them does anyway."

Putting his chin in his hand and his elbow on the table he stared at Jase while completely ignoring his brother. Matt looked to the polystyrene ceiling for help.

"Love the red hat by the way, it definitely adds a certain something. So what's your story, soldier boy? Apart from the fact you used to fancy the pants off my brother. And what self-respecting rim-raider wouldn't? He's gorgeous, just like me."

Still muttering to himself, Matt beat a hasty retreat as Jase sat and watched the Chris Show. This youngster might be able to wrap everyone else around his little finger, but he had interrogated all sorts of emotional young men over the last ten years. This one was hiding something behind the bravado. He'd always found chatty prisoners easier to question, eventually they always felt the need to fill the silence.

"Strong and silent type, huh? I can work with that. Hopefully you'll get so pissed off with me babbling, that you'll do something to shut me up. Personally I prefer being pinned down and silenced with a hot mouth. Or a fat dick. How about you? I'd guess you're a dedicated top, which certainly floats my boat, although if you like switching, I can–"

"I'm not buying the act."

Chris cocked his head to one side, making his dark curls bounce. His grin appearing forced for the first time.

"See? I knew I'd get you to talk, but I'll take a rain-check on the smile, it could take all night and I can't let any one fan monopolise the star of the event. I'm off to make some grannies blush, but you, Eddie Bull, are firmly on my 'to-do' list. See ya."

Jase watched as Chris bounced to his feet and then homed in on Mrs Budgen who was almost wiggling in her seat because she wanted to dance although no one had asked her. With a theatrical bow, which tugged a smile from Jase's lips, he pulled the stout pensioner who'd been his and Matt's playschool teacher to her feet and led her to the dance floor as 'Angels' came on.

CHAPTER 7

Chris

Everywhere he went, he felt the soldier's eyes on him and it wasn't comfortable. Matt's friends and neighbours treated him like an entertainment act and he was more than happy to play the airhead. It stopped people looking any closer, stopped them finding the real him, because they certainly wouldn't like what they found.

Instead of worrying about Jase, he threw himself into making sure everyone had a bloody good time, from the smallest child, to the wreck who had sired him. It was what he did at the club, although his act was severely toned down in these circumstances. He danced, told jokes, pulled faces at the kids, got drinks and plates of food for Matt and Kate's guests, even though the happy couple had left for their week long honeymoon in Scotland an hour ago. He didn't eat himself, because food often yo-yoed when he was in full 'busy' mode.

As usual, the more he did, the more nervous energy he produced. His head buzzed, his mind going faster than his body. What he needed to slow the spin was a good three hour work out on one of the club podiums, but he was due to spend the night at Sarah's helping to babysit Ryan. Although he knew the 'grown-ups' had cooked up the scheme so someone would keep an eye on him. Wherever he was, sleep definitely wouldn't happen tonight.

Several of the drivers offered him alcohol but after the half a pint of lager Mike had pressed onto him, he switched to lemonade. As soft drinks went, he preferred diet coke, but they only had regular here and he didn't need the caffeine sending him higher. Alcohol had the effect of speeding him up even more, or it did until he overloaded and crashed dramatically. He didn't exactly make the best decisions when he was sober but when he was drunk, 'no' seemed to slip out of his vocabulary entirely.

He was lifting yet another ice cube filled pint to his lips when a hand gripped his wrist.

"That's your fourth pint in an hour, your ninth tonight. You'll flood yourself. I don't suppose Matt and Kate want to spend their wedding night in A and E watching you get emergency dialysis."

Soldier boy stood beside him, his green eyes steady and serious. "E's aren't usually harmful, but you have to watch what you drink with them. You also haven't eaten tonight and from what Kate said, you haven't had anything all day either. Even though it probably doesn't feel like it, you must be running on empty."

Frowning, Chris tried to move his arm, and found he couldn't. After transferring his drink to the other hand, he took two deep swallows before putting it down and turning to his annoying, self-appointed guardian angel, or should that be prison guard?

"I'm not using, I don't need to. What you see is what you get and if you ask nicely, you might get, but right now I have a kid to look after." Glancing down at the large hand still firmly around his wrist, he concluded Jase wasn't going to let him go anytime soon.

"I appreciate the enthusiasm Eddie, and I like being held down as much as the next guy, hell who am I kidding, I fucking love it, but maybe not here, eh? I need to find Ryan, you know, Kate's son? The kid I'm meant to be looking after?"

"Ryan went home with Sarah an hour ago." The smug expression on soldier boy's face because he thought he'd got one over on him, significantly pissed Chris off.

"I knew that. I was just trying to make an excuse to get the hell away from your sanctimonious arse."

Jase's continued grip on his wrist told him that his ability to shock wasn't working quite as well as it usually did. The domineering soldier leaned in till his breath tickled Chris's ear.

"We've established Matt's youngest responsibility is safe, but who's going to look after you tonight?"

A shiver of heat swept through Chris's body, ending in his groin. Yep, being 'looked after' for a few sweaty, energetic hours just might tip him over the edge into sleep. As Sarah had cleared off, he had Matt's house to himself for the night and whoever he chose to spend it with. This evening was getting better by the minute.

"And by that I mean making sure you eat, get home safely and get some sleep in your bed, on your own."

Chris pulled away in surprise. As proposals went, that had to be the crappiest he'd ever received.

The slight twitch of the older man's lips showed he'd known exactly where Chris's mind had been going, but two could play at the teasing game. And unless he'd missed something, he was at least as experienced as this guy at this game, probably more so.

Leaning in, he made sure his lips were almost touching Jase's. "Oh, I'd be happy to let you tuck me in, as long as you fancy having a Bacon sandwich before you turn in, then a full plate of crispy bacon for breakfast. You can choose the sauce."

Jase moved his lips to his ear, and Chris shivered as he felt breath tickling the delicate area. "I don't sleep with anyone unless I know their age and full name, so if you want it–"

Chris jerked away, anger replacing the delicious high at the prospect of falling into a post-coital, much needed sleep in the next three or four hours.

"Matt put you up to this, didn't he? Well fuck him and fuck you. No doubt I'll see you around hop-a-long, don't wait up."

Sticking his hands in his pockets, he made for the door. At least Matt's 'best man' wouldn't be able to tackle him like his brother had that first day. It was a five mile jog into town, but unless someone held him down and forced him to stay still, he'd have another sleepless night. He wasn't sure how many more he could survive before he imploded. Organising a wedding in a week had been intense, and as Matt and Kate needed to work, most of the work had fallen on his shoulders.

"Chris? Chris! Wait up, I can't bloody well chase you," Jase shouted from the door of the village hall as Chris headed out of the carpark.

"That's kind of the point," Chris mumbled as he broke into a jog. Maybe that big guy he'd met last Friday would be at the club. Yes, he still had the bruises, but at least the git had been able to stop his head fizzing. He'd slept for four hours straight afterwards, and the world had been far calmer and slower for the next couple of days.

The phone Matt had bought him vibrated in his pocket. "Yeah?"

"Come back. I promised Matt I'd look after you."

"Good for you GI Joe, but I'm quite capable of looking after myself, been doing it for years. I'll give you a shout tomorrow; you're staying with your folks next door, right?"

"Tell me where you are. I'll come and get you."

"And how the hell are you going to do that with only one leg? Sorry to say, but the cat's away and this mouse has got some serious playing to do. Sweet dreams, Gramps." He made a kissing noise down the phone, ended the call and turned it off.

It was ten past midnight. If he kept up this pace he would be in town in an hour. It gave him two hours before the club closed to find an energetic partner with a bed for the night.

Cars shot past him intermittently, blaring into the darkness, destroying the peace. He imagined them wanting to stop, longing for their engines to turn off, for their lights to go out, so they could cool and rest. But just like him, the cars weren't in charge of their own engines. He just wished his own petrol tank was a lot fucking smaller.

A vehicle slowed behind him, and he turned with a smile and his thumb up. A lift into town would be bloody useful. The smile dropped of his face as he recognised Matt's pick-up. The window wound down as it kept pace with him.

"Get in," Jase ordered from the driver's seat.

"Screw you." To his joy, the vehicle stopped. Hopefully, soldier boy was going to do a U-turn and go back to bed where he belonged.

Abruptly, he heard running feet behind him. A quick glance showed two of Matt's drivers gaining on him rapidly with huge grins on their faces. He took off. There was no way that two half-pissed blokes in their thirties could catch him.

The blue pick-up shot past him and pulled across his path. Chris stopped to prevent himself from running into the front wing. He was about to dodge around the back just as Stuart and Mike caught up.

"In you get." Stuart indicated the passenger seat.

"What is it with you lot? Can't a guy go to a club without the Gestapo tracking him down? Why are you following his orders anyway?"

"He's a sergeant. I was a corporal, Mike was a private."

Rolling his eyes, Chris reached for the door handle. "And if he told you to jump off a fucking bridge, you'd do it right?"

"Yep. You have to respect the chain of command," Stuart replied immediately.

"Bollocks, no one's in charge of me," Chris told them emphatically as he got in the front passenger seat and slammed the door shut.

"And yet here you are," Stuart said cheerfully as he climbed in behind him and Mike got in behind Jase.

"Your moonwalk sucked," Chris told Mike.

"Belt up," Jase instructed without looking at him.

"Should you even be driving?" Chris groused as he complied then folded his arms and hunched down in the seat.

"It's an automatic. My left ankle's buggered, not my right."

"What do you do in the army anyway, head of the 'being a bastard' corps?"

Stuart chuckled. "Nearly kid. He's a Redcap, military police."

"Fucking wonderful. Consider my previous offer of a blowjob rescinded."

"Aw fuck, Tigger, do you have to say stuff like that?" Mike moaned.

Chris grinned to himself. Payback was a bitch. "You should try it sometime mate, it tastes a bit salty, bit slimy, like uncooked egg white with extra salt. If you swallow quick when it hits the back of your throat, you hardly..." The sound of an electric window motor came from the back, followed by retching.

"You caused it, you get to clean it in the morning," Jase said as if discussing the weather.

"I'll do it when we get home if you like."

"When we get home, you are going to bed," Jase said firmly.

"So do you guys want some real live bacon baguette for breakfast, while I get my runny eggs?" The sound of another window opening and two stomachs emptying was music to his ears.

"You little shit, what the fuck am I meant to have in the transport café now? I'll never be able to look at a fry-up in the same way again," Mike moaned. "No bacon, no eggs and I'm sure as fuck never ordering sausage again."

"Will you shut the fuck up? I hadn't thought about sausage yet," Stuart told Mike. "And fuck I shouldn't have said that." The sound of retching filled the car again.

"Yeah, well, think twice about obeying 'I-fell-over-a-penguin,' here when it concerns me in the future."

Both men in the back roared with laughter. "Seriously, you got invalided out because you tripped over a penguin?"

Chris saw Jase scowl for the first time, and filed away the fact that insulting his 'machismo' pushed his buttons.

"That's what I told Matt, you know what a worrier he is. And if you tell him this I'll beat your arses, and even you won't enjoy that, Chris. My ankle is wired together because I got caught by a suicide bomber in Helmand. My colleague didn't make it. She was twenty-two, first tour. I discharged myself early from hospital to be here, so I could really do without this shit."

The word 'guilt' didn't really cover what Chris was feeling.

"I'm sorry, I didn't..." he started. He needed to say something, anything, to stop the oppressive silence in the vehicle.

"Shut it, just shut it, you stupid, selfish little shit."

The rest of the short ride was silent as the depth of his idiocy rolled around his head. *Why the hell were these good people, genuine heroes for fuck's sake, doing spending time on his useless hide?*

When they got back to Matt's house, Stuart jumped out and opened Jase's door. Mike retrieved a pair of crutches for the back and handed them over.

"You need a hand, with him or anything else, at any time, just give me or Mike a shout. We've both been over there."

"Thanks, but I think he'll behave himself now. Right, Chris?"

When he didn't answer, Jase got a little louder. "I said, 'right, Chris'?"

"Yeah, whatever." He didn't look at the others, no doubt they had smug, superior expressions on their faces but they deserved them.

"Actually, can you two come in for a minute?"

Chris looked up to see a hard, calculating expression on Jase's face.

Knowing he sounded immature, Chris heard himself huff as he used his key to get into Matt's house. The three military men followed him in, but he ignored them. Perhaps they were going to have a 'During the war' buddy bonding session.

"Hold him," Jase's voice rang out and Chris found himself on his knees, both hands twisted up his back and his face rammed into a sofa cushion.

"What the fuck," he shouted and tried to twist out of their grip but they held him tight.

"Matt's worried he's on something, and judging from his behaviour tonight, I have to agree. I think it's time we found out what and start to get him clean before Matt brings his new family back here, don't you?"

"He's always bloody lively, I'll give him that," Mike said.

"Right, we search him, then his room, and go from there," Jase ordered. "We're looking for pills, powders and needles." Suddenly there were hands touching him that he hadn't invited. His shirt was pulled over his head, effectively blindfolding him.

He twisted and struggled, but he couldn't get away.

"Where did you get the bruises, Chris? Did you let someone do that to buy a fix?" Jase's hard voice sounded from just behind him. "Check his arms for track marks."

"Get the fuck off me, I don't fucking use, I'd rather die," he shouted.

"Nothing here," Mike said from his right.

"Me neither," Stuart added from his left.

"There are other places, get his trousers."

They think I'm like her, but I am, I really fucking am. How long will it be before...

That was the moment he really started to fight, not against them, but against what was in his head.

"Calm down mate, we aren't going to do anything to you, we only want to help." Mike sounded as if he was gritting his teeth as he pushed down on his shoulder while he pulled his arm up his back. It meant that the hands on his trousers were Jase's.

"If you don't let me go, right fucking now, I'll be out of here the first chance I get. I hope you enjoy explaining to Matt, Kate and Ryan why I'm not here when they get back."

"I don't give a shit what you do. You turned up out of the blue, and you can fuck off the same way for all I care. They'll get over it far quicker than having a smack head in the house with a little kid and a baby around."

"I'm not a fucking addict, I've got fucking ADHD," he shouted.

The hands stilled, then released him, but they'd seen all his junk anyway. Why it mattered when he'd been intimate with so many guys he didn't know, but it did. Grabbing his trousers he hauled them up, turned over and tried to get up. Jase pushed him back down.

"Search his room."

Chris couldn't believe his ears. He looked up at the hard face. At least Mike and Stuart didn't seem quite so ready to obey his orders now. The decisive body language had morphed into drooping shoulders.

"Mate, he's hyperactive, that's why he can't sit still," Mike tried.

"And I've heard that excuse a hundred times," Jase said without a hint of sympathy. "Even if it's true, It doesn't explain the bruises or why he won't tell anyone his real name, date of birth, or previous address. For all we know he's a runaway fifteen-year-old, a rent boy, an absconder from a young offenders institution or all of the above. All of which would bring a pile of shit down on Matt's head that he really doesn't need."

Mike and Stuart looked at each other, but didn't speak.

"Seriously, how old do you think he is?" Jase asked them. "Just because he claims to have the same surname as an au pair who last worked here eighteen years ago doesn't mean the affair didn't go on after she left. Richard might be his father, but we've got no proof she's his mother."

They seemed to have it all worked out so Chris kept quiet, besides, they'd just stripped him naked and not because they fancied him. All sympathy for Jase and his heroic injury drained away like dirty bathwater down a plughole.

Stuart squatted down beside the sofa. Chris pulled the sides of his shirt together as best he could seeing as most of the buttons were missing, and wiped the snot off his face with the back of his hand. It was snot, definitely snot, he didn't cry, not anymore.

"How old are you? We can't help you if you don't let us in."

He indicted his ruined shirt, then looked each of them in the eye. "This is helping is it? I was better off living in the fucking tent. At least the guys who screwed me back then didn't pretend it was for my own fucking good."

Stuart and Mike both looked thoroughly ashamed. Jase stared at him impassively.

"I'll check his room. Make sure he doesn't piss off. As for you, when you give me a reason to trust you, I will."

Chris stared at him for a few seconds, neither giving in until Jase turned around and made his way slowly up the stairs, using the banisters to keep off his injured ankle.

Stuart flopped down beside him on the sofa. "Jase wasn't this intense at school," he said to no one in particular.

Mike parked his backside up against the back of one of the brown leather armchairs. "Four tours can do that to you."

"So can being a Redcap. Paranoia goes with the job," Stuart said.

"You know, giving him some personal details would go a long way to reassure him that you're not screwing over his best friend," Mike prompted.

Chris kept his lips firmly shut. Once he started talking, he probably wouldn't be able to stop. It was nice here, probably the best place he'd ever stayed, or at least it had been up to now.

"Without those details you won't be able to get a driving license, a proper job, a place of your own, or anything really. It sucks, but the world relies on those details," Stuart said carefully.

"I've got ADHD you stupid bastard, it doesn't mean I'm thick. Besides, who said I couldn't drive?"

"Why didn't you say you've got a licence? You can get a job with us lot," Mike said.

"Never said I've got a licence, just that I can drive, probably better than any of you," he muttered.

"When were you diagnosed?" Jase said as he appeared at the top of the stairs.

"I'm not telling you shit. If I can last nearly seven weeks with Matt and Kate trying to wheedle it out of me, I can survive you for a week. That is, if you can manage to keep me here."

"In case my dear brother didn't tell you, I don't sleep. But I bet you're going to need some hefty painkillers for that heroically buggered ankle. When the cat's asleep, this mouse is going to piss the fuck off."

"And go where? Back to living in a tent, living off scraps? Turning tricks in alleyways for cans of coke and sweeties?" Jase asked coldly.

The pity and contempt coming off the three men thickened the air until Chris felt he would choke on it. Didn't they get that he was the one who did the looking after? People didn't look after him, he looked after them or at least he'd tried. He'd fucked that up too. Jase was right, Matt, Kate and Ryan were better off without him.

"I'll be fine, I always am," he mumbled, but he didn't look at any of them.

"Oh yeah? So why, after seven weeks, are you still on antibiotics for a chronic lung infection, and pills for malnutrition?" Jase said as he held up the white pill bottles that had been beside his bed.

Chris knew he looked like a sulky teenager as he shrugged and focused on his knees, but he didn't have a choice.

"Get some sleep Sarge, I'll keep an eye on him for you," Stuart said.

"I'll just be next door if you need me," Jase said and made his way out the front door without sparing Chris another glance.

CHAPTER 8

Jase

Jase could hardly drag himself into the bathroom to do a strip wash when he got home. No light came from under his parents' door. When he'd wiped off the grime from the busy day, he went back to his room and flopped back onto the bed letting the towel fall away.

His dick didn't seem to be sharing his need for sleep, in fact, he was getting harder by the second. Seeing Matt again must be causing this unwanted boner. He'd tried telling his dick that Matt wasn't interested many times over the years, but it never seemed to listen. Going to sleep with sex on his mind was possible, but when he did that, he often had a wet dream. Semen stained sheets wouldn't be any easier to explain to his mother now than they'd been fifteen years ago.

He gripped his throbbing cock in his hand and started with gentle strokes, imagining entering Matt from behind. He'd long since stopped worrying about fantasising about Matt, as it'd always been the quickest way to get off. Tomorrow was going to be draining and he needed as much sleep as he could get.

His fingers gripped tightly around himself as he remembered how Matt's butt muscles had moved underneath his smooth skin in the school showers. Locking his fingers around his length, he stroked them up and down in a rhythm he knew would get him off quickly.

In his imagination, he was kissing those tender pink lips. Cupping his balls with his free hand, Jase slowly rolled them between his fingers, imagining Matt doing it. He groaned, as fantasy Matt replaced his hand with his tongue.

Strokes turned into tugs as he pumped into his hand at the same rate as Matt's imaginary mouth. When the familiar tingle started at the base of his spine, his hips bucked faster, thrusting him harder into Matt's mouth. He saw the dark eyes he'd fantasized about gazing up at him, pupils blown with lust. He tugged harder, imagining Matt's body tensing and working hard to bring about the explosion they both craved.

Heat soared through his balls, drawing them up. He came hard, imagining spilling into that hot mouth instead of across his own stomach. But it wasn't Matt's face he saw in those last few moments; it was Chris's. Cursing himself for being a dirty old man, Jase wiped himself clean. Carefully, he positioned himself to sleep with his injured ankle propped up on a pillow on top of the quilt.

* * *

Waking up in your childhood room when you were nearing thirty was odd. It was also rather sad that it was still the only place in the world that he thought of as home. Then again, Matt still lived in the house he'd been born in and it was where his kid would come into the world. The permanence and stability of his friend's life, after all the disruption and chaos he'd seen overseas, made it even more precious.

Thinking about Matt, he turned his mind to the task he'd been set. Crispy Bacon, Tigger, or whatever the hell his name was, was not only disrupting the smooth continuity of life next door, he was invading his fantasies too.

The kid was as nervous as a cat on a hot tin roof whenever anyone asked about his past. He was also so full of bravado that he strutted like a peacock shaking his tail feathers. Chris has certainly done a great deal of tail shaking last night, which was probably the cause of that highly inappropriate erotic fantasy.

He'd been so painfully hard when Chris had been talking about blowjobs, swallowing cum and bacon sandwiches in the car that he'd regretted bringing Matt's two drivers along. He'd known Stuart at school, the guy had been a few years older, not necessarily a friend but not an enemy either. Both were typical enlisted men, rough around the edges, but as loyal as they came.

But he never would've caught Chris without them. He wouldn't have been able to search him either. He pushed the thought of that bubble butt bent over the sofa last night out of his mind. He didn't have time to indulge himself again.

Even though he hadn't found anything illegal, he was positive Chris was hiding something apart from hyperactivity, but it probably wasn't hard drug abuse. It would be one thing off Matt's mind. However, his extreme reaction to the mention of drugs and his refusal to take even prescription sleeping pills was a big red arrow to some sort of adverse experience with substance abuse.

This brand new little brother was an intriguing puzzle who could occupy him, in a completely non-erotic way, while he healed enough to decide what the hell to do with the rest of his life.

As much as he loved spending time with Matt, working in the haulage firm's office didn't float his boat; besides, he didn't know squat about the legal aspects of haulage. Jase knew investigating crime and tracking down distressed, volatile squaddies and finding out why they'd gone AWOL. Which wasn't dissimilar to the situation next door.

Moving carefully, he rolled over and sat up. Even with the strong painkillers he'd taken as soon as he'd got home last night, he'd still had trouble sleeping because of the continual throb. Hopefully, he hadn't done his ankle too much damage chasing around last night. He'd said he was ok to drive, as the others had been drinking, but he really wasn't. Bending his leg, he winced at the large red tinged patch on the bandage. Yep, he'd busted something last night. Hopefully the wound was just seeping a little, rather than having opened up again. Facing more surgery was not on his agenda, even the thought of what it looked like made him queasy.

"Morning," he greeted his parents as he used both crutches to make his way into the kitchen. He wondered if either of his impromptu posse from the night before had medic training. If they didn't, he'd have to call Sarah and that would cause all sorts of problems. She'd probably confine him to bed and she'd definitely take Chris off his hands. The idea was surprisingly upsetting.

"Hello dear. Good night?" As usual his mother didn't wait for a reply as she launched into a blow by blow description of how they had spent the evening, even though he'd been in the same room most of the time.

"Matt's brother is really fun, don't you think? He certainly doesn't hide his light under a bushel. I remember his mother, pretty little Mediterranean looking thing, although there was a bit of an American twang there sometimes. She was always busy, with dark curly hair and flashing dark eyes, just like him. Such a good looking boy, and can't he dance well? Some of his moves were making the old folk blush, but Mrs Budgen was almost drooling. Jason, are you listening? I said Matt's brother, Chrisander, is a good looking boy."

He focused back on her rather than the pain. "How do you know his full name is Chrisander?"

She gave him a 'silly boy' look. "I don't, not really. I just remember Chrisander was her grandfather's name. He was the only relative she ever mentioned." She smiled to herself shaking her head slightly at the memory. "The pride when she spoke about him fighting the Fascists in Italy..." She smiled to herself. "I just assumed he was named aft—"

"Thanks Mum." He kissed the top of her head, which made his father lower his paper briefly.

"What was that for?" she asked.

"For having such an incredible memory. Do you remember anything else about her?"

"Just that her birthday is the same date as your father's, October 10th. She mentioned it when I took a piece of cake round for Gwen. I came back and got her a piece too, poor thing didn't get a single card or present. To be honest, I don't think she even told her family where she was, if she had one."

"You're a star. I'll see you later."

Keeping his weight entirely off his ankle, he put his shoe on, then made his way down his parents' driveway and up Matt's. Usually he would have hopped over the fence, but that wouldn't happen again any time soon.

He knocked gently on the door. Mike opened it a few seconds later. "I came round at six to take over from Stuart," he whispered. "Chris wasn't kidding about not sleeping, he only dozed off an hour and a half ago. Stuart took him for a walk about three because he was still bouncing off the walls. It's a good job Stuart's been working nights this week otherwise he never would've lasted."

Jase hobbled into the living room. Chris was asleep on the sofa on his back, his knees propped up as if sleep had snuck up on him when he wasn't looking. Without the grins and the scowls, he appeared younger and far more vulnerable than he had last night. His hand still held a pencil and a pad of paper with a half-finished portrait of Stuart lay on his lap. Other drawings spread across the coffee table. The one of himself with devil horns and a snarl mad him snort, but most were of people at the wedding, including many of Kate and Matt gazing lovingly at each other. Each picture captured a moment in time, an emotion or a thought. How had Chris had time to notice it all with the amount of energy he'd expended?

"He's good, isn't he?" Mike murmured.

"At drawing? Yeah, he is, but I think he's pretty screwed up otherwise."

Jase indicated with his head that they should go through to the kitchen, both to prevent waking Chris with their conversation, and because his ankle throbbed like a bitch.

"I don't buy the 'happy chappie' act for a minute. Do you?"

"I did, but after last night? I agree with you. He's a good lad, always helpful around the yard. He's always busy, never sits still unless he's got a pad of paper and a pencil in his hand. He's done a portrait of everyone in the firm, Matt's got them on the wall in the office. It's as if he takes a photo in his head and then just copies it out."

Jase shifted uncomfortably. "Sorry to change the subject, but this is bloody sore. Did you have medic training? The dressing needs checking and it's hard to see it myself properly."

"Yeah, no problem." Mike said. "Do you know where Matt keeps his supplies?"

Five minutes later, Jase had his foot up on the kitchen table and Mike was peeling the dressing off. His pinched expression told Jase everything he needed to know. He certainly wasn't going to look himself if it was making a trained army medic pull that face.

"That bad?"

"It's fucking horrible. How the hell did they let you out with this?"

Jase shrugged. "Best mate was getting married. What can I say? The nurse was sweet on me. Can you patch it up or not?"

Mike looked doubtful. "I can change the dressing, but unless you keep off it, and keep it elevated to take the swelling down, you're going to bust these stitches and it'll be slice and dice time again, that is, if they can save it."

"I'm sorry."

Jase turned to see a gloriously dishevelled Chris standing in the doorway. He looked as if he'd just crawled out of someone's bed after being thoroughly fucked all night. The only problem with the picture was that he hadn't been involved.

"No problem. It was my choice to come after you, Chrisander."

The youngster stiffened, but he didn't confirm it was his name, then again, he didn't deny it either.

"My mum remembers your mum talking about her grandad being in the war. You were named after him, right?"

Chris shrugged and looked away. "He's dead; I never met him."

"Matt said your mum's overseas, right?" That caused a scowl.

"What's this, twenty questions before breakfast? I thought you got the hint I don't want to talk about it last night."

Jase smiled. "Oh I got the memo, I'm just a stubborn git."

"Bastard."

"Nope, that would be you."

Mike's jaw dropped open, but after a second's pause, Chris chuckled. "You got that right, with big fucking bells on. Now, what's your plan for today? I'm going for a run. Fancy coming with?"

He cocked his head to the side, his eyes sparkling with mischief. "Oh right, you can't, can you?"

"Touché, but you're not going anywhere. Today you're going to be my legs."

Now that got a reaction. The grin dropped off Chris's face. "You can't be serious? I can't stay in here all day, I'll be climbing the walls in an hour."

"You won't be inside all day, you have a car to clean remember?"

The grin came back like a lightbulb turning on. "Oh yeah. Runny eggs. Fancy some breakfast, Mike? I'm cooking or do you want to donate?"

Mike turned a little green. "You're one sick fucker, you know that? I'm off. Call me if you need me Sarge, but if I've got to chase him down again, I'm bringing a gag and a cattle prod."

"And handcuffs, I just luurv handcuffs. Spreader bars are cool too," Chris called out as Mike made a hasty exit.

Plonking himself down in Mike's recently vacated chair he said, "Got to love those straight guys, they are so easy to wind up."

"Coffee," Jase instructed. With a roll of his eyes, Chris jumped back to his feet and put the kettle on.

"How do you like it, Eddie? Hot, white and so sweet it'll make your teeth ache?" Chris stuck his hip out and flicked his hair.

Jase couldn't help grinning. "Nope, black and bitter."

Chris dropped the act. "Crap, that's me out the frame then." He poured the coffee and put the mug on the table.

"You're not having one?"

"Coffee and me? You've got to be kidding. I'm jittery on orange juice, let alone Matt's extra strong cappuccino. That reminds me, drug time."

Gathering up the pill pots Jase had found in his room the night before, he tipped one of each into his hand, then swallowed them dry.

"Mmm, yum. Not having a gag reflex comes in handy in all sorts of situations, The green ones are bitter, but I can't get enough of the red ones. See? I can be responsible. What's next? Puke removal?"

The guy was as eager for action as a dog was for a walk. Jase had known a few soldiers who had mild ADHD, the constant action of training or patrolling suited them down to the ground. But he'd never met anyone quite like Chris.

"You're still wearing the same clothes as last night."

Chris lifted his armpit and sniffed. "Stale sweat doesn't do it for you then?"

"It does for you?"

Chris's face broke into a broad smile. "Aw, I knew you fancied me; trying to find out what floats my boat already are you? To tell you the truth, I really like it when a bloke—"

"Just get washed and dressed will you?" Exhaustion dragged at him already and he'd only been here half an hour. He didn't know how Chris was so bloody perky on less than two hours sleep, but the dark circles under his eyes showed the truth.

"Sure you don't want to come wash my back or anything else for that matter?" Chris said then ducked out of the room as Jase threw one of the plastic pill pots at him.

The dark marks under his eyes had vanished when Chris came down. He looked fresh, energetic and he exhausted the hell out Jase just by being in the same room. As Chris danced to a rhythm only he could hear as he moved around the kitchen, making the promised bacon sandwich, Jase noticed other slight blemishes on Chris's face had disappeared too. The make-up explained how Chris fooled so many people.

The day proceeded in much the same way, with Chris pushing him in every way possible, always with a grin and not so subtle innuendos. It didn't help matters that every time that cheeky bright smile appeared, Jase had the urge to hold him down and wipe it off with his own lips.

Watching Chris's lithe body bending over, scrubbing at the side of the pick-up made more than his ankle throb. Then he remembered the cane marks and other bruises lurking beneath the vest and shorts. His desire faded.

How many blokes had Chris slept with in his short life? Jase pushed the thought out of his mind. It didn't matter because he was Matt's little brother and Jase wasn't going there, even if being told he was attractive, almost constantly, didn't do his own ego any harm. The fact that

Chris flirted with everyone in his vicinity, even female geriatrics who had lost control of their bodily functions, negated the effect somewhat.

Washing the car, cleaning the house and cutting the grass on both properties, as well as forcing Chris to sit still long enough to eat a sandwich at midday, took them to mid-afternoon. Chris didn't seem to be flagging at all. Jase wanted to go back to bed, and he'd only been watching from a chair.

"You tired old man?" Chris mimed shadow boxing as he bobbed and weaved his way back up the garden path from the shed. He was wearing a pair of baggy green shorts and a blue tie-dye vest, but his skin was the same light tan colour all over.

Jase couldn't help remembering him pinned down on the sofa last night, ass bare. He bet Chris would be as exhausting in bed as he was everywhere else, holding him down forcefully might be the only way to do it. His dick seemed to like the idea of having the lithe body at its mercy. Recalling Chris's comment about handcuffs and spreader bars exacerbated the problem occurring in his boxers. *How does he know about spreader bars? I've never even seen one in real life.*

"You still with me, Sarge? Don't want to lie down or anything?"

"I think its coffee and foot up time again," he said and started to get up from the patio chair where he'd watched Chris cut the grass.

"Go park your ancient wrinkly arse. I'll get the coffee."

"I'm twenty seven you little shit, that's not old," he called as Chris shimmied around him and raced indoors.

"Are you, or are you not, about to be put out to pasture by the army?" he called out from the kitchen as Jase lowered himself onto the sofa feeling every bit a retired man.

"Well, yeah, but I could have signed on for longer if I'd wanted."

Chris came in carrying a mug and put it within Jase's reach before putting a cushion on the coffee table and lifted Jase's leg gently on to it.

"Thanks."

"You're welcome. At least you don't piss and shit yourself like the residents of Dad's nursing home."

From the bright smile on his face, Chris was still indulging in his slow torture routine, but two could play at that game.

"So, anything you want to ask me?" he said, then hastily qualified his question with, "anything apart from my sex life that is."

"Spoil sport." Chris cocked his head to one side. "Is this a case of I ask a question, then you ask one?"

"If you like."

"Well if you're not going to spill all the beans, I reserve the right to refuse to answer any of yours too."

"Fair enough. You first."

Chris pursed his lips then wiggled them from side to side as he thought.

"What do you want to be when you grow up?"

Jase blinked then burst out laughing. "Seriously?"

Chris grinned back. "You're cute when you laugh. You should do it more often."

He's just playing you, like he does everyone else.

"Yeah well, not much to laugh about recently," he indicated his foot.

"Not to mention the fact the guy you've had a crush on since you realised your dick was for more than pissing just got married." Chris looked at him from under his eyelashes as he took a sip of tea, gauging his reaction.

"That ship sailed a long time ago," Jase said, then a smile tickled his lips. If he was going to get Chris to open up, he had to share a little too. "Although I won't ever forget the look on his face the one time I tried to kiss him."

Chris's eyes lit up with glee. "You're kidding? You did? When? What did he do?"

"We were sixteen, GCSE results day. For a start his eyes nearly popped out, then he shoved me so hard I nearly landed on my arse. But your brother's a good man, he still spoke to me, after a while. Although him constantly trying to fix me up gets a bit old."

"Never been anyone else who matches up eh?"

"My turn for a question."

Chris held up his hand in a scout salute. "I hereby reserve the right not to answer any question that could incriminate me further." He folded his arms, hugging himself. "Shoot."

"What do you want to do when you grow up?"

He answered immediately. "Artist in the morning, model in the afternoon, dancer in the evening, porn star at night. Sleep's for wimps."

"You sure you're not a triplet?"

"Nah, only child...Crap." He scowled at Jase for getting a bit of personal information out of him. "You're a sneaky bugger, aren't you?"

Jase pretended to buff his fingernails on his shirt. "It's the result of years of training and possessing a natural in-built bullshit detector. Apart from the art, which coming from a complete art bellend, seems bloody good and dancing, which, although it pains me to say, you're also not too shabby at, what are you good at?"

"Bullshit."

Jase had to give him that one, the cheeky grin made him forget the pain in his foot.

"And that's two questions in a row for you. My turn again." Chris rubbed his hands together in glee. "Are you leaving the army because you're scared next time it won't be just an ankle that gets blown up, or are they throwing you to the knackers for being a lame horse?"

After taking a swig of coffee, he said, "Bit of both. If I never see another desert, I'll be happy. You have no idea how good all the 'green' here looks. Plus, field work with a weakness means my colleagues would have to take up the slack, which isn't fair. They were pushing me to take a commission before this happened and it was a requirement if I stayed with this." He patted his thigh. "The higher up you go, the more admin you get landed with. I don't mind following paper trails, tracking down information on a case, but endless performance evaluations and staff rotas? Not my thing. I'm a nosy bastard at heart, I want to know why people do the shit they do."

"I bet I piss you off big time, don't I?" Instead of the expected cocky smirk, Chris looked sad. To his surprise, Jase felt a stab of remorse himself, that face shouldn't be sad, it didn't look...right.

Chris seemed to shake himself out of whatever hole he'd drifted into. "So what now, Mr Redcap?"

Jase shrugged. "Staying here while I heal, back for check-ups and physio at the Queen Victoria in Birmingham. Maybe setting up my own private investigation business."

Chris held out his hand and wobbled it from side to side. "Can't quite see you as Ace Ventura, but..."

"Somebody stop meee."

Chris fell off the sofa laughing at Jase's woefully bad impression. "Oh fuck, that's funny, it's like the Queen saying, 'Eat my shorts'," he got out between gasps as he rolled on the floor.

Jase tried to look offended but couldn't resist Chris's infective laughter. When they wound down, he took a chance and asked a question he knew might offend.

"So what stops you?"

Chris eyed him suspiciously. "What d'you mean?"

"What stops you bouncing off the walls so you can sleep? I don't know much about ADHD, but I do know lack of sleep makes it worse."

Chris picked up his now probably cold tea and took a mouthful. "I've tried lots of things. I took Ritalin for a week when I was a kid but it made it worse. It also gave me a hard-on that lasted six hours which might be fun now, but it was fucking scary when I was eight. Alcohol knocks me out eventually, but a hangover when I'm hyper is bloody awful. So, as you probably noticed with your fucking detective skills last night, I don't drink much. And I don't, ever, take drugs. I mean that, never ever. That's what freaked me out last night, not being touched, cos that happens..." His voice faded away.

Chris accepting being touched intimately by complete strangers as normal, bothered him more than it should, considering their tenuous day-old relationship. However, Matt pussyfooting around Chris's issues for the last seven weeks, because he didn't want to send him off the deep-end, hadn't helped either.

"I was wrong last night, but you've got to admit, there were warning signs."

Chris shrugged, head down.

"What else works?" Jase prompted after the silence stretched for nearly a minute.

"Physical exhaustion, if I time it right. Too much, or an emotional upset at the wrong time puts me right back where I started or worse."

"Which is what happened last night," Jase filled in for him.

"I was getting there. I probably shouldn't be telling you this, but I have been known to do some pretty stupid things when I'm really buzzing."

He couldn't help grinning at the pointless confession. "No shit, Sherlock. So did I save you from yourself last night? Because that'd polish my ego no end."

Chris laughed. " 'Fraid not, Caped Crusader, I wasn't that bad last night. But it does get scary. Sometimes I can feel it taking over, everything buzzes like I've got ants on the inside. I know I'm fucking up, doing stupid shit, but I just can't stop myself." He snorted. "Like the Mask."

"So what would have happened if we hadn't caught you last night?" Jase asked quietly, not wanting to stop the flow of information.

Chris concentrated on the last dregs of his tea. "I would have gone to the club, danced till someone big, someone forceful, hit on me. Then back to his place." He shrugged. "Lots of rough sex, restraints if I'm lucky, then hopefully not being kicked out afterwards so I can get a few hours sleep."

"You like being tied up?" He knew he'd said the wrong thing when Chris glared at him.

"No, I don't like being 'tied up'. It forces me to stay still, gives me a chance to calm down enough to sleep. My mum used to hold me still in bed with her when I was small, when I was older she…Fuck." He shot to his feet and started pacing, every inch of him tight and defensive.

"Why the hell am I telling you all this crap? I'm fucked up. I know it and now you know it. Tell Matt his brother is a psycho he'd be better off without when he gets back. I don't give a shit."

"Sit down. I can't chase you, but I know a couple of guys who will. Save yourself, and me, the effort," Jase said quietly. Chris looked surprised to find he was on his feet and halfway towards the door.

With a dramatic sigh he flopped back down onto the sofa. But it only lasted a second before he hunched forward, and his leg jiggled up and down as if it had a mind of its own.

"Stop it."

"What?"

Jase indicated his leg with his eyes.

"Oh, sorry." Gritting his teeth, Chris managed to stop the movement.

"So apart from being physically forced to stop moving, what helps?"

Chris huffed and looked out the window. "Nothing when I've got to a certain level. I just have to wait it out till I crash. The longest I've gone without any sleep at all was three days, but it's been better since I've been here. I usually get a couple of hours a night, sometimes more."

"And how do you prevent getting to that level?"

"The normal boring shit."

"Don't go all stroppy teenager on me, even if you are one. If the people around you understand you a little more we can help you control it, just like you help other people. You made last night so much more enjoyable for a lot of people, and Kate said they love you down at the nursing home. So I'll ask again, what 'normal shit'?"

Chris huffed, then gave him a tight smile without an inch of his usual happiness.

"Routine and moderation, living like a fucking monk. Regular meals, regular exercise, staying in bed, even if I don't sleep, for a few hours every night. No booze, no caffeine, no sugar hits. No game consoles after five, having a bedtime routine, essentially being a fucking toddler."

"And your mum helped you with that? Before she left?"

He regretted the question immediately as Chris tensed up. There was something going on there, but pushing any further on that front probably wasn't going to work. "But that's not relevant now, what we need to do is get you back into a routine so things are calm for when Ryan comes to live with you."

Chris shrugged and looked out the window, but at least he didn't argue.

"Right, time for you to go visit your Dad at the home."

Chris blinked at him. "Now?"

"Yep, right now."

Shaking his head in disbelief, Chris stood up and went to get his shoes. He came back in with them on his feet and he was holding Jase's single shoe.

"I'm not going."

Chris frowned. "Then how am I...oh. It's four miles each way. Remember I said that if I get too tired, I'm worse?"

"I'll cope if it happens. When you get back, pop next door to my place, I'll tell mum there's going to be one more for dinner. I hope you like pie."

"What sort?"

"Bacon pie unless you get a move on. Dinner is at seven, and you make my mother wait at your peril."

The answering grin lit up Chris's face. "Don't worry, I've never met an old lady I can't charm."

CHAPTER 9

Chris

The visit with his dad was fun, or at least larking about with the nurses was entertaining. He'd found his father calling him 'Crispy Bacon' amusing at first but the fact that he still didn't understand he was his son, hurt.

He still felt adrift in the world, as if he was hanging on to reality and his own sanity with his fingertips. At least he was no longer in freefall, although he had slipped a bit last night. The verdant, English summer landscape around him as he jogged home let him think. It was something he usually avoided like the plague, being in his own head wasn't fun.

Sleep and his hyper demon played a never ending game of hide and seek. He tried not to notice sleep sneaking up on him, hoping it would bash the demon over the head before the bastard noticed it was there. It sucked that it had eyes in the back of its head. Even when he was virtually passing out from physical exhaustion, just as he was about to drift off, he always thought, *is this it? Am I going to sleep?* Then the moment, the opportunity, for unconsciousness evaporated.

There had been thousands of drawings of the demon over the years, dark, undefined images of creeping fear and endless frustration that went in the bin as soon as they were finished. Thinking about it, he hadn't drawn a 'demon' picture in what, three weeks? That was certainly a difference. He'd slept a little last night and that was an ongoing theme recently. He hadn't had a completely sleepless night for about a month, but it was still usually only an hour or two. Plus he was eating fairly regularly. Thanks to Jase, he'd had both breakfast and lunch today. It looked as if he was going to get dinner too.

This wasn't the first time he'd made these connections, but without someone pointing them out, he often let his routines slide and ended up back at square one or worse. Sleeping rough had definitely led to a major FUBAR situation. If he hadn't been ill and half starved, Matt would never have caught him that day, but he had. It had been the best thing to happened to him in a long time.

Living with Matt brought some much needed stability to his minute by minute, kaleidoscopic, swirling world. But his brother worked long hours and had been courting Kate from almost the first day. It hadn't left much time to supervise his stupid, hyperactive kid brother, not that he should have to babysit him. It meant he'd been able to keep most of his fucked-up-ness to himself.

On the other hand, in less than twenty-four hours, Sergeant Jason Rosewood, irritating, intense and fucking gorgeous Eddie Bull, appeared to have made him his personal pet project. Although it wasn't going all the domineering soldier's way. The way he'd been able to wheedle, or more likely irritate, personal details out him made him smile as his feet continued to eat up the tarmac.

He frowned. Crap. Jase had got far more information out of him than the other way around. Then again, the guy was a trained interrogator, so what was he expecting, an easy win? Strategizing took up his attention for the rest of his run.

Matt's house was empty when he let himself in. Did Jase think that just because he'd won last night, and Chris had played ball today, that he was going to roll over and admit defeat? Dinner with the parents, whom he already had under his thumb due to doing their outside chores for the last month, was an opportunity for points he couldn't pass up. Smiling to himself, he went to shower and change, the stiff upper lipped sod wouldn't know what hit him.

The look on Jase's face when he walked into his parents' living room was worth every second of pounding the eight miles of footpath. The guy didn't know whether to hide his face behind a cushion or drag him back out the door by his ear. But once outside, whether Jase wanted to beat the crap out of him, or strip him naked and fuck him to within an inch of his life, he wasn't sure. Whichever it was, his clothing definitely did not meet with Sarge's approval. *Score another one for Bacon.*

By the twitch on Susan's lips when she'd opened the door, he'd got it exactly right. Skin-tight purple stretch jeans and a bright pink t-shirt that ended three inches above his waistband with 'Too Fabulous to be Straight,' emblazoned across the front in gold glitter.

"Well what do you think?" He indicated his body with one hand while he put the other on his cocked hip.

"You look ridiculous. Go change," Jase ground out.

His puppy dog eyes and pout as he dropped the pose and hunched his shoulders would've melted an iceberg. Susan Rosewood didn't stand a chance.

Her arm went around him as she turned laser beam eyes on her son. "Leave him alone, Jason. If this is how he feels comfortable, this is how he should be. I think it's great that he doesn't try to hide who he is, unlike some. And yes dear, we know you're gay, but it might have been nice for you to tell us. I've been looking forward to your 'coming out' speech since you were fifteen." She sniffed and turned her attention back to him. Jase looked as if someone had blown him up again.

"I think you look wonderful, Chrisander."

"I prefer Chris," he mumbled.

"Chris it is," his mother said brightly. "Now come and tell me what you want to drink and we'll leave the two army fuddy duddies to talk tanks and marching."

Just as he was about to leave the room, he looked back over his shoulder and stuck his tongue out at Jase. David coughed to cover his laughter.

Chris was positive that he found dinner far more entertaining than Jase did, especially when Susan asked him for fashion advice. He'd waxed lyrically about fabric and how stripes were 'in' again. Thank god he'd watched morning TV a couple of times last week. Apart from 'bright, tight and often offensive' when it came to own clothes, his knowledge was pretty limited.

By nine, they'd retired to the living room after Jase's mother had done her best to stuff him like a Christmas turkey, in between comments such as 'you're too slim Chris, you need to eat more.' To which he'd replied, 'Yep, I agree, I'd love to get some more meat on my bones, and the sooner the better.' At which point he'd waggled his eyebrows at Jase who choked on his lager.

His request for extra cream with dessert because 'he could never get enough of that stuff,' elicited a look that could kill.

After having drawn a very flattering pencil portrait of Mr and Mrs Rosewood on printer paper, he was positive they were both eating out of the palm of his hand. Jase was about to blow a gasket. And he still had one more 'parent whispering' trick up his sleeve.

"You wouldn't have any pictures of Jase and my brother when they were little do you? Is it true they've been best friends since they were born?"

The beaming smile on Susan's face contrasted strongly with the heartfelt groan from her son. When she'd left the room, Jase levered his recliner armchair closed.

"Don't you think you should be turning in, Chris? You didn't get much sleep last night and it's getting late."

He gave Jase a toothy smile. "Not tired. I don't know if you've noticed lights on next door in the night since I arrived, David, but I'm a chronic insomniac. I hate to admit it, but the only thing that sends me off without fail is someone reading me a story."

"Oh come on, now I know you're pulling my leg," David said. "If a book sends you to sleep, why not read one yourself?"

"I can't read."

"Bollocks," Jase exploded. "Complete and utter bollocks. I've put up with you spouting crap all evening, and now—"

"Jason, that's enough." David's voice cut through Jase's tirade like a knife. "Whether he's telling the truth is immaterial; he's a guest in this house, my house may I remind you, and you will show him respect."

"Have you heard what he's been saying about cream and shit? And look what he's wearing, that's not exactly respectful is it?"

"You will not use that sort of language in my home." Mr Rosewood's finger jabbed towards his son.

Chris realised where Jase got some of his attitude from. This was a side of the older man he'd never seen, and he'd caused him to lose his cool, caused him to be upset with his son. This family had been happy before he'd poked his nose in. Just because he was a fucked-up bastard, it didn't mean he had the right to upset people who weren't.

"He made your mother smile, which is all I care about. If you can't cope with someone advertising–"

Glancing at the clock, Chris realised he'd have to get going to make to it to the Toolbox for the busiest part of the night. Throbbing music, mindless sweating bodies were what he needed to numb his mind rather than roaming Matt's empty home like a caged monkey on speed for the rest of the night.

"I'll go, I didn't mean to cause a family argument. I'm sorry." He made it out of the room and the front door before either male Rosewood could get out of his chair.

"Chris? What's wrong?" Susan called out behind him but he carried on going.

Why the fuck don't I have an 'off' switch? All I had to do was smile, make nice for a few hours and leave.

Just because my life's an inconsistent nightmare, it doesn't give me the right to ruin Jase's stability and happiness. The guy has enough on his plate without dealing with the fucked in the head neighbour from hell.

Matt would be home with his new bride and new family soon and he'd probably fuck up their lives too. Jase had already said as much. Stuart and Mike agreed with him. But being the good people they were, they felt an obligation to him because one old man had sought a little consolation from his au pair when his wife was dying. Knowing his mother, she hadn't exactly been innocent in the matter. The apple didn't fall far from the tree. Meaningless hook-ups happened all the time, he should know, he'd had enough of them. Just because he was the result of one, it didn't give him the right to impose his crap on these decent people.

He let himself into Matt's house and went straight to his room to put on the little bit of make-up he used for clubbing. A little waterproof mascara and eyeliner, plus more concealer for the bags under his eyes and a little lip gloss. 'Fresh' was the look club goers preferred from the dancers, not 'wired insomniacs'.

Leaving, and not only for a session at the club tonight, was the right thing to do. Unfortunately, if he just took off, he bet Jase would set his pair of bloodhounds on him again. Matt didn't need to come back to that much stress either.

Putting on a front, fabricating a new life he could go to without them all worrying was the way to go. Unfortunately, that was easier said than done. He'd exaggerated his lack of reading ability, but not by much. Employers tended to prefer people who could actually follow paperwork a little faster than a sentence a minute, that is, if he had the patience to sit and work it out, which was a pretty laughable goal.

The club, or one just like it was a possibility as they paid casual dancers cash. The Toolbox hadn't been his first dancing gig and it wouldn't be his last. He could probably earn a buck or two doing portraits on the street too. All he'd need to add to his backpack was a couple of folding stools and an easel.

After coming down the stairs two at a time, he grabbed his jacket off the hook by the door. He could kill two birds with one stone; speak to Russel to see if he knew of another club that could use his services, it didn't matter where it was as long as it wasn't here, and finding himself a partner with a bed for the night. Hopefully, he'd be able to get some sleep afterwards and everything would be a little clearer, a little slower.

When he opened the front door, Jase was camped on the doorstep like he was on sentry duty.

CHAPTER 10

Jase

"Son, that is not—" his father started his lecture as they heard Chris running down the front path.

"Sorry, Dad, but if I don't get round there he'll take off again. Running is his way of dealing with things. Matt will crucify me if I lose him. He doesn't make the best choices when he's upset and dressed like that. He might as well have 'victim' tattooed on his forehead."

"Well stop yapping and move then," his father pointed towards the door. "If you need me to drive, just shout, he's a great kid, he deserves a break."

Grabbing his crutches he made his way to Matt's front door as fast as he could. He was just about to knock when the door opened to reveal Chris, with one arm in his jacket. He looked like a rabbit caught in headlamps, a rabbit wearing make-up that made his eyes even more appealing.

Keeping his demeanour as relaxed as possible, because one, not so hard, shove would have him on his backside, he asked, "Going somewhere, mouse?"

Chris looked down then up at him through his black eyelashes and curly hair that drooped across his forehead. The way his face screwed up and his tongue touched his top lip was probably one of the sexiest things Jase had ever seen. He wondered if Chris knew how adorable he really was. He was one hundred percent sure he didn't realise the extent of his vulnerability. He'd seen countless kids, just like Chris, dead over the last decade. The world wasn't a friendly place for young pretty homosexual boys.

"Work. I dance at a club in town on Fridays and Saturdays."

Matt had said something about that, but he'd also mentioned Chris often didn't come home afterwards. It was probable that Chris would hook up with some random stranger tonight who would use him without a second thought. *Which was pretty much what I want to do to him.*

The urge to push him back inside, rip his garish clothes off and take him on the stairs was frighteningly strong. And he'd bet his last penny that Chris would be as up for that as he was. It still didn't mean it was the right thing to do. If he'd learned anything during his time as a Redcap it was that impulsive, risky behaviour didn't end well. Besides, Chris had enough impulsivity issues for a dozen people.

"Is that a good idea considering how little sleep you've had and the fact you've been on the go all day? Didn't you say over-exertion makes it worse?"

"Well, yeah, but–"

"You don't have a contract of employment do you?"

Chris didn't answer, so he continued. "So surely it's up to you, if and when you go in?"

Christ, watching him squirm is fun. Every emotion played across that expressive face like a book, and right now, Chris had been caught with his hand in the biscuit barrel.

"Or are you really going to the club to try and find someone to read you that bedtime story so you can sleep?"

Taking a step back, Chris held the door open so Jase could enter.

"Damn you're good at this detective stuff. Want a coffee?"

"At night?"

"You're not into hot chocolate before bed are you? Because that's just sad."

"Tea works for me, hot and sugarless."

Rolling his eyes, Chris took his jacket off and put it back on the hook before slouching his way to the kitchen. When they were sitting at the breakfast bar, Chris continued to shift restlessly.

"What's on your mind?" The question caused Chris to deflate before his eyes.

"I didn't mean to ruin your evening, or make your recovery more difficult. You, Matt and Kate have got a good thing going here. It's a nice place with nice people, including your folks, although Mike and Stuart are dicks. Let's face it, I'm a fish out of water here. I'm going to wait till Matt gets home, say goodbye properly, then move on."

If his own hair had been long enough to pull, he'd probably be doing it to relieve the frustration Chris caused even when he was trying to do the right thing. Instead, Jase settled for letting out an exasperated groan.

"And become what? 'Mr Fabulous' full time? How long do you think illiterate rent boys who sleep rough and don't mind violent clients last out there in the big wide world?"

Chris hunched even more and started picking at his nails. "Not a bright move?"

"No, not a bright move, especially for someone as talented as you. You've got a lot more going for you than a cute backside."

The smile on Chris's face as he straightened up was like the sun coming out.

"You think I'm cute?"

"As well as annoying, moody, having no sense of self-preservation..." Jase ticked the attributes off on his fingers, "Not to mention very dubious ideas about fashion, I mean stripes? My mother would look like a deckchair in stripes."

"Hey, stripes are in, that fashion dude on 'Good Morning' said last week. Besides, you think I'm cute," Chris confirmed with a smug smile.

Jase reached into his pocket and held out a fifty pound note. "Here."

The smile dropped off Chris's face as if he'd been slapped. "I don't charge. I'm not a rent boy."

"And you never will be if I can help it. My Dad gave me this for you. It's for the drawing."

Chris didn't reach for the money. "Keep it, I draw for my benefit, nobody else's. If they want to get me some more supplies, that'd be nice. I used up a lot last night. I thought Matt and Kate could give them out as 'thank you's' for the wedding presents."

Noticing that Chris still hadn't drunk his tea, Jase moved the mug an inch nearer to him. Chris picked it up and took a swallow without hesitation. He was amazingly compliant, if you knew what buttons to press, and Jase was learning more with every passing second.

"You're selling yourself short. You have a talent, maybe not international 'Banksy' class, but you could definitely make a living doing portraits. Get a website, get people to send you photos... Money in the bank. Legal, legitimate money you can be proud of, not ashamed of."

"Slight problem with that. One, I'm not ashamed of dancing for tips. Two, I don't have a computer. Three, I don't have a bank account and four I can't fucking read, remember?" Frustration and self-directed aggression rolled off him in waves. To prevent the forthcoming flight, which Jase knew he probably couldn't stop physically, he put his hand on his knee.

Chris froze, every muscle tense.

"There are many people who can do all that easily, very few can draw like you can. And now you can do something for me."

Chris swivelled round on his stool, then leaned in, his eyes on Jase's lips. It would have been so easy, so very easy to let him do what they both wanted, but he put his hand on Chris's chest, stopping him with an inch between their lips.

"I want to sleep with you tonight, Chris Bacon."

"I thought you'd never ask," those delectable pink lips murmured. "Don't worry, I'll do all the work; all you have to do is lay back and enjoy."

"Oh, I'll be laying back all right, and so will you." Jase couldn't help smiling at Chris's confused expression. There were probably multiple positions going through his mind as he tried to work out how they could get it on while they were both 'laying back'.

"Well, I'll try anything once," he started.

"Good, because tonight you are going to try sleeping, just sleeping with me."

Jase let out a bark of laughter at the crestfallen expression on his face. "You look like a spaniel puppy that's had its ball taken away."

Flopping his upper body forward onto the counter as if he'd been shot, Chris groaned, "I hate you."

"Come to think of it, using balls as treats is how we train spaniels as search dogs and with that hair, there is a certain resemblance. Maybe if you're a really good boy..."

Chris sat back up, looking much happier than he had a few seconds ago.

"Ha, ha very funny. If you think I'll sit up and beg for it, you've got another thing coming," he said, then squinted over at him. "That wouldn't work would it? I know some kinky sorts like puppy play, but it's not really my–"

Jase rolled his eyes. "No, it wouldn't work. I spent the time you were at the nursing home this afternoon looking up ADHD. You were right, sleep and a regular routine helps, so tonight I am personally going to make sure you stay in bed."

"I won't sleep and I'll keep you awake all night," Chris said quickly.

Jase patted his bad leg. "With the painkillers I'm on? I doubt that very much. Besides, I've slept under fire many times. When you've been in a war zone, when someone else is on watch, you sleep when you can because you don't know when you'll get the opportunity again."

A calculating look appeared on Chris's face, so Jase nipped whatever plan he was cooking in the bud. "And don't think you can sneak off when I'm asleep. Matt's old room had a lock on the door, and I'm going to keep the key.

"As punishment for making my mum sad, you are going to be stuck in that room with me, no TV, no pad and pencils, in fact nothing to distract you from sleeping until seven tomorrow morning, and if you wiggle or talk too much, I will tie you up and gag you."

"Promise?"

The cheeky grin on Chris's face made him wonder if he'd bitten off more than he could chew after all. A cell full of insurgents or belligerent squaddies would probably be a walk in the park in comparison.

"Bed," he said.

"Oh I love it when you come over dominant, Sarge. Is it alright if I call you Sarge, or would you prefer Sir? Should I salute? I can you know, although I was only in the boy scouts for a month. I got a prize for the size of my woggle, it was the biggest one in the troop. The Akela always complimented me on the fit of my shorts. Mum couldn't afford a new pair so I got given a pair from a kid several years younger. They were really, really tight–"

"Irritating me into leaving won't work. I once sat and stared at a prisoner silently for ten hours, he cracked."

"Bet that makes you a blast in the bedroom," Chris mumbled as he got up.

"Sorry? I didn't quite catch that."

"I said, we might as well get this over with."

"Right, you have a nice warm bath, and I'll get into bed."

Chris huffed as he turned back towards him. "Seriously? I'm nearly... I'm not a kid. A bath before bedtime?"

"And you just nearly told me how old you are. See? Patience is a virtue. Besides, you have to wash that crap off your face. You wouldn't want to wake up with panda eyes would you?"

Chris mouthed what he'd said sarcastically as he got up and slouched his way to the stairs, but his lack of protest told Jase that he wanted this, probably craved it. Not for the first time, he wondered how much attention and love Chris had received as a child. One moment he'd accept, even demand physical attention from anyone, good or bad, but if anyone tried to find out anything other than superficial information, he literally ran a mile.

Tonight would prove interesting, if probably very frustrating. Tomorrow was Saturday and either Mike or Stuart could watch Chris while he caught up on his sleep if he needed it.

CHAPTER 11

Chris

This was not how he'd imagined spending the night with Eddie Bull. Sitting in the foaming water, in the tiny ensuite bathroom, listening to the irritatingly good-looking, domineering man move about in the bedroom, he really couldn't work out what was going on.

Had he got it wrong about Jase fancying him? The way he'd caught Jase looking at him said no, but in that case, why was he refusing him? The uncomfortable conclusion was that although Jase found him attractive, and occasionally amusing, he wouldn't touch him with a barge pole because of his lifestyle. He probably wouldn't even give him the time of day if he hadn't been Matt's brother. People found porn stars attractive, it didn't mean they actually wanted to be intimate with them.

So far, he'd done his best to convince Jase he was a complete slut who regularly had sex with random, possibly dangerous strangers. Which was true. It was also not something he wanted to do for the rest of his life.

He paused. The rest of his life? He usually had trouble considering what he was going to do in the next hour, let alone next month, year or decade. Matt had changed that, and if he didn't piss him off too much, his brother might carry on caring. He had no problem believing his brother would kick his arse out if his behaviour brought trouble to his door. Even thinking the word 'responsible' left a bad taste in his mouth, but it was that or the road.

"Have you fallen down the plug hole?"

Jase's voice from the other room made him jump, and the rapidly cooling water sloshed toward the lip of the tub.

"Nah, I'm good."

Sliding down a little he dipped his head back to wet his hair and then leaned forward to pull the plug out. A quick shampoo removed the hair products and he used the shower attachment to rinse and give his face a final scrub to make sure the make-up was gone.

When he got out, the mirror confronted him as it always did. Without the tinted moisturiser, the finger shaped bruises on his hips and wrists, and the cane marks on his arse and upper thighs stood out starkly. *Crap.* The tube of make-up was still on the chest of drawers in the bedroom, with Jase. He also hadn't brought any clothes in with him and putting his 'Fabulous' shirt back on didn't seem appropriate.

"Erm, Jase? I've got nothing to wear in here."

"Don't tell me you're shy? Didn't you intend to be bumping, grinding and shaking your stuff in next to nothing in front of a couple of hundreds strangers right now?"

The persona he usually adopted, whom he'd come to think of as 'Tigger' over the last few weeks would stride out, shake his booty and try to make Jase blush and dismiss him as an airhead. But Jase had seen a little of Chris this afternoon, someone nobody had seen for... a very long time. No-one could hurt Tigger or his less sexual alter ego, 'Crispy Bacon,' but Chris was as vulnerable as it was possible to be.

"Chris? You ok?"

Tigger is easier.

"Yeah, Yeah I'm coming, but don't say I didn't warn you."

After giving his hair a rub, he wrapped a towel around his hips. Tigger didn't have anything to be ashamed about, he was all about the moment and fun without consequences. Nothing soldier boy said could affect him.

He unlocked the door and stepped out. The only light in the room was the lamp on the bedside table, where a glass of water stood. It looked, calm and cosy and it scared the living daylights out of him. The room and the man waiting for him expected, demanded, the one thing he couldn't do.

Jase was already on the bed, wearing a probably army issue set of khaki vest and boxers. Those startling green eyes were almost daring him to say or do something inappropriate. The dim light made Jase look softer somehow, more human. *Matt must have a bloody big screw lose for not grabbing him with both hands when he had the opportunity.*

Jase was on his side, facing the centre of the bed with his bad leg raised on a cushion and his head resting on his hand. Chris hadn't seen his leg bare before. The dark blue/black bruising stretched almost to his knee and the only part of his foot Chris could see because of the bandages, the ends of his toes, where equally dark.

"Fuck ..." Chris mentally zipped his lips before he said anything about how hideous it looked then glanced up at Jase's face, which had more than a hint of scruff at this late hour. *How would it feel scraping across my inner thighs?*

A smile played on Jase's lips. "I told you that's not going to happen." His voice sounded deeper, sexier than normal, as his eyes ran over Chris's body.

Chris actually felt his face getting warm. He hadn't bloody blushed for years. Hastily, he mentally shoved Chris behind Tigger because that part of him wouldn't have a damn clue how to handle this.

"Very funny. Now if you don't want to give yourself high blood pressure that'll bust your stitches Grandad, you'd better shut your eyes."

"I'm good."

Chris gaped at him. *He wants to see me naked? What happened to no sex?*

Pulling himself together, he said, 'Suit yourself, remember, you asked for it." Stepping over to the chest of drawers, he pulled out the first pair of underwear he came to, then without giving himself time to think, dropped the towel and pulled the shorts on. Thankfully, the awkwardness had dealt with the semi he'd had a few moments ago.

"Really?" Jase said when he turned around. Following his gaze he looked down at his black shorts. There was a multi-coloured stripe with the legend, 'If you want to taste the rainbow, just ask' next to it.

Chris stuck his hand on his hip. "I've got plenty more like this, they give them away at the club, same as the 'Fabulous' shirt. Want to see?" He turned back to the chest of drawers with enthusiasm. A fashion show would certainly kill some time.

"Not now. Now we sleep. Take your sleeping pill and get in."

"I haven't got any..." He turned around to see Jase holding a small white pot. "Dad drove me over to Sarah's this afternoon. Your antibiotic and vitamins are in here too. Seems you haven't been taking your pills, because there were a lot more left than there should have been. You also appear to have lost the sleeping pills altogether."

"You really are a controlling bastard, aren't you?"

Instead of replying, Jase rattled the pot. It sounded as if there were only a few in there so he was probably telling the truth about measuring out the correct dosages.

"I care about Matt, and he cares about you. Take your pills."

"I told you, I don't do sleeping pills."

"You've already had a few of these and you were fine, so–"

"I bloody well haven't."

"You bloody well have," Jase shot back. "Matt dosed you when you weren't looking." Jase's voice was matter of fact, but he wasn't in the least bit apologetic about the deception.

Chris stalked towards to door.

"Where are you going?"

"To call my brother and give him a piece of my mind. Drugging someone without their permission is–"

"Have you been sleeping better since you got here?" Jase interrupted.

"That's not the point, he shouldn't–"

"Answer the question."

Chris pushed his hand through his damp hair as he thought. "Not all the time, but sometimes, yeah, I've got a few more hours than... Oh."

"Take the pills, Chris. I'm here. Nothing is going to happen to you while you sleep. I promise."

"I'm not afraid of... fuck it." Scowling, he stomped back to the bedside table, grabbed the pot, opened it, up ended the contents into his hand and took the pills without looking at them. Slamming the pot down on the table, he threw back the quilt, climbed in, and turned the light off.

A pet project to please the love of his life, that's what I am. If Matt owned a dog that needed round the clock care, Jase would tackle the problem with equal enthusiasm. Soldier boy doesn't really give a shit about me and Matt only does because of that stupid DNA test. At least the guys at the club want me for what I can make them feel, not out of some misguided sense of obligation.

He didn't feel the least bit sleepy, in fact he felt so pissed off, that if by some miracle Jase relented, he'd be up and out of here faster than a bloody greyhound. The dance floor was where he wanted to be, music vibrating through his body as he left his mind behind and just moved. As he couldn't be there in reality, he imagined he was, enjoying the noise, the smells and the energy release he craved.

"You're very tense."

"Fuck off, I'm concentrating."

"On what?"

"Dancing," he said, then flipped over to face Jase. In the gloom, he could see the slightly mocking expression on that gorgeous masculine face. It pissed him off even more.

"Right now, I'm up on the central podium, wearing just a pair of purple Lycra shorts with 'I'm so gay I shit rainbows' on them and I'm shaking my arse as hard as I can. There are six guys drooling on themselves watching me."

"Does that work?"

"What?"

"Getting to sleep by keeping your mind busy while your body is still."

His smile was completely devoid of warmth. "Nope. I'm just killing time and I can talk for England. I don't see why I should suffer alone when this is your idea, not mine. Still think this is a good idea?"

Jase just blinked at him, his face expressionless.

Where the fuck does this dick get off with his smug superior attitude? He acts as if I'm a stroppy teenager and he's my headmaster. A bloody hot headmaster. Knowing my luck he doesn't even have a cane, and if he did, he wouldn't use it for fun.

"Has anyone told you you're a really boring bastard?"

"Yet my current health problems were caused when I was on the other side of the world fighting for international peace. Yours are self-inflicted."

Fucker. Chris turned over again, giving Jase his back. Staring into the darkness, he wondered how long it would take Jase to fall asleep so he could get up. The hyper demon was having a fucking ball and he'd be fucked if he was going to lay here all night listening to it taking the piss out of him. Jase was bad enough. Yes, he was a fuck-up. He knew it, Jase and everyone else knew it, but it still bloody hurt to have his nose rubbed in it and that was all Jase seemed to want to do.

If I'm quiet, I could probably do some sit-ups or something once he nods off. What are the chances of breaking a leg if I go out the window? Being in plaster would probably send me stark staring mad. Maybe I'll get a nice padded cell and a straitjacket. I could spend all day bouncing around like I'm in a permanent bouncy castle, could be worse. Then again, I wouldn't be able to draw or paint, they probably don't allow nutters to have pointy objects. That would suck.

Is there anything in the room, or the bathroom I can draw or paint with? The walls in here are too boring anyway. Toothpaste and blue hair gel are possibilities, if I mix them together I might get a pretty decent consistency. Might drip though. Or I could carve the soap into something with my eyebrow tweezers. I could do Jase's ugly face then melt him in hot water. That'd take up at least a couple of...

"What did your mum do to help you sleep, apart from reading to you?"

"Not telling." *Christ, I sound like a petulant brat, but Jase thinks I'm a fuck-up anyway so why should I bother changing his mind?*

"She didn't sing did she? Cos I'm not doing that. I sound like a strangled cat."

Chris snorted in amusement. "Nice to know there's something you're not superior at."

"There are a lot of things I can't do, but I know what I'm good at and I use my abilities to my advantage. You can do that too, once your life stops revolving around sleeping."

"It doesn't—" he started and then stopped to think for a moment. "Crap. It does, it fucking well does. I think I hate you even more you sanctimonious know-it-all."

"So, we start beating the arse of this insomnia now. What have you discovered that works apart from routine, not getting over tired, being read to—"

"I take it rampant sex and being held all night is out?"

Seconds ticked by. Jase must havr dropped off. Even though there was someone only a few inches away, the insomnia made him feel horribly alone.

"What is it about being held that works?"

Chris stared into the shadows in the corner of the room. "It's daft."

"So's being frightened of rabbits but I am, no idea why. Creepy little furry bastards get everywhere. A magician with a top hat has me running for cover in case he pulls one out."

Chris flipped over again. "Seriously? You're scared of little fluffy bunnies?" He could just make out the slight smile on the other man's face.

"No, I'm just yanking your chain, I like bunnies, the animal sort, not the girls. But the smell of disinfectant and blokes in white coats bring me out in a cold sweat, which is a bit of a bastard considering the amount of surgery I'm probably going to have to go through with this leg."

"You're going to have to have more?"

"Probably. I might even lose the foot, but don't tell anyone. I can't stand the sympathy looks. That's why I made up the penguin story, if people knew I'd been blown up, they'd be watching me for signs of PTSD all the time."

"Have you got it?"

Jase shrugged slightly. "A bit. I get the occasional nightmare and I don't know how I'll deal with a car backfiring or thunder yet. Now it's your turn for a confession. Why does being held help you sleep?"

Chris couldn't believe how much Jase had shared, it made his own reluctance to talk rather pathetic.

"I guess so I know where the other person is. If they leave, I'll know. I won't wake up on my own and people can't creep up on me. Well they could, but it's less likely if I'm with someone, especially if they're bigger than me. Makes me feel secure, even if they're a stranger. It helps me relax, stupid huh?"

"Turn around."

Chris complied. An arm went around his abdomen and he was pulled back against a broad chest. Jase's thumb started to move, up and down on his pec just below his nipple. It was only a fraction of an inch at a time, in time with his breathing. It was a slow, steady rhythm he concentrated on, to the exclusion of anything else.

"Go to sleep Chrisander, I've got you."

"Don't call me that," he murmured automatically, but it didn't stop his eyes drifting shut.

CHAPTER 12

Jase

An hour later, Jase was still awake and he didn't know why. Perhaps Chris's insomnia needed a home because judging by the soft snores coming from the region of his chest, it had been evicted from its normal victim. Chris's confession of his abandonment issues could have prompted 'guard duty' behaviour. By far, the more worrying option was that he was thoroughly enjoying holding Matt's mostly naked little brother and he didn't want to miss a minute of it by sleeping.

Chris was like a pinball in a machine, madly bouncing around, throwing himself into one risky situation after another, craving a connection with another person to anchor him for a few hours. He needed looking after just as much as five-year-old Ryan. The question he needed to answer was did he have the will or even the right to slip into the role this vibrant, incredibly sexy, train-wreck-waiting-to-happen, so badly needed? Because if there was one thing he knew, if he decided to do it for longer than Matt was away, and then backed off at a later date, he wasn't sure Chris could cope with being abandoned again.

He'd never been attracted to flamboyant types before, but although Chris put himself out there, dramatically so, there was a desperation to be loved, to please, that tugged at his heart-strings. He had an idea that if someone actually paid attention to him long term, Chris would do absolutely anything to keep that connection, even if it was toxic. If he had 'abuse me' tattooed on his forehead it couldn't be any more obvious.

His career, his own personality had always been about control and enforcing correct behaviour in others. The one time he'd taken a real personal risk, when he'd confessed his feelings to Matt as a teenager, it hadn't gone well. His few, always temporary, relationships had been with people similar to himself and he'd always made his position quite clear before starting anything. Two people in the same situation, looking for a little companionship away from home. Once the posting was over, so was the relationship.

That wouldn't happen with Chris. This would be an all or nothing situation at a point in his own life when he was adrift. Setting up his own business would take a great deal of time and effort, as would the person in his arms. Did he want to take on an emotionally scarred, incredibly needy and often irrational person who wouldn't admit what he was running from or even how old he was?

Chris turned over and burrowed into his chest, pressing his face up against him. He found himself stroking his soft, curly hair as he whispered, 'I've got you' till he quietened again. This felt right. Really, scarily right. But he wasn't the only person involved.

It was definitely time to put the anchors on his emotions and wait to find out if this was just lust and protectiveness before involving anyone else's emotions including Chris and Matt's. In the meantime, he'd do his damnedest to find out everything he could about the enigma he held in his arms. Decision made, he closed his eyes and drifted off.

He was sitting on a plush leather sofa, totally relaxed with his shirt and trousers open. Chris was kneeling between his spread thighs, looking up at him with lust and adoration. Apart from a black leather collar encircling his neck he was naked, because that was what Jase had ordered.

Chris's olive skin was perfect, his muscles gently sculpted rather than bold and overly defined. A body that was active, with a vibrancy that drew the eye of everyone who saw him, yet Chris belonged to him, and him alone.

"You're beautiful, Master," Chris murmured as he traced Jase's abdomen with a finger, then he kissed both of his lightly haired thighs in turn. "Can I Master? Can I please you?"

The smile that appeared on Chris's face when he inclined his head in permission was joy personified. Even though he knew this was all his slave lived for, it still pleased him to have it confirmed. His property began by wrapping his thumb and forefinger around the base of his cock, before tracing one of the veins from root to tip with his tongue. Just that one careful, considered movement had him shuddering in anticipation.

He let him continue, licking, kissing and tracing till the suspense was almost overwhelming, but Chris seemed to know the exact moment to move to the next stage. He knew his master so well, but however many times he did this to him, it still felt as good as the first.

Then he felt delicate, fine boned fingers on his balls. Chris rolled them gently, reverently, then drew circles on them with his tongue before drawing them, one by one into his mouth and sucking lightly. The need to feel his hot wetness surrounding him burned higher and he reached down, fastening a fist in those soft curls to draw him up to where he wanted him. Those sweet lips locked around the tip of his dick, then sank down without hesitation till he hit the back of his throat. Jase took over, gripping his hair and using his slave's mouth to bring himself the pleasure he knew his property was born to give.

The pleasure was interrupted by a sharp pain in his leg, as he shifted to give his 'slave' more room. The fantastic dream dissolved into an incredibly disturbing reality. Chris really was between his legs, and both Jase's hands had handfuls of his hair while he forced him down onto his dick.

"Shit, fuck, stop," he gasped and let go of his hair as if it'd burned him. Chris wrapped an arm across his belly anchoring himself, clearly not willing to give up his prize.

Taking another firmer grip in those curls he hauled Chris off. "I said, stop it."

"What the fuck? I know you were enjoying it, I can bloody taste it, so what's the problem? Can't a guy say thank you?"

Jase pulled his shorts back up his thighs. "Thank you is two words, not a bloody blowjob."

Chris rolled to his feet. His expression bore little resemblance to the grateful, compliant face in Jase's dream.

"Thank you is what you say to your granny when she passes you the ketchup. You just gave me the first decent sleep I've had in," he cocked his head to one side as if considering, "probably more than a year, maybe two. That deserved a little more, don't you think?"

"No, I don't. Why don't you go put the coffee on?"

Chris scowled. "You know, it wouldn't hurt you to think with your dick for once, you know, have a little F.U.N.? Or does your little red hat come with an in-built 'happy removal' device?"

When Jase just continued to look at him, because he was starting to wonder the same thing, Chris rolled his eyes and held out his hand. "Key?"

Time for a little payback. "You don't need a key. I never locked it."

The amount of feeling Chris got into the single word 'bastard' as he opened the bedroom door and stormed out made him smile. A shower and dealing with his disobedient dick before he saw Chris again was definitely a good idea.

When Jase opened the ensuite door again, he stopped in his tracks. Chris was laid out on the bed, naked as the day he was born. The leg furthest away from him was slightly bent and he was stroking himself, his mouth slightly open, his face tense in concentration. It was probably the most erotic thing Jase had ever seen.

I should stop him, I shouldn't let this continue.

Chris's free hand, the one nearest Jase, wandered slowly across his chest, then he pinched his own dark flat nipple and moaned. Even though Jase had brought himself to a strong climax two minutes before, blood rushed to his cock. Chris was so impossibly sensuous and sexy as he almost undulated in his self-administered pleasure. Even the bruises on his hips turned Jase on. He imagined he'd put them there, that he'd had Chris squirming and begging for more beneath him, that he'd had to exert strong control to make sure they both got what they wanted.

Rather than moving his hand up and down, Chris kept it still and used his hips to provide the movement, the friction, that was bringing him such obvious pleasure. His whole body was working, then he tensed, arm, abs and jaw were all caught up in the sensations he was giving himself. *Pleasure I could be giving him.*

"Ah, I need it, fuck, please, give it to me," Chris moaned as he twisted and worked his body feverishly, then he was exploding, shooting a ribbon of cum onto his chest. His hips made a few more fast, hard thrusts, milking the pleasure from himself before he slowed and stopped, his round, muscular backside finally collapsing back onto the bed.

It was only then that Jase realised he'd just intruded on a very private moment that he'd had no right to see, and certainly no right to enjoy so much.

Eyes still shut, Chris's fingers slowly ran through his own cum, moving it up till his fingers hit his nipple and rubbed it into the tender flesh. Jase's dick twitched again. He looked higher up and almost jerked back a step as Chris's dark eyes focused on him.

"That's what you missed, old man. Doesn't it suck to be you?" he said coldly, then rolled to his feet and stalked out of the bedroom totally at ease with his nakedness.

That kid's going to be the death of me. He needs locking up for his own protection. Who am I kidding? I need locking up for imagining some of the things I'm thinking of doing to my best friend's little brother.

Getting dressed, he tried to remove the image of what he'd just witnessed and replace it with the vulnerable person he'd looked after in the night.

The sight of Chris's naked bubble butt, complete with faint cane marks as he made coffee in the kitchen put paid to that.

"Would you please put some clothes on?"

"Why? You were so keen to see it on Thursday night that you had your straight mates hold me down so you could get an eyeful."

Jase sighed. "Just do it will you?"

Chris did an abrupt about face and Jase had to work hard to keep his expression neutral and his eyes up. Unfortunately, Chris's face, with his eyebrows raised over those dark eyes, and the slight scruff on his face that proved he was indeed an adult, wasn't much less of a problem. He blew at a curl that had fallen into his eye with a puff of breath.

"You do know that frowning all the time will give you even more wrinkles?"

Jase forced himself to stare impassively back, till Chris dropped his gaze. Huffing 'killjoy' he stalked past to the stairs.

Thank fuck for that.

CHAPTER 13

Chris

"So what's on the list of prison activities today, Boss man?" Chris said as he came back into the kitchen.

He still wasn't sure teasing Jase this morning had been a good idea, to be honest he was even beginning to wonder if the bloke was as gay as everyone said. Who the hell turned down an ongoing blowjob? A fucking good blowjob even if he said so himself. Then again, judging from the tent in Jase's towel after he'd finished his little show, there was something there. Either that or he just wasn't Jase's type. Maybe he liked big brawny soldiers who beat his arse into submission, although Jase didn't strike him as a bottom.

"Stuart's coming round after breakfast to pick you up. You get to wash lorries today."

"Fantastic. What are you going to do?"

"I'm going to get my leg checked, then get some more sleep."

Fuck. I kept him awake all night and he's just out of hospital. "Hey, don't look like that. Last night was my choice and you look far better this morning for it. When was the last time you slept for seven hours straight?"

Chris blinked in surprise. "Seven hours, really?" On impulse he threw his arms around Jase.

Moving back slightly he gazed into Jase's eyes, there was no disgust there; in fact, Jase looked as if he wanted to eat him alive. He leaned in to kiss him. Strong hands held his biceps.

"No. It was no this morning, and it's no now. I'm not going to take advantage because you feel grateful for my help."

Dropping his arms, he moved back, the familiar emotions of shame and anger washing over him. "Right. Of course, poor confused Chris can't make his own decisions about who he wants to sleep with. I'll go wash the lorries because that's what I always do on a Saturday, not because you've told me too. Then I'm going to work, because, horror of horrors, even though I'm a little kiddie, I have a job."

"At the gay club." Jase looked as if he'd sucked on a lemon.

"Yes, at the gay club," he said sarcastically. "They don't usually pay twinks to go-go dance on a podium in straight clubs."

They ate in silence. A car horn outside had Chris getting to his feet.

"Pills," Jase said, not looking up from his smartphone.

"Oh sorry Sir, perhaps you could remind me to wipe my arse as well, because I often forget that too."

He grabbed the pot Jase held up, and as he had last night, he swallowed the few pills in it without looking.

"What time do you have to leave for work?"

"About eight," he lied.

"I'll meet you here at seven for dinner then I'll give you a lift."

Chris ignored him and went to the door.

"I said, I'll–"

"I heard you," Chris replied as he walked out the door.

"Alright?" Stuart asked as Chris climbed into his BMW.

"Nope, but why should you give a shit?"

"Sarge is only giving you a hard time because he cares."

Chris kept his mouth shut that he was actually pissed off because dear old 'Sarge' hadn't given him a hard time at all.

"No he doesn't. He cares about your boss, my brother. Now are you going to shunt lorries around so I can scrub bird shit off them or not?"

He finished in record time, even for him, then Stuart dropped him back. It was only five thirty, but Chris grabbed a lightning quick shower, stuffed his club gear in a bag and ran to catch the bus into town. Jase could stuff his lift right up his tight and incredibly righteous arsehole.

* * *

The familiar throb of music, the admiring glances and cat calls, the sneaked squeezes, pinches and propositions soon had his ego back where it belonged. Floating around near the roof.

He'd been dancing non-stop for what seemed like hours, but he only wanted more mindless movement. A huge muscled, bald, thirty something, hard looking man appeared beside his podium. Russel was the manager of the Toolbox and had started out in the industry as a doorman. He indicated with his head that he wanted Chris to follow him. With a sigh, Chris jumped down.

His head didn't even come up to the top of Russel's shoulder, but he liked that about the man. The man had given him a job without any questions after he'd sneaked into the club and started dancing the first night he'd arrived in town. Russel had helped him out on several occasions with over-enthusiastic patrons and paying him back with a few blowjobs in the office wasn't a problem. It looked as if that was going to be the case again.

Even as his dick twitched in anticipation, there was a niggle at the back of his mind that Jase would be disappointed in him. But he'd offered it on a plate to him several times now, and been knocked back. If Jase only wanted 'platonic' that was fine, but a guy had to get his jollies somewhere.

His five current groupies groaned as he left. "Don't worry fellas, I'll be back in a bit."

A hand squeezed his butt hard, and he gave the guy a grin. "Hold that thought, sweetheart," he said then followed the broad back of his boss towards the door to the staff area.

"What do you need? It's manic out there, I've been groped more tonight that I was the whole of last weekend," Chris said closing the office door behind himself.

Pushing Chris against the wall, Russel grabbed his face with both huge hands. "This…"

Russel's lips crashed into his and his tongue forced its way into his mouth. The kiss was rough, animalistic and it made Chris's knees go fuzzy with the high of being wanted.

Russel pulled back, breathing deeply. "Sorry, I just need to taste you, you look so damn good tonight, I don't know what it is, but all those guys out there can see it too, you're on fucking fire. I've been hard for the last two hours watching you."

Chris smiled, it was always good to know he was appreciated. "Oh yeah?" His hand rubbed at the front of his boss's trousers. "Crap you are. Wow, you could hammer nails with this."

The frustration Jase had caused this morning had haunted him all day, it had made him feel inadequate, unwanted and undesirable. As a result, he'd been trying harder than usual to turn the clubbers on tonight. It seemed to have worked.

"Lock the door."

Chris almost ran to the door, someone wanted him, needed what he could do for them. It gave him even more of a rush than it normally did because Russel could have his pick of probably fifty or more blokes tonight, and out of all of them, he'd chosen him.

Russel was on him before he fully turned around, attacking his neck with his lips, insistent fingers tearing at his black latex shorts as he removed the material separating them. The man was nearly eight inches taller and almost double Chris's width. He'd also found out that his dick matched the rest of him when he'd first blown him. It had been a real test of his skills, but Russel seemed to have enjoyed it enough to come back for seconds, thirds and fourths.

"Get over there," he growled, Chris almost fell as Russel pushed him towards the desk. There was no respite as the older, larger man followed him, pulling at his own belt. Backed up to the desk, Russel pulled Chris's shorts down quickly then turned his attention to his shirt. Last time he'd blown him, Chris had remained fully clothed. A niggle of worry started that this wasn't going to be the normal blowjob situation.

Within seconds, his t-shirt was on the floor and Russel's mouth was on his chest, licking, sucking and biting. It only lasted a moment before Russel grabbed his waist and flipped him around, pushing at his shoulders so he fell across the desk.

"Fuck, I need you," he growled and Chris heard the unmissable sound of trousers being pushed down and a foil wrapper being opened. Without waiting for a reply, he felt cool lube fall on his hole, followed by a finger.

"Crap, you're so tight for such a little slut." For some reason, instead of the dirty talk turning him on like it usually did, he felt as he'd been hit in the face with a wet fish.

The next second, Russel was pressing inside and pain spiked through him.

"Shit, ow, fuck that hurts, slow down," he cried out as he tried to get free but Russel held him firmly and continued to fuck him, one harsh thrust after another. One large forearm went across his upper chest, the other was on his hip holding him still for the onslaught. "That's it, squirm for me boy, I love it when you wiggle."

Russel didn't care what his real name was, that he was a nut job who couldn't read, he just wanted him, craved him enough to risk being caught in a compromising position. The enthusiasm of his partner gradually overcame the pain as the endorphin buzz kicked in. Rather than trying to pull away, Chris started to flex back against him as Russel nailed his prostate again and again.

"Fuck you feel good, this isn't going to take long," came the panting voice behind him.

Knowing it was what he wanted, Chris said, " Harder, do it harder."

"Like this?" Russel growled as his hands held on tight enough to bruise and hammered in to him so hard the heavy desk moved a fraction and the pot of pens fell over.

Gritting his teeth, Chris clenched his backside rhythmically for all he was worth.

"Oh fuck, that's, fuck just like that, do it, do it, *ah fuck.*" Russel pulled him hard against himself as he emptied into the condom.

Chris winced as Russel pulled out abruptly, then jumped as his hand came down on his backside.

"Ow, what the fuck was that for?" Chris looked back over his shoulder and started to pull up his shorts feeling more than a little battered.

Russel smirked. "You know you can always sleep on the couch in here for a couple of nights, right?"

"Yeah," Chris replied although he wasn't really listening as he tried to stuff his semi back into his shorts. They were stretchy, but there was a limit. He definitely wasn't going to try sitting down for the next few hours.

"And don't go tugging that off in the bathroom, the punters like to see hard dicks on the dancers. I'll sort you out later if you haven't found anyone to take you home. Now get out there and shake it some more. Horny blokes are thirsty blokes."

"Thanks a bunch," Chris grumbled as he bent to pick up his cropped, vest style shirt that had a picture of a hotdog with the legend 'I like a big one in my bun' on the front and went to check what he looked like in the mirror. There was a bloody huge bite mark on his neck. Tilting his chin up, he pulled the neck of his shirt down to get a better look at the hickie.

"Fucking hell, Russel, I look like I've been got at by a fucking vampire; what the hell did you do that for?"

Russel grinned back. "Just showing the weirdo with the crutches that hasn't taken his eyes off you all night that you're a free agent. He was giving evils to any guy who tucked something in your shorts."

Fuck, fuck, fuckity fuck with big fucking bells on.

"You know him then? Old boyfriend is he?"

"Just a friend of the family who knows what's best for me, if you know what I mean."

"I know the type. You sure you don't want to crash here for a while?"

Chris pulled the neck of his vest up, as he squinted into the mirror; it was no good, the mark was like a fucking traffic light and the shirt didn't cover it. "Can I get back to you on that?"

"Course. Do you want Cuddles to chuck him out?"

"No, god no, he'd probably break his arms. Jase is some sort of military special forces ninja. I'll sort it."

Getting back to his podium with the number of hands going for his rapidly softening dick wasn't easy.

"Aw, didn't he sort you out cutie?"

"Just come to the bogs, I'll have you purring in seconds and it won't be your neck I'll be sucking on."

He grinned, pushed away hands, made non-committal answers to the proposals and eventually made it.

"Help me up guys?" he shouted to two of his hard core fans, and they boosted him up with some significant arse squeezing thrown in for good measure. Both men had already tipped him significantly tonight; they deserved a little something for their cash.

He'd arrived halfway through a song, and by the time it ended, the face he didn't want to see, especially as it looked as if it was chewing on a wasp, was looking up at him.

"Get down. You're coming home, right now."

"Sorry?" Chris pretended he couldn't hear him and carried on dancing as the next song picked up speed.

A hand grabbed his ankle, which was at hip height for most of the patrons.

"Hey, rules are that you don't touch, unless you're tucking tips," fan number one told Jase loudly.

"I don't a give shit what the rules are, he's underage and he's coming home with me." Most of the guys around the podium looked up at him as if he'd suddenly developed an extra head.

"Fuck off will you? I'm not underage, I'm just short and skinny."

The faces around him looked dubious. "Oh for fuck's sake, haven't you ever seen a jealous ex before?" Chris said and jumped down off the podium. Without waiting to see if Jase was following, he headed for the staff area.

This was a no-win situation. Yes, he could get Cuddles to throw Jase out and carry on working, but he wouldn't be able to go home and his relationship with his brother, Kate, Ryan and his niece or nephew-to-be would go down the toilet. If he stayed, Jase would continue to heckle and either he'd get thrown out with the same result, or Russel would sack him for causing trouble. A rumour of underage dancers could close this place down. Russel wouldn't risk that for a bit of tail even if his ass was the best he'd ever had, and with Russel's track record, that was highly unlikely.

A formal accusation would result in Russel demanding to see his birth certificate which wasn't going to happen. If there was one thing Chris's mother had impressed upon him, it was to keep his identity to himself. This had been the perfect gig, and now thanks to bloody do-gooding Jase, it was buggered up, maybe permanently.

"Fucking bastard!" he shouted as he slammed through the door to the private area of the club. It was just his epic luck that Russel was coming out of his office.

"Chris? What's up?"

"Nothing you can help with, just that guy making a pain of himself. I'm sorry but I've got to go. I'll try and get back in the week but I'll definitely be back next Friday."

"Is he the reason you weren't here last night?"

His mind whirled as he tried to think of an answer that would let him keep his job.

"Listen Chris, if you need somewhere to stay, I'm here for you, but I need you to turn up when you say you will. Those podiums need to be filled. The customers come here for dancers."

Dropping his shoulders, he glanced down at his feet and then up again. 'Adorable' often worked with big protective types like Russel. "Yeah, I know, I'm sorry. I really need this job, but things are a bit fucked up at home. My brother's away on honeymoon and this guy is his best friend, he thinks he's on a mission to 'save' me, he–"

The door at the end of the corridor opened and a crutch appeared.

"Oh fuck," Chris said to himself as Jase came through the door with a scowl that matched Russel's.

"Are you in charge here?" Jase said, every inch the army officer who expected to be obeyed, even though Russel had two inches in height and around a three to four stone weight advantage. Not to mention two fully functioning legs. It didn't seem to bother Jase.

"Yes he is and I'm just coming. I've just got to get my stuff." He turned back to Russel. "Sorry to leave you in the lurch, but I'll be back next week when my brother comes home."

"Do you allow your young employees to be abused at work on a regular basis Mr?"

"Denman. Russel Denman. You are?" Russel asked making every hour he spent in the gym show as he folded his arms across his bodybuilder chest. The display didn't seem to faze Jase in the least but Chris's backside clenched painfully as he remembered being under that a few minutes ago. If he wasn't so sore, he'd quite like to do it again, as long as Russel took a little more time getting him ready.

"Sergeant Jason Rosewood. I'm this young man's temporary guardian while his brother is away."

"Christ, get over yourself Jase. You're not my guardian," he said but both men ignored him. Macho posturing was clearly far more important than anything he had to say. He didn't matter any more than a piece on a game board to these two.

"He came back here, with you, half an hour ago. He walked out fifteen minutes later, obviously in discomfort and with that mark on his neck. Is abusing, raping, vulnerable youngsters unable to defend themselves how you enjoy yourself, Mr Denman?"

"Oh for fuck's sake, you know what? I've had it up to here with your holier than thou attitude."

At the back of his mind, he knew he was starting to spiral out of control. The fact that he was shouting, almost at the top of his voice, didn't matter as he waved his hands around.

"He was horny, I was horny and he fucked me like a musclebound Duracell Bunny over his desk. Did he ask politely and get me to sign a consent form in triplicate? Buy me dinner, chocolates and fucking flowers first? No, he didn't. Was he rough? Yes, he fucking well was and I loved it because he's got a dick the size of a fucking rolling pin and he knows how to use it.

"You know why I looked uncomfortable when I came out? Because I didn't get off. He left me high and dry just like you did this morning so I'm going home to have a fucking good WANK."

"Chris wait, you can't leave on your own, there's been a threat..."

"Just watch me, grandad."

The two men stood in complete shock as Chris grabbed his phone, leaving the rest of his stuff with his jacket on the staff coatrack beside him. Skirting past Jase, he stormed through the door of the private area and walked out into complete silence, which rapidly became a giant round of applause.

He closed his eyes, sighed, plastered a smile on his scarlet face then bowed left and right to his audience.

"I wouldn't leave you high and dry," an unidentified voice shouted. It was followed by at least forty other similar offers. Giving them the finger and a smile, because there wasn't anything else he could do, he walked towards the exit with no keys, no wallet and dressed like a, well, like an out of work go-go dancer. Because that was exactly what he was now.

CHAPTER 14

Chris

As he stepped out into the cold evening, a voice he didn't recognize spoke from behind him.

"You look like you could do with a good drink and a bed for the night."

Chris turned to see an olive-skinned, sharply attractive man with hooded dark eyes and a fag in his mouth. He was leaning up against the wall in the club's designated smoking area. His lips pulled on the cigarette, sucking the smoke into his lungs, his eyes closed in sensuous enjoyment. Chris's neglected cock twitched. *If this guy sucks a ciggie with this much passion how will he be in bed?*

His accent was as exotic as his looks, eastern European by the sound of it. This could be exactly the distraction he needed from the FUBAR situation Jase had created.

"You offering?"

The guy nodded, dropped his half smoked cigarette and stubbed it out with his shoe, his very shiny, expensive looking shoe. He was wearing a tailored mid-grey suit so he didn't look like the normal Toolbox type. Then again, who was he to judge what was normal? A partner with a bit of class would make an interesting change.

"Car's that way," the man said and indicated a dark four-by-four parked at the far end of the car park.

"Lead on," Chris said with what he hoped was an attractive smile. Giving Jase time to cool off before he saw him again was an excellent idea.

"After you, I want to watch that ass," his hook-up said. Chris started walking, it was always nice to be admired.

"Your name is Chris? Correct?"

"That's right, what's yours?"

"Dimitar. Your family name is Kemp, yes?"

Chris considered the question. It wasn't the name on his birth certificate, then again, neither was 'Bacon', but he was Richard Kemp's son. He'd also been hanging around the haulage yard where everyone knew he was Matt's brother. It gave him a warm fuzzy feeling to know he was being connected to Matt by people he didn't know. This guy must fancy the hell out of him to have gone to the trouble of investigating him. Being wanted was his number one turn on.

"I don't use it, but yeah I suppose it is. Why?"

As he got to within a few feet of the car, the rear passenger door started to open. Chris stopped in his tracks. Another olive skinned man got out. This one wasn't smiling and he wasn't hot. In fact he looked like the ugly uncle who couldn't pick up a date without paying for it.

Chris turned towards the first man, holding up his hands in apology. "Thanks for the offer, but no thanks, I'm not into group stuff."

Dimitar smiled broadly, shrugged and stepped towards him. "No hard feelings, eh?"

"Chris!"

Chris turned to see Russel standing beside Jase. The big bald man started to run towards him as Jase shouted, "Watch ou–"

Something hit him hard across the shoulders; his hands and knees hit the gravel. Rolling onto his side, he tried to kick at the big ugly sod who was grabbing at his arm.

"You fight, and I will shoot your friend, Mr Kemp," Dimitar said calmly as if it was the most normal thing to say in the world.

Dimitar had a gun in his hand, an actual fucking gun, or at least Chris thought it was. It could be one of those replicas, but he wasn't going to take that chance. If someone had told him his life depended on him moving right then, he couldn't have twitched a muscle. How the fuck did Jase deal with shit like this? Then he realised the gun wasn't actually pointing at him.

"Let him go, whatever you want, whatever he's done, we can talk about it. You haven't done anything illegal yet." Jase's voice was so bloody calm, he could have been talking about how much sugar he wanted in his tea. In contrast, Chris thought it was highly likely he was going to lose control of his bladder any second. Couldn't Jase see that the guy had a fucking GUN for God's sake?

Dimitar chuckled, and he was even better looking than he'd been earlier. *Wanker.*

"Oh, but we have and this little pigeon is just one in a long line of successful business arrangements. If our instructions are not followed, his brother will still get him back, but not in this condition."

Cold, creeping dread filled Chris's stomach.

"It'd be a shame to spoil his pretty face for the sake of a few unlocked lorries in Calais, no?"

Like some sort of magic trick, his limbs started working again and he scrambled to his feet. The second man grabbed him around the chest, lifting him off his feet. As he kicked and struggled he could see Jase and Russel about twenty feet away. The bouncers were stopping anyone leaving the club.

The man holding him started to haul him backwards towards the car. It was the last place he wanted to go and he fought even harder.

"Stop, we need you breathing, nothing more," the man said against his ear in a thick, eastern European accent.

"Do what they say. I'll get you out of there, I promise," Jase called out as he moved forward at the same pace that they were retreating. Russel hadn't moved since the gun appeared. Chris didn't blame him in the least.

"Stay calm, do what you're told and you'll get him back. Call the police and you'll never see him again. Some people will pay well for a boy like this."

When they were against the side of the car, he heard another door open.

"Say goodbye," Ugly Uncle said as he pulled Chris's arm straight out. Another hand appeared, holding a needle.

Adrenaline flooding his system; he heard Jase shouting but all he could see was the needle heading towards his arm. The man holding him tightened his grip till Chris's bones creaked and still he tried to fight.

"I'll be good, please, please don't do that. Whatever you want, I'll do it, just don't, please don't–" With tears flooding down his face, and unable to get free, he begged for his life, as he'd begged his mother not to be dead. It hadn't worked four years ago and it didn't work now.

The needle pierced his skin but he barely felt it. All it took was a count of four before he spiralled away from the fear and the world. He could still see the hands holding his arm, still feel the arm around his chest, the leg wrapped around his own, but he just didn't give a shit any more. *Was this how mum felt? Was this why she'd done it?* He felt... nice, more than nice. It was fucking wonderful and it should be scaring the shit out of him. The world faded as he became lost in the sensations that overwhelmed him.

"What did you give him?" Jase's tight voice came from a distance, which was odd. *Isn't he holding me tight and snug? Why isn't he happy when I feel so good?*

"Nothing that will do permanent damage as long as his brother does what he's told. But the longer he fails to comply..."

His eyes were so heavy. Every blink lasted longer, until they refused to open altogether. His legs gave way and his head fell back against Jase's chest as he wondered vaguely how a man on crutches with only one good leg was holding him up. It didn't matter, nothing mattered except this wonderful floaty feeling.

"What do you want?"

"Ask his brother, if he had obeyed in the first place, this unpleasantness wouldn't have happened."

Then he was moving, laying down on the back seat of a car. Someone was shouting, saying he would get him back, but it didn't stop the lead in his limbs and his brain, taking over entirely as the car hummed to life and started moving.

CHAPTER 15

Jase

"If you're calling the police, disconnect, right fucking now," Jase growled at Chris's arsehole boss as they watched the car disappear out of the car park.

"But..."

"Do you want to get him killed or sold to some pervert? You might think of him only as a convenient fuck and a disposable crowd pleaser, but I happen to want him back, and not in pieces. I'll sort it."

"You? How the fuck are you going to go up against a bunch of foreign terrorists? You haven't even got two good legs. Leave it to the experts."

Jase eyed the body builder who clearly spent more time on his muscles than he'd ever done on thinking. "They weren't terrorists. They were people traffickers. And as for being able to sort it? It's what I do for a living, and I have a lot of friends with far bigger guns than the peashooter that bastard had. Go play with your barbells, and leave Chris to me."

Russel looked relieved, but he didn't immediately about face. "Look I'm sorry about earlier. I do care about him, he's a good kid but..."

"Kid is right, did you even bother to ask how old he was before you employed him? Before you..." Jase pursed his lips together. This wasn't helping, but seeing the fear on Chris's face when the bastard stuck a needle in him, was the most painful thing he'd ever seen. He'd been absolutely terrified. It made him want to hit something. Although planting his fist in this prick's face would make him feel better, it wouldn't help Chris and knowing his luck, the big, musclebound bastard would hit him back. Making the phone calls he needed to with a broken jaw would be significantly uncomfortable.

Instead, he settled for, "Just fuck off, will you?"

"You'll let me know if you need any help and when you find him?"

Jase simply stared at him. The man dropped his gaze, turned and walked back into his seedy club.

Jase got out his phone. The people Matt loved were in danger, and although Chris might have been the most accessible target, he wasn't the most vulnerable.

"Sarah? It's Jase."

"Is everything alright? Is Chris hurt?" The immediate concern in her sleepy voice almost made him smile; the fact that her first thought was that Chris had gotten himself into trouble, didn't.

"I know it's late. Is Ryan with you?"

"It's one in the morning, where else would he be?"

"Just check for me please."

He listened to soft quick footsteps, then a door creaking open.

"He's safe in bed, what the hell's going on?"

"You can actually see his face, it's not just a lump under the covers?"

"Yes I can see his face, he's sucking his thumb. What the hell is going on?"

Jase heaved a sigh of relief, one down, two to go.

"Thanks, just keep a close eye on him, and I mean in the same room with your phone handy. I'll get back to you."

He hung up and dialled again.

"Jase, what the fuck?" His best friend sounded out of breath.

"Hi Jase, you have impeccably good timing," Kate giggled in the background.

He regretted spoiling Kate's honeymoon; he didn't regret spoiling Matt's.

"Why didn't you tell me you were being threatened by people traffickers?"

Matt sighed. "Shit, there hasn't been another one of those creepy letters has there?"

Jase's jaw creaked it was so tight. "No Mathew, no new letters and no phone calls. They made good on their threat. They've taken Chris. They shot him full of something, probably heroin or ketamine judging by the way he collapsed, right in front of me. And there wasn't a fucking thing I could do about it, seeing as there was a gun up my nose at the time. I think you'd better come home, don't you?" He hung up and dialled Mike.

"Mmm?" a sleepy voice said.

"Get over to Sarah's place, you're on guard duty. Chris has been snatched and Ryan's next on the list."

The snappy 'Sir' acknowledgement went a long way to settle his nerves.

He made his way over to Matt's pick-up. Somebody was going to pay for this fuck up and he hoped to god it wasn't Chris. He'd seen plenty of dead bodies in his time, the sheer lack of life, the stillness was what was horrific. The image of Chris's eyes open, fixed and dull, his mouth slack in death, made his stomach clench. He vomited violently, completely caught out by his body's reaction.

When his stomach was empty, he spat to clear the acidic taste. He didn't have time to indulge in fear or any other emotion. He had a job to do and he'd need help.

Getting into the truck, he picked up his phone and started calling in favours. The getaway car and descriptions of the three kidnappers were his first and only clues till Matt gave him more details about the threats, if he had them.

If he'd just carried out a more thorough search yesterday he might have found the threatening letter in Matt's sideboard in time to prevent this happening. But he hadn't acted quickly enough; just like Matt he hadn't taken it seriously enough, and Chris was paying the price. Berating himself wasn't helping the situation. *Focus Rosewood.* He'd seen all three kidnappers fairly clearly although only one had spoken, and he'd had an Eastern European accent. It was a damn shame Chris wasn't here to draw them for him.

Twelve hours later, he sat at Matt's dining room table, with two of his Redcap colleagues, plus Matt and Stuart. Mike was catching up on his sleep in the spare room upstairs and Kate was playing with Ryan in the living room.

"So you've got two coming back into Dover on Monday night?"

"Yeah. Roger and Will are running back together with a load of factory machinery. They would have been back today but France has a no commercial vehicles transit law on Sundays."

"The instructions are to stop in a certain layby, wait for an hour and then carry on without checking the load, right?" Jase confirmed.

"Yep. I told the drivers to avoid it like the plague. I get a two grand fine for each illegal that's found by customs. So far, we've avoided getting one. We don't often do curtain siders and box trailers which are the main targets." Matt looked knackered, having driven all night to get here, but Jase had little sympathy.

"But there are places on those loads where people could hide?"

Matt rubbed his forehead. "Sure, but not many. One here, one there."

"Are these drivers ex-army?"

Matt nodded.

"Tell them to do it and why. We need to keep the kidnappers happy while we investigate. We don't want to give them any reason to hurt him. The guy I heard was eastern European and they aren't exactly known for being gay friendly."

"And Chris is...?" Mark, one of Jase's previous tour 'hook-ups' asked.

"Camper than a field at Glastonbury," Stuart said. At Jase's glare he added, "What? I didn't say it bothered me did I? But anyone who wears 'I'm so gay I fart rainbows,' shirts isn't exactly in the closet."

Mark snorted in amusement. "Sounds like quite a character."

"If you've all finished laughing at him, perhaps we can get on with finding him before he ends up dead?" Jase said in a tight voice.

"Jase please, we've all been up all night, we're all worried," Matt started.

"And how do you think Chris's day is going?"

They all returned to their jobs, mostly accessing CCTV of the local area trying to follow the route the kidnappers' vehicle had taken.

Matt's phone beeped and he picked it up. "Oh, Christ."

Jase looked up, Matt's face was paler than he'd ever seen it. He reached across and took the phone out of his friend's frozen hand.

Chris was lying on his back on a bare mattress, hopefully either asleep or unconscious. The second picture was of him on his stomach. Both views showed bruising to his hips and neck and there was a distinct handprint on his backside.

"This is all my fault, if..." Matt started, but Jase interrupted. His friend didn't need more pain that was necessary.

"He probably had most of those marks before he was taken, he–"

Matt lunged across the table. Jase found himself, and his chair, falling backwards. His jaw felt as if it had come into contact with one of Matt's lorries, not his fist.

"Two fucking nights, I left him with you for two fucking nights. You couldn't wait to get your hands on him once my back was turned could you? Just because I turned you down all those years ago, you decided to take it out on my little brother?"

"Mate, calm down. Me and Mike were with Chris all of Thursday night, Jase spent the night at home," Stuart said as Mark helped Jase up.

"What about Friday? Go on, Jason, look me right in the eye and tell me you didn't sleep with him."

Knowing this would come out all wrong, Jase said it anyway. "It wasn't like that. Yes, I stayed with him overnight, but it was to help him sleep. He told me that he doesn't like sleeping alone. I got him to take a sleeping pill and–"

"You drugged him first? How is that better than what those bas–"

Matt's face was scarlet, there were veins standing out on his temples. Jase had never seen Matt this angry, but arguing amongst themselves wouldn't help Chris.

"Would you shut the fuck up? I didn't bloody well touch him. I've got more respect for him, and for you for that matter, which is a damn sight more respect than he has for himself. We talked, he went to sleep. I woke up with him..." He shook his head. "It doesn't matter, I stopped it. But he uses sex to say thank you and to get guys to stay with him overnight so he can sleep. He's scared to sleep on his own, something to do with his mother abandoning him."

Matt deflated as if all the energy had gone out of him. "He's been here for nearly two months, and I had no idea. How the hell did you get it out of him?"

"I didn't let him dazzle me with bullshit, he's damn good at it though."

Matt gave a tight-lipped smile. "That he is."

Jase felt the brief rift in their relationship heal.

"So who did hurt him?" Mark spoke up.

"His boss at the club. It seemed pretty much consensual but it wasn't Chris's idea by any means. If anything I think he felt obliged to go along with it to keep his job. I was having a little 'chat' with said boss when Chris stormed off."

"Wow what a surprise, Tigger galloping off into the sunset when things get rocky," Stuart said almost to himself.

"Well he's not galloping anywhere now, is he? Shall we get back to it?" Mark said.

Jase looked at the pictures on Matt's phone again. "That's artificial light, so it was either taken last night, in the last few hours, or he's in a room with no windows. A very small room by the look of it."

"He'll go batty if he spends any time in there, unless he's drugged up to the eyeballs," Stuart said as he leaned over Jase's shoulder to look at the phone.

CHAPTER 16

Chris

He tried to keep hold of the bone deep relaxation that went with being asleep for a long time. It didn't happen very often and he didn't want to lose it. But something wasn't right. He couldn't feel a warm body touching him, and he didn't usually sleep well when he was alone. And this bed...stank. Of piss and sweat.

Then it came back to him and he catapulted upright. He was on a mattress on the floor of a tiny, empty, windowless room that looked like an cupboard. It was dark, but there was natural light coming from the crack under the door. There was nothing else in the room apart from the mattress he was on and a black bucket. He got up, and ignoring the fact he was naked, banged on the door that didn't have a handle.

"Hey! Anybody out there?" There was no reply so he started banging again. After a minute, he decided to both entertain and distract himself by trying out different rhythms. After what seemed an age, he decided that either there was nobody out there, or if they were, they were deaf. As his hands were starting to ache, he began singing. Loudly and badly. Queen's 'I want to break free,' seemed appropriate.

He lost track of time as he moved through every song he knew, from modern ones to the Christmas carols he'd learnt at school. Even though he knew it was daft, he kept concentrating on the door because if he looked behind him, the tiny, bare space would close in on him. It was getting cold, and the light was diminishing under the door before he heard anything. The sound of a key in a door had him freezing between one word and the next.

Despite having wanted someone to come, suddenly he wasn't so sure. Heavy footstep on some sort of hard, stone flooring came closer. He retreated to the mattress and sat down in an attempt to cover himself up a little. He wasn't embarrassed about his body, but he did feel vulnerable.

The light under the door was interrupted as he heard bolts being undone.

As the door creaked opened he tried for a friendly tone. If they liked him, hopefully they'd be less likely to hurt him.

"Hi, erm, sorry about the noise, I got a bit bored, I..." was as far as he got before the older man he'd christened 'Ugly Uncle' walked in and smacked him hard around the head.

"Be quiet, faggot," he growled although Chris could hardly hear him because of the ringing in his ears. Then he hit him again on the other side of his face. This time it knocked him over and he held up his hand to stop any more.

"I'm sorry, I'm sorry, I can't help it. I can't keep still. I need something to do."

The man stared impassively at him as Chris wiped a trickle of blood from his nose. "How long am I going to be here?"

Ugly Uncle didn't move speak or even twitch.

"Not very chatty are you? Is there anything I can do that'll speed this up, because I really..." The man lunged forward again. Chris rolled into a ball, his arms protecting his head. *Fuck fuck fuck.*

After a few seconds, when a blow didn't come, he peeked out from under his arm.

The man's face was inches away from him. "I no like faggots."

"Your choice, but..."

The man hit him again. This time it made him dizzy. *You really should shut your mouth.* But as good as his own advice was, as soon as the room swam into focus he opened it again.

"I've got ADHD. I can't help it, when I'm nervous, I–"

The man roared wordlessly in his face then turned and left.

"Well that wasn't very polite," Chris said to himself, just to fill the silence. After wiping his still sluggishly bleeding nose, he probed the left side of his face, which hurt worse than the right.

"I bet I look like I've been five rounds with Tyson Fury, and he doesn't like gays either. I definitely won't be able to dance in the club for a while."

Footsteps at the door had him buttoning his swollen lip.

This time it was the guy who had propositioned him at the club. The smiling, slick bastard who had started all this. And he still had a flawless white shirt and neatly pressed trousers. Chris felt the urge to bleed on the git. *Try getting blood out of that get up, you fucker.*

Dimitar walked in, closed the door behind himself and sucked his breath through his teeth. "You have upset Avni. It is not a healthy thing to do."

"I didn't mean–"

He held up a finger, "Ah, ah. Keeping quiet when your betters are talking is common politeness that children should learn at a very young age. Avni said you have something that sounded like a disease. Do you?"

Chris's mind worked overtime. Would they let him go if they thought he was going to get really ill if he didn't have medication?

"Truth, little peacock, always the truth." The man smiled. *Why couldn't he be an ugly fucker like the other one?*

"I'm hyperactive. I can't be still or quiet and I don't sleep much. Hitting me won't stop it, I can't help it. It's like I've got ants under my skin, I've just got to move."

The man grunted. "Thank you for being honest, but we cannot have you making that much noise; the neighbours, you understand, yes?"

Chris nodded. "I'll try, I really will, promise."

"You will be here for at least a couple of weeks, maybe more."

A few hours he might manage, but weeks of being still and quiet? I've got more chance of growing wings and flying out of here.

"Why? I mean what do you want?" They hadn't mentioned his mother, or the nameless people she had always been scared of finding them, but if that wasn't it, what was it?

"We only wish your brother to stop his lorries in a certain place outside Calais for a little while."

"You're people traffickers?" Chris blurted out then clapped a hand over his mouth, which hurt his lip.

The man frowned briefly but his crocodile smile returned almost instantly. Chris bet he could charm the birds from the trees if he wanted to, it had certainly worked on him.

"We help asylum seekers. Unfortunate people who by accidents of birth, were not lucky enough to be born in such a wonderful country as yours."

"So do you do this kidnap and blackmail thing a lot? Because you seem pretty damn good at it."

The man's smile widened. "You are very odd, even for a faggot. I will get you some food, then you will rest."

"I'm not tired, can't you just–"

The smile dropped off his face. "It was not a request."

Ten minutes later, the door opened again. Dimitar placed a plate on the floor wordlessly then backed out again.

"Seriously? A cheese sandwich is the best you can do?" he called out, but nobody replied.

He glanced towards the bucket. Maybe eating wasn't such a good idea, if he ate, he might have to use that and it wouldn't be nice to spend time in here with his own waste. Besides, his mouth was bloody sore. Ignoring the plate, he started to probe his teeth with his tongue. Nothing seemed too loose. Examining his injuries, especially without a mirror was fast losing his interest.

He started to hum, then stopped because that hurt too. With a flash of inspiration, he grabbed the still empty bucket, turned it upside down and instantly had a drum. Using only his forefingers, he started tapping out a quiet rhythm.

It was almost too dark to see by the time he heard footsteps again. The door opened and a light shone straight at him, causing him to lift his forearm to protect his dark adjusted eyes.

"Crap, warn a guy first will–" was far as he got before a large figure strode forward.

"Shit, I'm behaving, don't–" he shouted as adrenaline fuelled fear shot through him.

Dimitar's voice dripped regret. "I'm sorry, but you haven't complied Mr Kemp, so poor Chris has to pay the price for your failure."

The kick to his ribs stole his breath, his mouth worked but nothing came out. *Fuck that hurts.*

"Now, little Chris, would you like another like that, or would you like some more happy juice?"

Happy juice? It clicked what he meant and even though his ribs screamed, he scooted back as quickly as he could till his back was up against the wall.

"No, no please don't do that. I'll be quiet as a mouse, promise."

"I'm afraid, my little peacock, that this isn't about that. I'm not a murderer, and I don't chop little bits off people and send their relatives soggy parcels. Far too messy. What I do, if they don't comply, is either find someone who would like a little peacock to play with permanently, or I return their loved one with a habit. Now, I would like you to have a little chat with your brother."

He handed his mobile phone over, and Chris realised he'd been on video.

"Matt?"

"Oh God Chris, I'm so, so sorry. We'll get you out of there, I swear we will. Have any of them... touched you?"

Chris started to laugh, but stopped quickly because it hurt everywhere.

"You're worried about me getting felt up and fucked by a stranger? Hell, that happens nearly every night at the club anyway. Have you seen my fucking face? I bet I look like Quasimodo, look." As quickly as he could, he turned the phone around and pointed it at the three men standing in the doorway. He was sure Jase would be watching too. If they could identify who had him...

CHAPTER 17

Jase

The flash of three men with dark clothes was swiftly followed by a scream of pain that made everyone in the room either gasp or wince. As the sounds of a struggle continued, Matt shouted Chris's name. Then it went ominously silent.

"You bastards, you fucking bastards, what have you done to him?"

"Your brother has been very silly, Mr Kemp. I'm afraid we need to take measures to ensure he cannot repeat these impulsive acts. He explained that he has trouble resting. He will no longer have that problem. Make sure your drivers stop where they are meant to next time, or he may never have a problem with keeping still again."

"That wasn't my fault, the police waved the drivers on, they couldn't stop."

"Next time, make sure they have a breakdown, Mr Kemp."

The phone showed a brief flash of a naked, bruised and battered Chris lying bonelessly on the grubby mattress with a needle hanging out of his arm, before it cut off.

"Get that video up again, see if there's enough for facial recognition," Mark said.

They worked in silence, till Kate insisted they stop for food. Her suggestion that she take Ryan home was met with vehement denial from everybody sitting at the table.

"You both stay here, where its safe, until this is sorted. Just because they've got Chris, it doesn't mean they won't try for you and Ryan, and I couldn't cope with that," Matt said. He wrapped his arms around his new wife, his head on her abdomen as she stood next to him.

"They'll be safe, I promise," Jase said, but it seemed so inadequate.

* * *

"Why don't you get some sleep?" Mike asked as Jase pinched the bridge of his nose and tried to refocus on the video footage. He had more than enough willing volunteers ready and able to go on a rescue mission. But without a location, there wasn't a lot they could do. The plates on the car had been stolen. The images Chris had suffered significant injury to get were too dark to get a hit off facial recognition software.

Chris's behaviour was also puzzling. He was scared and hurt, and yet he'd reacted more pissed off than anything when Matt had mentioned the possibility that he'd been sexually abused. Most people would have reacted with shame, horror or at least distress at the suggestion; Chris had laughed and hadn't denied it had happened. Yet when he'd been threatened with another dose of heroin, he'd gone bananas, just as he'd done in the car park.

It wasn't the reaction of someone who'd never had any contact with drugs. Chris wouldn't even touch sleeping pills he'd been prescribed without a fight, even though it was clear he desperately needed them.

Was he a former addict, a rent boy shying away from any sort of sedatives in case it brought the cravings back? With the investigation going nowhere, it was time to solve this puzzle and there was one person on the planet that would probably know.

"Matt? Has Chris ever talked about his mother? Her name's Marietta right?"

* * *

Two weeks later, by calling in every favour possible, the video footage had been enhanced, quietly, by a leader in the field. Two of Chris's captors, known people traffickers, one from Bulgaria, the other from Turkey, had been identified.

It hadn't helped. There were no contact details held by any agency in Europe, they weren't even known to be in the UK. His Redcap colleagues had been forced to return to work. Both had promised to continue to help if they could. But without further information, there wasn't a lot to do. They had resigned themselves to waiting out the kidnappers, obeying every instruction, and hoping.

Matt and Kate had both returned to work, Ryan had returned to school. Apart from the fact that Richard was playing merry hell at the nursing home because he thought Matt had somehow stopped Crispy Bacon from visiting, everything seemed 'normal' except the house was too damn quiet without Chris.

Apart from the first hiccup, the lorries coming back into Britain had consistently managed to stop in the designated places. According to the drivers, including Mike and Stuart, they had carried two or three clandestine passengers across the channel each trip.

The low numbers of stowaways each time, the usual heavy machinery loads and their previously squeaky clean record meant Kemp International Haulage vehicles were seldom checked. Which was probably why they had been targeted. These people wanted their clients to have guaranteed passage.

Every day, around eleven pm, they got a brief video of Chris. Although he didn't appear to getting any more bruises, his physical and mental condition was clearly deteriorating. It was heart breaking to see and Matt had stopped showing the images to Kate because they upset her so much. All he said was 'he's the same'. But he wasn't.

The back chat had stopped, the life and energy had gone out of his eyes. Even the fight when they injected him was diminishing.

Tonight, as always, they were waiting for the contact with Matt's phone linked to a laptop. It beeped showing a video message had been received.

The scene showed a figure on the familiar mattress with a grubby sleeping bag. It was the only thing they permitted Chris to cover himself. When Matt had asked why they didn't let Chris have clothes on the third day, Jase wearily told him it was an interrogation technique. Being naked kept people off-balance, it would make most people hesitate before escaping outside. Not that he thought that would apply to Chris.

"Wake up, time to say hello to your brother," the voice behind the phone said.

Chris didn't respond. A booted foot appeared and nudged him, none too gently, but it wasn't exactly a kick. Chris was noticeably thinner, and he hadn't had any spare flesh to lose in the first place.

Chris pulled himself to a sitting position, looked around blankly, blinked, licked cracked lips and presented his arm. He wasn't given anything to eat or drink but it didn't seem to bother him.

Both men watching fought hard to control their reactions to Chris's complete capitulation. A figure, face carefully shielded from the camera, administered the injection. Chris slumped wordlessly back down. It was probably one of the most disturbing things Jase had witnessed, what made it far worse, was that he couldn't do a damn thing about it.

"I'm going to bed," Matt said, his voice thick with emotion. Jase could only nod. They were way past the 'it'll be alright,' platitude stage.

Instead, he continued to search for Chris's mother. The more information he had about him, hopefully the more they could help when they got him back. He couldn't entertain the possibility that they wouldn't. He'd only been with him for a couple of days, but the attachment he was experiencing seemed as strong as what Matt, Kate and the drivers felt. Chris had the ability to produce strong emotions, both positive and negative, whether he was trying to or not.

After finding no trace of a 'Marietta Bacon' he'd started to try different variations of the name with the partial date of birth his mother had supplied, along with an age range of five years. Everyone who had met Marietta all those years ago agreed that she had been in her early to mid-twenties and spoke with a refined American accent.

It took several more days to get a positive hit with the name Marie Baccioni. The death certificate showed Marie's life had ended in a squat via an opiate overdose four years ago. The reporting person was listed as her fourteen-year-old son, Chrisander.

"Poor little bastard," he murmured to himself. No wonder Chris was scared stiff of needles.

The coroner's report detailed a sad existence of a woman using prostitution to fund her heroin addiction. He wondered why the state hadn't intervened to protect Chris from such a hideous childhood, but maybe they hadn't known.

Many addicts didn't have permanent addresses. It was likely Chris had moved from one squat to another most of his life. It certainly explained his fear of sleeping alone when his mother was out getting the cash for her next fix. It also explained his cavalier attitude to sex. Hopefully she hadn't 'worked' with Chris present, but who knew? Rather than delving into his own feelings about Chris's abusive childhood, he concentrated on the information on his screen.

After his mother's death, Chris had been put into a foster home, where he'd stayed for precisely five days. The rest of the record consisted of him being returned to social care in various parts of London and the south east, often by the police. Persistent truancy, expulsion from several schools for complete non-compliance, petty shoplifting, pick pocketing, being the victim and/or perpetrator in minor assaults, vagrancy, the list went on. Drug use didn't appear anywhere on the record, which fit with Chris's behaviour. Most of the issues could be put down, in part, to his ADHD and deprived childhood. Chris's teachers must have deserved medals to deal with him as part of a class of thirty, although by the look of it, not many of them had made the effort with such a 'problem' child.

The last item on his care record was a report of him absconding from a children's home, an hour after he'd arrived, six months before his sixteenth birthday. Jase sat, looking at the date on his computer for twenty minutes before going to the General Registrar Office online and ordering copies of Chris's birth certificate and his mother's death certificate. Chrisander Baccioni had turned eighteen three days ago. After checking the time, he closed the laptop down. It was three in the morning.

He didn't miss the irony that while Chris was getting more sleep than he'd probably ever had in his life, he was becoming an insomniac. The redcap motto was 'By example, we lead,' but he was failing at that just as much as he was failing Chris and Matt.

He was due back at Catterick tomorrow to have his final medical assessment and then be formally discharged. His parents were driving him up. It would be a matter of performing like a trained poodle for a series of doctors, then collecting his paperwork from the personnel office. Hardly a an auspicious ending to ten years of service, although if he'd let it be known he was leaving, he knew some of his colleagues would make a fuss. A party under the current circumstances didn't seem appropriate.

Chris had been in his life for such a short time and yet, apart from Matt and his own parents, perhaps his Auntie Jean too, he couldn't think of another individual who had made this much impact on him. The extreme mix of spirit and vulnerability, the overt, crass sexuality... No, that wasn't right. Chris wasn't crass, he was just comfortable with himself, or at least he was comfortable with his sexuality. Unlike himself. He'd told himself it wasn't anyone else's business, but deep down he knew he'd hid it, from his parents and his colleagues.

The fact that his parents had known, had been waiting for years for him to share that part of himself with them, made him feel damn stupid. It was Chris leading him by example, not the other way around. Quietly, he let himself out of Matt's house and went back to his own. Although it wasn't his, it was his parents' place. He had no home of his own, no job and no real purpose in life except finding Chrisander Baccioni, alive. Day by day, hour by hour, that was looking to be an increasingly unlikely outcome.

* * *

The medical wasn't a great deal of fun, especially after spending three hours in his Dad's Volvo getting to Yorkshire. After doing all the normal checks, they concentrated on his ankle. X-rays and then a session with an orthopaedic physiotherapist, whom Jase was seriously convinced was a sadist.

"You've been walking on this," she said with a frown.

"Yeah, well, I've been looking after–"

She cut him off. "Look after yourself first, or you won't be able to look after anyone else. This is healing, but not at the rate I would have expected from your records. At least the scars are healing well, which is surprising considering the amount of swelling you still have."

After manipulating his ankle for what seemed like hours, she got him to circle and flex it, then asked him to stand and walk a few steps.

"I think you can go down to one crutch now, but minimize walking. Now that you have no open wounds, what you need to do is swim. Daily. Hydrotherapy will be the making of this ankle. If you look after it, you might get nearly full function back again, but it'll probably always ache a bit."

"I can live with that."

Two hours later, he was back in the family Volvo, with his smug father and his significantly annoyed mother. Her strident voice made him wince. His father shouted or gave disapproving looks when angry. His mum did a shrill, rapid fire 'daffy duck' impression that most sane people would do anything to stop, if they could get a word in edgeways. Chris's 'make a run for it' technique seemed quite appealing, even with his buggered ankle.

"And why didn't you tell us you'd been blown up?"

He opened his mouth, but to his surprise, his father took the bullet for him. "Because he didn't want us to worry, because he didn't want to be treated any differently, because he was just doing his job. Right son?"

He smiled gratefully. Although he wouldn't have put it as eloquently as that, it was true.

His mum wiggled in her seat. "My son's a hero!"

His dad chuckled. "He always was love. He doesn't need brass on his chest to prove it." Watching them briefly hold hands brought a lump to his throat, then he palmed his forehead as his mother started planning a special 'congratulations' dinner complete with rolling out his terminally ill aunt. She was right, Jean would enjoy such an event, but the timing sucked.

Even though it was the last thing he wanted, he was powerless to stop his mum in full planning mode. He'd kept the situation with Chris from them, from anyone that wasn't immediately involved to prevent the risk of the police finding out. That could very well be the signature on Chris's death warrant.

"So I know you've still got some healing to do, but have you decided what you want to do on civvy street? I can get you an interview at the Bailiffs office, if you–"

He headed the question off quickly.

"I'm really not sure what I want to do right now. It hasn't been long since it happened and I'm still getting my head around it to be honest."

He wasn't being truthful, but if he hadn't come up with a believable excuse, they'd keep on digging. Thinking about the future, meant putting Chris behind him, and he couldn't do that, not yet, not when there was still hope.

It felt stupidly good sitting in the back seat of his Dad's car, being looked after as if he was a little kid again. The radio, the drone of the engine and his lack of sleep, soon had him dozing.

His phone beeping with a text message from Matt woke him.

Searched at Calais, passengers found.
What will they do to C?

Don't know. I'll be home in an hour.

There wasn't anything else he could say. The happiness he'd felt earlier, vanished to be replaced by guilt.

"What's up, you look like you've seen a ghost?" his Mum asked as she twisted around to look at him.

"Have you had an argument with Chris? I noticed he hasn't cut the grass for a fortnight. You two need to talk, I know he can be a bit temperamental, but–"

"Leave it, Susan, it's his business. I'm sure he's old enough to sort out his own relationships. Just because he hasn't told us about them, it doesn't mean he's new at dating."

They thought they'd had a lover's tiff. He didn't even know if Chris was still alive. Gritting his teeth against the unexpected and unwelcome tears that were prickling his eyes, he concentrated on the passing countryside. To his surprise, his father pulled off the road at the next layby, parked and turned around in his seat.

"If he means this much to you, find him and apologise. It doesn't matter which one of you was in the wrong. Hell, get on your knees and beg, but make it right. Whatever caused the argument, it's not worth losing someone you love."

"I don't..." he started but his father gave him a hard look.

"Yes, you do. I know it's quick, but when you find the right one, that's it, done and dusted. You've been a shadow of yourself for the past fortnight. The only time I've ever seen you like this before was after you had that argument with Matt just before you signed up. And don't tell me you still would have joined up if that conversation had gone the way you wanted."

Jase gaped as his father's perception. "How...?"

"Because we're two peas in a pod, except that I fell for a wonderful girl instead of a wonderful boy. Just because it didn't work out with Matt, it doesn't mean things can't work with Chris. When we get home, you're going round there, and you're going to make him listen to you."

"I can't. He's—"

His mum couldn't help putting in her two pennies worth. "How many times have I told you that can't is just can with a 'T'? There's no—"

"Would you stop interrupting? I can't talk to him, I wish I could. He's..." Jase lost the 'stiff upper lip' battle and a tear slipped down his face which he swiped at angrily. The sympathy on both their faces for what they assumed was a lovers quarrel pissed him off. As if a dam had broken, he started telling them.

By the time he'd finished, his mum was in the back seat with her arms around him, and he'd made a wet patch on her blouse. He hadn't done that since he'd turned twelve but being held by her felt so right. He'd been keeping it together for so long, both in Afghanistan and here.

"So his mother's dead?" his father said quietly.

He nodded. "Chris found her, he was fourteen. She still had the needle in her arm. He sat with the body for hours before he went for help, the squat they were in didn't have a phone, electricity, or running water. They don't know whether she did it on purpose or whether it was an accident."

His mum gave him a squeeze. "It's going to be alright, but you really should talk to the police."

"No!" father and son said at the same time. "Honey, if they get one whiff that the police are involved, they'll... Well they'll make sure Chris won't be talking."

"They might do that anyway," she said and then put her hand over her mouth. "Oh love, I didn't mean that, he'll be fine, he..."

Jase patted her hand and smiled tightly. "I know Mum, I know."

CHAPTER 18

Chris

He finally understood why she'd done it. Everything went away when he was high. The fear, the pain, the worry and his head hadn't buzzed since...He briefly tried to work out how long he'd been here, but he gave up after a few seconds. It didn't matter, nothing mattered.

The cracks on the ceiling moved and swirled as he watched them. They were like clouds, every time he concentrated just a little more, they made different shapes, told different stories. It was like his mother was here, telling him stories in the night, keeping him calm, letting him sleep.

"Thanks Mum, I do love you, even though I don't say it," he murmured because it was important that she knew.

"I am not your mother, but it is nearly time for you to go home. Up you get." Dimitar's masculine voice woke something else in him.

He wanted to be close to someone, wanted to be held and touched. When he normally had sex, it was always hard, urgent and over quickly; now he felt as if a climax could last for hours, days even and he wanted to make someone else feel as good as he did.

He reached for the well-muscled, jean clad leg crouching next to his mattress. A hand closed around his wrist. He marvelled at how it moved, how all the blood, bones and ligaments beneath the skin worked together. How the individual hairs were each perfectly inserted into the skin. He could almost see the blood rushing through the tiny little tubes, it was like having x-ray vision.

"Not yet, but soon. It's time to make sure your brother doesn't come knocking on our door."

Chris frowned. "Matt's here?"

"No. Now come on, up you get, it's time for you to get ready for your going home party."

With Dimitar's hand wrapped around his upper arm to steady him, Chris found himself on his feet. His head spun and he staggered a little.

"Whoa, who's moving the floor?" he mumbled but didn't get an answer.

When he felt himself moving towards the door, he frowned and pulled back. It was safe in here, he knew what happened in here.

"Come on, time to get cleaned up; you can't go to a party smelling bad can you?"

It made as much sense as anything else did. He blinked against the light as he stepped out of his cupboard and into the large kitchen of an old farmhouse. The ceiling was low, the floor had flagstones and there was a huge wooden kitchen table. It was dark outside the small window.

"Wow, this place is old," Chris heard himself say. His voice sounded oddly unfamiliar.

"And you've never seen it have you?" his captor replied as he guided him to another door.

It took a while for his foggy mind to work out what Dimitar was on about. "Erm no, no I haven't."

He could hear a mummer of voices coming from deeper into the house.

"Good boy," Dimitar said and pushed him into a small bathroom next to a heavy wooden external door. "Get yourself clean, we wouldn't want your brother to think we were neglecting you would we?"

"You're letting me go?"

The handsome man smiled, pinched his cheek and closed the door on him.

The room was uniformly white, with a toilet, sink and a small shower cubicle. After glancing in the mirror, he wished he hadn't. Sallow skin, bruises that ranged from black to green, a swollen eye and a fat lip met his eyes. His scruffy, sparse beard covered a little of it. Luckily the mirror wasn't big enough to see the rest of his body. He looked down in surprise, he'd forgotten he was naked. There was a toothbrush and a tube of toothpaste on the back on the sink. He had no idea how long it had been since he'd brushed his teeth, so he squeezed a little out. The way it moved was fascinating. Before he realised what he was doing, he'd produced a long, toothpaste snake on the back of the sink.

"Come on Bacon, focus," he told himself and picked up the brush. After he managed to brush his teeth, without drifting off in a haze more than once, he turned to the shower.

By concentrating hard, he got through a brief wash and shampooed his hair before the water droplets on the glass door stole his attention. What made one drop run, when another one, that looked exactly the same stayed put? He imagined each drop was trying to pick up as many of its friends as it ran down the glass.

The next thing he knew he was being hauled out of the cubicle by his upper arm, and a towel was thrust into his chest. He dried himself roughly as his captor took another towel and rubbed at his hair.

"Come on sleepy head, time to shave," Dimitar said and handed him an electric shaver.

Chris stared at it, then turned it over in his hand, the colours reflecting in the metal were fascinating. It was snatched off him.

"If I had wanted to be a babysitter, I would have stayed at home," Dimitar muttered to himself as he grasped Chris's hair and tilted his head back, before attacking his facial hair.

When he was satisfied, he let his head go and opened the bathroom door.

Chris hesitated, something wasn't quite right if he was going to a party, then it occurred to him. "I'm not dressed," he mumbled.

"Doesn't matter," his captor said and pushed him out of the bathroom. There was a glass of coke sitting on the table. "Drink it."

"I don't..." he started. To be honest, going back to his mattress for another sleep sounded like a much better idea.

"Drink it or I call someone who will enjoy forcing you. It is roofie. It won't hurt you, but it'll make you forget what you see as we take you home. We can't have you telling people where you've been, understand?"

Chris took a deep breath, picked up the coke and downed it.

"Good boy, now let's go see your party guests."

Dimitar pushed another wooden door open and pushed Chris through it. The living room was large, filled with musty 'granny' furniture and men, lots of olive-skinned men. Chris tried to back out immediately but Dimitar stopped him. "Oh no,++++++++ little peacock, you are going nowhere."

He spoke in a language Chris didn't recognise, then pushed him towards two of the men that were walking forward with eager grins on their faces.

One grabbed him around the waist and pulled him into the room. "We party, yes?"

Hands started to touch and fondle him, stroking his ass and rubbing his dick, he started to fight, but he found himself pushed down onto a sofa as words he didn't understand rumbled around him.

"Get the fuck off me," he said as he tried to defend his groin from two sets of hands. All he could see was a wall of dark, mostly hairy skin. Someone grabbed his wrists and started talking gently in a language he didn't understand. He couldn't help relaxing as a wave of dizziness swept over him.

"That's it, it's getting to him. Remember, camera on him only, no faces. I don't want to have to edit too much." Dimitar's voice came from a distance at the same time that he was turned onto his belly. His hips were pulled up, as his face was forced into the cushions. He still tried to struggle weakly, but it was getting more and more difficult to work out which way was up. Laughter and words that sounded like encouragement came from all around him, then there was pain.

He tried to escape it as the laughter continued, but the wall of flesh prevented it. By the time the first man had finished, the rohypnol have fully taken effect and on top of the last dose of heroin, he no longer knew or cared what was happening.

CHAPTER 19

Jase

I t had been four days since the first lorry had been searched and every lorry had been stopped since then. The UK Border Agency had found hidden clandestines on two occasions, but although a third lorry had stopped in the indicated place, nobody had stowed away. It appeared that their usefulness was at an end, but nobody voiced the fact that the need to keep Chris alive had also passed.

The daily snippets of film had stopped, as had all other contact with the kidnappers. They tried to call them, but none of the burn phones they'd used received incoming calls. Each phone had probably been discarded as soon as a message had been sent. It's what he would have done in the same circumstances.

They were all on edge, each playing scenarios through their minds and keeping them to themselves, just in case the imagination of the others wasn't as horrific as their own. Plus, they had to keep things as normal as possible for Ryan. As far as he was concerned, his new, very entertaining uncle was on holiday.

Jase put out all the feelers for information that he possibly could, but it was now a not so simple matter of waiting. Kate had tried to up their spirits by saying 'no news is good news' about an hour earlier, but her comment had only made him wince. No news was far more sinister than receiving another video of Chris being beaten and drugged. At least they proved he was still alive.

It was one a.m. on Monday night, and Jase had been thinking about going next door to bed but he couldn't bring himself to move from Matt's sofa. Even though he knew Matt would call him if he got a message, he didn't want to leave, just in case. He, Matt and Kate were pretending to watch some action film, but none of them were paying attention.

His own phone buzzing made him jump. Pulling it out, he didn't recognize the number.

"Jason Rosewood."

"Is that Chris's soldier friend?" a male voice said. Jase sat forward on the sofa, conscious that both Matt and Kate were watching him intently.

"That's right, who's this?"

"Russel Denman, at the Toolbox. He's here. A car just pulled into the car park and pushed him out. He's drugged or something; eyes are open but nobody's home. Do I call an ambulance? He's pretty beaten up, naked and someone's been... I've got him in my office."

"Put him in the recovery position and keep an eye on his breathing, I'm on my way with a doctor."

He was already on his feet, as were Matt and Kate, their faces daring to hope. "He's at the club, phone Sarah and get her to meet me there."

"I'm coming too," Matt said as he snatched his shoes off the rack in the hall.

"No, you'd better stay here," Jase said quickly.

"No fucking way, he's my brother," Matt glared at him.

"I know, but those bastards are in the area, and they might be out for more leverage. Do you really want to leave Ryan and Kate unprotected?"

"I'll be fine, go," Kate said quickly.

Matt looked from one to the other, then put his shoes back. "So help me Jase if you don't–"

"I'll call, promise," Jase said quickly. "Call Sarah," he reminded them as he grabbed Matt's keys as he hopped/ran as fast as he could out the door.

If anyone had offered a million pounds for the details, Jase wouldn't have been able to recall a single car he passed or what colour the traffic lights were as he went through the high street.

He swerved into the car park, sending the gravel spraying and all but abandoned the vehicle next to the entrance.

The doorman waved him straight through. Nobody was dancing and the few patrons that were left were getting ready to leave. Shutting up early tonight was one of Russel's smarter decisions.

The office door was shut, but he didn't bother knocking. The first thing he saw was the back of a dark-haired male stranger who appeared to be injecting something into Chris's unresponsive arm as he lay on a battered, red leather sofa.

"What the fuck," he leaned forward and pulled the guy away by his shoulder. He found himself looking into surprised, startling blue eyes.

"I'm a paramedic. Sarah called me because I was closer. I'm just giving him some naloxone, it counteracts heroin, and by the look of him, he's been having quite a bit."

Jase was mortified as he looked at the needle that was still hanging out of the inside of Chris's elbow. "Fuck, I'm so sorry I thought... Shit I don't know what I was thinking."

The man smiled reassuringly. "No problem. Sarah didn't say anything apart from to get over here as quickly as possible as there could be an overdose case. I do a bit of drug counselling so I carry naloxone as a matter of course. I can see this place from my flat. Russel told me he's a kidnap victim?"

Jase ignored the question as he watched Chris's pale, unresponsive face. "Is he going to be alright?"

Somehow, even though he'd seen the bruises on a screen too many times to count, it was a hundred times worse in reality. Chris looked even younger, even more vulnerable than Jase remembered. A grey blanket covered him from mid torso to his shins. The fact that his feet were bare as they stuck out the end, made tears prickle at his eyes.

"I've been here less than five minutes. He's breathing and responsive to pain, even if he is out of—"

"You hurt him?" Jase said then remembered his own first aid training. "Sorry, standard test right?"

"Can I ask how you know him?" the medic asked.

"He's my... friend. I grew up with his older brother."

"Not him?"

"No, not him. His brother didn't even know he existed until a couple of months ago. I met him a few days before he was taken, that was just over two weeks ago." Jase watched as the man lifted Chris's eyelids in turn.

"Good. His pupils are starting to respond, he should start coming round in a minute. I'll just check the rest of him."

"They beat him up on the videos they sent his brother," Jase told him.

"Fucking bastards, I mean why? He's harmless." Russel spoke for the first time from where he stood, with his backside up against his desk at the back of the office.

"Because they could, which is exactly the same reason you used him. I tracked down his birth certificate. He turned eighteen a few days ago."

Jase decided Russel had at least a few brain cells as he didn't try to justify not making sure how old Chris was before employing him, or having sex with him. He did however, look significantly sick at the news.

The door opened just as the paramedic folded the blanket down on Chris's pale chest. Jase heaved a sigh of relief as Sarah appeared around the door.

"Thanks so much for charging to the rescue, Nate. How is he?"

The following brief conversation, as Sarah opened her bag and got out a stethoscope and blood pressure cuff, was full of medical terms which mostly went over Jase's head. He turned to Russel and a skill he did understand.

"Did anyone see the car or anyone that dumped him?"

"The doorman saw the car, a silver Discovery, but he didn't take the plate number as he was more concerned about Chris. They turned around at the top of the car park, then just pushed him out, almost at his feet, before they gunned it. One other thing, this was thrown out with him." Russel handed him a DVD. "I've got a machine if you want to watch it."

"He's awake," Nate said quietly. Jase immediately went back to the couch. Sarah was already trying to talk to him, but one look told him that although Chris's eyes were open, nobody was really 'home' as he blinked and stared at nothing.

"Chris? Chris can you hear me? It's me, Sarah, do you know where you are?"

Seemingly with a great deal of difficulty, as a frown appeared on his face, he tried to focus on her, but he didn't say anything or move.

"Does it hurt anywhere? We need to know if you've got any serious injuries."

Chris didn't respond.

"Shouldn't that stuff you gave him be working by now?" Jase said, not caring that his voice sounded strained.

Sarah looked up at him. "It is working, but it only works on opiates. I think he's been given something that'll mess with his memory too."

"Bastards," Russel growled from behind them.

Jase turned to look at him. "It's better than the alternative way to stop him talking, don't you think? Let's look at that DVD while the medics work."

Russel shoved the disc into the slot on the small portable TV sitting on a filing cabinet.

The blue screen held the message, *'This will be released to the net, if you call police'*. Then it morphed into a silent scene of male bodies, some naked, some partially dressed, but all were below the level of faces.

The crowd of flesh moved and Jase felt as if he'd been punched in the gut. Chris was on his knees, being held up around the hips by the figure taking his backside. His face was being used by another headless male who had a two handed grip in his hair, moving Chris up and down on himself. From the tone of his muscles, Chris wasn't entirely unconscious, but he certainly wasn't fighting or being complicit in what was happening to him.

"Christ," Russel swore and reached to turn it off.

"No, leave it. We need to know what happened to him, but I don't think he'd want you to see this," Jase told him.

Nate stood up and came over. After glancing at the screen he said, "I don't think he'd want you to see it either. Why don't you wait outside while Sarah and I finish the examination and see if there's anything on here, medically speaking, that we need to know about?"

Tearing his gaze away from the graphic, horrific pictures he nodded and without looking at Chris, he walked out of the room.

The shutters were down on the bar and the lights were bright and harsh as Jase walked back into the club. Glasses still sat on the tables and the place smelled of stale sweat and beer. *Why on earth does Chris want to be here so much?*

"I called last orders as soon as…" Russel trailed off.

"And you want a pat on the back for that?" Jase snapped.

"Take a seat," the club manager said and indicated one of the tall stools at the bar, while he moved behind it and pressed a hidden button that started the metal shutter rising.

"Drink? You look like you need one."

"Do you really think a drink drive conviction would make this any better?"

"Coffee then? I've got a feeling this is going to be a long night, one of many since I last saw you judging by the bags under your eyes."

Jase inclined his head, and within a minute, there was a cup of black coffee sitting in front of him. "How did you know I like it black?"

The big man shrugged. "Just a guess. Chris likes his caffeine free, white and sweet." There was an awkward pause.

"I did try, to look after him, I mean. I offered him the office to sleep in for as long as he wanted, he always refused. He also swore he was over eighteen and I did ask. He certainly acted like it."

Jase sighed. He knew how difficult Chris could be, how frustratingly independent, bolshie and full of bullshit he was. It'd taken all his skill to pry the few bits of information he had out of him, even Matt hadn't had any success.

"He might have taken you up on the offer if you'd offered him a place in your bed. He can't relax enough to sleep when he's on his own. Knowing him, he didn't tell you that or that he's got ADHD."

"That was never going to happen. I don't do relationships, not anymore."

Jase looked up at the shuttered face. "Got burnt?"

"Got widowed. Lawrence was going to a job interview in the city when some bastard decided to become a martyr on the tube train he was on."

"I'm sorry," Jase said, knowing how inadequate it was.

"Yeah, so am I, about Lawrence and about Chris. I dropped the ball with him, too caught up in my own world I guess. I believed the 'I'm alright' act because it was what I wanted to believe."

Jase snorted, then chuckled a little. "Yeah, he's a lying little shit, isn't he?"

Russel lifted his cup. "To lying little shits everywhere, what the hell would we do without them?"

After he'd finished his coffee, Russel moved around the bar and started collecting glasses.

"A manager's job is never done eh? I'd help, but..." He tapped his leg.

"The staff usually do the clearing up, but I thought the fewer tongues wagging the better. Although it was probably pretty pointless as my doorman carried him in, right through the bar."

"We'll make up some story about a prank gone wrong. As you said, people believe what they want to believe, especially if the alternative is harder."

"What happened to your leg if you don't mind me asking?"

"A teenage boy in Helmand decided to become a martyr."

"That's shitty."

"Yeah it was, but I chose to go, knowing the risks. Your husband assumed he was safe, and he should have been in his own capital city. Part of the reason I went."

Russel put the tray of empties he'd gathered on the bar. "So what about Chris? Is he a pet project while you heal before you go back overseas, or is he something more? Just because I'm not up for a relationship, it doesn't mean I'm blind to someone who needs stability more than his next breath."

Jase frowned, anger starting to bubble again. "And this is coming from the guy who pulled him off a podium, fucked and marked him, then sent him back to work within twenty minutes? Yeah, you really fucking care."

The door to the back area slammed open and Sarah stormed through it. "If you two have quite finished trying to work out which one of you failed that poor kid more, maybe you'd like to join the queue? None of us is without blame in this, we all took him at face value. I'm his doctor and I did exactly the same thing."

The way she was standing there, with her hands on her hips, eyes sparking with anger, made him see why Matt had fallen for her equally fiery sister.

"Now would you like to know how the latest set of people to use and abuse him have left him?"

Jase nodded as he got of the stool, hoping that he didn't look as much of a scolded schoolboy as Russel did. She took a deep breath, shutting off her emotions as she went back into 'doctor' mode.

"He's got a lot of bruising, but as far as I can tell, there are no broken bones, although he might have a cracked rib or two. There's nothing but rest to be done about those. There are signs of multiple injections on both arms. I'd say they've kept him topped up with heroin almost permanently, probably to keep him quiet. It's likely he'll suffer some physical withdrawal symptoms, but those probably won't last for more than seventy-two hours. It'll be rough, especially with his hyperactivity, but he'll get over that."

"He told you about that?" Jase asked in surprise.

"Why do think I prescribed him sleeping pills as well as antibiotics and vitamins the first time I examined him? But he didn't tell me his age, real name or any of the other stuff you found out. Matt filled me in as I was driving over here, he thought it was relevant, and it is."

"His background makes his mental recovery more of a problem, as does what happened on that video." She sighed and rubbed her forehead as she seemed to deflate.

"I'm not going to lie, it was bad, really bad. The only good thing I can say is that they appeared to all be using condoms. Judging from his physical condition, the video was taken earlier this evening. He's battered, bruised and raw, but it doesn't look as if any permanent damage has been done. Hopefully he won't remember a great deal, if anything at all. I think they gave him rohypnol so he won't be able to identify the men involved. I'm not sure how damaging it will be for him to find out the exact details, he's resilient but this is..." After a pause, she took a deep breath and carried on.

"As a GP, I'm really not experienced with this type of trauma, but Nate is a volunteer drug councillor amongst other things. He can help with the withdrawal period and provide counselling for any issues he has about his mother's habit. Your, Matt's, Kate's and Ryan's jobs will be to keep things stable, and as calm as possible to prevent him disappearing again.

"Russel, your job is to be the safe haven, the link with his past that he will hopefully run to first when ironman here pisses him off too much. ADHD means he has little control over impulses, and together with a latent heroin addiction, and growing up with prostitution and no permanent home, all makes him a ticking time bomb waiting to go off. Am I making myself clear?" She looked from one to the other. Jase glanced at Russel who nodded back. They could be civil to each other for Chris's sake.

Jase hobbled over to her and enfolded her in his arms. The rigidness went out of her body as she leaned into him briefly. She stiffened as Russel spoke.

"So hopefully I'll get a head's up if he's likely to be turning up? I'll shut him in my office till someone comes to get him."

Sarah pulled away from Jase. "Didn't you hear me? This place has to be a safe haven for him, so he'll come here if he feels under pressure rather than disappearing into the wild blue yonder. If he turns up, you let him in. You let him dance, up there on one of those stupid podiums if he wants to, actually it might be better than being on the floor because it'll be easier to keep an eye on him. But no booze and no going off with anyone. You call, me, Nate, his brother, or Jase, whichever one of us hasn't pissed him off to pick him up at the end of the night when he's got it out of his system. Dancing, flirting and a safe, supervised, place to spend the evening, that's it, got it?"

Jase decided if he'd been on the receiving end of Sarah's little speech, he would have been standing to attention and saluting with a snappy 'Yes, ma'am'.

Sarah's phone rang, and she looked at it before handing it to Jase.

"It helps to actually bring your phone into the building when you tell someone you'll tell them everything that's going on. I've already told Kate the medical facts."

"I'll beat the crap out of you later for not phoning," Matt's voice made him smile. "We've got his room sorted out, is he able to walk yet?"

"I think he's still pretty out of it, Sarah chased us out while she and a paramedic pal of hers checked him out. But yeah we should be home soo–" he broke off as Sarah made a cutting gesture across her neck. "Hang on a minute," he said, "I'll call you back."

"He can't go back there, not in the state he's in. It'll freak Ryan out. My place is only one bed, and I've got work all week. He shouldn't be left alone for the foreseeable future."

"He can stay at my place," Jase said immediately.

Sarah frowned, "Don't you mean your parents' place? Don't you think you should ask them first? Besides, I don't think Chris is up to being sociable."

"He can stay with me," Nate said as he came into the bar. "I've dealt with people suffering from withdrawal before, and I've got room for someone else to stay with him so he won't be alone when I'm working. A familiar, non-judgemental, non-patronising face who won't treat him as if he's made of glass or responsible for what's happened to him…"

All eyes turned to him and none of them looked particularly convinced.

"What? I can do that," he protested.

The expression on Sarah's face said she didn't believe him. "You're a policeman, you can't help being judgemental; it's in the job description."

Jase drew on every ounce of his trained to stop himself snapping back at her. "I also deal with victims, and that's what Chris is."

A crash from the back room had all of them rushing back down the corridor. Chris was sitting on the floor, stark naked, the remains of a glass shattered around him. He was looking at a cut on his finger with fascination and didn't appear to have noticed the room now contained four more people.

Jase crouched down next to him. "Chris?"

He didn't respond, still focused on the scarlet drops that were forming on his index finger.

Jase put a finger on his chin and slowly moved his face toward him. The blank expression slowly turned into a frown.

"Jase?" he whispered, then looked past him at his surroundings and then up at the people surrounding him.

"I'm back?"

At Jase's gentle smile and nod, Chris's face crumpled and he started to cry. Jase enfolded him in his arms, and nothing in his life had ever felt more right.

CHAPTER 20

Chris

His face was up against a t-shirt covered chest and there was something over his waist that felt suspiciously like an arm. He moved his foot slightly. He had a quilt over him, and a sheet under him. Neither smelt like pee.

For one brilliant, sparkling moment, he actually thought he'd dreamed it, that all that shit hadn't happened and he was still in bed, in his room at Matt's with Jase. The body he was cuddled up against certainly smelt like Jase, but this wasn't his room. There was an air of space outside his little cocoon that he didn't want to know about. His body ached, but by far the worst pain was in his backside, he didn't want to think about why.

More than anything, he wanted to go back to sleep, back to oblivion, but he could feel the familiar restlessness starting in his toes. If he made a noise, they'd come and hurt him again, although if he was awake, the next shot must be due and then it'd be ok. But this wasn't his mattress, wasn't his little windowless room, so where was he?

He fought to keep his mind in the here and now, wherever here was. The arm around his waist tightened. He tensed and continued to push at his fuzzy mind for answers that just wasn't there.

"Chris? You awake?"

He stayed quiet. At least he could confirm that it was Jase behind him, but if Jase knew he was awake, he'd expect answers. Problem was, he didn't have a clue what to say. Even figuring which way was up was like the bloody Krypton Factor.

The chest moved and he was rolled onto his back. He found himself looking up into a pair of concerned green eyes. Eyes that seemed to have more lines around the corners than he remembered.

"You ok?" The voice he'd been convinced he'd never hear again sounded scratchy.

What the hell am I meant to say? Just peachy thank you? Or should I tell him I've been drugged, beaten up, kept in a cupboard and by the feel of my arse, used as a fucking dart board by most of eastern Europe?

He kept his mouth firmly shut.

"You don't remember?" The hope on Jase's face gave Chris the out he needed, and he vowed to exploit it with every ounce of his soul.

"What's the last thing you do remember?"

"The club..."

"That's where they dumped you last night. We're at the home of a friend of Sarah's, do you remember Nate? He came to the club last night, helped you, and brought us back here."

Chris didn't remember any of that, although that must have been what Dimitar intended. It was a shame that they hadn't given him that memory stuff the whole time. Then it occurred to him that Jase and Matt wouldn't know that; he could plead complete ignorance and never have to discuss any of it ever again. It sounded like a bloody good plan.

"Chris? Do you remember being at the club last night?" Jase prompted again, concern in his eyes at Chris's silence.

"I remember you were pissed off because I had a quickie with Russ, then I headed into the car park. There was some sharp looking bloke in a suit..." He frowned as if trying to recall what had happened next.

Jase sighed and briefly closed his eyes. There was pain in them when he opened them. "I don't know how to tell you this, but that was just over two weeks ago. You've been held by a group of blackmailers; they forced Matt to let his lorries carry illegals over the channel."

Chris didn't have to try too hard to look surprised, he had no idea it'd been that long. Getting back to normal by pretending nothing had happened was his strategy.

"Two weeks? Pull the other one, I just went on a bender. Nice try for a wind-up, but no cigar."

He threw the covers back and sat up on the side of the bed, which made his butt hurt even more. Even though his head was swimming, he could see that the room was vast. Plush cream carpet, that he could actually sink his toes into, stretched for nearly ten feet before it hit a wall. A quick glance showed there was an equally huge distance all around the bed. Everywhere screamed money, buckets of it.

"Whoa, I think I like this dream, but why are you in it? I could have had Aiden Turner instead, cos you're tasty but he's–"

"Chris, they shot you up with heroin and probably roofies, that's why you can't remember."

Why couldn't Jase just keep his damn mouth shut?

111

"They sent us videos, every night..." Jase looked as if he was trying to keep it together, even though he'd been blown up in Afghanistan. It couldn't have been that bad, could it? Memories of needles, of being hit, of being...

"Whatever happened, Matt, Kate and I, the drivers that helped, even Russel and the Toolbox staff, we all know it wasn't your choice, wasn't your–"

Hoping that the door nearest to him led outside the room, or at least into a bathroom so he could put some distance between himself, Jase and the hideous reality, he lurched to his feet and found that the carpet really was soft, up close.

"Shit, you alright?"

The voice, the hand on his back and the one on his arm, dripped with pity. He hated it with a passion so deep it felt as if every cell in his body was exploding with it.

"Fuck off! Just fuck the hell off, nothing happened, nothing fucking happened," he shouted as he scooted away from Jase. He needed to get out, needed to leave this place and everyone that knew behind him. This was just another horrible chapter in his life and he could leave it behind, just like he'd done before.

Getting to his feet, he grabbed the first door handle he came to. *A fucking walk in wardrobe. Who the hell is this Nate guy?*

"Chris please, you can't run away from this," Jase pleaded.

Using the wall to balance himself as his legs shook, he turned and faced Jase. "Watch me. I don't need you, I don't need Matt and I–"

"Didn't need your mum? I found out what happened to her, that you found her. That's why we need to–"

Chris felt all the blood drain out of his face, then rage boiled through him. "You bastard, you fucking BASTARD."

The walls were closing in on him. It was happening again; he'd be shuffled from one patronizing adult to the next, with none of them actually giving a shit except to get the box on their fucking form ticked and a bonus in their pay packet or a feather in their do-gooder hat.

He pulled open another door and to his relief, found a bathroom. He was inside, with the door locked within a heartbeat.

"What the hell is going on?" The masculine voice wasn't one he recognised, so he imagined it was the owner of this fantastic pad. Hell, he didn't even know if he was in a flat or a house, no change there then. At least this was better than a piss soaked mattress in a cupboard, although in many ways it was so much worse.

When he'd been with Dimitar, they hadn't looked down on him. Well, Uncle Ugly had, but that because he was a homophobic arsehole, it wasn't personal. He'd performed a function there, he'd been needed. Now? Now he was just an object of pity to be looked after, just like his senile father.

He listened as the two do-gooders discussed their latest case. It mainly consisted of Jase apologising for being a tit, and the other guy agreeing with him. Apparently confronting a 'fragile' patient with the truth as soon as he was conscious, wasn't the preferred procedure.

"I'm not fucking fragile, I'm pissed off because he's a nosey fucker," Chris called out, then wondered why the hell he couldn't keep his mouth shut.

He'd managed to keep quiet for days in his cupboard. Then again, he'd had the added advantage of being bombed out of his brainbox on smack. Two weeks. Shit. He'd really had no idea it had been that long. But that was what smack did to you, it took away the worries of the moment and made you feel wonderful, even if the world was going to shit around you. *Crap, I want a fix.*

Instead of dwelling on his craving for oblivion, he looked at his arms. There were bruises and small scabs on the inside of both arms. He'd been given a lot. Which meant he was probably starting to go into withdrawal. As he'd found with his mum and numerous others, the physical stuff wasn't nice, but it was hardly the worst thing in the world. The problem was dealing with the world without the buffer of drugs between you and reality.

People thought the drugs were the cause of an addict's problems, but they often started out as a temporary relief from existing crap. The downside was, when you came down, the problem was still there, and had usually got worse while you were in Never Never Land. So you took some more. Things could spiral out of control before you knew it.

His mother hadn't been able to cope with the real world, even with him doing his best to help her. Was he stronger than she was? Or would little Ryan walk in on him lifeless on the floor, kneeling as if he'd just touched his forehead to the floorboards for a second before getting to his feet, with a needle still in his arm? Would Ryan sit and look at his body, frozen in time forever, willing it not to be true, willing him to get up but scared shitless to touch him in case it turned out that the person you loved really was dead?

He tore his mind away from the memory that he kept locked up when he was awake. When he was asleep, it wasn't so easy, although with Dimitar's 'happy juice' it hadn't been a problem.

His mother hadn't been a bad person, she'd just wanted out from spending another night in with him bouncing off the walls and the worry that her hated family would catch up with her.

If Dimitar opened that door right now, would he hold out his arm or would he fight like he had the first few times. If a syringe rolled under the door, would he use it? Right now, having everything just fade away again was bloody tempting.

CHAPTER 21

Chris

A light tapping at the door broke him out of his thoughts.

"Chris? It's Nate. We met last night, we're at my place. We thought it would be easier on Ryan if you started your recovery here rather than at home; he and Kate moved in to your brother's while you were away. I'm a paramedic and a drug counsellor.

"And Jase is a prat. A well-meaning prat, but a prat all the same. I've sent him off to polish his boots, military TYPES like that stuff. If that doesn't keep him out of mischief I've got some ironing he can do. But I can't be here all the time, and someone needs to stay with you. It's not nice, it's not fair, but it's the way it has to be until you get your shit together."

"My shit is together," he said automatically.

"Your bullshit might be, as for the rest, you'll have to prove it because from what I just heard, we have a little work to do. You've suffered a trauma, several traumas by the sound of it and there's no escaping that. The choice you have to make is whether you're going to let the shitty things that have happened to you in the past, shape your future."

And there was the crux of the matter. This guy was almost as bad as Jase, although he wasn't quite as blunt and confrontational.

"Come on, out you come, I've got plans for you."

"Like what?"

"It's going to be a barrel of laughs, I promise. Heroin withdrawal always is."

Chris couldn't help snorting in amusement, "You're going to be a complete pain in the arse aren't you?"

"I aim to please. I also aim to get you back to the state you were in before all this shit happened to you."

"So tell me, Nate, why do you give a shit? And so help me, if you say anything about 'giving something back to the community, I'm going to...'"

He paused. He didn't know what he could do, seeing as he was sitting in the guy's fucking plush bathroom and by the look of it, wearing his underwear. Because sure as shit stank, neither he nor Jase owned black silk boxers.

As the silence stretched, Chris concluded that Mr Fancy Pants was desperately trying to think up a good answer. Another bleeding heart, 'do-gooder' looking for brownie points wasn't what he needed.

The quiet voice from the other side of the door took every ounce of his attention. "My older brother died from a self-inflicted cocaine overdose. I idolised him. He was happy, sporty, conscientious and driven about his work. He had a steady girlfriend and a great future running the family retail company. We didn't even know he was using until it was too late. He'd been an addict for four years. He kept a diary, and I've read it a hundred times. People that take drugs aren't evil or pathetic, they've just found a solution to stress that takes over before they realise it's got them by the balls."

Chris didn't know what to say, but at least this guy had a genuine understanding and a reason to help.

"So, opening the door time?"

With a sigh, he got off the toilet and opened the door, making sure he didn't look in the full length mirror opposite the bath. The fact that his backside felt as if an industrial drain rod had been used on it didn't bode well for the state of the rest of him.

Opening the door, he immediately wished he'd paid more attention to his appearance. Nate the do-gooder was seriously gorgeous. Even if he was just wearing sweatpants and a t-shirt, he was tall, dark-haired and had stunningly intense blue eyes. He couldn't help thinking about Nate's 'designer stubble' making his own face, and other places, raw with passionate friction.

Chris's 'flirt' switch flipped on automatically. His Tigger persona was easy to hide behind than having 'Chris the victim' out on parade.

"Got anything else I can wear apart from your underwear? Because I'm damn sure I've never worn anything so plain in my life. Although I'm liking the silk," he said as he looked down at the plain black boxers.

"I think they're rather fetching. They do say less is more," Nate said, a slight smile on his face.

The day is looking up.

"As much as I'd like to ogle you all day, Jase has asked your brother to bring some of your stuff over later."

And there it goes, hurtling back down again, thanks Jase. What the hell am I going to say to Matt?

"I know seeing family might not be easy after what happened, but the longer you leave it, the worse it'll get. If it helps, he'll be feeling awkward too. Try putting yourself in his position."

Chris shrugged, trying to convince himself, and Nate, that it didn't bother him. "I have that effect on people anyway. No biggie."

He was grateful when Nate let the lie go. Jase wouldn't have. The man wanted everything just so, all I's had to be dotted and all T's crossed as soon as possible, so that he could move on the next item on his neat little agenda. Chris didn't know if he was happy or sad that he wasn't another item on Jase's list that could be dealt with so easily.

* * *

Twenty minutes later, after Nate had done his medical checks, and given him an embarrassingly large tube of antibiotic and anaesthetic cream for his arse, Chris was in the kitchen of what proved to be a penthouse. Nate nonchalantly told him it took up the top floor of a department store. Looking out the window, Chris knew exactly where he was. Cooper's wasn't a shop he could afford to patronise, not that it sold the stuff he wore anyway.

Wearing the dark blue towelling bath robe Nate had provided, he moved an inch to the right as he looked out the window. The flat roof of the two storey building he could just see, was actually the Toolbox. The living room windows looked out over the river running through the centre of town. This had to be the best, most expensive property in town. He felt awkward just being in it. Matt's cosy, three bed, family home had been pretty amazing, but this? This was so far out of his league he didn't know which way to turn. All he knew was that he didn't feel comfortable, and he had some work to do if he was going to get out of here any time soon.

Jase, looking every inch the military man, dressed in combats and a black t-shirt, plated up three portions of scrambled eggs and toast. Keeping 'bullshit' firmly in mind, Chris huffed as he sat down a little gingerly.

"Is that it? I've been starved for a fortnight, and all I get is this?"

"That's why. You need to get your stomach used to food again. Too much and you'll bring it back," Jase informed him as if he were a child.

This would be so much easier if he looked like a potato. Chris tore his eyes away from Jase's pecs that showed clearly through the tight cotton.

Distance, he needed distance to stop himself from giving in to everything Jase asked, just he'd done with Dimitar. He'd seen Jase's type before. Men like him enjoyed the process of moulding weak willed idiots into what they wanted, but the final product didn't hold their interest for long. Once he was nothing but what Jase wanted, he'd move on to another project and leave him a cardboard cut-out of a person.

As Jase would probably refuse to give him space, Chris decided to produce his own.

"Now that's an idea. My best pals, slut, ADHD, dyslexia and the new member of the crew, junkie, are looking for a new best friend. Bulimia would fit right in, don't you think?"

Jase shot him a look that could kill and left the room without saying a word or eating a bite. Even though it was what he'd wanted, seeing the stiffness in Jase's shoulders as he walked away, hurt.

Nate tucked into his food silently. Chris wasn't hungry and not only because he felt guilty for pissing Jase off. He'd seen his mum in withdrawal many times, and if he had the timing right, he'd be talking to god on the Great White Telephone within the next four or five hours, unless he got another fix. And with his do-gooder double act on duty, that was hardly likely. Which was good, really good, because at the moment, he still didn't know if he'd take a hit if it was offered.

"Not eating?" Nate asked.

"Don't fancy it coming back. He might not realise it, but we both know that I'm going to be sick as a dog in a few hours."

"Been through withdrawal before?" Nate asked as if drug withdrawal was normal. The problem was, it was, for both of them.

He shrugged. "Only from your side. I'm sure Mr Information has told you, but my mum was an addict, so were most of her friends. I grew up with it. I've got the shakes, the shits, puking, a snotty nose, belly aches, paranoia and generally a shitty time for the next three or four days."

"And you don't want Jason to see that."

Chris frowned. Great, just what he needed, a perceptive do-gooder. "Would you want anyone to see you crapping yourself as you heaved your guts up while you shook and shivered with snot running down your face?"

"Not anyone I cared about. And you do care about him, don't you?"

Chris opened then shut his mouth again as he scowled at Nate. That was a bloody big question. Jase was a domineering git, but he'd pushed him and got him to open up more than anyone else had in years. Jase saw through the bullshit, and that was damn scary, because so far, he was still here. Nevertheless, he'd only actually spent two and a half days with him, and most of that time they'd been sniping at each other.

"Or don't you think you deserve him? Are you consciously, or unconsciously, trying to push him away to save his sexy military 'together' backside from whatever you think you are?"

"His up-tight controlling arse you mean," Chris growled as he pulled the plate of eggs towards himself and started eating.

"And having a relationship with someone who helps you to be a little more stable and consistent would be a bad thing? Yin and yang together, works for some."

"For a start, we only met two days before the fun and games started. And second, Jase doesn't want me that way, I've offered it to him on a plate several times. He's definitely a Star Trek kinda bloke," Chris said, keeping his eyes on his plate as he shovelled a forkful of egg into his mouth. It was really rather good, probably because it was the first hot thing he'd eaten in a fortnight.

"Sorry?" Nate asked in total confusion.

"He wants to boldly go where no man has gone before. I'm more like bloody Deep Space Nine with the number of visitors I've had."

117

"You're positive about his feelings?"

Chris shrugged. It was time for someone else to be in the spotlight for a change.

"So Nate, who's the yin to your yang? And how the fuck do you afford a place like this on a paramedic's wages?"

"I am currently yin-less, and before you ask, no I'm not looking. And as for this place, my surname's Cooper."

Chris stopped eating. "You mean like the…" he pointed downward.

Nate grinned. "Yep. It's also why most of my relationships end. I'll let you in on a little secret, gold diggers are the pits. Take my advice, if someone is just after you for your money, ditch them."

Chris grinned. "Oh yeah, I agree, every time. There was one guy last year who only wanted me for my tent."

Nate smiled back. "Big one is it?"

"Two man. It's awesome. It even has a special 'lived in' fragrance that I've worked on for nearly two years."

"You haven't still got it have you? I was thinking of doing a back to basics trip, all this luxury gets kinda boring after a while."

"Bastard."

"If you've got it, flaunt it, and from what I've seen in the club over the last couple of months, you've certainly got both of those fully covered."

Chris blinked. "You've watched me dance?"

"Oh, yeah. And the sooner we get you back up on that podium, the happier the gay population of this town will be."

Nate grinned and for the first time since he'd woken up, Chris felt accepted, warts and all.

* * *

Twenty minutes later Chris was standing on the roof of the building, still in Nate's bathrobe, with his eyes bugging out.

"Oh, my, fucking, God. They bloody well killed me and I've gone to heaven," Chris said as he stared at the swim spa where Jase was swimming against the artificial current with long, lazy strokes.

"Yeah, he's not bad looking is he?" Nate said from beside him. Chris aimed a slap at his chest.

"I meant the bloody paddling pool, you git," Chris growled, but he couldn't keep the smile off his face.

"I might believe you if you manage to roll your tongue back in. As for Star Trek, I don't know about the virginal thing, but he's definitely not the sort to go for an emotionless one night stand. If you want him, you're going to have to put in the effort and I don't mean for a night or two."

Chris gazed at the man stretching his muscles in the pool, completely oblivious to being watched. Jase wasn't as big or as muscly as Russel, wasn't as good looking or as rich as Nate. There wasn't a shred of flamboyance or brightness in him. He didn't even dance or go out of his way to please anybody.

Jason Rosewood was as straight as they came, for a gay bloke. He'd had a stable upbringing, his parents were still married and they'd supported him both emotionally and financially all his life. In turn, he tried to do his best for his country, his family and his friends, even if it didn't make him popular.

So why the hell was Jase here, instead of running a mile from such a fucked up individual as him? And why did Jase's interest in him make Chris almost more nervous than the thought of getting clean?

CHAPTER 22

Jase

A loud chime broke his concentration on keeping his movements smooth. He let the current push him to the back of the swim spa before he stood up. This was literally what the doctor, or rather the physiotherapist, had ordered. Although Nate had told him it was up here and he could use it anytime he liked, he hadn't actually believed him until he'd stepped out onto the roof terrace.

They'd talked for a while after they'd settled Chris in bed last night. Nate seemed to be a genuinely nice bloke despite his silver spoon up-bringing, although he hadn't had it all his own way. But if anyone could turn Chris's fickle head, it was a rich, handsome man who understood him.

He'd spent hours, as he'd held Chris's disturbingly unresponsive body last night, wondering if Chris was shallow enough to have his head turned by such a man. If it came to it, could he win a fight for Chris's affections with Nate? Did he even want to? Even if he did, was it right to try and prevent Chris benefitting from all the resources Nate could provide? After all, what could he, a crippled, out of work, ex-army sergeant offer?

Getting to his feet in the four foot end, he winced as he put weight on his damaged leg. Maybe he had pushed it a bit, but getting his muscles working again after so long had felt fantastic. Before the bomb, he'd run at least five miles a day, no matter where in the world he'd been, but he guessed those days were over.

"You ok?" Chris's voice coming from next to the spa made him look up.

He still looked like a kid who'd borrowed his dad's dressing gown, a kid who'd received one hell of a beating. Jase reached for the proffered hand as he climbed out of the water. Although he didn't think Chris could actually hold him up if his leg did give way; he barely looked strong enough to keep himself upright.

"Yeah, I'm good. I need to take my own advice though, I got a bit carried away with the exercise. I used to run a lot before this happened, it's tough not being able to move when you want to."

"Welcome to my world, Sarge," Chris said as he handed him the navy towel that was sitting on the small wooden table beside the spa.

"Is that why you stopped fighting the injections?" Jase asked and then kicked himself mentally as Chris seemed to deflate briefly.

To his joy, instead of making a run for it, Chris glared at him.

"Have I got a fucking neon message display on my forehead or something? Cos you seem to be able to look into my head anytime you damn well want, and to be honest, its bloody uncomfortable."

Yet again, Chris had surprised him with his fast switch between not letting him in at all, and brutal honesty.

He grinned. "It's a skill."

Disappointment washed over him as rather than making a clever comeback, Chris's gaze wandered south.

Sex was just another technique Chris used to distract himself from his problems or gain himself temporary resources. Although personally, he'd never gone for deep and meaningful relationships, he also didn't do one night stands. Sharing your body, your most intimate, vulnerable moments with someone, required at least trust and mutual respect, or it did for him. Unfortunately, Chris didn't respect or trust himself, so he didn't expect anyone else to, but with help, hopefully his help, he could change.

"Eyes up," he reminded him.

Chris pursed his lips and scowled. "Didn't anyone ever tell you there's no harm in looking?"

"Do you find yanking my chain entertaining?" He knew he'd said exactly the wrong, or maybe the right thing, as Chris grinned. For the first time since they'd got him back, Chris's pale, multi-coloured face became animated with happiness rather than fear, anger or shame.

Jase pointed a finger at him. "Don't answer that," he said, not bothering to hide his smile.

Chris spread his hands, palm up, trying to keep an innocent, 'who me?' expression intact.

"Chris?"

Jase looked over Chris's shoulder and saw Matt standing with Nate. Chris's smile vanished. Jase could understand his nervousness. Each time he met someone who knew what had happened, it must be like facing it all over again, and he'd started out this morning by listing all the people that knew. No wonder Chris had tried to run from him.

Nate indicated that Jase should follow him as Matt walked forward and simply enfolded Chris in his arms.

Once they'd walked down the open wood and glass staircase to the main floor, Nate kept on going till he got to the kitchen and flipped the kettle on.

"Well done on cheering him up, I really put my foot in it," Jase said, forestalling any criticism, although he deserved it.

"Coffee or tea?" Nate asked.

"Black coffee, please."

"You sure? It's going to be a long night. If you can get a couple of hours more sleep now, I'd go for it."

"I'm good," Jase replied, then went into the main bathroom to put his clothes back on.

Once he was settled back at the kitchen table and they had their drinks, Nate spoke up. "I need to get a baseline of what's normal for him so I can gauge how he's coping with the withdrawal. I've seen him dancing at the club, but apart from being flirty and energetic, I don't know much about his personality. Is he always so volatile?"

Jase started explaining what he'd found out about Chris, and his habit of running as a first line of defence. Nate was an attentive listener.

"And how do you feel about him, personally?"

Jase frowned. "And how is that relevant to his medical care?"

"Because drug addiction isn't just about the physical. Heroin was the worst possible choice those bastards could have made for him, because it does things that he can't do for himself. Simply put, from what I've heard and what I've seen, Chris is a smack head waiting to happen." Nate started ticking points off on his fingers.

"He's got a history of family addiction. He chooses to avoid problems by physically distancing himself from them, rather than confronting them, and there's no better way to get away from problems in your own head than heroin. He's hyperactive, and quite unable to calm down enough to rest without engaging in extreme activity, including risky sex.

"Sarah pushed the samples we took last night, he's clear of anything horrible apart from neglect and a very abused backside. She gave him a long acting antibiotic shot, just in case, and some anaesthetic cream. He claims not to remember much, which may or may not be true. He feels worthless, damaged and a burden to people who matter, which as far as he's concerned, has never included him. All of that disappears if he shoots up, and he knows it."

Jase shifted uncomfortably under Nate's intense gaze. "He knows Matt is likely to want to help him, because he's family and that's the sort of guy he is. You, on the other hand, have no obligation to him whatsoever. He's tried to pay you back with the only currency he possesses, his body, and you've refused him, more than once. To put it bluntly, you confuse the shit out of him. One minute you're holding him all night, the next you're battering at his walls as if the only thing you want is reduce him to a pile of mental rubble."

Jase gave his companion a hard stare. "That might be what it looks like, but it's not true. He needs to confront his problems, not run away from them. Doing that hasn't helped him so far has it?"

"And are you going to be around, long-term, to help him do that?"

Jase clenched his jaw, then relaxed it. Nate was doing exactly what he'd tried to do with Chris, and it was damn uncomfortable. The difference was, his style was to confront problems head on, not run from them. Then again, he'd always had the back-up of a stable family.

"Are you?" he countered.

"As a friend? Yes. If I was looking for a relationship, possibly something could develop over time, but I'm not looking, which is what I told him. He's also a little too confrontational for my personal tastes. With his ADHD, Chris is always going to need fairly intensive attention and with my work, I need to relax when I get time off."

Jase let out a breath that he didn't know he'd been holding.

Nate put his chin on his fist, as he scrutinised him. "Did you know he thinks you don't want sex or a relationship with him because he's damaged goods? I understand if that's true, he's a lot to take on, but if it is, you need to back the hell off before you confuse him even more. Because if he starts to depend on you, and you abandon him, that'll send him sprinting back to smack faster than Usain Bolt with a cattle prod up his arse.

"You'll also need to acknowledge that sex is a huge part of what makes Chris tick. Most people see sex as an additional part of a romantic relationship, an important part, but not the main aspect. Chris's whole psyche revolves around physicality; for him sex isn't about deep and meaningful feelings, it's about trading favours, recreation and forgetting."

Suddenly the exhaustion of the last two weeks, hell, the last couple of months, seemed to catch up with Jase all at once and he rubbed at his forehead. Maybe Nate could help him sort out his own head as well as Chris's.

"You can't enter a relationship when one party doesn't know his arse from his elbow. And to be honest, right now I'm not a lot better than he is. I got medically discharged from the army a matter of days ago because I was on the wrong end of a suicide bomber. I don't have a home of my own, a car or even a job; everything I own fits into a couple of duffle bags. Chris needs stability, not more uncertainty."

"He needs emotional stability, not a detached house in suburbia filled with flat packed Swedish furniture and cocoa every night at nine. He was happy living in a tent for fuck's sake."

The sound of footsteps on the stairs stopped the conversation.

"He's shivering," Matt announced as he guided Chris into the kitchen.

Chris scowled at his brother as he pulled the oversized robe tightly around himself. "So?"

Matt indicated a bag Jase hadn't noticed near the door. "I brought you some clothes and some art supplies. Thought it'd take your mind off things."

"Great, I'll just draw unicorns and rainbows and everything will be sunshine and flowers," Chris said as he slumped onto a chair, then shifted uncomfortably.

"He's only trying to help Chris," Jase started.

"I don't need any help, and I don't need to be watched like a science experiment," Chris spat back but he was hugging himself as if his belly hurt.

Jase and Matt exchanged a glance, but Nate ignored Chris's discomfort.

"Do you usually draw unicorns? 'Cos I pegged you more as a 'still life' kinda guy."

EMMA JAYE

Chris looked up. "Seriously? Grapes and shit? Not my thing."

"So what is?"

Jase had to admire the way that Nate, in just a few words, distracted Chris from what were clearly symptoms of withdrawal.

Chris got half way through a portrait of Nate, before he either twigged he was being manipulated or his pain had increased.

Putting his pencil down, he said, "I don't feel like doing this anymore; I'm tired."

Nate glanced over at Jase and indicated the drawing with his eyes.

"Giving up so soon? I thought you had more guts than that," Jase said.

Chris shot him a look that could kill and pulled the pad back towards himself, his whole body tense as he started again wordlessly. He continued, in fierce silence, for another twenty minutes before he put the pencil down again.

"That's it, I'm done."

"You haven't–" Jase started.

Chris interrupted him by holding his hand out, palm down. It shook dramatically. "See? I can't," he said then folded his arms across his belly and put his forehead on the table with an audible thump, but he wasn't relaxed.

"Do want to watch a bit of telly?" Matt suggested.

"No, I want a fucking fix." His voice was strained, angry even, but he didn't attempt to move.

"A word?" Nate said.

Silently, Jase and Matt followed him towards the door of the apartment.

"It's going to get ugly for a while," he said.

"Don't care," Matt said emphatically. "I let him down once, I won't do it again."

Jase put his hand on Matt's shoulder. "I think he means that Chris won't appreciate you seeing him like this."

"And he's alright with you seeing it?" Matt said incredulously. "I must have been wrong about him fancying you."

They were interrupted by the sound of Chris throwing up. Jase avoided looking at either of the others, hearing Chris in distress wasn't easy, but if he could make him feel better, just a little, he was staying.

"What's this, a mother's meeting?" a tired voice asked. They turned to see Chris, with his oversized dressing gown pulled tight around himself.

"Are you alright?" Matt asked then shut up as he realised the stupidity of his words.

"Just dandy bruv, but you watching, and listening, to me do that and worse for the next day or two won't help either of us. This isn't your fault, any more than its Jase's. I was a tit for being a diva at the club that night and–"

"This is not your fault," exploded out of Jase's mouth as he stepped toward Chris, as if his physical presence could stop Chris blaming himself.

Chris jerked back a little and blinked. "Wow, passion. I didn't know you had it in you, Sarge."

"Playing the blame game isn't helpful folks," Nate said quietly.

"So you want me to go?" Matt asked.

Chris closed his eyes and blew out a breath. "You're my brother and I love you, but I also don't want you to remember this every time you think about me. So yeah, can you please piss off?" He wiped his nose with the back of his hand as he looked at the floor.

Matt grinned. "Anything for you, Chris," he said then wrapped his arms around his brother and lifted him off the ground in a bear hug.

"Ah, fuck, put me down," Chris cried out.

Matt did so immediately. "Shit, did I hurt you?"

Chris had a pained expression on his face. "Nah, but squeezing me at the moment might give everyone...Oh fuck, work it out for yourselves."

"What about Jase?" Nate asked.

"What about him?" Chris replied, still a little red-faced and clearly uncomfortable.

"He means, do you want me to stay or go?"

Chris cocked his head to one side. "That depends on whether I'm right or Nate is."

"About what?" Jase asked.

"About whether there's a chance of you and me getting together at some point."

"You don't beat around the bush, do you?"

"Question is, do you ever want to?" This time, Chris didn't meet his eyes. It seemed that even his bravado had a limit, or at least it did right now. Jase glanced at Matt, who was looking most uncomfortable.

"I don't think this is the..." Jase started to say.

"The time? The place? Well I do." Chris said as he straightened up. "If there is even a slight chance that you could ever think of me in that way, I don't want you here right now. If there isn't, for whatever reason, and let's face it, there are fucking hundreds of them, including the fact that you're my brother's best friend and a control freak, and I'm... Then you can stay. But for some reason I haven't got a handle on yet, I'd like you to go, so you can stay, later. And if that makes any sense at all you're brighter than I'll ever be. I've done everything else in my life on my own, and I can do this withdrawal thing too."

Chris turned to Nate. "Go to work if you have to, just lock the front door and the one up to the roof and take the keys with you."

"Why the key to the roof? You're not feeling suicidal are you?" Matt asked quickly, his face abruptly pale.

Chris grinned. "Fuck no, I'm a too much of an arsehole to put you all out of my misery, but I might take a dip in that wonderful swim spa up there and bugger up the filters. Puke city, remember?"

Jase wondered if Chris would ever stop surprising him. He hoped not.

"Is he safe on his own, if you go to work?" he asked Nate.

"I wouldn't recommend it, but I haven't got a shift till tomorrow night. But I'm sure I could get a colleague or Sarah to spell me if I need it."

Without another word, Jase walked back to the bedroom and picked up his keys and wallet.

"Can you give me a lift, Matt?" he asked not looking at Chris as he got to the door.

"What? You mean?" Chris stuttered from behind him.

Jase turned back to the bewildered, brave young man who was rapidly stealing his heart.

"I mean I will carry on waiting until you are ready for the kind of relationship I want to have with you. Ask your brother, I'm a stubborn git who is used to getting my own way. And you, Chrisander Baccioni, seem to be taking up residence on my 'to do' list, even if you irritate the hell out of me ninety-nine percent of the time. You intrigue me and I'd like to explore that further. Besides, you're a sexy little shit."

Even though he looked like death warmed up, the compliment about his sex appeal lit up Chris's face. Nate had been right, for Chris, it was physical first, emotion later if he let anyone in at all. If that was how it had to be, he had to see if he could give it a whirl because the idea of Chris giving that grin, or anything else for that matter, to another man made his stomach churn.

CHAPTER 23

Chris

'Not fun' was a fair description of the last forty-eight hours. The only one on the list of symptoms of withdrawal that he hadn't suffered so far was diarrhoea. Probably because he hadn't had anything solid inside him for... a period of time he didn't want to think about. Some of it he put down to his hyperness, restlessness, anxiety, particularly over Jase, and insomnia. Other symptoms, such as the shakes, joint aches, belly cramps, tearing eyes, snotty nose and heart palpitations were one hundred percent pure heroin withdrawal.

Nate and Sarah took his tears, his anger and his moroseness on the chin as they kept him hydrated, clean and eating as much as his poor belly could take, which was virtually nothing. All he wanted to do was curl into a ball in a bed that he didn't care was damp with his own sweat and give up on the outside world while he twitched, shivered and groaned. Unfortunately, the pair kept bugging him. He wondered if medics were born sadistic, or if it was part of the training.

"Come on, blood pressure time, then it's a shower and soup for you," Sarah said as the quilt was pulled away from his huddled up body.

"Too tired. Later," he said as he kept his eyed closed, hoping she'd go away and leave him to rot.

"Now, Chris. It's midday and Nate will be coming home soon and I'm not handing over a stinking, dehydrated patient. Put it this way, either you get up, get washed and dressed and get some food inside you, or I'll be calling Jase to help you do it."

Chris's eyes creaked open. Although the stickiness left over from the grizzling session that had finally exhausted him enough to allow him to sleep around seven a.m. didn't make it easy.

"You wouldn't; I'm a mess."

"Well you'd better get up then, just in case I do."

"Bitch," he mumbled as he pushed himself to a sitting position. He was still wearing Nate's dressing gown, which he had to admit, looked, and smelled, a little worse for wear.

Half an hour later, he was sitting in Nate's incredible kitchen wearing the least flamboyant shirt Matt had brought over. It was black with long sleeves with a small rainbow over his right pec. At least it covered the bruises on his arms and body, not to mention his prominent ribs. His previously tight black jeans were horribly loose, but even if he asked Nate, he didn't think he'd have a belt small enough to fit him. If he didn't put on some weight soon, he'd have to start shopping in the kids department.

Sarah fetched the clipboard she and Nate were using to note his vitals and her ever present black doctor's bag.

"Do you ever go anywhere without that?" he grumbled.

"Nope," she said brightly. "I even take it to the bathroom. Arm?"

He pulled his sleeve up and presented his arm, then tried not to flinch as she turned it over and examined the injection sites.

"These won't scar, I can hardly tell where some of them were already. At least the person who injected you knew what he was doing."

"Dimitar did. The others, not so much."

"You know who did this to you?" Sarah said. He could tell she was trying to keep her voice neutral as she got out the blood pressure cuff.

He shrugged. "First names, faces, that's all."

"I've thought about this a lot over the last few days. I took an oath to do no harm when I became a doctor, but this is a no-win situation. You're probably one of the most resilient people I've ever met and I'm a hundred percent sure you'll be right as rain, given time. But the evidence all points toward you being just one in a line of victims, some of whom might not deal with it as well as you have. I know it's a horrible burden to put on your shoulders, but have you thought about talking to the police?"

A wave of nausea swept over him. Someone was in that cupboard right now, suffering as he had done. He'd been lucky that none of his main captors had been gay. The assaults he'd suffered hadn't been sexual till the end, but a woman might not be so lucky. The thought of what Ugly Uncle would do to a girl made him feel physically sick.

"Chris? You still with me?"

He nodded automatically and focused back on her as she continued, her entire face tight with concern.

"To be honest, I'm worried about Ryan. Not right now, but when the Border Agency's level of suspicion about Matt's lorries calms down in six months, a year from now? He could become a target, just like you could be again. That DVD is a horribly effective blackmail tactic."

"What DVD?" The question fell out of his mouth automatically, but he had a horrible suspicion what she was talking about. He'd been hoping that those vague memories were just another withdrawal fuelled nightmare.

The pity on her face made his heart drop. "You remember how sore your back passage was when you woke up?"

He shrugged, not willing to admit anything.

"I'm so sorry, but they filmed what happened; they said they'd put it on the internet if Matt went to the police."

"Have you seen it?"

"Unfortunately, yes. But don't worry, only Nate and I have seen all of it. Jase and your boss at the club saw the first minute or so, but Nate sent them out, and I'm glad he did. I'm also glad they gave you rohypnol. No one should have to remember that," she said tightly as she finished the blood pressure reading and put her things away.

A bowl of steaming chicken noodle soup appeared in front of him a few moments later. He picked up his spoon, then put it down again. Even though the sight and smell hadn't sent him running for the bathroom again, he had no appetite.

"Where is it, the disc?"

"Nate took it out of the machine at the club, but I don't know what he did with it after that."

"I want to see it."

Sarah's face hardened. "That's not a good idea right now, and it probably never will be. I shouldn't have said anything; it's just that Kate and Ryan are my only family—"

Anger rumbled. "They're my family too, and I'd do anything to stop that—"

Sarah reached across the table and gripped his wrist in sympathy. "You'll get over this, I promise. You're stronger than you think you are, to have survived a childhood like—"

"My mum loved me, and she did the best she could," he snapped and pulled his hand away. Nate might understand how good people could get sucked into drugs, but Sarah certainly didn't.

"I'm sure she did, being a single parent is never easy and coupled with a drug habit..." Sarah had that condescending 'sympathy' expression all social workers wore.

He dredged up the smile that he'd used for all do-gooders; right before he buggered off. "Mum never judged me and she always encouraged my art. She made me the fabulous person I am today."

"I'm sure she loved you very much."

Chris decided that he had probably never seen such a fake smile in his life. Maybe he was a poor deluded sod, but at least he didn't lie about what he thought of people.

He was saved by Sarah's phone ringing. As she answered it, she got up and walked away, clearly not wanting him to hear her important call. Just like every other do-gooder, she thought she was better than him. Even though she probably was, what with her being a doctor.

She ended the call and came back into the room. "I'm sorry, that was work. My colleague who was taking afternoon surgery called in sick, I've got to cover. Will you be ok here on your own? You seem to be over the worst of it and Nate will be back by seven."

"No problem. I'm still pretty tired, I'll probably just go back to bed anyway." Why such a clever woman believed his bullshit, he didn't know. Actually he did; she wanted to believe him because it was easier than the alternative which was finding someone else to babysit him at short notice.

As soon as the front door locked behind her, he trotted up the corridor to Nate's room. The plan was, find the DVD, watch it so it didn't have any nasty surprises if the kidnappers made good on their threat. He didn't matter, but he wanted to find out if Matt or anyone else he cared about had been identified, because that would complicate matters. If the DVD wasn't here, he'd have to do some serious bullshitting to make sure he got some alone time at Matt's and then Jase's place to find it.

If it was here, after he'd watched it, he'd pick the lock on the front door, trundle down to the cop shop on the high street and spill the beans before any one could stop him. Plan made, he got going before he chickened out.

Nate's personal suite was as tasteful, and even more vast than the two guest suites in the penthouse. As well as an ensuite bathroom and a walk in wardrobe, it also had an office with a desk. The fine piece of furniture had a single locked drawer. Nate couldn't have made it any easier to find if it'd had a bloody big arrow pointing at it.

Along with pickpocketing and shop lifting, lock-picking was a skill one of his mum's many and varied 'friends' had taught him. Sitting down in Nate's plush leather desk chair, which probably cost more than most families paid for an annual holiday, he found some paperclips and set to work making himself a lock-pick and probe.

Twenty minutes later he was sitting on the sofa in the living room with the disc in his hand.

"Right Bacon, even if it gets put on the internet, how many people watch gay gangbang porn anyway? Besides, you're not a blushing virgin with a glowing reputation to keep intact. Hell, I shake it for a living, everyone probably thinks I do this shit anyway. Those bastards lucked out if they thought a sex tape would stop me."

Despite his thorough pep talk, he hesitated as he reached towards the DVD player. Lock-picking took a steady hand. The sick look on Sarah's face when she had mentioned this thing might or might not mean something; she might be a complete prude or a closet homophobe. The thought of watching lesbian porn made him a little green around the gills too. Nevertheless, sorting the lock out on the front door might be better done before he watched it. As would doing sketches of the kidnappers he remembered clearly.

It only took an hour to get everything ready. The penthouse door was open, the sketches were done, and he even had his red and white basketball boots on for a quick getaway. Taking a steadying breath, he pushed the disc into the slot and pressed the play button.

Yep, that was a lot of bodies, and given the choice, most of them weren't blokes he'd choose to sleep with. Plus he looked really out of it; his eyes were barely open. The three 'bears' surrounding him were having to hold him up as they groped him. He was vaguely trying to push their hands away, but his efforts were about as effective as a chocolate teapot. It wasn't good by any means, but what had he been expecting - dinner, flowers and Daniel Craig in a tuxedo?

Seeing himself doing things that he didn't remember was weird. If he blocked out the fact that the scene on the screen involved him; it didn't look too different to any of the 'gangbang' porn he'd seen. What was really disturbing was that it was making his dick wake up for the first time since he'd gotten back. And by the look of it, he'd been turned on, at least some of time, during the abuse too.

None of the men on screen had 'porn star' attractive bodies, although they were all enthusiastic about getting in on the act. Even when on screen Chris started crying that it hurt and pleading for that big bugger to stop when he'd... as the rest laughed and encouraged their friend to go further, he'd had a hard on, or at least a semi.

Christ Almighty, I am one sick puppy. It turned me on, even drugged up to the eyeballs, it turned me on.

Jase, Matt, Nate and everyone else were stupid to be wasting their valuable time on him. What he deserved was the gutter, while they spent their time on people who weren't sick in the head. He certainly wasn't a suitable role model for Ryan or his new niece or nephew. Ryan almost hero worshipped him already, what if he followed his lead as he got older?

CHAPTER 24

Jase

"He's gone."

Those were the words Jason Rosewood dreaded ever hearing again. For the last three days, it had been better than when Chris was being held, but not by much. The thought of him suffering with only a stranger, a hot, wealthy stranger, for company wasn't easy. Was Nate helping Chris sleep like he had done?

Instead of wondering if something was happening between Nate and Chris that he couldn't change, he decided he needed to start making plans about where his own life was going. He was a grown man and he needed to move his arse out of his parents' house, get a job and some transport.

The fact that Chris also needed somewhere to live was an additional incentive. Besides the awkwardness of living with a pair of newlyweds, Sarah was right that Chris living with Ryan full-time was not good idea.

He might find Chris fascinating, but his mood swings were not an example a five-year-old needed to see on a regular basis, even if there were huge reasons for them. The realisation that he was planning a life with Chris, at least in the short term, was a bit of an eye opener. He'd spent many hours considering what he wanted, what he could provide and what Chris needed.

His previous relationships had been mutual ones, yes, he preferred to top rather than bottom, but he'd never sought out partners he could, or needed to dominate. And that was just what Chris needed, at least until he was stable enough to sort out his own affairs. Back in the army, he'd always dreamed of starting up his own private investigation business, but that would take a great deal of time and effort, just like Chris. Setting up a business could wait, Chris couldn't. What he needed right now was stable regular and not overly taxing employment.

Another essential item on his agenda was something to occupy Chris. Because left to his own devices, a bored Chris would get into trouble, even if he was home with him every evening and every night. With the decision made to provide Chris with the stability he needed, Jase spent his time researching formal art classes, sorting out a job as High Court bailiff and arranging to take on Kate's two bedroom flat.

Now that Kate and Matt were living together she had spoken about renting it out. The location, above a kebab shop in the seedier part of town wasn't ideal, but beggars couldn't be choosers. It was a ready-made, inexpensive, and quick solution he couldn't pass up. For the last twenty-four hours, he'd been waiting for a call from Nate to say Chris was ready for visitors again. Breaking the news in person, and hopefully seeing a smile on Chris's face had been something he'd been greatly anticipating. It appeared he'd waited too long.

Taking a hard grip on his anger, he said, "What d'you mean, he's gone? How the hell is he missing if he hasn't been left alone?"

"Sarah sent me a text an hour ago, saying that she had to go into work, but that Chris was doing well, eating, getting dressed, being his normal obnoxious self. She thought he'd be alright for a couple of–"

"That's not important now. So he's been gone for an hour at most?"

"Could be two. I phoned her back; she was phoning between patients. There was an emergency and she couldn't text me straight away."

"Have you phoned Russel?"

"Yep, no joy, but it doesn't look good."

Jase's heart dropped. "What d'you mean?"

"I think you need to see for yourself; have you got transport?" The worry in Nate's voice had all sorts of alarm bells ringing in Jase's head.

"I bought a car yesterday."

"Anything nice?"

Jase rolled his eyes at the question from Mr Silver Spoon. "It's a brand new Ferrari, what do you think an unemployed ex-army sergeant can afford? I'll be there in fifteen," he said and broke the connection after Nate gave him the code to the underground car park of the department store.

As he drove the seven-year-old silver Fiesta towards town, he wondered if rushing to find a missing Chris would be an on-going occupation. Maybe he should fit him with a tracking device like Matt had on his lorries. The rest of his journey was taken up with trying to work out how he'd get Chris to carry it, because if he knew what it was, he probably wouldn't.

When he pressed the buzzer next to the discreet door at the side of Cooper's, it immediately clicked open. The short, wooden floored corridor led to a stairwell and Nate's private lift. There wasn't a choice about which he should take. Yes, he could probably get up all those stairs now, the shop had four floors, but it'd take bloody ages and he'd be useless once he got to the top.

The door of Nate's penthouse was open when he got there. He tapped on it and walked in. Nate stood in the kitchen, the first room to the right off the entrance hall. He looked worried, and more to the point, damn guilty. Shutting off his own emotions, Jase started to work the case as Nate began confessing.

"This is how I found it, front door wide open and..." he trailed off and indicated the living room. "I've got no idea how he found it. It was in a locked drawer in my desk."

The television screen was on pause. It showed Chris's face in close-up, bruised, battered and creased with pain. Tearing his eyes away from the disturbing image, he saw a scattered pile of pencil drawings. Two were of the men who had taken Chris that night at the club. The others consisted of detailed drawings of two other men Jase didn't recognise, as well as several less distinct images. An eye, the side of a face, a jaw line, a geometric tattoo.

Chris had been trying to remember, trying to identify his abusers but it appeared that it'd been too much for him. The immediate risk was that he was out looking for a fix to take it all away again.

"Where would he go to score?"

"There are only four or five dealers in town, but I'm not sure he'd know where to find them, if that's what he's doing. To be honest, I'm not sure he is. He was doing really well, I've seldom see anyone so determined to put drugs behind them. Then again, most addicts start abusing voluntarily. When they are trying to kick hard drugs, most try replacing one addiction with another they perceive as less damaging, such as alcohol, tobacco, cannabis, acid or ecstasy. Chris hasn't gone near the drinks cabinet or the packet of fags I left in the kitchen. I don't smoke, but a fag can help dial down the agitation of withdrawal."

"So he's not after drugs, and as he's not at the club, he's not after company... have you checked the roof?"

Nate blinked, then turned and jogged to the stairs off the kitchen. Jase heard him trot up the wooden staircase and rattle the door.

"Still locked," he called as he came back down. "He's left everything else he opened just that, open. He wasn't trying to hide what he did. He's a damn fine lock-pick though."

Making a mental note to investigate that aspect of Chris's past when, not if, he found him, he asked, "Was the door to the building open?"

Nate's face fell. "Shit, I never even thought of that. It was shut, but it's weighted to close automatically. At least we'll be able to find out when he left and what direction he took; the shop has security cameras down there. I'll be back in about ten minutes; being the son of the owner has certain advantages."

Nate was out of the door almost before he finished talking. Jase was left in silence with the frozen TV. How did Chris know that the DVD was here, or that it even existed? Had he been hunting for something else in Nate's locked desk and just come across it? Drugs or money perhaps? But if that was true, why did he leave everything open and sit down to sketch and watch an unlabelled DVD?

Logically, it didn't make sense, but logic wasn't one of Chris's strong points. Nevertheless, this had all the hallmarks of a systematic plan to gather evidence to present to someone. *Me?* Jase didn't think so; Chris hadn't wanted him to witness his withdrawal symptoms, let alone the stuff on the DVD.

It wasn't difficult to work out that Chris had been planning on taking evidence of his abduction and abuse to the police. He'd even opened the front door so he could leave as soon as he'd finished watching. His plan must have been forgotten when the DVD proved too much. Chris was braver than any of them had been on his behalf. They'd all been trying to save him from further trauma, but Chris had intended to put himself through what would be an absolute hell of an investigation to see justice done. Then again, maybe Chris didn't realise that every aspect of his past would be dredged up in such a case.

His phone beeped with a text.

Door opened and shut, he didn't come out.
He's still there.

Jase shoved his phone back in his pocket, and went to Chris's previous bolt hole of choice, the bathroom off the first guest bedroom he'd been using. Nate might have tried it already, but if there was one thing he'd learned, it was that civilians couldn't search properly to save their lives. The door was open, but he still checked behind it with no joy. He then did a lightning quick search of the other three bathrooms in the property, again with no luck. Time for another tactic.

"Chris? I know you're in here. It'll be a lot easier if you just say where you are, because I'm not leaving till I find you."

Silence met his ears. "No one's cross with you, in fact, Nate's bloody impressed with your lock picking skills. He wants you to show him how to do it."

Again, not a murmur. He never should have taken Nate's word that he was safe, never should have listened to Chris's appeal for him to go. He had one last trick up his sleeve before he started to take the place apart. Chris had never managed to stay silent when he was being needled.

"Don't tell me you're playing hard to get now?"

The immediate retort he'd hoped for didn't happen. Nate's voice came from behind him.

"That's a bit strong isn't it?"

"You start that end, I'll start this, but if you find him, call me," he told the medic. Nate had dropped the ball as far as he was concerned, and he wasn't going to give him the opportunity to do it again.

Nate hurried off towards his own bedroom suite which was on the other side of the reception areas. Jase returned to the guest section. The room he and Chris had used was nearest the kitchen, so he carried on towards the second guest suite. Systematic searching and seeing, rather than just looking, was the key to any investigation.

After checking the bathroom and under the bed, the only other place in the room large enough to hide was the walk-in wardrobe. It was just as full of clothes as the one in Chris's room. Most of the clothing still had tags on.

As he opened the door, some of the trousers hanging at the back of the six by six space moved slightly. It could have been the draft caused by him opening the door, but he didn't think so. Getting out his phone he texted Nate that he'd found him, and he'd call if he needed him; then he put it on silent.

"Chris? I'm here now; you're safe."

A sniff came from behind the swaying trousers. He'd never heard a sweeter sound.

"Are you coming out, or am I coming in?" he asked.

"Go away." The stroppy, nasal comeback made him smile.

"Not going to happen. So unless you've found the entrance to Narnia behind some Armani trousers, I'm coming in."

Getting down on his hands and knees, he crawled into the cupboard and moved trousers, that he couldn't even begin to guess how much they were worth, to one side. Not looking at the hunched figure right in the corner, he settled down with his knees drawn up and readjusted the clothing that screened them from the world.

"Nice here, isn't it?" His inane comment produced a derisive snort from Chris, but he didn't say anything.

"Have you got any idea how much it'll cost him to get all this lot dry cleaned if you've snotted on it? I'd have to re-mortgage my Fiesta to pay for it."

"You got a car?"

"More of a skip with wheels, but yep, yours truly is mobile. The advantage is, it's already so banged up that it won't matter if you prang it when we get you your provisional licence."

Chris didn't answer, he just hugged his knees and laid his forehead on them. Reaching over, Jase put his arm around his shoulder and pulled him toward himself. At first he resisted; then he moaned and let Jase sit him on his lap.

Having his arms around him, having Chris cling to him as if he was the most important person in the world, felt more right than he ever thought it could. His dispassionate, logical considerations of the last few days went out the window as his protective instincts took over.

"I've got you and I'm never going to leave you again, even if you try to send me away." Jase took his hand and grazed his knuckled with his lips.

Chris stiffened. "You can't. You haven't seen, you don't–"

Jase held him tighter. "I've never been so sure of anything in my life. And whatever happened to you, doesn't change that. I'll watch it if that's what you want, but it won't change a thing. You didn't have a choice."

Chris's next words were polar opposites to what his body was almost screaming as he held on to Jase for dear life.

"It'll never work. I'm so different to you. I'm a mess, you know it, I know it, fuck, everyone bloody knows it. I'll drag you–"

Jase tilted Chris's chin up till he could look into his eyes. "That is complete and utter bullshit. You make me a better person, Chrisander Baccioni. Just having you around makes me want to get on with things.

"In the last forty-eight hours, because of you, I've bought a car, got us somewhere to live, sorted you out some art classes and applied for a job. You're good for me Chris, and I'm going to make sure I'm good for you.

"Now, can we get out of this cupboard before my arse goes to sleep permanently?"

CHAPTER 25

Chris

T he wardrobe no longer provided a safe haven. He'd crawled in here to get away from the world and his own fucked-up-ness. But the world, in the form of Jason Rosewood, had followed.

He desperately wanted to believe in the fairy tale Jase was dangling like a carrot in front of him. A stable future, a home, art classes, formal driving lessons rather than the joy riding he'd done as a kid, but it all depended on someone else. One wrong word, one argument, one fuck up, and he'd be back where he'd been, on his own, broke and homeless, but with another huge hole in his heart.

Once he crawled out of the wardrobe, he had no idea where to go. Jase would follow him like a bloody bloodhound, and the thought of going outside with all those people staring at him was just as uncomfortable now as it had been an hour ago.

"I'm not a child, I don't need looking after," he said as he stood up even though they both knew he lied.

Jase came up behind him, turned him around, smiled and kissed the end of his nose.

"Believe me, you'll be earning your way."

Chris blinked, then stiffened, the only thing he was really good at was dancing, vertically and horizontally. From the DVD, it appeared that he could do the horizontal version well enough to produce a room full of satisfied customers even when mostly unconscious.

Was Jase proposing he provide sexual favours in return for a home? Did that class as 'earning'? He couldn't mean going on the game, could he? He'd had enough offers at the club to just jump right in; would that be so bad? He wasn't naïve enough to think that the pushers had given his mum drugs for free. It ran in the family, so why not if it got him a permanent home?

Another explanation shot into his mind. Perhaps Jase was just a really kinky git. BDSM was ok as a bedroom game, but as a hard core, permanent lifestyle choice? He could probably do it as long as Jase didn't get off on inflicting extreme pain. Spanking and bondage was one thing, but–

"Stop thinking," Jase said. A smile tickled his lips a moment before he took Chris's lips passionately. One hand took a handful of his hair, the other curled around his hip and ground them together. All thoughts drifted away as Jase dominated his body and his mind. As a first kiss, it was a doozy.

Pulling away because he was getting dizzy, Chris buried his face in Jase's shoulder. He inhaled the natural scent of the man he'd be happy to say yes to, whatever he bloody well wanted. The thought of being on his own again was a scarier prospect than going back to Dimitar's. Jase had the ability to ground and settle him like no one else, not that anyone had ever really tried, not for more than a night anyway.

He needed, deep down inside, to show Jase just how much he appreciated what he was doing for him. His chest, his gut, his whole body ached to be joined to him, to drive him to the heights of ecstasy, but his backside was still too sore to take him. Having watched the DVD, he now knew why, but Jase didn't. If his case ever went to court, Jase would find out. It would be so much worse if he got dumped, weeks or months in the future, than it would be if it happened now. After all, all they had shared so far was a bed for a few nights and a bloody hot kiss.

Chris groaned as Jase rubbed his rock hard dick. He'd been hard since he'd watched the film, but he'd refused to touch himself. Getting turned on by watching himself being abused was so fucked up he didn't even want to think about it. He needed to stop this, needed to make Jase watch it so he understood what a truly fucked up bastard he was before he wasted any more of his valuable time on him.

"You're not making this easy are you? We can't do this now," he murmured but he didn't push Jase away, he couldn't.

Jase's hand moved to the back of his head, moving his head until his lips were at Chris's ear. He nibbled at it briefly, sending a shiver through Chris's entire body.

"I know you're probably still sore and I won't go near your hole. Last time I checked, we have an advantage over straight couples."

Chris froze; did Jase mean what he thought he did?

"You want me to top you? Cos I'm not very–"

Jase put his fingers over Chris's lips, silencing him. "Ah, no, not my style; I don't think it's yours either. I was thinking we could continue what you started that morning at Matt's place. You have no idea how difficult it was to pull you away from me. I've been dreaming about it ever since."

His mouth must have been hanging open because Jase chuckled and pushed his chin up with a finger.

"Not that hard to believe is it? You must have guessed I liked it, and the show you gave me afterwards. I've had blue balls ever since because I wanted to hold you down and give you even more of a reason to groan.

"Russel doing exactly what I was dreaming of doing to you, made me... You have no idea how angry at myself I've been over what my jealousy caused. If I hadn't kicked up such a fuss, you wouldn't have run and... But I'd do it again in a heartbeat, I can't help myself."

Chris's mind whirled. This was really happening, Jase wanted him warts and all, but he didn't know about what happened on the DVD yet. Jase was as jealous as they came and seeing him enjoying being used like a bloody blow up doll, might change his mind as quickly as flipping a light switch.

Do I have to make a choice between getting my own happy ever after and saving some other person, possibly Ryan, from going through what I did? How would a naive straight boy, or a young girl cope?

A finger stroking his cheek brought him back. "If there's one thing I don't want to do, it's to push you into something you're not ready for. We can take things as slow as you need."

Chris managed a shaky smile. They were talking, make that thinking in his case, at cross purposes. He didn't know how to bring up his depravity without making Jase run for the hills.

Instead, he said, "What did I do to deserve you?"

Jase smiled gently and kissed his forehead. "You were your extraordinary self. Now, we're going to go get a drink, something to eat, and you're going to tell me all about how and why you were watching that DVD. Come on." Jase took his hand and towed him out of the room.

Nate was putting the kettle on in the kitchen. "Remind me never to play hide and seek with you, although sardines could be fun. Tea?"

"I'm sorry I broke into your desk." Apologising quickly often deflected anger from those in authority, although he wasn't usually sorry in the least. In this case, he genuinely regretted seeing that DVD.

"No problem. You didn't break anything. I would have given it to you if you'd asked, although I wouldn't have recommended you watching it on your own."

Without Jase's hand on the small of his back, he might have made another run for it. It was bad enough that Nate and Sarah had seen him getting off when he'd been drugged up and abused on camera, without anyone witnessing the same when he was completely lucid.

Nate put three steaming mugs on the table, the one he pushed towards Jase was black coffee. Chris had hot sweet tea, the standard British treatment for shock.

"What I'm more interested in, is how you knew it was in there," Nate stated.

Chris sat down with Jase close beside him. He took a sip of the tea and shrugged. "Sarah told me about it, although she didn't know exactly where it was. It wasn't difficult to find; that was the only locked drawer in the entire place."

Jase and Nate exchanged a glance. "So what prompted that conversation?" Jase asked.

Knowing Jase wouldn't leave the subject alone, he told them about what Sarah had said about Ryan. "I was going to go to the police, to stop it happening to anyone else, but I wanted to see what they would see first. So I..." The disturbing images replayed in his mind.

"If that's what you want to do, I'll go with you, but giving a statement won't be easy. A court case will be worse. I'm not trying to put you off, but I dealt with that sort of thing for a living."

Knowing he could be scuppering the best thing that'd ever happened to him, Chris took a deep breath and spoke. "I want you to watch it. If it goes to court, you'll hear about it anyway and that could take months, if not years. If we're together till then, I couldn't take it if you changed your mind, because of..."

He trailed off and kept his eyes on the remains of his tea. Looking either of them in the eye wasn't going to happen; they'd be wearing 'pity' faces that he didn't deserve.

"Alright."

Chris looked up sharply. He hadn't expected such a matter of fact response from Jase.

"We can watch it together, then we can report it to the police," Jase finished.

"Hang on a minute, have you thought this through, Chris? I want to stop these bastards as much as anyone, but a court case will be harrowing. I don't think you–"

Chris interrupted Nate. "I'll cope. I know you don't think I can, but I will. Some other poor sod might not. It's not as if I've got a squeaky clean reputation, a relationship or a job that would be ruined if they put it online. Those bastards have done it before, and they'll do it again, unless I do something about it." The next second, he was enveloped in Jase's arms.

"God, you're so fucking brave," Jase whispered against his ear.

Will he still want to hold me when he finds out I'm not brave, just horny and depraved?

Jase pulled back, wiping at his eyes. "Right, let's do this thing," he said as he stood up.

"Do you mind if I don't watch it again?" Chris asked quickly. "I stopped it, so if there's anything else I need to know about after that bit, you can tell me, ok?" he turned to Nate. "Can I take a turn in the spa? I think I'm over the stomach problems and I need to do something active to take my mind off things."

Nate gave him a tight smile. "Sure, I'll come up with you."

Nate only stayed long enough to make sure he knew how to operate the spa and to kit him out with a pair of trunks. Unsurprisingly, he had lots of spares in a whole variety of sizes.

An hour of very welcome exercise later, the jet on the spa turned off. Chris stood up, the water coming half way up his chest and turned to see Jase climbing into the spa fully clothed. Without a word Chris went to him, and was enfolded in his arms. It literally felt as if a huge weight had been taken off his shoulders. He'd spent the last hour wondering if Jase would ever talk to him again. He wouldn't have blamed him if he'd walked away and never looked back.

After being held, silently, for nearly ten minutes, in a light breeze, he started to get goose bumps.

"You ok?" Chris finally asked hesitantly.

"You're so fucking wonderful, I can't believe how you coped with–" Jase choked out.

Chris's heart fell. He must have missed something for Jase to be this upset.

"Did anything different happen after I paused it?"

"Not really. They moved you into a kitchen for a bit more, but you passed out completely soon after that, not that you were very with it anyway. They didn't seem to find a completely unconscious victim as entertaining. Can you really not remember?"

Chris backed off and focused on the buildings in the distance. "I remember a kitchen table, not when they were...but before that. The cupboard I was kept in was off the kitchen, but I only saw it that last day. Dimitar said I had to get ready for my going away party. I had a shower, Dimitar shaved me cos I couldn't do it, then he gave me a doped coke. After that I've got vague recollections; probably from the first few minutes of the DVD. That's where the partial drawings came from. But the vast majority of it? I haven't got a clue. Which is partly why I freaked out. I mean, not remembering that? I was—"

Jase wrapped his arms around him from behind. "It's over. You're safe now and I'm never going to let that happen to you again."

Chris blew out a breath. It was now or never. "You watched it and you still don't get it do you? Truth is, I got off on it. Even drugged up to my eyeballs and in pain, I was still hard nearly all the way through. Even watching it gave me a—"

He turned around and faced Jase, every fibre of his being felt filthy as he forced a slight smile. "Now do you get why you should run a mile? I'm wrong in the head, and in so many different ways that I've lost count. I don't matter, I never have done, but it could be happening to someone else right now; someone that does matter. It could happen to Ryan in the future if they aren't stopped. I couldn't live with that."

To his ultimate surprise, Jase rested his chin on the top of his head instead of leaving as fast as his bum leg would let him.

"Firstly, if you ever say you don't matter again, I'm going to spank your arse till it matches my red hat. I might even wear it while I do it. Secondly, has it occurred to you that they might have slipped you a Viagra to make the blackmail even more effective?"

Chris blinked. It hadn't, but it didn't explain his reaction today.

"When you were sleeping it off the night we got you back, Nate explained some of the symptoms of withdrawal. When the depressive effect of opiates end, for some men, it can cause things to erm, 'bounce back' with more enthusiasm than normal. Believe me, you're not sick, you were just reacting, perfectly normally, to the drugs they forced on you."

As he was trying to digest the information that he wasn't quite as warped as he assumed, Jase continued. "If you still want to go to the police, I'll take you tomorrow. But I'd already identified two of the men you drew from that trick you pulled with the phone, which was bloody stupid by the way. The rules are, when you get captured, you do what they say and trust others get you out. That was my job, not yours."

Chris moved away just a fraction. "Strangely enough, I missed the whole 'what to do if you're captured by people traffickers' training. I thought grabbing the phone would help. I didn't know they were going to beat the crap out of me. I didn't do it again. Rough sex is one thing, but that? I'm thick, but I'm not that fucking stu—"

Chris found a finger on his lips. "I'm not having a go at you. You were braver than anyone could have been–"

"Oh yeah? Then why did I just spent most of the day hiding in a fucking wardrobe because I got a boner watching myself being gangbanged and fisted? I'm so fucking brave that I held out my arm to make it easier for–" This time Jase put his hand over his mouth.

Chris gave him the evil eye but didn't reach to move the hand. It felt good that Jase was stopping him spiralling up into a state that he knew he didn't have a hope of controlling on his own.

"What I was trying to get in edgeways, was that I still have friends in the intelligence services. Those bastards are known all over Europe. Your evidence will just add to the pile when they are caught, and they will be."

Chris glanced pointedly down at Jase's hand then up at his face and raised his eyebrows.

Jase's lips twitched in amusement. "Not yet. What you need to know is that the police, in several countries, are already looking for them. Yes, your evidence will help secure a conviction, but it doesn't mean you have to gallop to the police station right now. And I have already given Sarah a piece of my mind for putting you through unnecessary upset.

"For your information, in case you haven't guessed, I like being in control in the bedroom and I don't consider myself sick. The fact that you get turned on by being on the receiving end, doesn't make you sick either. What it makes us is compatible. Although nothing like that DVD will ever be repeated, because one, I don't enjoy seeing you frightened, and two, I'm jealous as fuck and I don't share. Ever," he said, then gingerly removed his hand.

Even if this was the result of drug withdrawal, Jase's behaviour and words were making Chris's body and mind buzz with desire. Showing Jase just how much he appreciated his words, his time, seemed to be a bloody good idea.

CHAPTER 26

Jase

"You're all wet," Chris said as he bit his lower lip and ran a finger down Jase's soaked t-shirt.

Jase blinked then threw his head back and groaned, half in amusement, half in frustration. "I don't think I'm ever going to get used to the way you mentally change direction, but yeah, I'm all wet. Comes of standing in a swim spa with my clothes on because I couldn't wait to get my hands on the most adorable, fickle, brave and frustrating man I've ever met."

His mind rolled back to what he and Nate had discussed after they had both watched the DVD. It hadn't been easy, even though he tried to be dispassionate and look for identifying characteristics of the abusers for possible future prosecution. Watching Chris be humiliated and used made him want to hit something.

"He won't have seen this in the same way you are," Nate said.

"Of course he wouldn't, it happened to him not me."

"That's not what I mean. He has a very skewed view of sex. For him, it's not about being intimate or love, it's about his own ego and controlling resources. He tries to turn every situation toward sex because it's what he's comfortable with. Simply put, if people want him, he feels more worthwhile, more powerful." Nate pressed his lips together as if he knew what he was about to say would be classed as offensive.

"With that in mind, whatever bothered him about that DVD, and something really did, it probably wasn't the actual sex."

Jase shot to his feet. "You've got to be kidding? That, that was hideous. He couldn't sit down without being in pain for days, he was crying for fuck's sake."

"Yes, he was, and he's pretty torn up, but I'm far more worried about his state of mind than any long term physical effects of his ordeal. The fact that he didn't run for it, which is typical 'Chris' behaviour when he's distressed, is worrying."

"When I tried to kiss him earlier, he pushed me away after a few seconds even though I'm sure he was enjoying it."

"Odd, significantly odd. He fancies the crap out of you. Put it this way, if Matt hadn't turned up the first day, I think he would've let you do anything you wanted to him, even in that state."

"I wouldn't have touched him and you know it." Revulsion at the suggestion of taking advantage of Chris in that way boiled up.

"I do, but from what you said, and him hiding rather than running just now, something's changed. We need to get him mentally back where he was before; only then can we start boosting his ego with other things."

Jase's eyes narrowed. "I'm not fucking him in this state, and you certainly aren't. He's weak, abused, confused and he's only just turned eighteen."

Nate got to his feet. "I know that, probably more than you do, medic remember? As for his age, you're what, in your late twenties? How long have you been sexually active? How many lovers have you had? Unless I'm very wrong about you, Chris has a higher count than either of us; he could even have been sexually active longer than we have. Kids brought up in drug dens, surrounded by prostitution, don't stay virgins for long.

"You need to get it into your head that sex and emotional intimacy are two very different things for him, but maybe with time, understanding, and a lot of effort on your part, he might come around to a more conventional view. But here and now is not the time to start preaching and looking down on him. What it is time for is accepting him, warts and all.

"Besides, I wasn't suggesting you take his arse. He's still damaged back there and if that's the only move you know, I don't hold out much hope for a long term relationship."

"He needs affection and stability, not more meaningless sex," Jase reiterated.

Nate shrugged as he moved towards the door. "Have it your own way, but he doesn't think about it in the same way we do. Don't get me wrong, I'm with you all the way, but neither of us grew up with sex as currency and no moral compass. You don't get that good at lock-picking without a lot of practice. To be honest, it's a miracle he isn't already an addict and banged up. It says a lot about him that he's fought going down that route, but he's been lucky so far. Legally, he's an adult now. How do you think he'll fare in prison?"

Jase shuddered at the thought. But there was a more pressing issued right now. "And if I don't do it, I take it you'll be providing the therapy yourself?"

Nate's serious blue eyes focused on him, and he was struck by how gorgeous the man was yet again. "Right now, he trusts me as a friend and a medic, which is a pretty big thing. You and I both know he can get sex anywhere. If you don't provide it he'll get it elsewhere just as he's always done. And we both know that every time he goes off with another stranger, he's risking his life. I can flirt with him till the cows come home as a 'safe' person and I think that's important. I doubt he's ever had a gay friend who isn't trying to get into his underwear. Besides, I don't want him long-term, and I think you do.

"Long-term stability is what he needs, but first we need to find out what's going on in that head of his and to get him back to being Chris rather than a mouse. Impulsivity and profound mental disturbance do not make for a happy outcome. And yes, I mean exactly what that sounds like."

It felt as if his gut had dropped all the way to the street four storeys below. "You think he'd attempt suicide?"

"Mate, Chris wouldn't attempt anything, he'd do. Impulsivity, remember?"

"And you let him go up on the roof on his own?" Jase got hastily to his feet, wincing as pain shot through his ankle.

"He's swimming, nothing more," Nate replied calmly and turned his phone revealing that he had a CCTV camera up there.

"Turn that off," he growled as he made his way to the stairs.

"Spoilsport."

* * *

Ten minutes later, he knew he'd gotten the reason for Chris's meltdown wrong, but bit by bit, he was starting to work out the puzzle that was Chrisander Baccioni. Chris was certainly a lot happier than he'd been an hour ago, and all it had taken was an overt demonstration that he still found him attractive, a touch of speculative bullshitting and some medical insights.

Right now, Chris was doing the most amazing puppy dog eyes impression; the bugger was even pouting at him.

"Aw, poor Eddie, all frustrated."

His dick twitched to life as Chris's hand landed on his butt and squeezed. The borrowed swim trunks didn't do much to hide Chris's enthusiasm either.

Jase couldn't help smiling as Chris leaned forward and kissed his collarbone. "I'd better take these clothes off; if I'm going to get them dry again."

"That's the best idea you've had all day," Chris murmured as he reached for Jase's fly.

Chris's confidence had roared back to life with a vengeance. It was good to see him like this, but it was also rather sad that a little sexual attention made such a difference to him. Nevertheless, this was what Chris needed, so he ploughed on with as much bravado as he could manage.

"Actually, you sucking me till I'm within an inch of losing my sanity is the best idea I've had all day."

Chris's head shot up. "You're serious?"

In reply, Jase took his face in his hands, hovered his lips over Chris's for a second, then almost attacked his mouth. Reaching down between them, he slipped a hand inside Chris's trunks and moulded his fingers around his rigid dick. He smiled into his mouth as Chris let out a throaty moan.

Chris pulled away and scrambled at Jase's fly, then gave up and tried to pull his t-shirt over his head.

"Too many clothes," he mumbled as he fought to divest Jase of the wet, clinging cloth between them.

To check that his own misgivings weren't justified, Jase asked, "Are you sure this is what you want right now? Cos we can wait if you want to."

The confident smile on Chris's face said it all. "Slide your stuff off and sit on the edge, you are about to get a Bacon special you will not believe."

Jase did as he was told, dropping his soaking combats, shirt and boxers over the side of the spa. He perched on the edge of the wooden platform above the three seats in the shallow end that also served as steps to get in and out of the deeper water. It also positioned his back towards the camera that Nate might, or might not, be watching.

Chris was in his arms, kissing his throat hungrily a moment later, his body moving as if he had his own private music playing in his head. It was a rhythm only Chris could hear, but Jase could enjoy it too.

Unlike his own lightly haired chest, Chris's body was nearly smooth, except from the dark line leading down from his navel to his groin. His facial bruises were turning yellow and green, although the one on his ribs was still reddish against his olive skin. The marks made Jase want to provide gentle care to counteract the violence he'd suffered, but it appeared that this was the sort of caring Chris craved far more than anything else.

The bastards hadn't needed to hit, frighten and abuse Chris; merely holding him would have achieved the same result with Matt. Jase would never forgive them for that. The other person on his Chris related 'never forgive' list was Marie Baccioni. Because she had been weak, Chris had grown up thinking he was worthless, and probably still did. It was a thousand miles from the truth.

Built like a distance runner, Chris had a body that needed to be active and in the sunshine, not shut away in the dark. And boy was he being active now.

Blow jobs were an integral part of gay relationships, but Chris took it to a fine art. Most guys just got straight down to it, but to his surprise Chris started by picking up his hand and sucking his thumb slowly, and then hard, moving his tongue around it as he slowly got to his knees between Jase's thighs. If Chris sucking his thumb felt this good, his ability to hold out for more than thirty seconds when he finally touched his dick would be non-existent.

He kissed up one thigh, then just as those pink lips were about to reach his groin, Chris switched to the other leg and treated it to the same torture. Jase reached a hand out to cup Chris's face, intending to draw him in for a kiss, but Chris leaned back out of reach.

"Ah, ah. I want to see your expression when I touch you."

Trailing his fingers over Jase's abdomen took another few seconds, before he took hold of his dick. Jase groaned.

"You like that, huh, Sarge? Well you ain't seen nothing yet."

Chris dipped, and kissed the top of the head. Jase's dick twitched. It was as if the damn thing was waving Chris on all on its own. Then he knelt up again, and moved in for a kiss which Jase happily accepted. He put his fingers into Chris's hair to control the kiss, but when Chris squeezed his shaft and sucked on his tongue, his toes literally curled.

Smiling against his lips, Chris pulled back and headed south again. When his lips finally closed over the head of his dick, Jase added a mouth that should be certified as a deadly weapon to Chris's list of attributes. And he hadn't even sucked him yet.

He licked the tip, kissed it, then slid his mouth back over it, but he didn't use his tongue like Jase was almost begging him to. All thoughts of abuse, of feeling sorry for Chris, evaporated as he concentrated on the sensations he created.

When Chris pulled off, and blew cold air on the tip, Jase's whole body jerked. He feathered the tip briefly, flattened his back, extended his neck and took Jase all the way down to his balls without gagging. Jase knew he wasn't huge and he certainly couldn't claim Russel's apparent 'rolling pin' dimensions, but he couldn't remember anyone managing to do this to him before. He must be halfway down Chris's throat.

"Oh fuck," he groaned, then jerked again as Chris swallowed around him. A second later he realised he had both hands fisted in Chris's curly hair, and was pushing his hips up hard to get even further down his throat.

He let go immediately. "Fuck, I'm sorry."

Chris pulled off him with an audible 'pop'. "Don't be; I like pushing you to lose control. As long as you don't storm off like you did last time, cos that was a bit bruising to the old ego. I'm good with this, more than good in fact."

Chris gave him an adorably sexy grin. "There is only one person in this relationship who gets to do any storming off, and that's me. So stay put and do whatever feels good. Don't worry, I'll let you know if I don't like it."

Knowing that there probably wasn't a great deal Chris would ever object to, and not sure about how he felt about that, Jase placed his hand on the top of Chris's head and guided him back down. Chris took his time, varying the tension and speed as he sucked, licked, nibbled and kissed his way up and down Jase's cock, occasionally taking it to the back of his throat, causing an involuntary groan of pleasure. A long fingered hand pushed firmly on Jase's chest. Complying with Chris's unspoken command, he leaned back on his elbows.

Pushing his knees apart even further, Chris gently took each ball in his mouth and rolled it briefly before putting his hands under Jase's thighs and encouraging him to lift his legs. Using his tongue, he drew a gentle line from behind his balls down to his hole. Jase tensed with anticipation of feeling his mouth there, but Chris changed direction before using his hands to separate his cheeks.

"I can't believe you're letting me do this, but I'm so fucking happy about it."

Tugging on his hair, Jase forced Chris to look up at him. "I am the lucky one, not you, and one day I'm going to make you believe it too."

With a 'yeah right' shrug, Chris bent to his task again. After working Jase to the state where his hips were rocking unconsciously, Chris pushed his legs up a little further and Jase felt his warm breath on his chilly damp skin, a moment before he kissed his hole. When he pressed his tongue inside, Jase couldn't help crying out, "Oh, fuck, that's good."

"You like me eating you, Eddie? Cos I'm loving–"

"So help me, if you stop now, I'm going to throttle you," Jase ground out.

With a chuckle, Chris returned to his task. With every soft thrust, Jase felt his hole relax a little more, then without warning, Chris moved back up to take his dick in his mouth. He took him deep, sucking strongly on the way back up, then bobbed over the head as he pressed the tip of his finger inside him. Jase briefly worried that Chris was preparing to penetrate him with more than his finger, but if that was what he wanted, he'd cope, even if it wasn't what he usually preferred. A second finger joined the first, it burned a little and Jase grunted slightly in discomfort.

Chris lifted his head. "If you don't like it, I can stop."

"Don't be daft, if you enjoy–"

Chris's fingers disappeared from inside him and he stood up. "Is this what this is about? You think it'll somehow make it better if I hurt you? Well, bollocks to that because, argh!" Chris yelled as the firm push on his chest sent him backwards into the deeper water which closed over his head.

He came up spluttering. "What the hell was that for?"

"To stop you going off the deep-end again. What I was going to say was that if you enjoy it, it must be worth putting up with a bit of pain. Now get up here and show me what appeals to you."

Chris wading the few steps towards him, lust in his eyes and droplets of water glistening on his black hair and olive skin. Without another word, Chris put Jase's ankles on his shoulders.

The grin on Chris's face made Jase feel more than a little worried, as he spat on his fingers and rubbed the saliva onto Jase's hole.

"Last chance to back out, soldier boy. You ready?"

Not wanting his voice to sound weak, Jase just nodded, then sucked in a sharp breath as Chris took him deep again and pushed first one and then a second finger inside him. The contrast between pleasure and pain was extraordinary. He started to get an idea why Chris liked to bottom so much, but he couldn't imagine letting anyone else have this much control over him. Working with hands, lips and body, Chris didn't give him a chance to think about anything but the growing need to come.

It wasn't the hard, straight in/out thrusting Jase did, either with his fingers or with his dick. As always, it seemed that Chris did things his own sweet way. There was no halt in his movements as he changed direction, rather he kept up a constantly varying circular motion until his fingers hit a particular spot. The rush of pleasure made Jase gasp as his neck and abdominal muscles contracted automatically.

"Oh fuck, that's...more, do that more," he found himself gasping, but it seemed Chris was way ahead of him. He was already hitting the same spot again and again. He'd always thought that the guys he fucked were being overly dramatic when he hit their prostate, but he'd been wrong, so very wrong, as he found himself groaning as loudly as any porn star.

Chris sped up, pounding into him with his fingers as he bobbed and sucked with his mouth and tugged on his balls with his other hand.

To his amazement, Jase found himself gasping, "Yes, oh fuck, yes," as a familiar buzzing sensation fizzed down his spine; the pressure on his prostate seemed to magnify it.

"Ah, fuck," he cried out as he spilled into Chris's mouth, his eyes tightly shut and every muscle straining. When he came back to himself, it was to feel Chris still stroking him slowly and gently. He opened his eyes to see Chris grinning down at him.

"You have the most stunning 'cum face'," he said and leant forward to kiss him gently. "Thank you letting me do that."

"You're thanking me? I literally saw stars," Jase blurted out, then frowned. "I was a bit distracted, did you?"

Chris pecked him on the lips quickly, too quickly. "I'm good. Come on, let's see if Nate can spare any of his huge designer wardrobe for you while we get your things dried off." Chris said as he started to climb out of the spa.

"Hold it. I thought you weren't going to run from me anymore? Sit," he ordered.

With a huff and hunched shoulders Chris sat down beside him, and just like that, the normal dynamic between them was restored. For a little while, it hadn't been him in charge, and he'd found it a little uncomfortable, if highly pleasurable.

"So what's with the not finishing thing? Didn't I do it for you?"

Chris immediately straightened, his dark eyes wide in surprise. "Christ, no. You're really hot, I mean you're seriously smoking, one of–"

Jase put a hand on his leg. "I get it. So is it what happened on the DVD? Or something else?"

"I erm..." Chris looked down at his knees.

"Spit it out. We need to–"

Chris snorted. "I can't; I already swal–"

"Grow up for once will you?" Jase replied but he couldn't help grinning. "What I was going to say is that we need to be honest with each other if this is going to work. So tell me."

Chris didn't meet his eyes. "It really doesn't matter, I really got a kick out of doing that, but I was focused on you; I couldn't relax enough to..." Jase pushed him down onto his back, and loomed over him.

"You matter. I don't know how many times I'm going to tell you before you get it, but I'll carry on saying it until you do. You need to communicate, to tell me what you're feeling and what you want because I'm going to have no problem fully enjoying you. Do you know what I'd like to do now?"

"What?" Chris asked, although he looked a little worried.

Jase bet he was nervous about him going near his arse, but that wasn't going to happen for a while. Knowing Chris, he'd probably let him though.

"Seeing you jerk off that morning was probably the most erotic thing I've ever seen. The way you pushed your hips up instead of moving your hand? Magic. I want to watch that again." He kissed him quickly as he ran his hand down Chris's flat stomach.

"I want to hold your balls as they tighten up just before you come," he said as he bit at Chris's throat, eliciting a gasp from his victim. "I want to be kissing you as you explode, I want to feel you gasp and writhe with it," he said as he wrapped a hand around Chris and stroked. Chris's dick had softened to a semi, but within moments, he was hard again.

Jase moved down to fondle his balls as Chris's hand found his own cock. As before, Chris's whole body moved and Jase feasted on the sight.

"Does that feel good?" Jase said, hovering over him, flicking his nipples.

"Uh, yeah, yeah it does," Chris gasped, his jaw tense.

"I want to fuck you so much right now, but I won't, not until you're ready. I'll decide that, not you, all you have to do is enjoy and be who you are." Tugging gently on his balls, he went with the rhythm Chris set, but it seemed he could no longer keep up with his desire just with his hips as his hand moved faster.

"That's it, faster, harder, do it, come for me," Jase murmured a fraction of an inch away from Chris's open mouth. He felt Chris's balls tighten and pressed his lips over his as the beautiful boy who had taken his heart tensed, trembled and shook with his climax.

Jase pulled back to watch as Chris relaxed, swallowed and then opened his pleasure dilated eyes.

"Better?"

Chris blew out a breath, closed his eyes and relaxed before wrapping his arms around Jase's neck.

"Yes, thanks, Boss."

Jase snorted in amusement. "Boss now is it? How many more names are you going to have for me?"

Chris shrugged. "Can't answer that, but now you'd better take me to bed."

Jase blinked in surprise. "You can go again, already?"

Chris chuckled as his arms flopped back down onto the decking. "Nah, I need to sleep, I wasn't kidding about sex being my off switch."

He did indeed look more relaxed than Jase had ever seen him while he was conscious.

"Sure, after we've had a bite to eat. From the look of it, all you've had today is some soup."

"Nope. If I don't use it, I'll lose it."

"But your hair's soaking wet."

"I'll put a towel on the bed," he mumbled as he pulled himself to his feet and headed, a little unsteadily, for the stairs.

CHAPTER 27

Chris

It was seven in the evening and he'd woken up alone an hour ago. He'd had to check the clock twice before believing that he'd actually slept for eighteen hours. After a swim to get rid of the cobwebs, he'd made his way back downstairs, irritated that he felt wobbly.

There was a large pizza box on the table as he walked back into the kitchen after getting dressed in his room. Both significantly hot men turned to watch him. Having Nate look at him as if he was a piece of glass about to shatter was getting a little old. Jase seemed to have relented a little but it wasn't enough by a long shot. The physical symptoms of withdrawal were virtually gone, apart from feeling pathetically weak and not having an appetite. It was time to put this whole sorry episode behind all of them.

Although speaking of behinds, his was still tender, but hopefully the cream he'd applied before he dressed would start working soon. He smiled to himself as he wondered how Jase was doing in that department. When it'd become clear that Eddie Bull hadn't been familiar with being on the receiving end, Chris had been far gentler than people usually were with him. Jase seemed to have gotten a kick out of it in the end so it wasn't off the list of bedroom antics just yet.

"What's next on the agenda? Do we all traipse down to the cop shop, or do you reckon we can wait a while? Because as much as it's the right thing to do, I'd rather not spend the rest of the day talking to a victim support officer, they're even worse than sodding social workers."

He took a quick slurp out of the glass of lemonade Nate pushed in his direction, picked a slice of pizza, took a bite and continued before either of the others could speak. "Come to think of it, I think I'm ready to go home. Living with you is good and all, but I'm constantly scared shitless that I'm going to bugger up your designer gear. Besides, the breaking in to your desk thing has left a bit of an atmosphere, don't you think?"

"What, you don't think so?" he prompted a silent, open mouthed, Nate.

"I'd say he's over his withdrawal," Jase said with a smile. "Nathan Cooper, welcome to the real Chris Bacon."

Chris grinned, put the pizza down and stuck his hand out towards the dark haired man who was sitting on the other side of the table looking a little shell-shocked.

"Pleased to meet you loaded, anti-drugs, paramedic dude. My name's Chris and I'm loud, proud, and fucking irritating. And you really shouldn't have let me sleep so long."

Jase burst out laughing at Nate's goldfish impression. Chris decided that Jase didn't deserve to have everything his own way either. Just because he'd been a mouse for the last few days, it didn't mean that those kidnapping bastards were going to stop him being who he was.

"I don't know what you're laughing about Sarge, just because I agreed to be your boyfriend, it doesn't mean that you're going it have it all your own way. Actually you never asked me." He tilted his head to one side. "Do you want to be my boyfriend, Mr Rosewood?"

"Erm, yes?" Jase looked a little gobsmacked too, but then again, Chris often had that effect on people. He liked it.

"Good, cos that sounds good, not that I've got any experience of dating. As a complete virgin to the boyfriend thing, I have to say I expect regular, interesting dates. I'm not ready for slippers and cocoa yet."

"What kind of dates?" Jase asked quickly.

Chris gave him his best cheeky grin and took another bite of pizza. "I have faith in your creativity. In the meantime, I'm going dancing," he said as he held one hand in the air and did a seated bump and grind, just to emphasise he was back in every sense of the word. It didn't even make his backside hurt too much. Way to go magic arse cream.

"I've got to burn this pizza off somehow. You two can both sit at the bar, admire my sexy ass and growl at my groupies."

Nate piped up. "Not a good idea, not yet. This is the first solid meal you've eaten in weeks. Apart from the risk of you throwing up or passing out on the dance floor, which will not please Russel, you need to put a bit of weight back on. That is unless Jase prefers the skeleton look, which if he does, makes him an arsehole."

"I don't. No clubbing," Jase said confirmed.

Chris scowled at the pair of them. Nevertheless, it felt good to be getting back to his old, obnoxious self.

"Well, what do you suggest then? I'm buzzing here, I've never slept that long in my life. How about a visit to Matt's? I want to see how my mini-me is getting on."

"Ryan's got Beavers tonight, then he'll be going to bed," Jase told him. "If we turn up he'll be falling asleep at his desk tomorrow."

Chris was about to say that it never did him any harm but changed his mind. His school career was certainly nothing to boast about. He'd spent more time in detention than in class, and more time out of school than in it. He'd often been the target of bullies when he joined a school. Most of them left him alone after he proved that he was willing to defend himself physically, although usually he just made people laugh which stopped the majority of fights before they started. A smart mouth, puppy dog eyes and taking the piss out of teachers usually gained him a fan club, amongst the girls anyway.

"How about a drive in your new car then? Come on, I haven't been out and about for too fucking long." Putting his chin in his hand, he hit the poor sods with his patented puppy dog eyes expression. "The world misses me guys; you can't deprive it of me forever."

"You could have gone out yesterday, but you didn't," Nate said.

The reminder of his epic failure to leave the safety of the building brought him plummeting back down. Without thinking, he put the slice of pizza back in the box, feeling rather sick.

Jase got to his feet. "Come on."

"Where are you taking him?" Nate asked.

"Out, not that I need your permission. If it's ok with you, I'll bring him back here tonight but I'll be staying again too. If you'd rather we not, I'll take him to my parents' place. I'm going to move my stuff into Kate's old flat tomorrow and Chris is coming with me."

Chris looked between the two older men. Both were dominant, forceful, and bloody hot, and they were arguing over him. It had been a long time since anyone had actually cared about him, other than wanting to get into his underwear. Now he had Jase and his parents, Nate, Matt, Kate and Sarah, not to mention the majority of the Kemp International drivers, and the nursing staff of his dad's home, all looking out for him. It was nice, but it was also pressure he wasn't used to. The opportunity to disappoint them all was fucking huge. When he'd been on his own, hell when he'd been with his mum, nobody had cared what he did from one week to the next.

"Hey, don't fight over me; there's enough of me to go around." Due to the fact that Jase bore a startling resemblance to Bruce Banner just before he turned green, he realised he'd put his foot in it again. "And I didn't mean that like it sounded. Nate, you're hot and all, fucking smoking to be honest, and under different circumstance I would really be up for–"

Nate started chuckling as Jase stood up and hauled Chris to his feet by his arm.

"Before you start giving him any more ideas, I think we'd better go."

"Believe me, I've already had a vast range of ideas concerning Chris, his dancing really doesn't leave much to the imagination," Nate said as he smiled and waggled his eyebrows.

"I bet I can give you a few m–" Chris managed to say over his shoulder as Jase dragged him from the room with a growl.

Five minutes later they were heading down in the lift. Chris's anxiety levels were rising with every few feet they descended. If someone had thought to bring his make-up over he might have felt a little more confident about going out in public. It had sounded like an excellent idea in the kitchen, but the reality wasn't nearly so appealing.

"Remember what I said about talking to me? What's up? You being quiet is a bloody loud alarm bell."

Chris looked everywhere but at Jase, although there wasn't a lot of scope in the lift. He could literally feel Jase's eyes boring into the side of his face. Even thinking about artwork to brighten the lift up didn't distract him.

"Did I tell you that the mind reading thing is bloody annoying?"

"Yes. Now what's up? We can do this another time if you like, but putting it off isn't going to make it any easier. In fact, the longer you leave it, the worse it could get."

"The bruises won't get worse," he said and then regretted it.

The lift came to a halt, the doors opened. Jase didn't make a move, so neither did he.

"You don't want anyone to wonder or ask about them or where you've been. I get it," Jase said as he draped an arm over Chris's shoulders and gave him a squeeze. "How about I field any awkward questions and give anyone that looks as if they're going to bug you my patented 'hard stare'? It worked on Taliban insurgents so I don't think I'll have a problem with the locals around here."

Chris turned to look at him. He was going to have to spell it out. "You do know they'll think you did them."

Jase shrugged, his green eyes unconcerned. "And why I should care about that? The people that matter know the truth. Anybody else can take a running jump."

Could he let Jase take the blame for what Dimitar and his cronies did? It didn't feel right, but...

Jase guided him forward out of the lift and to the door of the building, his walking stick clinking on the wooden floor. He hadn't used it within Nate's flat, but it was clear his ankle wasn't fully healed yet.

"Stop overthinking it. It'll be fine," he said and drew Chris out into the warm late afternoon sunshine.

There were only a few people going about their business in the pedestrianised area outside Cooper's department store. Jase guided him unerringly to the right.

"Where're we going?" Chris asked as he kept his hands in his pockets and his head down.

The club was this way, and despite saying he wanted to go dancing earlier, now that he'd thought about it, it was the last place he wanted to be. Even though he couldn't remember being there the night Dimitar's lot had dropped him off, plenty of people would have seen him. And thanks to the DVD, he knew exactly what state he'd been in.

"We are going for a gentle walk and then I'm going to buy you dinner. You didn't eat much of that pizza. If I remember rightly, and it's been a few years, I think it's called a date."

Chris grinned and bumped him with his shoulder. "A date, Jase? Big, bad, 'I'm not out' Sarge is taking his twink on a date, right out in public, in his home town?"

Jase scowled. "You're not a twink and I've never hidden my preferences; I just don't shout about it."

Chris stopped, forcing Jase to turn back to him. He cocked his hip and put his hand on it, knowing it would emphasise his skinny frame. "I know I'm not wearing one of my kinky rainbow shirts, but on the twink scale of one to ten, I'm an eight and we both know it. I've been working on the camp voice and gestures, but I haven't quite got it yet."

Pouting, he fluttered his eyelashes at Jase, who was shaking his head and looking up to the darkening sky for inspiration.

"Aw Eddie, are you an itty bit embarrassed to be out with me?" he asked in a daft kiddie voice.

"Nope, but you might be when I put you over my knee and paddle your arse right here."

If Jase was expecting a threat like that to work, he was sadly mistaken. Chris ran over to the nearest bench. Bending over, he looked over his shoulder and wiggled his backside.

Instead of the red face Chris expected, Jase's jaw clenched and he strode towards him, his limp hardly noticeable as he carried his walking stick. He looked strong, dominant and definitely pissed off. He wouldn't really make good on his threat, would he? Chris straightened up as not only did Jase walk up to him, he didn't stop till his face was less than an inch away from his.

"Bit much?" he offered with an apologetic smile.

"Oh no twinkle toes, it's not too much for me, but it might be a little over the top for the head teacher of your new college, who is just over there." He nodded in the direction of a middle-aged couple who were walking towards them.

"Oh fuck," Chris exclaimed, then clapped his hand over his mouth as the couple glared at them as they walked by.

"Sorry, I'm not usually so rude, Mr, Mrs–" Chris called loudly then whispered to Jase, "which one is it and what's their name?"

Jase burst out laughing. "I've got no bloody idea, but the look on your face is classic."

He slapped Jase's chest hard with the back of his hand. "I hate you," he said but couldn't stop himself from grinning, this playful side of Jase was a revelation.

Jase rubbed his chest. "Careful with the slaps, I'm delicate."

Chris slipped his arm around Jase's waist and they started walking again. "Yeah and I'm Jaws out of Moonraker."

"You're a Bond fan?"

"Mum liked them. Come to think of it, you've got a bit of a Daniel Craig look about you, all blond, mean and moody."

The snort of laughter Jase let out made his heart leap. Yep, he'd thawed the iceman.

Two minutes later, they arrived outside McDonald's.

Jase waved a hand in the direction of the entrance and bowed slightly. "I present, your supper venue for this evening."

"And here was I thinking you were a cheapskate." Chris grinned.

"Nothing but the best for my boyfriend. I'll even spring for a large meal if you promise me sexual favours in return." This time, Jase avoided the slap.

"Behave, I still have my handcuffs," he said quietly as he held the door open.

"Promises, promises," Chris whispered back as they went in.

A few minutes later they were sitting in the quieter upstairs part of the restaurant, with Chris tackling a 'Big Tasty'. Jase had a quarter-pounder with cheese meal.

Chris eyed his huge sloppy burger with suspicion before taking a bite.

"You enjoying that?" Jase asked with slightly raised eyebrows.

"Not really," he said as he put it down and sucked some sauce off his finger, thoroughly enjoying Jase's discomfort as he focused on his lips. After yesterday, Chris knew exactly what Jase was thinking, because that had been his exact intention.

"Why did you order it then?"

"Just wanted to see the look on that guy's face when I said I really needed him to give me a big tasty one."

"Any joy?" Jase asked with a completely straight face.

Chris reached into the brown paper bag and pulled out a slip of paper with a telephone number on it.

Jase chuckled. "You're dreadful."

"Yeah, but you love me anyway," Chris said automatically, then stopped and glanced up at Jase. His heart almost stopped beating as Jase reached across the table and took his hand.

" I think you're right."

For once in his life, Chris didn't have a clue what to say. But he didn't pull his hand away as he looked into the green eyes that had fascinated him ever since he'd first seen them at Matt's wedding, less than a month ago.

The sincerity he saw there was scary; he wasn't worth the confidence Jase had in him. It felt as if he was about to discover that his foot didn't fit the glass slipper after all and that Prince Charming would move on to someone far more worthy.

And love? What was that all about? Yeah, Jase made him feel secure, he thought about him a lot and liked being around him, most of the time, and he certainly fancied him like crazy, but love? Hell, he didn't know what he was going to do or feel in the next thirty seconds, let alone making a life-long declaration.

A self-deprecating smile tickled Jase's lips. "Don't worry about saying it back, in fact I'd rather you didn't until you're sure."

Chris opened his mouth, knowing he needed to say something, but Jase spoke first.

"Nope, don't say anything. You've been through hell and that's going to take time to come to terms with. I just want you to know that I'm here for you, and I'm not going anywhere."

"This is erm… a lot," Chris finally managed as he looked down at their joined hands as Jase's thumb rubbed over the back of his hand. It was more intimate than what they'd done in the spa; that had been about sex, he was more than familiar with that, but this was….

"Tigger!" a voice called out. He looked up to see four men from the club walking towards them.

"Shit, that's all I need," he murmured.

"Who are they?" Jase asked quietly as the four approached.

"Remember I mentioned club groupies?"

They were all single, somewhat dominant gay men who enjoyed watching twinks dance. All of them pushed paper in one form or another for a living. The other thing that linked them, the one he didn't want to think about or mention to Jase, was that he'd had sex with three of them. This was not going to be pleasant.

"Where the fuck have you been, Tigger? We've missed your cute backside at the Toolbox," Ollie said.

He was the youngest of the quartet, and the only one Chris hadn't slept with, although he'd tried it on several times. As Ollie still lived with his parents and had been unable to offer Chris a bed for the night, he'd turned him down. Besides, he was a bit of a dick.

Despite the glare Jase directed at them, Harry and Ollie sat on either side of him. Steve and Dave pulled up seats behind him. It left Jase isolated on the other side of the table and him feeling particularly uncomfortable.

"Been a bit busy," he mumbled and picked up a fry as a distraction. Harry grabbed his chin, turning his face to one side before he batted his hand away. "Hey, club rules apply, no touching."

"I'll second that. Who are you?" Jase asked tightly.

Pointed to each of his fans in turn, he introduced them. "Harry, Steve, Dave and Ollie, meet Jason Rosewood, my boyfriend." The word felt strange in his mouth, but he didn't want to think about the expression on Jase's face if he introduced him as just another friend. Having this descend into a 'does he do that with you' type conversation was not going to happen.

"So you're the current 'busy'?" Dave asked. "It's been nearly a month since any of us have seen you; we were talking about it last night. Must be an all-time record; mind you, more than one night is unusual–"

"Leave it out will you?" Chris ground out.

"You finished with that?" Jase said as he gestured at Chris's abandoned meal.

Harry indicated Chris's face with a finger as he focused on Jase. "It doesn't look like you've been leaving it out though, what's with the bruises? We all know he likes it rough, but–"

Jase was on his feet in an instant, followed by Harry and Steve, the most forceful pair out of the quartet.

Crap. Chris tried to get up too, but Dave's hand on his shoulder kept him in his seat.

Keeping his eyes on Harry and Steve, Jase growled, "Hands off. Chris is with me now, and whatever relationship any of you thought you had with him is over."

"Can we just calm down? We're just concerned about him," Dave said, but he did remove his hand from his shoulder. "We heard he left the club nearly a month ago after an argument with someone who fits your description, not to mention crap about him being kidnapped. And now he turns up with you, quiet as a mouse, looking as if he's been beaten up and hasn't eaten for a fortnight."

As far as Chris could see, this situation was fast going tits up. Jase might be trained, but he was still injured. It would be four on one and he really didn't fancy an enforced trip to the cop shop. Being locked in a cell was not something he wanted to experience again any time soon, especially without any of Dimitar's 'happy juice'.

"I got caught up in stupid end of term university scavenger hunt. 'Twink' was on the list; they held me for a week and it got a bit ugly. Jase is ex-military police and my brother's best mate. He tracked me down and got me out."

"Hero type, huh?" Ollie said, eyeing Jase with interest. A surge of jealousy so intense it made his gut clench swept through Chris. He stood up.

"Yep, and he's my hero type. Get used to it, I'm off the market."

Steve snorted. "Yeah right, I'll believe that when I see it. You're a buffet kind of guy, and we all know it. No way will you be happy eating off the same plate for more than a week or so."

"Watch me. Besides, why would I want to carry on trying different vol-au-vents when I've got my very own meat and two veg at home?"

Ollie burst out laughing. "I can't wait to tell the others down the club that he called you lot 'vol-au-vents'." The table dissolved into good natured banter as Jase indicated with a twitch of his head that they should leave and started for the stairs.

Harry caught Chris's arm as he got up. "You know I'm around if you need me, Steve too. Give me a ring, yeah?"

Nodding caused the hand to let go and Chris followed Jase out. He hadn't hidden the fact he'd been promiscuous, but being confronted with a whole clutch of 'ex's' even before he'd actually done the deed with Jase had to be a bit of kick to the nuts. Hopefully Jase had meant what he said about loving him, because what had just happened would send any decent bloke running for the hills.

CHAPTER 28

Jase

With his hands in his pockets and his head down, Chris walked silently beside him.

"You ok?"

Chris glanced over at him. "You're asking me? I'm not the one who was just confronted with three blokes who have slept with my boyfriend."

Reached out an arm, he pulled Chris into his good side. "Are you going to sleep with anyone else while we're together?"

Stopping in his tracks, Chris turned to him wearing a frown. "Of course not, but it must piss you off that I've been with–" Jase silenced him with a kiss.

"It doesn't bother me." He paused. *If I want him to tell me the truth, I ought to do the same.* "Well it does, but it's not something I can change so I'll live with it. You can't change that I've got a knackered ankle either."

"But you didn't choose to get blown up, I..."

"Which ones did you hit on, rather than the other way around?"

Chris tried to pull away, but Jase held him close with his hand on his lower back.

"How. Many?"

"None. But I didn't exactly play hard to get either."

"And how many men have you slept with since you moved in with Matt, apart from Russel and me?"

"I didn't sleep with Russel, he's never invited me up to his flat. If you're talking about sex, other than Russel, four, it was–"

"And that I don't want to know," Jase interrupted. "Do you want to go back to Nate's now?"

"What's the time?"

Jase pulled out his phone to check. "Half eight. We'll have to sort you out another phone."

Chris sighed and dropped his shoulders. "You can't keep on buying me stuff. You're not exactly rolling in it yourself."

As if someone had lit a fire inside him, Chris straightened up. "Tell you what, let's go over to the club. We can pick up my last wages and see how Russel feels about me working again."

His enthusiasm was wonderful to see, his eyes were bright and alive again, but the idea that prompted the mood swing wasn't. The one time he'd seen Chris dance, it'd been almost impossible to keep his seat at the bar as he watched all those other guys drool over him, and in many cases, touch him. Chris hadn't encouraged the groping, but he hadn't exactly been upset by it either. There was no way he was going to let Chris be groped by multiple blokes every time he went to work.

"No podium dancing," he said firmly. It caused a frown to mar that beautiful face.

"I wasn't going to, not tonight. As I said, all I want to do is talk to Russel and–"

"No more podium dancing, full stop," Jase interrupted Chris's mile-a-minute speech before he could pick up too much momentum.

The frown deepened. Without another word, Chris turned and walked away.

"Wait."

Chris paused, and let his head fall back as he looked to the stars, but he didn't turn around. When Jase caught up with him, he took his arm and indicated a nearby bench. If there was one thing he'd learnt, it was that letting Chris run off and stew on something only led to more trouble.

Chris flopped down on the bench like a stroppy teenager. *Which is exactly what he is.* It didn't mean he was going to let him get away with such behaviour, just that he understood it. Chris had grown up without boundaries because no one had cared enough to set them, but he had people that could do that for him now. It remained to be seen if Chris would see it as helpful, or a reason to run again.

Sitting next to him, Jase waited patiently for Chris to speak, even though the temperature was dropping as the sun dropped lower. Several people passed by as they sat in silence; individuals making their way home from a late night at work, a few groups looking for entertainment, couples on dates, an older man walking his dog.

Sighing, Chris sat forward, his elbows on his knees, his head hanging down. "I really, really appreciate what you're doing for me, sorting me out somewhere to live, a college course, everything, but... it's also a bit much." Chris glanced over at him, probably to see if he was angry.

"Go on," Jase prompted quietly. This was a moment he'd been hoping wouldn't happen.

Looking down again, Chris continued. "It feels as if you're trying to turn me into someone else, someone... better."

Jase opened his mouth to protest, but Chris got there first. "Just listen, please. I know who and what I am, and it's nothing to boast about. I'm not sure if I can ever be what you want."

"You're worried that if you don't live up to my expectations I'll kick you out." Jase summarised.

Keeping his head down, Chris shrugged silently. Jase draped his arm over the young man's shoulders that he was currently confusing.

"Give me a month. Just one month to show you that life will be better with me than without me. I don't mind you working at the club, but I don't want people groping you. I don't care if people look, because they're going to, you're gorgeous. I certainly don't expect you to wear sackcloth and never speak to other blokes."

Chris snorted. "Like that's ever going to happen."

Ignoring his comment as the attempt at distraction it was, Jase carried on. "The one thing I can't do is share you in that way. I can't sit at home knowing other guys are going to be groping you, knowing that you might not feel able to say no. I couldn't cope with seeing marks on you that weren't made by me. When I saw that... thing Russel put on your neck–"

Chris sat upright again. "I don't know what you think I am but I'm quite capable of saying no–"

Reminding him that he hadn't objected to one of the men at McDonalds's holding him in his seat, or that he'd agreed to call one wasn't going to be helpful.

"The flat has two bedrooms. We can be housemates, nothing more, if that's what you want. My house rules include no drugs and that you come home every night, alone."

The hurt in Chris's eyes was clear. "You don't want me in your bed?"

Picking up Chris's fine–boned, artistic hand, Jase kissed the back of it. "Oh I want you in my bed alright, I just don't want you in anyone else's if we're in a relationship. And as you're so bloody gorgeous and sexy, that means you are going to have to learn to say 'no'. No laters, maybes, I'll call you's or running away to avoid the issue. Just straight out, 'no'. Do you think you can do that?"

"No, I don't think I can," he said sadly, then his face lit up with a grin. "How'd I do?"

Jase wiped his hand down his face, more to hide his own smile than anything else. "Do you enjoy being spanked?"

Chris's grin got wider as he stood up. Carefully facing his butt in the opposite direction, he held up his finger and announced, "No, I don't. See what I did there? I'm getting good at this."

Jase stood up, making sure he took most of his weight on his good leg. "Getting good at what, saying no or lying?"

"What do you think?" Chris asked.

He was almost expecting it when the younger man's arm went around his waist, but he jerked a little when he felt a hand push inside the back of his combats and squeeze his arse firmly.

"I think you need a lot more practice at both. I also think you need to get your hand out of my boxers before the group of skinheads that will be coming out of the Red Lion in about two minutes sees us."

Chris's hand shot out, leaving a rapidly cooling empty spot.

"You had any trouble with homophobia in town?" Jase asked as Chris checked out the front of the pub they were approaching.

"Nah, but you might."

"And how do you work that one out? I was in the army for the last ten years, and no one worked out I wasn't straight, whereas one look at you…"

Chris patted him on the shoulder. "The reason that I don't have any trouble with them is because the buggers can't catch me. Whereas you, you poor old sod, couldn't outrun a fairy cake."

"I have a better weapon than fast feet, and don't forget it."

"What's that?"

"Something you will never have my padawan, patience and the ability to talk sense."

Chris nodded sagely as the continued to walk. "Yep, boring people to death will definitely work."

Pulling him close, Jase whispered in his ear. "I can guarantee you one hundred percent that I won't bore you. I intend to wear you out so thoroughly that you'll never have to worry about insomnia ever again."

"Speaking of bed, would you mind if we go back to Nate's instead of going to the club, I'm kinda tired."

"After sleeping for most of the last twenty-four hours? You're lying ability needs a little more work, although the university prank story you told in McDonald's was pretty good."

Chris grinned at him. "Why thank you, kind sir. So where're we going?"

"We are going to the club so we can both cross a few things off our 'to do' lists. We've got a busy day tomorrow so you need a good night's sleep and you won't get one if you're not physically tired."

* * *

As soon as they walked into the car park, a deep voice shouted, "Tigger!"

Jase stopped in his tracks as Chris sprinted across the tarmac and literally threw himself up and into the arms of the hulking doorman. The man whirled Chris around in a circle, his grin as wide as Chris's.

Jase wasn't smiling. Hadn't they just had a 'no touching' talk? Perhaps Chris hadn't understood the rule also applied to him touching other people. Although if the big bloke didn't stop spinning Chris around, he was probably going to get his suit decorated with half a 'Big Tasty'.

"Chris?" he asked politely. The two looked over at the third wheel who was interrupting their little celebration. The big man didn't release Chris, although it looked as if he had merely forgotten he was holding him a foot and a half off the ground rather than being possessive.

Jase looked pointedly at the doorman, then back at him.

"Oh, right, sorry. Can you put me down, Cuddles? He's the jealous type."

'Cuddles' started laughing, but he did put a flushed Chris back on his own two feet.

"Name's Will. Don't worry, he's not my type; I'm just pleased to see him in such good nick. I was working when those bastards dropped him off. I carried him into the club. I just wish I could get my hands on them."

Will stuck out his hand and Jase shook it. "That makes two of us. And by not your type you mean..."

Chris huffed and grabbed his arm to propel him through the purple painted doors, calling 'see you later, Cuddles," to Will.

"For a gay bloke, your gaydar is shot to pieces. Cuddles is as straight as they come. He met his wife while he was working the door of a normal club. She didn't like all the girls hitting on him, so he took a job here."

Jase looked at him incredulously. "She'd rather he get hit on by gay blokes every night?"

"When I said he's really straight, I mean he likes curves, lots and lots of curves. His missus has got tits like barrage balloons and an arse like a bouncy castle. Put it this way, she wouldn't need airbags in a car crash." He held his hands out about a foot away from his body and wobbled from side to side as he walked through the red-carpeted lobby area.

Jase suppressed a shudder at the thought of all that wobbling flesh. The wall of sound that assaulted his ears as Chris pushed through the fire doors and into the club proper made him wince. Despite Chris saying he was tired earlier, the atmosphere seemed to act like a shot of instant adrenaline for him.

Chris answered the many shouts of welcome from around the large space with smiles and waves. He also did his best to avoid the hands and hugs of most of his admirers, but the sheer volume of people was defeating him. Jase settled for putting an arm around his waist and giving the men that approached Chris with an obvious physical greeting in mind a hard stare.

"Is he in?" Chris shouted at the good-looking tattooed guy behind the bar.

Even though he had his hands full pulling a pint, the guy indicated the admin area with his chin. They managed to get through the nondescript door without any more hands grabbing Chris's backside although Jase couldn't say the same for his own.

As the door closed behind them, he rubbed his pinched butt cheek. "Friendly lot in here aren't they?"

Chris grinned and bumped him with his shoulder. "Yeah, but don't take it too seriously. People treat this place like Vegas, whatever happens in here, stays in here. Put in this way, if this was a straight club, half the kids in the local primary school would be called stall one, two or three."

"What?"

Chris rolled his eyes. "You know the current trend of naming kids after where they were conceived? Brooklyn, Paris, India? These toilets have seen a lot of action. Put it this way, the cleaner fills up the condom machine more often than he does the soap dispensers." Jase's face twisted in disgust.

The grin on Chris's face was automatic. "Hey, don't knock it till you've tried it. Actually, thinking about it, my name could have been 'washing machine,' although 'shed' and 'garage' have a certain ring to them."

With that cheerful revelation, he knocked on the door of the office where Jase had seen him right after he'd been dumped by the kidnappers.

"Come," Russel's deep voice came from inside.

Chris pushed open the door, "If you insist, but I think Jase might have something to say about that." He turned and raised his eyebrows at Jase. "Unless you're into that?"

The look Jase gave him had quelled hardened soldiers on many occasions, but Chris just turned back to Russel.

"Apparently that's a no on the coming, and on the team sports. Personally I used to like playing tag, but—"

"Get to the point; I've got to close up in four hours."

"Can I have my wages and my job back?"

Before Russel could answer, Jase interrupted. "Not the same job though. He's not podium dancing anymore," Jase said firmly. "He's too vulnerable to temptation up there and as much as I wish it wasn't true, 'no' doesn't seem to be in his vocabulary."

Russel leaned down, opened a drawer and placed a small brown envelope on the desk. "How about if I stick him in a cage so no one can touch him? I'm thinking of getting a couple anyway. A guy fell off last night."

"I've never fallen off," Chris said, clearly offended. "What is he, blind or something?"

"Pretty much, yeah."

"Oh, sorry, my bad," Chris replied immediately. The news that a blind guy wanted to dance on a podium clearly didn't faze Chris as much as it did him. Maybe he wasn't as 'inclusive' as he'd always thought.

"No reason why he shouldn't be safe when he's shaking his stuff. Now about that cage..." Chris looked hopefully towards him.

"You're not a piece of meat," he said firmly.

"How about glass collecting?" Russel asked Jase directly.

"Even worse. He won't be able to defend himself with his hands full."

Russel frowned. "He's not big enough to be door staff, and I sort out the paperwork."

"He'd have trouble with that anyway, he's dyslexic."

"Cleaner?" Russel suggested but Chris was already heading towards the door.

"Where are you going?" Jase asked.

"Who me? I thought I'd go and do something useful while you two decided my future. And by the way, I'm not cleaning vomit and bogs or picking up used condoms for a living." He wiggled his fingers at them. "These were meant to create and excite, not do manual labour involving bleach," he told them, then walked out the door.

"You should go after him," Russel said.

"No, we should go after him. It's your club and your customers that I'm likely to be hitting if anyone's touching him."

Russel got to his feet. "I would say you're being paranoid, but then again, this is Chris we're talking about."

As he reached for the door, he added, "It's good to see him back to normal. I never would've believed anyone could bounce back from that so quickly, but as I said, this is Chris."

Jase preceded the taller, broader man out of the door. "He's not 'back' as you call it. This is all a front that he's trying to convince himself is true. Which is why I don't want anyone touching him without his express permission. I brought him here mainly to show him that he can still function around other people. This is the first time he's been outside since it happened. I found him hiding in a wardrobe yesterday because he saw that damn DVD, he'd been in there for hours. I hope your doorman knows not to let him leave on his own."

"He'd better, or he'll be looking for another job," Russel growled as they entered the club proper. Both scanned the dance floor for Chris. Jase's anxiety levels soared as he didn't see him amongst the gyrating bodies.

Russel tapped him on the shoulder. "I think I've found him a job," he said and nodded towards the bar.

Chris was on the other side, confidently serving and smiling at the customers as he swayed to the music.

"He's safe enough behind there isn't he? We have two bar staff on Fridays and Saturday, but we could do with a third, especially one that moves like he does. I could also use him as cover during the week occasionally. I pay one fifty over minimum wage; it's not great, but we've got tight margins. You keep an eye while I go sort out a contract of employment; I want everything above board this time. I've learnt my lesson with that one."

Russel left him leaning up against the wall, watching Chris in the world that he'd made his own. It was as if Chris had a light inside him and everyone else, including himself, were moths being drawn to it. Even though he couldn't hear him above the thumping music, from Chris's expressions, winks and grins, he was working the crowd as much as he'd done on a podium.

Expecting him to say no, to reject people he'd either wittingly or unwittingly encouraged was probably too high a goal. Even working behind the bar, Chris would be at risk from admirers after he finished a shift. Jase decided that he'd be here to pick Chris up every night he worked, and he'd be here at least half an hour before the end of each shift.

Russel appearing beside him, broke him away from his planning.

"Contract is on my desk. I'll give him the good news then you can go look over it together. He can start on Friday, if you think he's up for it?" Russel almost shouted at him.

It was too loud to have a proper conversation, so he just nodded and patted Russel's shoulder in acknowledgment, then wished he hadn't. Russel was built like a tank, and he thanked his lucky stars the man hadn't taken exception to his high handedness on each of the occasions that they'd met. As much as he didn't want to like the man, he decided that if he'd had any submissive tendencies whatsoever, Russel would be quite a catch. Just like Nate. And yet, Chris was coming home with him instead.

He just hoped he could be the man Chris needed, because there were several better looking, far wealthier men without knackered legs ready to take over, if only temporarily. Going to the gym was definitely going up on his list of priorities.

As he watched, Russel went behind the bar, leaned close Chris and spoke directly into his ear. Chris pulled back, his eyes incredulous. Russel smiled and nodded. It felt as if his heart was freezing over as Chris threw his arms around the big man. It thawed as Chris immediately looked over with a huge grin. Not waiting for Russel to back up out of his way in the confined space, Chris climbed over the bar and was dodging through the bodies towards him a second later.

When Chris reached him, his arms snaked into the air, and he started to do a victory dance that involved a great deal of wiggling and gyrating. Jase wasn't the only one admiring his sinuously body, so he grabbed him by the arm and pulled him into the staff area.

"Better get your name on the dotted line before he changes his mind," Jase said and gave his arse a firm slap. His eyes were drawn to the area as Chris rubbed his abused cheek.

"Well if you're going to get all dominant on me–"

Jase pushed him up against the wall, pinning him with his larger body. "You'll do what?"

Chris swallowed, his pupils dilating rapidly. "I'll shout for help. Help," he whispered a second before Jase's hands found his jaw and his hip, and lips found his mouth.

Chris pushed his hips against him, and moaned as Jase plundered his mouth. When Chris's hands started to knead his backside, privacy became far more important.

"Come on," he breathed into his mouth, then gathered a fistful of Chris's shirt and pulled him into Russel's office.

Chris pulled away and hurried over to the desk and the single printed sheet of paper on it.

"Do you mind giving this contract a quick look over for me? Cos, you know, reading isn't my thing."

"You looked so beautiful in the water yesterday," Jase said as he locked the door and advanced across the office.

"What are you doing? We can't do this here," Chris kept glancing toward the door, but Jase kept advancing till he had him backed up against the desk.

He flattened his palm against Chris's rapidly moving chest. Chris moved his own to cover it, forcing Jase to stop moving.

"Seriously, we can't do this here. Someone could come in any minute; I don't want to fuck this job up."

"Everyone's busy out there. Are you saying you don't want me to do this?" he murmured as he slid his hand down into the waistband of Chris's jeans, causing him to swallow convulsively. When he took hold of his cock, Chris let out a delicious moan. If there was one thing he'd learned about Chris, it was that he had trouble resisting distractions. This was going to be as much of a distraction as Jase could manage.

"Don't overthink it, just close your eyes and enjoy."

"We really shouldn't..." Chris continued to protest weakly but his hard dick sent a completely different message. Jase dropped to his knees and pulled Chris's beautiful cock from his jock strap.

A bead of pre-cum glistened at the tip, begging for attention and Jase didn't hesitate to taste it.

"Christ, can't you wait till we get home?"

"No. I'm on a mission to replace every memory of other blokes you have with me. Whenever you think of this office now, you'll think of me, not Russel."

"Someone could come in."

"I locked the door."

"They'll hear."

"I doubt it with all that music, but you might want to try and keep quiet, just in case."

Not waiting for another excuse, Jase wasted no time in tasting him again, wanting to hear him groan with pleasure. It only took a few seconds before Chris was pushing his hips forward, desperate to sink deeper into what he was offering. Jase didn't want this to end quite so quickly, easing Chris's jeans and underwear down further, he gave himself greater access to his goal. Running his tongue slowly up from the base to the tip, he gently rolled Chris's almost hairless balls with the hand that wasn't kneading his firm rounded butt. He couldn't wait to feel it up against his groin as he buried himself inside, but he would, because he never wanted to see Chris in pain, either physically or emotionally, ever again.

His time in the army, and his various temporary relationships meant that he'd seen plenty of arses in his time, but he'd never seen anything as gorgeous as Chris's before. However, right now, concentrating on it might spook him again, so he turned his attention back to his cock, and took it as deep as he could without gagging.

He wasn't as proficient at this as Chris, but he hoped enthusiasm would make up for his lack of technical merit. It wasn't as if he'd any complaints from previous partners although usually his partner went down on him rather than the other way around. But Chris was well, Chris, and he wanted to taste and experience him in every way possible.

The gasp from above him, and the hand on the back of his head pressing him forward, proved that he wasn't doing too bad a job. He'd imagined doing this too many times to count over the last five weeks. At the same time, dread had stalked him that it'd never happen because Chris was either dead or wouldn't want his knackered old carcass.

Even after they'd gotten him back, there had been a real chance that he'd been so traumatised that he'd never be the same person again. Chris might not remember the night he'd lain senseless and battered on the sofa behind them, but Jase did. And he needed to erase that memory.

"Christ, Jase, that's... fuck," Chris groaned and moved against him as Jase sucked strongly. Knowing that he was nearly there, Jase quickly wetted his index finger, and trailed it down his hairless taint towards his hole.

Instead of pulling away as Jase had feared he might, Chris widened his stance, giving him more access. Alert for any signs of pain, he slowly pushed his finger inside as he continued to distract Chris with his mouth. Although his hip movements slowed a little, Chris didn't pull away or tell him to stop. So he continued with the gentle movement, going a fraction deeper with each slow push.

Without warning, Chris reached behind himself and pushed Jase's hand in deeper as he cried out, "Yeah, there, right there."

Jase immediately increased the pressure. Chris exploded in his mouth a fraction of a second later as he let out a wordless gasp of ecstasy. The tension in Chris's body drained out of him along with his climax. Jase got to his feet, using the desk as support, tucked Chris's rapidly softening dick back into his underwear and did his jeans back up.

Chris's eyes were still closed, his face relaxed in post orgasmic bliss. Pride swelled in Jase's chest. He wanted to protect this wonderful, beautiful young man more than he'd wanted to do anything else in the world. Gently, tenderly, he kissed his slightly open, pink lips. Chris's blinked open.

"Can we go home now? I feel about as energetic as overcooked spaghetti."

"I'll call us a cab. While we wait, I'll go over the contract."

"Cool," Chris murmured and started to eye the sofa.

"Ah, ah, no sleeping yet. I can't carry you."

Twenty minutes later, Jase cajoled Chris to keep going as he guided him into the lift at Nate's place.

As they walked into the penthouse, Nate was waiting for them. He took one look at Chris, and glared at Jase.

"What the hell did you do to him? He looks nearly as bad as he did a week ago."

"I'm fine, just tired. Can we argue about this in the morning?"

"No way, I want to take your vitals first, make sure no one has slipped you anything." Nate strode across the room to grab his med kit.

"Ah fuck, Nate, no one slipped me anything, in fact it was me doing the—"

"And the less said about that the better," Jase interrupted.

Nate's eyebrows nearly hit the roof as Chris cupped his hand around his mouth and stage whispered, "Sarge is a very naughty boy. I'll give you the highlights in the morn—" was as far as Jase let him get before he put both hands on Chris's shoulders and directed him towards their bedroom.

Once in the bedroom Chris headed straight for the bed as if he was going to face plant.

"Strip first," Jase ordered.

"Again? Look I appreciate the enthusiasm, but—"

"We'll be sleeping, nothing else. If you're not comfortable, you'll wake yourself up."

Shooting him a look that could kill, Chris toed his trainers off, pulled his shirt off, undid his jeans, shoved them halfway down his legs then fell back on the bed. Sighing, Jase pulled Chris's jeans off him, undressed himself, turned the light off then slipped into bed and pulled the quilt over the pair of them.

Chris rolled over till he was snuggled against his chest. "Thanks," he murmured and started to snore softly.

CHAPTER 29

Chris

Jase was still in the land of nod when Chris woke up. The sun was streaming through the gap in the curtains as he carefully slipped out of bed. Just because he didn't usually sleep much, it didn't mean other people didn't need eight hours. A quick look at Jase's phone showed it was five past six. Considering he'd slept for eighteen hours the day before, he was amazed he'd slept last night at all, but Jase's efforts at the Toolbox must have had something to do with it.

Someone giving him pleasure without expecting or demanding it in return was a very rare event, then again, Jason Rosewood was a very rare man. Why the hell he wanted a fuck-up like him Chris didn't know, but he was going to go with it for as long as Jase let him. When it all went pear-shaped at some point in the near or distant future, at least he would have the memories.

Grabbing a clean pair of jeans and a t-shirt he put them on as quietly as he could then started to towards the bedroom door. Jase's damaged leg was on top of the quilt and he stopped to get a closer look. They'd gotten naked together in the spa, but he hadn't been paying attention to this particular part of Jase's anatomy.

It was pretty fucking horrible. Wide, angry red lines ran from his foot to five or six inches above his ankle, and the area was still a little swollen even after a month. Walking all that way last night hadn't been a good idea. Jase needed looking after just as much as he did, but persuading him to take things slow today, probably wasn't going to be easy.

When he walked into the kitchen, he found Nate coming down the stairs from his roof terrace wearing a towel around his waist and rubbing his dark hair with another. That dark chest hair just begged to be played with, but Chris was a one man bloke now. It felt pretty damn good.

"Good night last night?"

Chris grinned at him. "Yep. I got a new job. May I introduce. Chris Bacon, barman extraordinaire," he said with a theatrical bow.

Nate smiled back and inclined his head. "Congratulations. Now I'd like to do your final vitals before you gallop off into the sunset."

Scowling, Chris sat down at the table. "Do all you white coat types have OCD as far as stethoscopes and blood pressure cuffs are concerned?" He held his arms out like a zombie. "Must check blood pressure," he said in a monotone.

"Yes we do, now stick your arm out," he said as he went to rummage in the ever present black bag.

Rolling his eyes, Chris complied. After Nate had blown his arm up and listened to his chest, he got out the chart he and Sarah had set up and started scribbling on it.

"Well, am I going to make it doc?" he asked as he put the back of his hand to his forehead and pretended to swoon.

Shaking his head, Nate put his things back in his bag. "Yep, you're going to make it. But–" Chris rolled his eyes as Nate continued. "It probably won't all be plain sailing. You're far better off than most people that fall for drugs, because you didn't choose it and you have a good support network around you, including me." Nate put his pen down and gave Chris a serious look.

"At some point, you will be tempted; it's inevitable. I'm on the other end of the phone, any time, day or night. Phone me; I mean it. Hopefully before you do something you might regret, but don't ever worry about talking to me if you think things have gone completely tits up. People fuck up all the time, nothing is too bad that it can't be worked on. I'm here for you, always will be."

Chris shifted uncomfortably, he'd started the day full of optimism. Now he felt as if he was teetering on the edge of an abyss, with everyone watching and waiting for him to fall. He wondered if this was what floated Nate's boat, constantly hoping to catch someone falling and picking them up when they did.

"Do you hear me, Chris?"

He looked up into the earnest, do-gooder face and nodded. "Yeah, I hear you, not that it's ever going to happen. If I was going to be an addict, I would've taken up the habit when I was surrounded by it as a kid."

Nate's condescending raised eyebrows had his anger boiling.

"You've only just turned eighteen, and although I think you're a great guy, you're not exactly the most together person in the world."

"So you're saying that if I'm prepared to fuck up it'll be easier when I do? I'm not an addict. I'm not like them, never have been, never will be. When Jase wakes up, and please don't wake him because he did too much on that ankle last night, tell him I'm at the flat."

"You haven't got any keys; you'll be stuck on the doorstep."

Chris smiled coldly at him. "I might not have fallen into drug taking as a kid, but I learned a few other things. Remember your desk? Believe me, I won't be on the doorstep."

He took the stairs to burn off a little of his angry energy. To his surprise, Nate wasn't waiting by the lift doors when he got to the bottom. Maybe he did trust him a little after all. Now he just had to trust himself. *Going out on your own is not a big deal. Stop being a wimp and just do it.*

As he stepped out into the early morning sunshine, there was a brief moment of panic and he had to stop himself from retreating back inside. Taking a deep breath, he forced himself to look around. The only people about were a couple of street cleaners and a lorry driver unloading at the front of one of the other shops. Breaking into a jog, he headed towards the outskirts of town where Kate's old flat was located.

It took about fifteen minutes to get to the small parade of shops. Despite his boast to Nate, without a set of picks, opening the door wasn't going to be easy. Instead of sitting on the cast iron steps at the back of the parade and waiting for Jase to turn up, he decided to run the extra mile to the nursing home and pick up a key from Kate, if she was there. He'd visit his dad while he was there too. His poor bewildered parent would either not realise he'd been away, or would have forgotten him completely.

The genuine smile on Kate's face as she unlocked the main door of the nursing home for him was touching.

"Great to see you. Have you come to pick up the keys?" She frowned. "Actually, how did you know I was on an early today? I only found out Linda was off sick last night."

He gave her his best sunny smile. "I didn't; I just felt like touching base with the old man."

She glanced behind him. "You're here on your own?"

He scowled at her. "Contrary to popular belief, I'm a big boy now. I can actually go out without a real grown-up holding my toddler reins. Is he up yet?"

"Does anyone know you're here?"

"Again with the 'big boy now'. I'll meet Jase at the flat later. Now, are you going to let me see my father or not?"

"He's in the dining room," she said still not looking happy. If he'd had it, Chris would have bet a thousand quid that she'd be on the phone to Jase as soon as his back was turned.

Chris located his father sitting with two other old fossils at a table near the window. He pulled up a seat. The other old man at the table didn't even acknowledge he existed, the old lady gave him a vacant, toothless smile. His father frowned at him.

"Where the hell have you been?"

"I was kidnapped by people traffickers to force Matt to carry immigrants across the channel hidden in his lorries," Chris told him the truth on a whim. To his joy, his father looked quite perturbed.

"You alright now?"

"Yeah, pops, I'm getting there. Matt did what they said and they let me go after a couple of weeks."

His father reached out a gnarled and veiny hand and patted his arm. "It's good to see my boys caring for each other after all these years."

Chris's jaw nearly hit the floor and tears prickled at his eyes. "You know?" he managed to say.

His father gave him a wry smile. "I do today; tomorrow, who knows? You look like your mother. How is she?"

He felt a tear trail down his face. "She died, four years ago."

His father patted his hand again. "Those drugs again was it? It was why I asked her to leave; I couldn't have that around Mathew. She didn't tell me she was pregnant until after you were born, I tried to find you several times, but your mum moved so often, I never could. I'm sorry that I let you down, son."

Chris was on his knees, hugging his father a moment later. After a few minutes, his dad patted his shoulder.

"Up you get boy, otherwise you'll leave a wet patch on my shirt. The nurses will think I've started dribbling like Edith."

Chris choked out a half-laugh and wiped his face as he sat back in the chair. His dad smiled at him. "Now then, how's your mother? I haven't seen her for years, naughty little thing she was, if you get my drift," he said and winked.

The sense of loss was deep, but at least he'd found out his father had indeed looked for him, had cared.

"She's fine, still having fun."

The old man nodded and smiled to himself. "She did like to have fun, my wife."

At that moment, Kate came over with plates of food. "Everything alright? I've got to help Mrs Collins and Mr Henderson with their breakfast now, but you're welcome to stay."

"Nah, I'd better get off. Jase will have a fit if I'm not at the flat when he gets there."

Kate winced in apology. "Sorry. I, erm..."

"Phoned him to say I'm here? Don't worry about it; I suppose paranoia is going to follow me around for a while. You care, I get it."

He stood up and Kate enveloped him in a hug. She was just about the same height as him, but those inbuilt airbags meant that they couldn't get too close.

"You have no idea how much they went through when you were... I don't think either Matt or Jason slept more than five hours in one go for the entire time. Those nightly videos killed both of them."

Chris pulled back to stare at her in confusion. "They sent video every night?"

"Mostly it was you getting injected and when you stopped fighting...Well it wasn't easy to watch."

A little voice at the back of Chris's mind said it was probably far easier to have been the one getting the injections than watching it happen to someone you cared about. To be honest, he didn't remember a great deal about any of it.

Kate sniffed and patted his shoulder. "Well off you go then, he's outside waiting."

CHAPTER 30

Chris

Feeling more than a little shell-shocked, Chris made his way outside. Jase was leaning up against a somewhat battered silver fiesta. He looked pissed off and bloody hot, then again, even covered in mud in the middle of the arctic, Jase would deserve the name 'Eddie Bull'.

Walking straight over, he moulded himself to Jase's chest, wrapping his arms around him. Jase reciprocated immediately and held him just as firmly.

"Hey, hey, what's up?"

"I'm sorry," he murmured into the neck that smelled of safety, acceptance and one hundred percent Jase.

"What for? You came to visit your dad; that's nothing to apologise for," Jase said against his hair as he continued to hold him.

"I should have told you I was coming here and I'm sorry that you had to watch those videos every night. I can't imagine how crappy that was."

"Kate?" Jase asked and Chris nodded. "It's behind us now. And how could you have told me? You didn't have your phone."

"I haven't got a…" he started then paused as Jase reached behind him. Untangling himself from Jase he saw him holding out a small box.

"You have now." Chris looked at it, then up at Jase in stunned silence.

"Don't tell me you're not happy about accepting presents? Because that's going to be a bit of a problem."

For the second time that morning, he felt tears prickling his eyes and pressed forward into Jase's arms again. After a few moments of being silently held, he pulled back and wiped at his eyes with a wry chuckled.

"I'm not doing much to dispel the idea that gays are crybabies am I?"

"It's only a 5530, now if it'd been an iPhone, I could understand the waterworks, but–"

"My dad knows who I am. He said he looked for me for years, but because we moved around so much… Then he forgot again. I feel like a bloody yo-yo, and it's getting boring. And if there's one thing I hate, it's being bored and boring."

Jase gave him a one armed hug, and steered him towards the passenger door. "In that case, shall we go sort this flat out? I've commandeered Matt's transit. Mum and Dad are supervising Mike and Stuart loading it up with a few bits and pieces. They'll meet us over there in about half an hour."

Five minutes later, they pulled into the distinctly seedy car park at the back of the small parade of shops on the outskirts of town. It served the local residents with small, everyday items that they didn't want to go into the main town to purchase. There was a post office, a dry cleaners, a chemist, an 'open all hours' convenience store and the Kebab/pizza house that was underneath their new home.

Chris took the key from Jase and bounced up the stairs two at a time. He let himself into the slightly musty flat and looked around. Compared to Nate's place, it was tiny. The living/kitchen room could have fitted into Nate's kitchen with room to spare. There was a baggy, much used tan leather sofa, a single black fabric armchair, a TV on a wooden corner unit and a faded, pale blue carpet. The kitchen counter had three stools in front of it, but there wasn't a table, probably because there wasn't room.

Wandering through the property, he had to smile at the camouflage themed smaller bedroom, now devoid of anything but a 'road' play carpet, a small child's bed and a battered wardrobe covered in stickers. The main bedroom was…lilac. He'd never taken Kate for an ultra-feminine type but the evidence was staring him in the face. Complete with delicate floral wallpaper. It made him shudder, more than a little.

The creak of the front door showed that Jase had finally made it up the stairs. Chris made the epic trip, all five feet of corridor, back into the living/kitchen room. Seeing Jase looking around himself with a less than enthusiastic expression, Chris vaulted over the back of the sofa and landed in a prone position. He grabbed the TV remote sitting on the arm of the sofa.

"Looks like they decorated for us already. Guess which room's yours?"

Jase didn't move from his position by the door. "I just luurv lilac," Jase said in an effeminate voice that had Chris turning to look at him so quickly he nearly gave himself whiplash.

"Shut your mouth; you'll be catching flies in a minute," Jase said, a smirk on those delicious lips. Chris did so.

"Actually, I thought it might be more practical to share the big room, after we redecorate it, and turn Ryan's old room into a study/art room for you. That way I won't be constantly tripping over easels, paint and all the other shit you artistic types leave around."

Chris stood up and walked over to Jase, trying to look 'superior'. "I'll have you know, I'm very tidy with my things, especially my art supplies. An artist always looks after his tools." As he said 'tools' he palmed the front of Jase's combats, causing him to jerk a little. Then he leaned in for a kiss. Hopefully they'd be able to christen every room in the flat by the end of the day.

"Fuck, Tigger, put him down will you?" Mike's voice came from the open door behind Jase.

"Drat, foiled again," Chris whispered against Jase's currently smooth cheek, before giving him a quick peck.

"Where do you want this?" Stuart's voice came from behind them as Chris pulled away.

Jase pointed to the kitchen counter, and the brown-eyed, brown-haired, six-foot-tall, ex-soldier walked over and deposited the brown cardboard box. When he turned back, to Chris's surprise, he found himself enveloped in a hug.

"Good to see you; you had us all worried," Stuart whispered against his hair.

Chris hugged him back briefly, then had a horrible thought. "You haven't seen the..." he trailed off. The thought of any of this lot seeing that damn DVD, was mortifying.

A familiar hand landed on his shoulder. "They saw some of the nightly videos, but by no means everything. Matt thought it was important to get the drivers on board as it was them bringing the people across the channel."

The look Jase gave him said he didn't have to worry.

"So you saw the erm..." he mimed injecting his arm.

"And the beating," the heavily tattooed Mike added as he came through the door with another box. "And if I ever see one of those bastards—"

"You'll get in line behind the rest of us," Stuart interrupted. "Although I doubt there'll be much to play with after Matt and Jase get through with them."

All this talk was bringing back memories he'd successfully buried for the last few hours. This was meant to be a new start, but if everyone here looked at him with pity every time they saw him, it might not work.

"And that's enough about that," Jase said firmly. Chris looked up, not realising he'd hunched his shoulders and was staring at the carpet. He gave his saviour a weak smile of thanks.

"Now, can you three bring up the rest of the stuff while I do something far more important and make the tea?"

Chris snapped to attention and saluted. "Yes Sir, Sergeant Sir." He had to admit that Stuart and Mike did a far better job at saluting than he did, but when Jase also straightened into 'attention' and saluted back, his dick became so instantly hard he almost groaned.

"You have got to do that for me later," he said out loud.

"Purleese. Can't you knock it off for more than a minute, Tigger?" Mike said and then paused as a pained expression appeared on his face. "And I've just got an image in my head about that nickname that means I will never, ever use it again."

Chris grinned. "Yeah, I'm Tigger." As the three made their way to the door, Chris bounced up and down, using their shoulders to get a little more height as he started to sing the 'Tigger' song that had entertained him as a child. The DVD had been one of the few things that had always moved from place to place with them. Along with the cuddly Tigger toy that had always shared whatever bed, sofa or floor he'd slept on.

"A wonderful thing is a Tigger, a Tigger's a wonderful thing. Their tops are made out of rubber, their bottoms are made out of springs. They're bouncy, bouncy, bouncy, bouncy, fun, fun, fun, fun, fun. The most wonderful thing about Tiggers is, that I'm... the only one." He grinned as both men rolled their eyes then he started from the beginning again.

As they got to the end of the balcony, Mike clapped his hands over his ears. "Somebody please make it stop," but he had a smile on his face.

He wasn't sure what he was expecting when they got to the van, but it certainly wasn't boxes of new stuff. There was quite a lot of flat-pack furniture and black bin liners of clothes, a few of which were his.

"What's all this lot? Jase hasn't bought the entire contents of Ikea has he?" Chris asked Stuart, as Mike, the more musclebound of the pair, simply grabbed a large box as if it was filled with tissue paper and started back up the stairs.

"We all chipped in. Because, you irritating little shit, we want you to stick around, although god knows why when you're so fucking annoying."

Without hesitation, Chris jumped up into Stuart's very surprised arms and wrapped his arms and legs around him. He wanted to kiss him too, but from the look on Stuart's face, that would probably be a step too far. He settled for a hug instead, then moved his head back until he could see Stuart's red face.

"Awkward?" he asked with a grin.

"Just a bit," Stuart said. Just to annoy him a little more, Chris stayed exactly where he was for a few more seconds as he watched Stuart's face get progressively redder.

"Hey, put him down; you're here to hump furniture, not my boyfriend," Jase called down from the balcony.

Stuart firmly pulled Chris off himself. "You are going to get me into trouble," he announced stiffly.

"I can't get you into trouble," Chris said with a grin. "Firstly, unless you've got a torch in your pocket, you're a bloke. Secondly, I've never been that good with pussy. Although I did try it once, there was this bi dude and..."

Stuart held up his hand, "Spare me the details, please, for fuck's sake, spare me the details." Reaching into the van, he picked up a bin liner of clothes and threw it at him.

Chris caught it, but did stagger back a step. "Hey, watch it, I'm delicate."

"Delicate my ars–" Stuart started then changed what he was about to say. "Never mind."

"Aw, Stuwie, were you going to say 'arse' because that's one of my..."

With a groan, Stuart grabbed a box and walked away.

Grinning to himself, instead of following Stuart up the stairs, he walked along the back of the next two shops till he was underneath where Jase stood leaning over the balcony.

"Catch, Eeyore," he called up before he crouched slightly to get a bit of momentum going and chucked the bag up to Jase.

"Eeyore?" Jase asked as he deftly caught the bag.

"Unless you'd like to be Pooh, the bear of very little brain, or Rabbit, the boring stuck-up one. Although thinking about it, that might be–" He grunted slightly as the bag landed back on his chest, making him take a step back.

"Play nice, or I'll have to think of some ways to get the bounce out of Tigger."

"Don't make promises you can't keep, Sarge," Chris called as he lobbed the bag back up.

"Bring the next bag up with you, tea's ready, and I bet you haven't eaten anything today yet, have you?"

Muttering "Yes sir, no sir, three bags full sir," he went back to the van and picked up the next couple of bags of clothing.

When he got up to the flat, Mike and Stuart were slurping tea and munching chocolate digestives that had been in the first box that was brought up.

"So what do you think, Tigger? Eeyore, Rabbit or Pooh for Jason?" Mike asked.

Chris's tea went down the wrong way, and he started coughing. Mike was the last person he expected to start making gay innuendo jokes. Jase smacked him on the back.

Mike's innocent, confused face, followed by his, "What did I say?" sent him swiftly back to the land of hysterical laughter.

Jase's lips were twitching as Stuart rolled his eyes and started to explain. "Mate, they're gay. Calling Jase 'Pooh' is a little too close for comfort, don't you think?"

Mike's face turned an immediate shade of deep red.

"What the fuck?" he jabbed a finger in Chris's direction. "You've got to have the dirtiest mind I've ever come across."

Sometimes Chris wished he wasn't so impulsive, but now wasn't one of them. "Sorry," he said. But couldn't stop the laughter bubbling up again as he finished, "It was a joke, not a dick, don't take it so hard."

Jase lost the battle with laughter, as did Stuart, and in the end, Mike chuckled too after punching Stuart on the arm.

The day carried on in much the same way, with all of them working to get the flat ready for habitation. Chris did his best to make it as fun as possible. At least it kept his mind off the fact that all these people, some of which he didn't actually know very well, had all chipped in their time and apparently money, to make him a home. It was more than a little overwhelming.

As he came back into the flat after helping Mike carry Ryan's old single bed down to the van for disposal, he found Jase on his knees in the small bedroom, about to take up the road carpet.

"Does Ryan want that?" he asked.

"He's got the old spare room at Matt's; it's bigger than this so they're going to get him a new one."

"Can I keep it?"

Jase knelt upright from being on all fours. "Seriously? You want a kiddie carpet in your study?"

Chris shrugged, "Why not? It'll give me ideas, you know, people, places, different lives."

Jase nodded thoughtfully. "I don't suppose some model cars, not toys of course, would help with this quest for inspiration?"

Chris grinned. "Busted?"

"Well and truly."

Chris fetched them all huge kebabs from the shop underneath the flat at lunch time with his wages and supplied them with copious amounts of tea as they argued into the afternoon about putting the flat-packed chests of drawers and wardrobes together.

Matt, Kate and Ryan turned up at around five, just as Mike, Stuart and Jase were getting to screaming point with the second flat packed bedside table as a part had been left out.

"I brought cars," Ryan announced as he held up his Thomas the Tank Engine back pack.

"Cool. Let's leave these boring grown-ups to play with their construction toys and make the biggest traffic jam we can."

An hour later, he was still sitting on the floor of the small bedroom, drawing yet another bus to make up the numbers. He'd already drawn about thirty vehicles from bicycles and motorbikes to the Batmobile and several Kemp International lorries. Each had been roughly torn out while Ryan babbled away about what was happening in his imaginary world.

A knock at the door had them both looking up. "Shall we let them in, or shall we hide?" Chris whispered.

Ryan's face screwed up and his little hands turned into fists. "Always tell my mummy and my new daddy where you are. They got really worried and sad when you went on holiday and didn't tell them. Uncle Jason even had some of his army friends looking for you. They were at the house for days and I couldn't go out to play."

Keeping the smile on his face took considerable effort. "I'll tell you what, I'll try as hard as I can to be good, if you do the same. If I'm good, you can come over and play cars again. If you're good, I'll come and draw some cars on your new bedroom wall for you."

The door opened slowly and Matt poked his head around it, but as he was behind Ryan, the boy didn't see him.

"Can I have dragons instead? I like cars and lorries, but I think Daddy likes them more."

Chris grinned. "I think you might be right. You have a think about what you'd like and we'll sort something out, ok?"

Ryan got up and gave him a hug. "I'm glad you came back, Uncle Chris."

Looking up at his brother, he held Ryan close. "I'm glad I came back too. Now off you go before we both get in trouble with your mum."

He let the little boy go and they started to put his toys back in his rucksack. Matt knelt down and lent a hand.

"What about the paper cars? They'll get all crinkly," Ryan said.

"Don't worry, I'll do you some new ones next time," Chris reassured him.

"Tell you what, put them in the front pocket and I'll take them to work and laminate them, then they'll stay uncrinkly forever," Matt said.

"Yay," Ryan cheered and jumped to his feet.

"Dinner on Saturday?" Matt asked as he guided Ryan towards the door.

"Love to," Chris replied. "And Matt? Thanks."

His brother smiled. "Hey, we're family, it's what we do."

When he walked into the living area, Kate was saying goodbye to Jase. "I've left you two a lasagne in the fridge. Believe me, you don't want to be eating out of that kebab house too often. See you Saturday." She wiggled her fingers at him, and after giving Jase a quick hug, followed her husband and son out.

*　*　*

Later that night, full of homemade lasagne and in the first place he had ever really been able to call his own, Chris lay curled up on the sofa. He was lying in-between Jase's legs, his shoulder tucked up against his balls, his head resting on his lower belly. There was an action film on the TV, but Chris wasn't watching. Instead, he was enjoying Jase playing with his hair, wrapping one short curl around his fingers after another.

He'd had sex with too many people to count, but he'd never done this with anyone he'd had sex with. The only person he'd shared something like this with had been his mum. And even then, most of the time she'd been high as a kite and it had been him holding her, trying to keep her safe, not the other way around.

Yes, Jase was a touch controlling, but he needed that, even though it was uncomfortable to admit. Jase made him feel worthwhile, loved and cared for, and not just because it was his job, what it said on a birth certificate or because he wanted to fuck him, even if he did. And even on that subject Jase was waiting for him to be ready, because he cared more about him than his own pleasure.

Well this time, it was going to be Jase getting as much pleasure as Chris could produce. He started to rub his cheek on Jase's groin and felt his dick start to swell beneath him. Shuffling around, he moved his hand up so he could undo his Jase's fly and release his hardening cock. As he took him in his mouth, Jase sighed in contentment.

Taking it slow, he breathed in Jase's scent, committing it to memory as he traced the large vein on the underside of his shaft with his tongue. He alternated between licking, kissing, flicking the head with his tongue and taking him deep. When Jase's hand on the back of his head started to exert a little more pressure, he tugged on Jase's trousers and they both stood and undressed.

As soon as they were both naked, Jase pulled him in for a passionate kiss. He broke off to pepper small bites on the side of Chris's neck as he squeezed his arse with both hands.

"Christ Almighty, Chris, how did you get to be so damn fuckable?"

"Sit down," Chris ordered breathlessly.

"I thought we were going to the bedroom?"

"Oh we will, and we'll be doing every other surface in this place too, but right now, I want to show you a far better reason to call me Tigger."

Jase looked confused, which made Chris grin. "Bouncy, bouncy, remember?"

"It's too soon–" Jase started but Chris gave him a hard push so he landed on the sofa, then climbed up to straddle his lap.

Reaching down, he took both their dicks in one hand and started to rub them together as he leaned forward and kissed Jase gently.

"It's my hole, not yours. I'll control things and I promise to stop if it hurts too much, but I think if I don't get you inside me soon, I'm going to explode and not in a good way."

"Lube, no arguments."

Chris grinned and hopped off the sofa, "Where is it?"

"My holdall, in the bedroom."

Chris grinned as he found the extra-large pump action bottle of 'Backdoor slide and glide.' He held it up as he walked back into the living room. Jase had moved so he was now reclining against the arm of the sofa.

"Too soon is it? So why are you packing a porn star size bottle of lube?"

Jase's answering wolfish grin made his knees go fuzzy. "I was a boy scout. I always try to be prepared. Get your sexy self over here."

After covering himself with a more than generous amount of lube, he handed the bottle to Jase and started to turn around because that was what he usually did.

"No. I want to see the look on your face as I fill you up."

Facing his partner was a rarity, most guys didn't care about his face, they just wanted his body, but Jase wasn't most guys. And this mattered, it mattered a lot. Would Jase be put off by his experience? Should he pretend he didn't know as much as he did?

As instructed, he slowly straddled Jase as he watched him slick himself up as his mind continued to whirl about how he should approach this.

Closing his eyes, he started to reach behind him, when he felt Jase's hand cup his face.

"Stop thinking; just do what feels right. If you don't want to do this yet, or ever for that matter, that's fine. It's you I want, not just your body. Although, I have to admit, it's a pretty bloody big bonus."

Not wanting to be talked out of this, Chris positioned Jase and pushed down onto him. Jase wasn't Russel, but he wasn't tiny either. Even with the numbing magic arse cream he'd used earlier and the lube, it hurt, but not nearly as much as he'd feared.

A hand gripped his thigh, "Stop, that's hurting."

"No, it's good, I promise. You probably think it's weird, but a little pain, not a lot mind you, makes it better; it stops my head spinning quite so fast. Can I move now, please?"

"You are seriously odd, but if that's what you want, I–"

Chris didn't wait for him to finish, instead he pushed down sharply until his butt cheeks hit Jase's thighs. He hardly heard Jase's 'ah fuck' of pleasure as he concentrated on the breathtakingly intense burn. Before it faded, he started to move back up, he was slow for only the first few seconds, before he started bouncing up and down.

He opened his eyes to see Jase watching him with profound lust in his heavy lidded eyes. Leaning over he went in for a quick kiss, which was all he usually managed to steal during sex as the majority of his partners were focused on getting off, not tenderness. Instead, a hand on the back of his head stopped him pulling away, and the kiss turned into a long, languid exploration.

When he pulled back, the urgency, the buzz had vanished, to be replaced by an emotion he didn't associate with sex, deep affection, maybe even the 'L' word.

"We've got all night, there's no rush, there's nowhere either of us has to be, no one's going to knock on the door and disturb us."

Chris opened and closed his mouth, but didn't say anything. A finger stroked down his face.

"Tell me," Jase said softly.

"I erm... I don't know how to do slow," he said, but this wasn't about the speed of their coupling.

Jase looked down to where their bodies were joined. "It doesn't look like you're enjoying fast too much either."

Chris didn't have to look to know he'd lost his erection. Sex was meant to be his thing, and he'd failed to meet Jase's expectations on two of the three times they'd been intimate. 'Defensive' was too mild a word for what he was feeling.

"Aren't I allowed to concentrate on you? Don't you think seeing and feeling you enjoy me is good? Shit." He pulled off with a wince, as the moment had gone. Leaving Jase on the sofa, he headed for the bedroom.

Why did Jase have to spoil things? He would've come at some point tonight; what did it matter if it was after Jase, or if one of them had more orgasms than the other? He was one hundred percent certain it wouldn't have bothered Jase if this was happening the other way around. Why did Jase get to be the selfless one?

His immediate impulse was to get dressed and go for a run, maybe to the club to lose himself on the dance floor. Knowing Jase, even if he did manage to leave the flat, he'd track him down like a bloody bloodhound, worried that he'd hook up with some stranger. Jase didn't trust him with other men; hell he didn't even trust him to construct flat pack furniture or tie his own shoelaces. He wouldn't be surprised if he got reminded to brush his teeth, eat his greens and currently, put cream on his arse.

He'd looked after himself, hell he'd looked after his mother and half her druggy friends since he'd been five years old. He wasn't a fucking child. The overwhelming urge was to punch the wall, scream and shout, but none of those options would help the situation. If he carried on acting irresponsibly, that's how Jase and everyone else would continue to treat him, but the walls were closing in. He wanted to calm down, needed to calm down, but he had no idea how to do it within the confines of the flat.

Going to the window, he peeked through the curtains and watched a group of laughing teenagers coming out of the kebab shop below. A boy had his arm around a girl's waist, and he gave her a peck on the cheek before handing over an open packet of chips. One of the blokes shook up a can of drink and opened it in the direction of another; a chase ensued. Nobody was angry, it was just teens larking about, having fun, enjoying a normal night. Their lives probably consisted of school, dating, homework, maybe a Saturday job and arguments about staying out too late with their parents. He felt old, and bloody envious.

He felt more than heard Jase move up behind him. The words 'I'm sorry' fell from his lips automatically.

Jase's lips caressed his shoulder and he felt material up against his naked butt. Jase had dressed again. It sent the clear message that he didn't want to be intimate with him. Of all the many things he was crap at, he'd assumed sex wasn't one of them. He'd been wrong.

"What are you sorry for?"

He didn't answer, because saying he was a fuck-up who couldn't even get sex right would only make Jase start on yet another 'you're worth it' pep talk.

That maddeningly calm and controlled voice came again. "What do you want to do, right now?"

I want to run till I fall down. I want to dance till I'm dizzy. I want to get fucked out of my tiny stupid mind by some built, random stranger. I want to get so pissed I can't stand up and I really, really want a fix so all this goes away.

He didn't say any of those things. He hoped he wouldn't do any of them either because that would hurt people who, for some unknown reason, cared about him.

After all the years spent wanting someone to truly care about him, rather than the contents of a syringe, now that he had it, he couldn't handle it. Nate had been right, he was an addict waiting to happen, because right now, sinking back into the happy oblivion that he'd experienced in Dimitar's cupboard would be just dandy.

Jase turned him around, but he resolutely refused to look at him. Even when he wrapped him in his arms, Chris held himself stiffly.

"I knew it was too soon. I shouldn't have listened to Nate."

Great, the grown-ups sat down and had a cosy little chat about my sex life.

"How about we take things down a notch? Come on, let's get some sleep, I'm sure things will look better in the morning. Besides, you've got an appointment at the college at ten. Do you want a sleeping pill? Sarah left another prescription with Nate. It's in the bathroom cabinet."

Wordlessly, Chris pulled away and went to the small bathroom opposite Ryan's old bedroom in the middle of the rectangular flat. As promised, there was a small white plastic pot with his name, his real name on it. He'd always found it somewhat ironic that a kid with dyslexia ended up with such a long name. Chris Bacon was easier to be and easier to spell than Chrisander Baccioni.

Picking up the pot, he sat on the side of the bath and opened it. There must have been over thirty smooth and probably sugar coated pills in it. Each and every one was designed to send him into a dreamless, restful sleep. If he took the lot, he wouldn't have to worry about sleep ever again, he wouldn't have to worry about anything ever again. Had his mum felt like this before she'd taken that final dose, or had it been an accident as the social worker had told him?

The expression on Ryan's face this afternoon, as he'd told him off for upsetting Kate and Matt came back to him. He couldn't do that to the kid, couldn't cause the cycle to repeat again and again. Maybe his mum had experienced something similar as a child; she'd certainly never spoken about her childhood.

Carefully, he up-ended the pot down the toilet and left them sitting in the bowl. Knowing his luck, if he did flush them, Jase would call an ambulance and he'd end up getting his stomached pumped, no matter what he said.

Instead of going back to the bedroom and Jase, he went to Ryan's old room with the intention of doing some designs for a mural for Ryan's new bedroom.

CHAPTER 31

Jase

Why can I never say the right thing? Jase asked himself as a naked, silent Chris walked away from him yet again. What the hell had possessed me to criticise, to correct, hell to decide on Chris's behalf what he should want? And now I've told him to go drug himself because he was upset. Way to go numbnuts. He's just getting over heroin withdrawal, and you just told him taking drugs is the answer to his problems.

He half expected to hear the front door open as Chris ran from him again and to be honest, he wouldn't have blamed him. Telling him that he didn't need to take a pill was the first step. The bathroom door was open. When he saw the empty pot on the side, his heart lurched.

"Chris!" he shouted and ran into the living room.

"In here," a resigned voice called from the second bedroom.

Chris looked totally relaxed, sitting cross-legged on the floor, still naked, with a pad covering his groin.

"Stay calm, I'll call an ambulance," he said, then realised his phone was in the living room. "Don't move," he said, holding hand up, as if Chris was a dog that would obey hand signals.

"For fuck's sake, you twat, I didn't take them. If you look in the bog you'll see I dumped them in there. I didn't like taking sleeping pills before, and I don't like taking them now."

Chris looked back down at his pad of paper and started sketching again, in the light from the open door. Jase moved to the side as he was blocking most of the light.

"You must be cold, I'll get you–"

With a sigh, Chris looked up again. "I'm fine. If I wanted something, I would have got it. I don't need wrapping up in cotton wool. I'm small, I get that, and I might even look younger than I am, but I've been looking after myself since I was five. Were you getting your own meals and making sure your parent ate every day at that age? Were you shoplifting food and housebreaking at eight? Was living with prostitutes, addicts and dealers normal for you? Well it was for me and although it wasn't always great, it wasn't always crap either."

Sitting down beside him, Jase kept two feet of distance between them so he that he didn't appear too intimidating. "I want to know all about it, all about you, and I promise I won't judge you or your mum. Now, for my sake, not yours, can you please put something on before I forget I'm not meant to be touching you?"

Chris scowled. "And who the fuck gave you the right to make that decision for me?"

To his surprise, instead of shrinking away, Chris put his pad down and swivelled around to face him.

"So what if I don't prefer 'slow and tender' like you do? It doesn't make me wrong, and even if it does, I really don't give a shit. You said I could still stay here even if we aren't sleeping together. So if the way I do it pisses you off so much, I'll sleep in here."

"But you don't sleep well on your own," Jase blurted out and immediately regretted it as Chris's eyes narrowed.

"I'll cope. And I'll tell you one thing for free, if I find out you're drugging my food like Matt did, I swear I'm out of here. I've got options."

"What options?" Jase couldn't help asking, as jealousy surged.

"I'm sure several of the guys at the club will put me up if I ask. Harry for one, probably Steve too and I've got a standing invitation to use to sofa in Russel's office."

"And you'll pay for your accommodation by letting them fuck you?"

Chris got to his feet, every fibre of his body radiating frustration. "Can't you get it through your thick squaddie head? I like getting fucked and the harder the better. I enjoy turning a powerful guy on so much that he forgets what he should be doing, what's right and what's wrong according to, who the fuck knows." He almost shouted as he waved his hands in the air.

Jase got to his feet, now certain about what he needed to do. "So if I asked you right now, if you'd share my bed tonight, you'd say no?"

Chris's dark eyes flashed. "Hell yes I'd say no. I'm not a fucking charity case, I–" was as far as he got before Jase pushed him sharply up against the wall and silenced him with his mouth.

When Chris immediately pushed against his chest, he grabbed both his wrists in one hand and pinned them above his head as he grabbed his butt with the other.

"This is mine, nobody else's," he growled against his mouth, then moved to bite at the tender skin of his throat. All the tension went out of Chris as he moaned and lifted his chin to give him better access.

Less than a minute later, he felt Chris's erection pressing against his thigh. Letting go of his wrists, he pushed on his shoulders. "Suck me like you mean it. If you do a good enough job, I might fuck you." Personally he thought he was laying it on way too thick, but the speed at which Chris's knees hit the floor and pulled down his sweatpants proved otherwise.

Then that hot, urgent mouth closed around him, and he didn't care anymore. Grasping the soft curls he obsessed over, he moved Chris on himself, setting a fast rhythm that made Chris gag a little. He nearly let go of his hair, but after taking a quick breath, Chris engulfed him again.

When he found himself thrusting into his mouth, chasing his own climax, he pulled him away. Breathless and bright-eyed, Chris looked up at him.

"Get on the bed," he ordered. Chris scrambled to comply.

His heart started to pound at the sight that met his eyes when he stalked into the bedroom having taken his sweatpants off. Chris was on his elbows and knees on the centre of the bed, looking back over his shoulder at him.

"Is this ok? Cos I can—"

"Did I ask you a question?" he said, channelling the sergeant major from his training days.

"No, but—"

"That's Sir, or Sarge to you, Private," Jase said in his official voice. It produced the most beautiful beaming smile he'd ever seen.

"Are you grinning at me, Private?" he asked, trying his best to retain his scowl.

"Yes, I mean no, Sarge," Chris said as he failed epically at wiping the grin off his face.

"I think I need to teach you how to respect your senior officers, Private."

Chris waggled his backside at him, so Jase smacked one cheek hard enough to leave a handprint. For a second, he thought he'd gone too far as Chris pulled in a sharp breath, but he didn't get up, in fact, he dropped his forehead to the mattress and widened his stance. If anything, Jase got harder, then he remembered the lube was still in the living room.

"Do. Not. Move," he instructed, and although Chris's body was almost vibrating with need, he froze.

The haste with which Jase galloped back into the living room and located the tube of lube from beside the sofa didn't fit the persona he'd created, but he didn't care.

Back in the bedroom, he swiftly slicked himself up, then added a more than generous amount to Chris's hole. It was the first time he'd seen it. Happily, it didn't seem to have suffered any damage from Chris's earlier enthusiasm, although it was a little redder than what he considered normal. Taking his time, to kiss and caress, to stroke and fondle, would have been his choice, but right now that wasn't what Chris wanted, what he needed. Maybe when he was a little more settled, a little more confident and trusting, hell a little more rational, things could change. In the meantime, it was better if it was him giving Chris what he craved, rather than anyone else, because unlike other people, he actually cared about him.

Chris let out a breathy little moan of pain as he pushed slowly inside. He immediately froze.

"Please, don't spoil it," Chris said in a tight voice.

"Are you telling me what to do, Private?" Jase snapped.

"No, no Sarge."

"Well just take it then," Jase tried to keep his voice angry, but to be honest, he was grateful that he'd finally found a way to shut Chris down, at least in one situation anyway.

As he slowly pushed in deeper, giving Chris's body ample time to adjust, Chris relaxed as he surrendered himself entirely. Jase started to thrust slowly, but the contact only between their thighs and groins wasn't enough. Pulling out, he pushed Chris roughly onto his back, thrust his thighs up and apart and eased back in. Grabbing one of his ankles, he pulled it around his waist. Chris immediately followed his lead, clinging to him with both arms and legs as Jase took his mouth.

Compared to when Chris had been riding him, there wasn't a great deal of movement, maybe only an inch or so, but when Chris gasped into his mouth, he knew he'd hit the right spot. Concentrating, he jackhammered as fast and as hard as he could. Chris's dick was like an iron bar between them, and he was doing his best to get some friction going between them by tilting his pelvis up and down without disturbing Jase's rhythm.

He pulled back just enough to see the expression on Chris's face as he put all his weight on one arm and forced his other between their bodies to grasp Chris's weeping cock.

"Ah fuck, shit, I'm..." Chris gasped before he convulsed underneath him, hot cum spurted into his hand and between their bodies. When Chris relaxed, he opened heavy lidded eyes and looked up at him.

"Do it, fill me up; I need to feel it." Jase had never heard anything sexier in his life. He pulled back, hooked Chris's ankles over his shoulders, and started thrusting again, but this time he was nearly withdrawing all the way before slamming back in. The increased friction along his length, and the smell, the sight, and feel of Chris beneath him had his balls boiling and erupting in white hot bliss less than a minute later.

He came back to himself, his cheek leaning against Chris's damp temple a few moments later. "Fuck Chris, that was..." he paused unable to find a suitable adjective.

"Yeah, sleep now," Chris murmured, not bothering to open his eyes.

"Wash first, then sleep," Jase told him as he pulled out, even though he didn't particularly want to move either.

"Nah, it'll wake me up," Chris mumbled and rolled over on his side. His hand reached for a pillow and pulled it under his head. After he'd rubbed his cheek against it a couple of times, every muscle of his body relaxed into sleep.

Jase blinked in surprise, Chris hadn't been kidding about sex curing his insomnia. It was certainly a far more entertaining option than the pills currently lying at the bottom of the toilet bowl.

Gently, he pulled the quilt over him and went to wash. Chris might not care about waking up crusty, but it wasn't something he enjoyed.

CHAPTER 32

Chris

Sunlight was streaming through the gap in the curtains when Chris woke. The soft snore from right behind him made him grin. Last night had been bloody fantastic, eventually. He couldn't believe how Jase had fallen into the role play so easily, but he was damn glad he had. The way he'd taken charge, had taken all responsibility away from him, had been magic.

The euphoria lasted until he moved and the quilt cover stayed stuck to his belly. Ugh. knowing it wasn't a bright move, he lifted the quilt and sniffed. Good God Almighty, he stank to high heaven. Detaching himself from the quilt with a grimace, he slipped out of bed as quietly as possible and headed to the bathroom. There was a damp towel in the washing basket that hadn't been there last night. Jase must have showered sometime in the night, although his memory of what had happened after Jase had coated his insides was more than a little fuzzy. All he knew, was that thanks to Jase, he'd had a good, drug free, night's sleep.

Smiling to himself, he decided to make Jase breakfast after he got cleaned up. When he was dressed, he took a quick look in the fridge; shopping was required. To prevent Jase worrying, he got his pad and quickly sketched a stickman figure holding shopping bags and left it on the side. There wasn't a lot left in his pay-packet after he'd bought lunch for everyone yesterday, but this was important.

The bacon was just about ready by the time Jase wandered in, sniffing. He looked adorably rumpled, with stubble on his chin that Chris couldn't wait to feel against his own, now smooth again, skin. Then he realised that there was no reason to wait. Walking up to him, he wrapped his arms around his neck and pulled him down into a soft kiss.

"Mornin' sleepy head," he said and smiled against Jase's lips. He tried to move back, but Jase's arms snaked around his hips and pulled him back in for another kiss.

"Bacon?" he managed to ask against Jase's hungry lips.

"I'll have double, starting with you." A hand landed on his butt, and anther pushed through his hair. Chris decided that breakfast could wait.

With a groan, Jase pulled away. "What time is it?"

"Ten, why?"

"Crap, you've got an interview at the college in an hour. Go put something appropriate on while I finished breakfast."

With a sigh, Chris pulled away then jumped as a hand smacked his arse. "Emphasis on appropriate."

Once in the bedroom he opened the chest of drawers that still smelled of wood glue and looked at his range of t-shirts.

None of them looked 'appropriate'. The hotdog shirt had been lost when he was kidnapped. 'I'm so gay I fart rainbows' and 'I have no gag reflex' were probably out too. In the end he settled for a blue shirt with huge rainbow 'kissy' lips on it and his blue skinny jeans.

When he walked back into the kitchen/living room, Jase paused as he was putting the bacon sandwiches together.

"What? It's the least 'out' one I've got. Besides, this is an art college right? They expect odd. At least I'm not tattooed and pierced all over with green and pink hair," he said as he hopped up onto a stool.

"Do you want me to come in with you?"

"Will there be forms?" he replied as he leaned over to make sure the ketchup didn't drip onto his shirt.

"You can bet on it."

"In that case, one hundred percent, yes. You might also need to poke me if I start to say anything, you know, inappropriate. I don't have a good track record with teachers. Or social workers. Come to think of it, apart from you and Nate, I tend to piss off anyone with authority over me within the first five minutes of meeting them."

"You think I have authority over you?"

Chris smirked. "You have to ask after last night? Because that was just, wow." His grin got wider as Jase shifted uncomfortably on his stool.

Stuffing the rest of his sandwich into his mouth, he chewed and swallowed quickly, before noisily sucking his fingers clean, whilst staring into Jase's eyes.

"You shouldn't bolt your food, you'll get indigestion."

"Sarge, I can bolt anything down this throat, and you know it."

Jase groaned, leaned his elbows on the table and put his head in his hands.

"What am I going to do with you?" he asked then his head shot up. "And I do not want you to answer that. Just try to be polite to the college staff ok? If you get expelled, the next nearest one is half an hour away by train; you can walk to this one."

"So are we walking today?"

"Not a good idea for me yet, especially as I've got my first day at the bailiffs a week Monday."

"You sure you're up to working yet?"

"You sure you're up to college yet?"

Chris grinned. "Touché. I guess we both have to try right?"

"Yep. Those bills don't pay themselves."

Jase's comment made him feel distinctly uncomfortable. If he was at college, he couldn't possibly pay his way with this flat.

"Hey, stop it. And you will be paying your way, eventually. We're going to set up a website for your portraits and as well as you doing a few shifts at the club, we'll get there. I've got some savings, plus an army pension and this place isn't expensive."

Chris closed his eyes and snorted to himself, before looking over at a confused Jase. "Do you know what I thought you meant the first time you said I'd be paying my way?" Jase frowned as he carried on. "I thought you were going to pimp me out."

Jase looked as if he'd just found half a worm in his sandwich. "Not that I'm horribly offended that you'd think I'd do such a thing, but if that's the case, why did you agreed to live here?"

He shrugged. "It's a roof, but I'm bloody glad I got it wrong, especially after last night."

"What made the difference? I've never had complaints, but I don't think I'm that good in the sack."

"Don't you believe it," Chris said, getting up. This was getting way too close to serious.

Jase caught his wrist. "Talk to me. If I'm just a meal ticket, and at the moment I understand that, it won't change anything. I'm also not asking for a declaration of undying love; I just want to know if we're heading in the same direction."

Chris sighed and sat back down, looking at the crumbs on his plate. "Last night, you put yourself out for me, again. Just as you've done ever since we met, but I think what I feel is more than just appreciation for your help, and your very hot body."

His attempt at levity didn't work as Jase simply said, "Go on."

"As to what direction I'm going in, I haven't got a bloody clue. Except for finding my dad, I've never planned anything in my life beyond the next meal or the next place to sleep. I'm not looking for pity, that's just how it is. So much has happened in the last few years, it feels like I'm on a rollercoaster. I haven't got that barrier thing holding me in and I'm waiting for the next loop when I may or may not fall out and go splat on the concrete.

"I guess I just need to get used to depending on someone, depending on you, and I want to do that; but it's not easy, you know?" He kept his eyes on his plate, not wanting to see pity on Jase's face.

"You can depend on your brother. What we have is a bit different, don't you think? I want to know how you feel about me."

Chris let out a huge sigh then looked up at him. Sincerity and more than a little pain shone in Jase's green eyes, but he had just pretty much said he was with him because he provided a roof over his head. So he bit the bullet, and opened himself up for yet more pain.

"I can't stop thinking about you, wanting you, thinking about you touching me, me touching you. But that isn't all, it's not just physical, although that's fucking good too. I trust you Jase, really trust you, and that's not something I've ever felt before."

He stopped Jase speaking by putting his finger on his lips. "Don't say you trust me too, because you shouldn't. I don't trust me either, and I still have no idea why you want to be with such a fucked up–"

Jase enfolded Chris's hand in his. "I want to be with you, for as long as you'll have me, because I've never met anyone with more life in them than you have. In the last ten years, I've seen a lot of fucked up things. Daughters stoned to death by fathers because they'd been raped, sons doused in petrol and burnt because they happened to love another man, children being used as walking bombs for the glory of god. But the worst thing were the dead eyes, especially on people who were still alive. People just give up, stop living and just go through the motions, but you, you live every second and I'm drawn to you like a moth to a flame."

"Even though you know you might get burned?"

Jase nodded. "I hope not, but it's a chance you take with every relationship. I took a chance with your brother when I was younger than you; it didn't work, but I'm still glad I tried. Living with never ending regrets is no way to live, and I'd be kicking myself from now to eternity if I didn't give this my best shot."

"So, we're playing it by ear?"

Jase's face broke into a bright smile. Chris couldn't help grinning back. "Yep, but I can't guarantee 'Sarge' won't put in regular appearances if you're being a brat."

Chris narrowed his eyes. "Are you suggested being bratty will bring Sarge out of the closet, because if it does–"

"Sarge will be remaining firmly out of the bedroom if you're bratty. However, if you're good…"

Chris leaned in for a kiss, but Jase smiled and moved back a little.

"As much as I'd like to continue this, college, remember?"

CHAPTER 33

Chris

At least it looked a little different to school Chris decided, as they followed a woman with purple hair sticking out of an untidy Alice band down a tiled corridor. The reception area for the college looked virtually the same as any of the many secondary schools he'd been in over the years, but the extensive art department appeared far less formal. It smelt of paint, clay and something that if bottled, could probably be marketed as 'creativity'.

As they walked quickly down the corridor, the head of the department who insisted they call her Tracey, rather than Mrs Burdock, described what was going on in the various rooms. She was waving her arms like an airhostess doing a safety talk and Chris hoped there wasn't going to be a test because he was sure he wasn't taking in half of what she was saying.

"We cover a wide range of art forms here, from drawing to painting, ceramics, 3D design and sculpture, textiles, graphic design and even game design. Most of our BTEC courses involve producing a portfolio of work that can be used for future employment as well as for the qualification."

She turned and smiled at them, and gestured towards an office door. "If you'd like to come in, we'll have a little chat about how we can help you, Mr Baccioni."

Heart in his throat, Chris entered the office, which was reassuringly cluttered with various works of art, rather than stark and academic. He sat in the indicated seat, quite sure that if Jase wasn't blocking his route to the door, he'd be making a run for it. Because now, the focus would be on him.

"So, you're Chrisander Baccioni? We don't seem to have much information on you."

"I erm, prefer Chris Bacon; nobody has ever used my birth name."

"Any reason for that?" she asked brightly as if she shat rainbows and not in a gay way.

"You'd have to ask my mother, although unless you've got a direct link to the hereafter, you'll have trouble. She died when I was fourteen."

Her immediate 'sympathy' face pissed him off. "Oh, I am so sorry; it must have been such a blow to you and your father."

Chris measured the distance between himself and the door.

"Chris didn't have a very stable upbringing. His half-brother and I are trying to rectify that as much as possible now. He loves art, and although I'm not an expert, his portraits are quite exceptional."

Chris wanted to give him a high-five for changing the subject.

"And you are?"

"Jason Rosewood."

"And your relationship to Chris is?"

"Does it matter? He is over eighteen."

Chris pushed his arse to the edge of the plastic chair and slumped backwards, his arms folded over his chest. Despite Jase's assistance, this was going just as he'd expected. As soon as he'd stepped foot in the place they'd started to judge him, but he'd be damned if he was going to lie to please a stuck-up nosy 'do-gooder' like this.

"He's my boyfriend. My sugar daddy, the guy who pays the bills in return for–"

"Chris, quiet. Tracey is not the enemy, and you will be polite."

Yep, Sarge didn't just live in the bedroom.

Tracey looked a little flustered. "Well Chris, did you bring any of your artwork to show me? As you have no formal qualifications or educational records, we need to establish whether we can help you."

Before Chris could tell her not to bother, Jase replied for him. It was getting annoying.

"I'm sorry, we didn't. Could he do something for you now?"

Tracey's eyebrow drew together in a frown and Chris lost the battle to stop his knee bouncing. How long did he have to put up with this? She clearly didn't like him, and she certainly didn't want a fuck-up like him making waves in her school. They were wasting their time.

"It's not usual. But there's a life drawing class across the hall. He could sit in while we have a chat?"

The look Jase shot him convinced him that if he played up, 'Sarge's' next visit would not prove as enjoyable as last night.

"Fine. Point me at the pencils," he huffed and got to his feet. He followed Tracey to the classroom across the corridor and they waited while she went in and spoke to the young male teacher.

"Behave yourself. They're only trying to help," Jase murmured.

"Yeah? I bet I only got this far because I tick so many minority boxes. Although if I'd been a deaf Maori lesbian asylum seeker with a wooden leg I would've made a few more."

"You can do it, and I'll be right here if you need me. We arrived together and we will leave together. No. Running. Off. Got it?"

"Yeah, yeah," Chris said as he shuffled his feet.

Jase leaned in so close, Chris could feel his breath tickling his ear. "And if you ever call me your sugar daddy again, I'll spank your arse till you can't sit down for a week."

Tracey was opening the door with a smile on her face, before he could answer with a cheeky 'promise?'

"Peter said he'd be happy for you to sit in, they haven't started yet; just try not to obscure the view of any of the other students."

He moved into the classroom, feeling nervous as fuck. They had no right to make him feel like this, no right to look down on him, so he channelled his 'Tigger' persona.

Plonking himself down in an empty seat in front of an easel with an A3 sheet of paper already set up, he looked around for pencils. A very white hand put a box on the desk beside him. Looking over, he saw nothing more than the side of a dark grey t-shirt hoodie. He leaned forward and caught sight of an elfin male face, with droopy blond hair covering one eye before his helper moved, totally obscured his face again.

"Thanks, I'm Chris."

"Alex."

He waited a few seconds but the lad didn't say anything else.

"Mysterious silent type huh? I get it, can't do it personally, but I get it. Frankly, keeping my gob shut for more than thirty seconds is a challenge, unless there's something in it. So, what are we meant to be drawing?"

"Here he comes," Alex murmured and nodded towards a door at the other end of the classroom.

Chris's mouth dropped open before he hastily shut it again. It was the dick who'd told him he'd trade a blow job for a bed for the night, then buggered off when his wife texted him. It wouldn't have been so bad if he hadn't already fulfilled his part of the bargain. It'd been late enough that he hadn't been able to secure another bed for the night. He'd been forced to go back to that damn tent, and it'd been bloody cold in February.

The bastard clearly thought he was the best thing since sliced bread as he swaggered out, dressed only in a pair of swimming trunks and sat on a stool set on a slightly raised platform at the front of the class.

"Today I want you to use your imaginations to place our model in a scenario you think he'd enjoy. It can be anything, from being alone by a stream, in the middle of a Roman feast, the bridge of a spaceship, or anything else that tickles your fancy. You have an hour."

Chris smiled slightly as he started to sketch quickly. Revenge for what had happened six months ago was going to be very, very sweet.

"Oh my fucking god," Alex said then clapped a hand over his mouth.

Chris turned to grin at him. Alex's picture showed the bastard with devils around him, although it screamed emo, it was pretty good.

His own drawing consisted of the naked back of a struggling young man, his hands pushing against the model's thighs while his face was buried in the guy's crotch. The man's head was thrown back in obvious pleasure as his hands gripped the lad's curly hair to stop him escaping. Personally, he thought his depiction of the straining muscles on both figures was particularly good. The whole piece screamed action and tension.

The entire class turned towards them at Alex's expletive. Mr Trendy Teacher looked in their direction with interest.

"Have you got something to say to the class, Alex?"

The poor kid seemed to shrink in on himself at being singled out. It immediately pissed Chris off. He'd always been able to hold his own against bullies mainly because he never stayed around long enough to really piss anyone off, plus he was bloody fast and made people laugh. This shy kid clearly didn't have those advantages, in fact, the poor sod had 'target' written all over him.

Chris got to his feet. "He was just looking at my work, Sir. It's pretty awesome and true to life, even if I do say so myself."

The dickhead on the stool looked like a rabbit caught in the headlights. Chris wiggled his fingers in greeting and grinned at him.

"Remember me do you? Good, cos I remember you. Anyone want to see what Mr Respectable here gets up to when he tells his wife he's working late?" Chris started to turn his easel around.

"Don't, he's—" Alex said quickly, but it was too late. Chris had taken his picture from the easel and turned his picture to the class.

The silence in the room lasted perhaps five seconds before the other students started laughing and hooting. The model turned white and almost ran from the room. Mr Trendy Teacher turned beetroot and started to push his way through the tables towards him.

"Oh shit," Chris muttered, and forgetting that he still had his drawing in his hand he made for the door, hopping over an empty chair as two of the delighted students inadvertently blocked his way.

Luckily, Jase must have heard the commotion and was opening the door of the office when he came barrelling out of the classroom. Without hesitation, Chris scooting behind him as all hell broke loose. The teacher was shouting incoherently, stabbing his finger in Chris's direction. The students were all crowding out, hooting and hollering, to watch the fun. Tracey was calling for calm, but nobody listened to her.

"QUIET," Jase roared. Between one moment and the next, silence reigned. Sarge rocked, but giving Jase a high-five right at the moment probably wouldn't be considered appropriate.

"Tracey? If you wouldn't mind," Jase said in an exceptionally normal tone considering his last utterance had nearly brought the ceiling down.

"Peter, would you kindly dismiss your class and then join me in my office?"

Chris peeked out from behind Jase to see Alex standing a few feet away. He mouthed, "What the fuck?" at him.

For the first time, Chris saw a smile on the youth's beautiful face. "Brother-in-law," he mouthed back, then grinned at Chris's horror struck face.

With the help of glares from Tracey and Jase, the crowd of students slowly dispersed. Now that things were calming down, Chris straightened up and moved away from his flesh and blood riot shield.

"Where do you think you're going?" Jase growled.

"Just saying goodbye to Alex, Sarge." He grinned. "I made a friend."

"Sarge is right," he growled. "Be quick."

He moved all of two feet away from Jase and beckoned to Alex. After casting a quick look around, Alex sidled over, still with his hood up. Chris was surprised to find out the Alex actually had a couple of inches on him, he'd seemed smaller when he'd been slumped in his chair in the classroom.

"Is it always this screwy around here?" Chris asked with a grin.

"You are one crazy bastard, but I haven't had as much fun in months. How do you know Peter's brother-in-law?"

Chris put his hand over his heart and a mournful expression on his face. "It was an unhappy period in my life, but I've got Jase now. Sexy ass don't you think? If I get kicked out of here, which let's face it, is pretty fucking likely, you can catch me at the gay club in town. I just got promoted from go-go dancer to bar staff."

Alex's mouth hung open. Chris grinned, reached out and shut his mouth with a finger under his chin. "You don't want to be doing that around Peter's brother-in-law, unless you want something embarrassingly small stuck in there."

"Chris?" Jase's voice came from behind him.

"Got to go, kiddo, see you around," Chris winked at the shell-shocked boy, who was probably about the same age as him, then turned and ducked under Jase's arm into the office.

Tracey sat behind the desk, Peter sat in one of the two chairs in front of it.

"Sit," Jase ordered, and for the first time, the tightness in his voice registered. Sarge was not a happy bunny. He also folded his arms as if he was on guard duty as he stood by the door.

"Wouldn't you rather, cos of–"

"Park your arse, right now," Jase growled and Chris obeyed like one of Pavlov's dogs.

"Would you care to explain that?" Tracey pointed at the crumpled drawing still in his fist.

"This?" he asked as he unravelled it and laid it on the desk.

Tracey glanced at it, blinked, then picked it up.

"Peter told me to draw the model in a scene we thought he'd enjoy, and I know he enjoys this. It's what he made me do in return for a promise of a bed for the night when I was sleeping rough. Problem was, after he was done, he got a call from his wife. He told her his meeting had just finished and pissed off."

"Liar," Peter spat out.

"He's got an ugly ass mole on his belly, just above his pubes. I couldn't have seen that today, could I?"

"You could have seen that at a swimming pool or a gym," Peter said, but he didn't look confident anymore.

"Like I'd pay to go to public pool when I was sleeping rough. Work it out, Mr Education," Chris mumbled to himself as he picked at his nails. They weren't going to believe him anyway, so what was the point in continuing this torture?

"Why would he lie?" Jase said calmly. "He's never met you before, never been here before. And saying what he did, makes him look just as bad as your brother-in-law. If I were you, I'd get your sister to the doctor for some STI tests, Chris here is clean, but I don't suppose all the vulnerable youngsters your brother-in-law has exploited since... when did this happen?"

"February. It was bloody cold," he mumbled.

"Can say the same," Jase finished smoothly. "Now, is his artwork up to scratch for the course, or are you going to be as prejudiced against him for his past as everyone else?"

After looking intently at the drawing, Tracey handed it to Peter. Sighing, he glanced at it, then looked a little closer.

"Where did you learn to draw like this?" he asked.

Chris shrugged. "Here and there."

"Who was your teacher? What school did you go to? Where did you learn about anatomy?" Peter quick fired questions at him.

Chris gaped at him. "You want me list them? I can't even remember the ones I didn't get expelled from, let alone all the ones I did. The bones and stuff I picked up from looking at art and anatomy books in the library. You don't have to buy anything to stay inside when the weather is shitty as long as you're looking at a book."

He heard Jase sigh from behind him, and he swivelled in his seat so he could see him. "What, you want me to lie? I thought you were on a 'turn over a new leaf' honesty kick. Well I'm trying. I've kept all this shit to myself for so fucking long, and this is why. Everyone's looking at me as if I'm a turd, just like they always do. I–"

"Chris?" Tracey said to get his attention.

She indicated the drawing still in Peter's hands. "That is good, really good, even if the subject matter is... unfortunate. And I'd be pleased to offer you a place here. The term is over in four weeks, and the new courses don't start until September. How about you look at the timetable, find some classes that interest you, and do some 'taster' sessions before making a commitment?

"Our BTEC courses involve working in several different mediums, from digital graphics to ceramics and photography. I take it pencil is your preferred medium?"

"Never had the chance to try much else, not properly anyway. I don't think I ever spent more than six weeks in any one school, I had a bit of a crazy childhood. My–"

"Jason told me, you don't have to go over it again. And he's right about you having a future in art; raw talent like yours is rare, and believe me, we've see a lot of students here over the years. You're good Chris, and with a little help, you could be great."

"I am? I mean, I could?"

Tracey gave him a warm smile. "I believe so, but please, no more obscene artwork in class, ok?"

"I was careful not to draw an actual dick, apart from the model that is." He tilted his head to one side, considering for a second. "So you want me to do Action Man crotches?" At Tracey's confused look, he added, "You know, when you take the clothes off, there's still nothing there?" He waved in the general direction of his groin.

Jase snorted. "I think she means no porn scenes."

"Precisely. If OFSTED inspectors came on an unexpected visit, something like this, even if it does have artistic merit, would cause more than a few awkward questions, and not just for the model."

Chris could see the sense in that.

"Peter, can you get Chris a pad and coloured pencils? And then I think you'd better take the rest of the day off, don't you?"

The man nodded and got to his feet. "I'm sorry I shouted at you. My sister is expecting their second child. The drawing was a bit of a shock, but it does explain a few things. No hard feelings?" Peter said then winced at his choice of words.

With difficulty, Chris managed to ignore the unintentional innuendo, although he hoped Jase registered the fact too. "Sure. I wouldn't have done it if I knew you two were related. I wanted to embarrass him, not you or your family."

After Peter left, Tracey turned back to him. "I want you to come in on Monday, bright and early. In the meantime, I want you to draw what it feels like to be you."

"I can do a self-portrait," he confirmed as relief washed over him at the simplicity of the assignment.

She shook her head. "No, I want you to portray what it feels like inside your head, now or in the past, maybe what you hope for in the future, it's your choice. Emotions, how it feels to have ADHD, both good and bad."

"What's good about it?"

She smiled at him. "Some of the most talented people in the world are hyperactive. Richard Branson, Will Smith, Will.I.Am, Justin Timberlake, and not surprisingly, Jim Carey."

"Wow, you know a lot about it," he said. The Jim Carey thing definitely made sense, especially the 'Somebody stop me' line.

"It comes of having it myself; although I had a supportive family and didn't have the added complication of dyslexia, but the two often go hand in hand. My advice is to use it. Embrace the creative edge it provides, but don't let it rule you or those around you. Now if you'll excuse me? I need a snack." She looked up at Jase where he stood behind Chris. "That's another thing that helps, regular nutritious food, every three hours if possible. ADHD and sugar highs and lows do not mix well."

"I've noticed," Jase said dryly.

"I am still here you know," Chris groused.

"Yes, I know dear, but you really don't want to be, do you? Nevertheless, I think you've done exceptionally well today. Managing to concentrate enough to finish a piece as detailed as that in a new, pressurized environment is no small feat. Art is obviously a great help to you, just as it is to me, but I don't have the patience to do portraits. Abstract is my thing. Big, colourful and full of movement."

Jase leaned over and shook her hand, so Chris stood up and did the same.

Peter was waiting in the corridor with a new packet of colouring pencils as they left the office. "I'll be interested to see what you do with those."

Chris grinned at him. "I bet you are."

"Be nice," Jase murmured.

"Sorry," Chris apologised immediately.

Peter smiled wryly. "You are going to be quite a challenge, but I'm looking forward to it. To be honest, it's refreshing to get a student who is so open as well as so talented. We get a lot of mediocre students who can't stop blowing their own trumpets. With others, even when they are genuinely talented, it can be like getting blood out of a stone. I find myself pouncing on them if they say anything in class."

"Like Alex? Give me a week; I'll crack him for you."

Glancing between the worried looking teacher and a scowling Jase, he swiftly held up his hands, in a 'don't shoot me' gesture. "In a totally platonic, non-gay, bringing him out of his shell kinda way, nothing else. I don't even know if he is gay. Besides, I'm not into twinks, or emos, for that matter. Life throws too much shit at you to obsess over the bad stuff, besides I've–"

"We get the idea; you're not going to molest him," Jase said, but there was a slight smile twitching his lips.

Peter looked doubtful. "I wish you luck with that one. He's been here a year, and I think he's spoken more to you today that he has to anyone else the entire term."

CHAPTER 34

Jase

"That could've been worse," Chris said brightly before he trotted down the steps of the college and was forced to wait at the bottom for him.

"How exactly?"

The grin Chris shot him had Jase despairing. "I got in didn't I? Plus, I didn't hit anyone, no one hit me and I made a friend."

"And how do you think it would have gone if I hadn't been there?"

Chris pecked him on the cheek. "But you were. What's for lunch?"

Jase shook his head. This was like trying to train an excited puppy. "But I won't always be there. You need to—"

Chris's eyes went round. "You're not dumping me are you? Cos I'm sure I can—"

Both to reassure him, and to shut him up, Jase put an arm around his waist and pulled him against his body sharply.

"What didn't you get about what I said this morning? I'm in this for the long haul. But I do have to go to work. On Monday. Which means you have to get here, do a class and get home on your own."

"Oh," Chris said.

Jase could literally see Chris's good mood draining out of him as he drooped. He gave him a squeeze before he started him walking back in the direction of the car park.

"But we can phone Matt and Kate, see if anyone's available to bring you and pick you up."

Chris tried to pull away but Jase kept a firm grip on him. "What like they do for Ryan? I'm not a kid."

"No you're not, but you have just undergone one hell of a trauma. Getting your confidence back is going to take a little time; unfortunately that goes for me too. That kid with the hoodie had all sorts of alarm bells ringing in my paranoid mind. He didn't want to be seen, and where I've been working, that just screams suspicious."

Chris blinked. "Seriously? You were worried that Alex was a suicide bomber?"

Jase nodded towards two smartly dressed, thirty-something olive-skinned men walking towards them. "And you're telling me that if you were on your own, you wouldn't be worried by them?"

Chris tucked his new art materials under his arm, stuck his hands in his pockets and hunched his shoulders. He didn't need to say anything to broadcast his emotions to everyone in a thirty foot radius.

The 'stiff upper lip' mentality of the redcaps, and the way other military personnel clammed up as soon as they saw him in his uniform, or found out his regiment if he was in civvies, made Chris's heart on his sleeve mentality even more appealing.

"It's embarrassing," Chris finally muttered after the men had passed them, but he'd kept his eyes firmly on the pavement.

"It's not embarrassing, it's human."

"And it's not happening to anyone else," Chris said decisively. "Cop shop time."

That was the last thing Jase had expected to hear, then again, when had Chris ever done anything he expected?

"You sure?"

"Nope, but let's do it anyway."

* * *

Fifteen minutes later, they were walking into the front office of the local police station. Without hesitation, Chris marched up to the counter.

"I'd like to report a crime."

The middle-aged male civilian receptionist glanced up at him briefly. "All our officers are busy right now. If you'd like to take a seat I'll get someone to see you as soon as possible. But it could be a while. What's the nature of the crime?"

"An international human trafficking ring, kidnap, unlawful imprisonment, blackmail, gang rape, physical assault and erm... assault with a syringe? Does that about cover it?" he asked Jase nonchalantly as the receptionist's jaw dropped open.

Jase thought for a moment. "Actually, hostage taking might be more appropriate, and you forgot the various firearms charges but they could get quite technical. Administering opiate drugs without consent is actually a separate offence as is administering drugs to obtain intercourse. Maybe even procuring others to commit homosexual acts. Not to mention reckless driving."

"Really?" Chris asked in surprise.

"They did throw you out of a moving vehicle when you were naked and drugged up to your eyeballs."

"Oh yeah, I forgot about that."

"Hard to forget something you don't remember because they'd forced rohypnol down your throat."

"That's true." Chris turned a bright smile on the shell-shocked receptionist. "So, do we still have to wait, or do you think you could find someone to have a little chat?"

The receptionist dialled.

Jase pulled his phone out.

"Who you calling?"

"Matt."

Chris scowled. "I don't need him to sit in, I'm over eighteen."

"I know that, but the police will want to talk to him. As well as Sarah, Russel, Nate, Kate, Cuddles, my army buddies that—"

"Ok, ok I get it. Guess I didn't think all this through." He looked crestfallen for a second then grinned. "But I wouldn't be the adorable, impulsive guy you fell in love with if I had, right?"

Jase sent his identical warning text to all the parties involved then looked up as a middle-aged man and a woman, both in suits, came through the doors at the other end of the reception area.

"I hear you have quite a story for us, Mr?"

"Bacon. I mean Baccioni." Chris glanced over to him for reassurance, looking every inch the youngster he was. "Or maybe I should use Kemp; what d'you think?"

The officer sighed as he exchanged glances with his female colleague. "Shall we start with my name then? I'm Detective Inspector Baum, this is Sergeant Evans," he said as he indicated the woman. "You are?" he asked and Jase introduced himself as Chris's partner, as well as his former rank and position.

The senior officer nodded. "And you witnessed what happened to Chris?"

"Some of it directly, some via video. He was held for two weeks. They dumped him back a week ago. He's been going through medically supervised heroine withdrawal since. They were particularly thorough in letting us know what was happening. I have—"

"Perhaps we'd better discuss this somewhere more private? Sergeant Evans, will you start with Chris?" He motioned towards the door he'd just come through.

Chris was an open book as he tensed. "I've got to do this on my own?"

The woman put on a gentle smile. "Don't worry, we'll take it slow."

Jase winced at her choice of words, if there was one thing that would freak Chris out, it was the thought of spending hours going over everything in minute detail over and over again in a small room with a complete stranger staring at him.

Chris turned panicked eyes to him. "I'm not sure I can—"

"We stay in the same room. I know witness interview technique so I won't interfere, but he won't stay there very long on his own. As you can guess, this isn't an easy thing to talk about."

The inspector didn't look pleased, but he nodded. After giving Chris a reassuring smile, they entered the 'serious' part of the station. Jase hung back to talk to the inspector.

"He has ADHD and flight issues. The drugs bothered him far more than the sexual assaults. Tread carefully or he'll get very agitated. I have a great deal of evidence, the prime perpetrators are known all over Europe. He's convinced he needs to speak to you now to stop it happening to anyone else; I don't agree. I also think it is way too soon for him to be doing this."

Instead of getting all superior, the officer nodded. "I understand. Would it be easier if we looked at your evidence before talking to Chris?"

"I'll get everything brought here. Let him talk, just no questions about his background; he'll get defensive and either clam up or try to leave. I'll fill you in on what we know."

By the time they got home at nine, Jase was wondering if being blown up again might have been an easier option. Chris had raged, cried, paced, threw the cushions around in the soft interview area as well as refused all food and drink for the last eight hours. For the last hour, he'd sat slumped, hugging one of the cushions and giving monosyllabic answers to the probing questions.

The entire police station had almost come to a halt apart from Chris's case. Everyone Jase had contacted, except his two redcap colleagues, had turned up at the front desk within an hour. Jase had kept Chris occupied by asking him to sketch what he remembered of the interior of the house as they waited for the officers to watch the material and do the other interviews.

The painful amount of detail Chris put into the sketches of the room he'd been held in, compared to the far less distinct ones of a small bathroom and a kitchen was almost too much to bear. Keeping his expression encouraging and devoid of anything Chris could possibly interpret as pity was one of the hardest things he'd ever done.

"Enough," Jase announced as Sergeant Evans asked again about the sequence of events at the end of the first week of his captivity. "He doesn't remember; he was barely conscious. He needs a break, so do you, so do I. You know where we are and we can come back in the morning."

The drive home was silent, and despite being coaxed, Chris failed to eat more than a couple of bites of the sandwich Jase made him.

"Can I go to bed now?"

"Of course. Do you want me to come with you?"

The dark curls bobbed a little and they made their way through to the bedroom. The fact that Chris didn't strip entirely sent out the clear message that he didn't want to be intimate. Instead, he silently cuddled up to Jase's side, and as Jase held him close, he cried himself to sleep.

CHAPTER 35

Jase

The determination on Chris's face the next morning was amazing. Jase assumed that he'd refuse to go back to the station for more punishment today, but he was up at the crack of dawn, putting sausage sandwiches together.

"Thought I'd get some grub in me before we head back. They're going to be digging today aren't they?"

"Probably. They won't want any surprises when you take the witness stand. The prosecution will try and discredit your testimony, probably by saying you were already an addict, that you wanted what happened, maybe even asked for it." He paused and watched as Chris deftly sliced through the toast and pushed a plate towards him.

"It could get pretty ugly. You sure you want to do this today?"

Chris grinned around a mouthful. "Absolutely not."

Jase sighed. "But you're doing it anyway."

"You bet. I'm done with running. That's what my mum did and it didn't help her any. I loved her, but what she did, or didn't do, for me was out of order. It didn't really sink in till I saw how Kate is with Ryan. That's how it should be."

* * *

They walked back out of the station at four p.m. Chris looked as if a huge weight had been taken off his shoulders but Jase felt shell-shocked. He was appalled at the matter of fact way Chris had revealed details of his childhood as if they were normal. It had been particularly difficult to hear that he'd purposefully traded his virginity to a dealer in order to get a fix for his mum who was in withdrawal.

"What was his name?" Inspector Baum asked.

Chris frowned. "Not going to tell you. I pushed him into it. It was my idea, not his. Before you're wondering, I did make him use a condom, I'm not stupid."

"Did it hurt?" Evans asked, her voice dripping with sympathy.

"Erm duh, of course it did. I was thirteen. I'm small now and I've grown since then. Next question."

"So that's how you became a rent boy?"

Jase braced himself for an explosion, which surprisingly didn't come.

"Just because my mum was an addict and sold herself, it doesn't mean I did. It also didn't mean she was a bad person, just a weak one in a crappy situation. She could have pushed me into doing what she did, she could have pimped me out, but she didn't, even though she got plenty of offers. And for your information, I've never sold myself, but when I was sleeping rough I did occasionally go home with blokes that I might not have gone with, if it hadn't been for a promise of a bed, a shower, the use of a washing machine and breakfast in the morning. Next. Question."

The two police officers, despite their professionalism, were also looking a little green by the end of the interview. Just like him, if Marie Baccioni had still been alive, they looked as if they would've taken great delight in prosecuting her to the fullest extent of the law for child neglect that amounted to severe abuse. Although knowing Chris, he probably would've defended her.

Jase draped his arm over Chris's shoulders as they walked back to the car. As much as he wanted to go home and just hold Chris all night again, that would be treating him like a child, not the adult he was.

"How about we go home and get something to eat before you get ready for work."

Chris looked up sharply in confusion.

"It's Friday. Bar job, remember?" Jase prompted. As expected, Chris's face lit up like a Christmas tree. It deflated just as quickly.

"You're coming, right?"

Jase couldn't help smiling back. "Of course I am. Do you think I'd miss the opportunity to watch you do your thing all night, knowing it's me who gets to take you home?"

"So you don't mind if I flirt a bit?"

"It wouldn't be you if you didn't flirt, but as I said, no touching and you shut down any propositions as soon as they happen, but you don't have to be rude about it."

At five-thirty, Jase was sitting on a bar stool at the Toolbox, watching Russel take Chris through some of the more complex drinks. There were only a few after work drinkers and Jase was enjoying the relative peace.

At seven, the place got a little busier. Nevertheless, the dance floor was still empty and all three podiums were conspicuously devoid of dancers. The only area of the club that buzzed was the bar. The fifteen or so guys propping it up kept asking Chris for crisps and nuts which were stored on the bottom shelf.

Jase knew exactly why. His arse really did look cute in those latex black shorts which he'd combined with a vest bearing the Toolbox logo on the front. It hadn't been easy to keep his mouth shut when Chris had come back out of the staff area wearing his new uniform but as it was the same as the bar staff had been wearing every other time he'd been in here, he'd managed it.

"Hey cute stuff, you dancing tonight?" A 'bear' standing right beside Jase asked.

"Behind here I am," Chris replied and rolled his hips.

"How about you come and do that in my lap?"

"You offering me a ride home?"

Jase couldn't believe his ears, what had happened to 'no'? Impulsivity issues or no, he was sitting right here.

"I'll give you a ride you'll never forget," the man said and rubbed his own chest as he focused on Chris's crotch.

Chris grinned at him. "Maybe you can, maybe you can't, but I'm not into HGV's these days; I'm more of a military Humvee fan. Armoured, manoeuvrable and designed to protect. Mine's sitting right next to you."

The bearded man turned to him; Jase just stared back.

He indicated Chris, who was now serving someone else with his thumb. "He yours?"

"Yep."

"If he wiggles like that in the sack, you are one lucky bastard."

Jase let himself smile a little. "He does, and I am. Name's Jase."

"Dan. I haven't been to a gay bar for years, but I'm single again, so I thought I'd give it a try. Sorry if I offended by hitting on your boyfriend."

Dan was actually a decent guy, and he couldn't really blame him for hitting on Chris. He was the sexiest thing in the club.

At around ten, Nate wandered in. Jase introduced him to Dan, although conversation wasn't easy as the music volume had increased considerably. It turned out that Dan was a doctor who had just accepted a position at the local hospital and the pair had plenty to talk about.

The other bartender looked stressed and run off his feet. Chris was completely in his element, bopping away to the music as he served customer after customer. He hadn't looked this happy since the first day Jase had seen him at Matt's wedding. It was a glorious sight, and as much as having other blokes leering at him pissed him off, it was clear that Chris thrived on it.

The sound of breaking glass made him look towards the seating area. A group of six or seven men at a corner table were waving at the bar and pointing at the floor.

Chris appeared with a dustpan and brush. As Jase watched, he swivelled his way through the crowd of talking and gyrating bodies towards them. When he lost sight of him amongst the bodies, Jase stood up to get a higher perspective.

"He can handle himself; this is his element," Nate said.

"It's not him I'm worried about," Jase said, lifting up on his toes to keep Chris in sight as he bent over to clean up the breakage.

The only one of the group he recognised was Ollie, the youngest of the group from McDonalds. Chris shot upright and glared at Ollie who was sitting directly behind him. On autopilot, Jase started towards the group.

"Steady," Nate said as he held his forearm. "Give him a chance. It'll do his confidence no end of good if he manages to sort it out himself."

Against his better judgement, Jase held his position and watched as Ollie stood up and put his hand on Chris's hip as they faced each other. From this angle, Jase could only see Ollie's face and Chris's back. Chris looked down at the hand touching him, then back up at Ollie's face. A second later, Ollie's eyes were protruding as he bent slightly at the waist.

The other members of the group we're clearly finding the scene hilarious, as Ollie's face tensed in pain. Chris delivered a none too gentle pat to the other man's face then picked up dustpan off the floor and started to make his way back towards the bar. He didn't look happy.

Jase met him at the half-door that gave access behind the bar.

"What was that all about?"

"That was a twat trying to show off to his new work buddies. Can you believe it after we warned him off? He told me to go to the bogs and suck him and his friends off." His grin was full of delight. "I think he got a little more than he bargained for. Seems I was a touch heavy handed for his liking. While I had hold of his nuts, I told him that although I might bruise them, you'd tear them off if he touched me again."

Jase immediately started to walk purposefully in Ollie's direction. Chris grabbed his arm, the sound of the glass in the dustpan he had in his other hand tinkling above the music.

"What're you doing? I sorted it."

Jase paused. "I know that. I just wanted to see how protective his mates are of him. Ollie you can handle on your own any day of the week, if the others gang up on you…"

Jase looked over at the table. Ollie was leaving and his friends didn't seem unhappy about the situation, in fact the man was getting a distinctly frosty reception. One of them looked in their direction, then leaned forward to speak to the other two. All three straightened in their seats.

"Please leave it; I don't want any trouble on my first night."

Giving the three men one last stare, Jase retreated back to his bar stool. Nate was still there. Dan had wandered off, probably looking for an unattached hook-up.

The rest of the night was sheer torture. He found himself gritting his teeth every time Chris smiled at anyone, every time he laughed, winked or he caught some bloke eyeing him up.

"Calm down; he's not going to do anything," Nate said in his ear.

"I know, but shit, this is uncomfortable."

"Let's go outside," Nate suggested.

Jase waved at Chris, and mouthed, "Back in a minute." He didn't like the way Chris glanced over and made sure Russel was serving at the other end of the bar before nodding. It proved that he wasn't as confident as he made out. He hadn't been out from behind the bar since the incident with Ollie, although the other two bar staff consistently took turns in collecting glasses.

The quiet outside the club was heavenly.

"Everything alright?" The doorman whom Chris affectionately called Cuddles, asked.

"Just getting some air," Jase replied, but the heavily built man didn't look happy as he glanced at Nate.

"You're not cheating on him are you? Because if you are, I'll–"

"This is Nate. He's the paramedic who sorted Chris out that night. Nate, this is another one of Chris's many fans, although this one happens to be straight."

Nate stuck out his hand and the two tall men shook hands. Will looked over at Jase. "Sorry to jump to conclusions."

"Quite alright, I'm glad you asked. I'm hoping that Nate or I will be around most of the time he's working. Russel has promised to keep an eye out too, but I'd appreciate a heads up if you see him leaving without either of us. Chris is erm…" He paused, unsure of how to phrase things without making Chris out to be a complete airhead.

"Erm, is right. Don't worry, I'll stop him going off with anyone, or on his own for that matter, if I'm around. I was here the night they took him. The kid's too friendly for his own good."

"Thanks, I appreciate it."

Will nodded and turned back to confront a clearly drunk trio of women who didn't look in the least gay.

"Come on, let's take a walk," Nate said. "I just don't get why straight people want to go to gay clubs. There was a stand-up fight a few months ago because a straight guy got his arse pinched."

Jase blew out a breath and circled his shoulders. He hadn't realised just how tense he'd been inside the club, and yet, he wanted to get back in there as soon as possible. Even though Will was watching the door and Russel was watching Chris inside, it wasn't enough.

Russel had promised he wouldn't touch Chris again, but it didn't change the fact that he'd had sex with him. He also didn't have a clue how many of the other men currently in the club Chris had been with. Every time another bloke eyed Chris up, Jase couldn't help wondering if the lust was speculative, or the hope of a repeat performance.

"You really aren't enjoying this are you?" Nate asked as they made their way along the road outside the club, the noise of the thumping music gradually fading.

"I like seeing him happy, and I think he is in there," Jase hedged.

"I think he's enjoying himself, but he's also worried about you. You're making him uncomfortable."

Jase stopped walking. "How the hell am I doing that?"

"By giving anyone who smiles or flirts with him the evil eye. He's bar staff in a go-go dancing gay club. A little flirting is part of the role."

"Intellectually I know that, but I can't just sit there and pretend I'm happy with him being eye-fucked by everyone within a ten foot radius."

"Then don't come in. Drop him off and pick him up. You saw what happened with that other bloke, he can handle it."

The thought of doing what Nate suggested made his balls shrivel. "Not going to happen. If something upsets him, he could take off. Will might be keeping an eye, but it didn't stop what happened last time did it?"

To his surprise, a large arm went across his shoulder and squeezed. "This might not be easy to hear, but I think this is more about you than him. Did you ever get counselling for what happened in Helmand?"

It felt as if he'd had a bucket of icy water thrown over him. He had to use all his training to consider what Nate had said rather than telling him where to stick his opinion.

"You think I'm projecting PTSD onto him?"

"Could be. Remember, he's survived on his own for a long time. Here, I got you this." Nate reached into his pocket, pulled out a small black pouch and gave it to him. With a slight frown, Jase opened it and tipped the contents out into his hand. It contained a chunky leather wrist cuff with a silver bar across the top.

"It's got a GPS in it. Tell him you want him to wear it whenever he's away from you, he'll be stoked. You can activate it via an app on your phone. Battery lasts three months if it's not activated. You can tell him it's just an SOS device. If you turn the bar, there's a button on the underside that sends an immediate alert to a mobile. "

Jase had heard of these, and apart from what Nate had just said, he knew they were bloody expensive which was why the army didn't use them.

"How much?"

Nate smiled. "Hundred quid."

"Bollocks. How much?"

"What I paid for it, is worth it to me to know Chris is safe with you. Because if I wasn't sure, I'd probably take him on myself, and that wouldn't be a good idea."

A confusing wave of jealousy and defensiveness swept over him. "Why, what's wrong with him?"

Nate chuckled. "Nothing mate, he's just a bit loud for my tastes. Don't get me wrong, I like to be needed, but I'm not into battling. I have to have the biggest ego and personality in a relationship, which, before you say it, I know makes me a bit of a dick. Besides, although I like him a lot, I don't love him and you do, don't you?"

"Yeah, I think I do, or at least I'm going in that direction fast," he said after a pause. "Let's get back shall we?"

"Alright Mr Paranoia. After all, we've been away for what, ten whole minutes?"

Jase breathed a sigh of relief as he saw Chris still behind the bar when they walked back into the club. He was still bopping about as if he'd just started his shift, rather than having been on the go for the last six hours, not to mention his traumatic day at the police station.

As if he could sense his presence, Chris looked up from the pint he was pulling and his face lit up with the devastating smile Jase hoped he'd never get used to even if he saw it every day for the rest of his life.

"Break time?" he mouthed and tapped his watch.

Immediately, Chris moved over to Russel and the big man leaned down so Chris could speak into his ear. He really was a short arse, although Matt and their father weren't. He wondered if the Baccioni family were small in general, or if Chris's lack of stature was due to poor nutrition as a child. He couldn't remember Marie, or Marietta as he'd known her, being particularly petite, then again he'd been in primary school at the time.

The pair appeared to be having a slight disagreement. Russel pointed towards the door to the staff area, and Chris, with a face like thunder, stomped out from behind the bar toward it. There wasn't an exit from the staff area, so knowing that Chris would have to come back this way, he moved over to where Russel was serving.

Leaning over the bar, he shouted, "What's up with Chris?"

"I told him to go home; he's already worked two hours past the end of his shift."

Jase nodded, although he needed to have a longer conversation with Russel about Chris's hours when he could make himself heard. He needed to discover if Chris had made a conscious decision to work longer than necessary. Was he avoiding coming home with him or had he simply lost track of time because he was enjoying himself?

Chris came out, wearing his jeans and his own t-shirt. As he came over, he spoke to several patrons, but although he smiled, Jase could see him keeping a physical distance. Was he doing it because he knew his overly protective boyfriend was watching and wouldn't like it, or did he genuinely not want to be touched by strangers now? How would Chris behave if he knew he wasn't keeping a close eye on him?

"You're growling and he hasn't done anything wrong," Nate said in his ear as he stood up to greet Chris. Without pause, Nate enveloped a surprised Chris in a hug, lifting him off his feet.

When he put him down, Jase saw Nate mime dancing and nod towards the dance floor.

Chris's automatic smile vanished as his eyes shot to him to gauge his reaction. *Crap, he's even worried about accepting his drug counsellor's invitation to dance in case it pisses me off.* Yes, he wanted Chris to listen to him, but he didn't want to turn him into a 'yes sir' submissive who couldn't go to the bathroom without permission.

As he couldn't be heard over the music, he motioned with his hand for them to go ahead.

'You sure?' Chris mouthed. Jase smiled and motioned them on again. Chris's grin returned and he trotted the few feet between them.

"Thanks love, won't be long," he said into his ear and pecked him quickly on the cheek before scampering back to Nate.

Jase would have been more impressed with the endearment if he hadn't heard Chris say it to most of the blokes he'd served this evening.

Two songs later, they were back. Chris had been glancing over at him every few seconds the entire time. His dancing had been far more subdued than the night he'd been taken, or even when he'd been serving earlier. Trying to convince himself the change of behaviour was because Chris missed him, didn't work; Chris was worried about him being jealous and it was changing him. The question was, did he like what he was changing Chris into or not?

CHAPTER 36

Chris

Dancing with Nate was good, the man had some serious rhythm, but he could feel Jase's eyes on them and it wasn't comfortable. He enjoyed it when most blokes watched him dance, had loved being up on the podium because his audience got a kick out of watching him.

In contrast, Jase wasn't a happy bunny and hadn't been all night. It had definitely soured his own enjoyment. Although being back here, even if he wasn't dancing, felt like everything that had happened was now behind him. Jase clearly couldn't do that yet. Even though it'd been him who had been held, his experiences had been filtered through a haze of drugs. He might have suffered physically, but Jase had suffered emotionally. Big bad Sarge wasn't as together as he liked to think.

"Sorry Nate, but I think I'd better go; I can hear him growling from here."

"Don't let him get away with it. He'll have you wrapped up in cotton wool before you know it; unless that's what you want? If it is, I've read you really wrong," Nate said into his ear. "If you're not prepared to give up this part of your life, let him know it's not negotiable."

Giving him a quick hug, Chris made his way back over to Jase. It was strange not to have people reaching out to touch him, and as guilty as it made him feel, he missed it. It wasn't that he wanted to be intimate with any of them, but knowing he was desirable, that they took a risk to have a quick feel, was an ego boost he'd enjoyed.

Now I've got Jase, a guaranteed bed for the night with someone who cares about more than just my arse and I care about him too. This is a chance to get off the rollercoaster, permanently. For that, for him, I can deal with whatever he wants. Cotton wool doesn't sound too bad.

Plastering a smile on his face, he swivelled through the crowd toward his boyfriend, and didn't that sound fucking strange in his own head.

Pushing his way between Jase's knees as he sat on the barstool, he wrapped himself around him and gave him his best shot at a passionate kiss. Jase didn't respond; he didn't even lift a hand to touch him. Chris pulled away in confusion.

"Nate got you all hot and bothered did he?" Jase's face showed no emotion. This was probably the face he showed to the soldiers he interrogated. Just like that, his decision of a few moments ago to be whatever Jase wanted flipped on its head.

Nate was right, he was going to have to fight to stop Jase cutting him off from anyone he didn't see as 'appropriate' company. Jase might be happy to live his life in monochrome, but he was a rainbow type and he wasn't going to dull his colours for anyone. If Jase couldn't accept him, warts and all, then this relationship didn't have much of a future, although the thought of never seeing Jase again made his gut ache.

"Whatever. You going to take me home or do I go back to Nate?"

Jase got up, and taking his elbow, guided him to the entrance.

"You ok, Tigger?" Cuddles called out as Jase almost frogmarched him across the car park.

"I'm good," he called back over his shoulder. Jase didn't release his arm until he'd opened the passenger door of the Fiesta and shoved him inside.

The short ride back to the flat occurred in total silence as did the walk up the iron stairs to the flat. *Well this is going to be one hell of an evening.*

Jase was probably going to lock him in the flat to stop him sneaking out, not that he'd do that now. Post Dimitar, running alone in the chilly, silent darkness had lost a lot of its appeal. Still being shut in such a small space all night with a distant, pissed off Jase was not going to be fun. Yep, sleep wasn't going to be happening tonight.

As soon as they walked in the door, Jase locked it, grabbed him by the front of his shirt and pushed him up against the door.

"No talking," he growled before taking his lips. The passion of the man was overwhelming. Chris didn't resist, he opened for him immediately, going from one hundred percent pissed off to one hundred percent passion in the blink of an eye. His dick came to life as Jase ground his large, fit body against him.

He felt Jase's hand go between him and the door and it squeezed his arse so hard it made him gasp. Fuck, he loved it when Sarge came out to play. He wanted nothing more than to sink to his knees and suck him until it drove Jase out of his ever-loving mind. The grip in his hair and on his backside meant he couldn't move, so he did what he wanted to do to Jase's cock, to his mouth. Jase groaned when he sucked on his tongue and ground his erection into his thigh. He'd never been particularly upset about being short before, but a couple of extra inches would have meant he could rub his dick against Jase's when they were standing up. That would have to wait until at least one of them was horizontal.

Jase pushed one leg between his, and started to press against him in a rhythm older than time. The next second, his shirt was being pulled over his head, followed quickly by Jase's. His eyes focused on Jase's tight abs, and he couldn't help himself dipping to suck one dusky flat nipple.

In an instant, he had Jase's jeans undone and his hard as nails dick was in his hand.

"I did this," he muttered against Jase's lips as he started to stroke him.

"I've been thinking about this all night, it made me crazy seeing you smile at other guys."

Chris halted his movements. "But who am I with, Jase? Who did I come home with? Whose cock is going to be in my mouth in a second?"

Jase groaned and moved back slightly giving Chris the space to fall to his knees, but he stopped him as he dived towards his straining dick.

"Mine, always mine and mine alone, promise?"

"Promise. Can I have it now?" he said looking up through his eyelashes at Jase's face. When Jase moaned, and pushed his jeans and boxers off as if they were burning his skin, Chris knew he had him back. The silence on the way back made perfect sense now. Jase hadn't been pissed off with him, he'd just been bloody horny.

Sarge put his hands on the door behind Chris and he obediently opened and took him in. The smell, the taste and feel of his passion was overwhelming.

"Ah, fuck I love seeing you do that."

Chris couldn't reply, but he gave him an extra hard suck to show he loved it just as much. He ran his hands up Jase's body as it rocked into him, caressing, tweaking and playing him for all he was worth. Reaching up, he presented his fingers to Jase's lips and he took them in, sucking on them just as hard as Chris was doing to his dick. As soon as he pulled them out of his mouth, he slid his now slick fingers behind Jase's tight balls, and stroked his hole. Bobbing for all he was worth, he pushed a finger inside Jase's wet heat as he massaged his tight balls with his other hand.

"Ah, fuck," Jase exclaimed and used both hands to ram Chris's head onto himself as he came down his throat. Chris was gently cleaning him up, when Jase seemed to come back from whatever nirvana he'd managed to send him.

"Fuck, I love your mouth," Jase said as he helped Chris to his feet.

"Come on, let's get you clean and in bed."

Chris smiled at the thought of some soapy fun. Jase had most definitely got off, but he hadn't.

"Join me?"

"Nah, I'll have one in the morning. You need to wash that make-up and club stink off," Jase said as he wandered towards the bedroom stark naked.

"Fucking wonderful," Chris muttered to himself as he made his way towards the bathroom. So far in their relationship Jase had been paranoid that they both got off, but it looked as if he'd only been making the effort at the beginning. It didn't bode well for the future.

"Did you say something?"

"No," Chris huffed.

"Chris? No playing with yourself, your dick is mine. I want it ready when I want it."

It was probably the angriest, most uncomfortable shower Chris had ever had. His dick seemed to be waving at him like a kid trying to get his teacher's attention. It certainly had his attention, especially when he took the plunge and washed it. Jase moaning about his make-up pissed him off too. It wasn't as if he wore it as a matter of course, but he hadn't wanted anyone pointing out the slight bruises he still had at the club. So he hadn't been able to resist the mascara Russel left in the staff bathroom for the go-go boys, big deal.

Not that there had been any dancers tonight. He made a mental note to ask Russel about it tomorrow. Changing the format of the club probably wasn't a good idea, the place was known for its entertainment.

There was a towel lying on the bed when he wandered in, still damp and naked. Little stubby candles burned on the chest of drawers and both bedside tables. He paused, not sure he could live up to Jase's expectations. 'Romantic' wasn't something he'd ever done.

"Lay down."

Jase's voice coming from behind the door made him jump.

"I'm not sure I know how–"

"Do you remember me telling you that you were in trouble for your behaviour at college yesterday?"

"Yesss," he replied slowly, wondering where Jase was going with this.

"Well this is your penalty. I get to do exactly what I want to you, and you are going to do exactly what I say, when I say it. Tonight is all about my enjoyment, not yours. On the bed, on your belly, eyes closed. Do not open them until I tell you too."

Chris did as instructed, the anticipation giving him delicious butterflies. Was he going to get spanked, fucked, teased within an inch of his life? The worst thing he could think of was that Jase wouldn't touch him at all. After the day he'd had, he was buzzing; If Jase thought enforced immobility without being touched was a suitable punishment, he was bloody well right.

The bed dipped and Chris tensed. Two stuttering breaths later, a single finger touched the back of his neck, then slowly travelling down his spine, causing a wave of goose bumps to bloom over his damp skin.

The single finger was joined by one from Jase's other hand, and they traced his shoulders and back. He couldn't suppress the shiver as Jase's featherlight touch teased over both of his buttocks at the same time.

"So tense, so stressed..." Jase murmured.

"Yeah, I haven't exercised that much for–"

"Did I ask you a question?"

"No, but–"

"Toys need to be seen and played with, not heard. You are allowed to make noises if you wish, but no words, not unless I ask you a direct question. Understand?"

Chris grinned into the towel. He'd played this game before, not often, but he knew the rules. This wasn't romance, it was BDSM.

"Yes, Sarge."

Jase's strong fingers started to massage the area between his neck and shoulder. He couldn't help the sigh of pleasure, but it turned into a grunt of discomfort as Jase hit a knot.

"Let's see if I can loosen you up," Jase said decisively and got off the bed. He imagined Jase drinking in the sight of him stretched out on his belly, waiting and accepting everything he wanted to do to him.

The bed beside him depressed, and a trail of almost painfully hot oil hit his back, he gasped, but held his position as the trail snaked across his shoulders and down to the crack of his backside. It didn't hurt as much as melted wax, but there was no way he was going to tell Jase that he already had experience of this sort of thing. What he did know, was that blokes that were into this dominance thing wanted genuine reactions, loud, genuine reactions and the trust of their partners. Chris knew he could give him that.

Jase straddled his upper thighs and set to work spreading the oil into his skin with firm assurance. Chris let out a grunt as Jase's strong fingers found a sore spot caused by the tension of two days spilling his guts to strangers and then using his dancing muscles which hadn't been flexed for many weeks. It only took a few moments of attention for the knot to relax, and for Jase to find another.

The massage proceeded slowly, deliberately, and Chris found himself almost becoming one with the bed as inch by inch, he relaxed. After making sure his back was completely relaxed, Sarge shifted downwards and started treating his calves to the same procedure. This was what heaven had to be like, having someone paying attention to him in a good way.

He knew why people watched him at work, which was the main reason he loved it. He'd been an inconvenience for most of his life, so being wanted, really wanted, for whatever reason, felt fantastic. It was shallow, but true all the same. He'd hoped that Jase seeing other people watching him, knowing that it was him going home with the bloke everyone wanted would have been good for both of them. It hadn't been, because Jase hadn't enjoyed it. Then again, if this was a direct consequence of the green-eyed monster, maybe it wasn't such a bad idea.

Balancing his own social nature, and Jase's jealousy and possessiveness was going to be difficult. He really needed to stop thinking and just enjoy this, but that was why he didn't usually do slow. Unless things were full on, his damn hyperactive mind interrupted things.

Jase worked his way up his right thigh slowly and firmly. Chris moved his legs apart to give him more access in the hope that Jase would take the hint sooner rather than later. But if there was one thing he'd learnt about Jason Rosewood over the short time they'd been together, it was that the man did things according to his own timetable.

The still warm oil hitting his crack and balls made him twitch back to wakefulness. Holding still while Jase's thumbs rubbed gently over his balls was delicious torture, especially when the touch became firmer, and a finger stroked the delicate skin between his balls and his ass firmly. When he started to press his rapidly resurrecting erection into the mattress, he received a gently slap to his butt cheek. Taking the hint, he concentrated on keeping still while Jase continued to slowly explore his body. It took Jase's finger pressing into his hole lightly before it left to continue teasing his balls to make him moan in frustration.

"You're being a bastard again," he growled as Jase bypassed his hole for the fifth time.

"I always am, especially with someone I want, and I've never wanted anyone as much as I want you. Everything about you drives me crazy. Turn over, I want to see your face."

Chris flipped over quickly. Jase loomed over him. The lust in his eyes, the way he possessed the space between them, made Chris's heart stutter. *Crap, this is going to be good.*

Balancing on one hand, Jase firmly stroked Chris's straining erection. Hovering his mouth over his, Jase took in his involuntary gasp as he took his hand off his dick and forced two fingers inside him.

Keeping his mouth a hair's breadth away from his, Jase devoured each and every small reaction to what he was doing to him. His intense focus pushed Chris almost to breaking point. He'd been horny most of the night, watching other guys make out, feeling Jase's and Nate's eyes on him, not to mention numerous others. His poor dick had been up and down more times than a bloody yo-yo and it felt as if it was going to explode all on its own in the very near future.

"Please Sarge, I can't do this anymore. If you don't fuck me soon..." Chris could hear the roughness, desperation and desire in his own voice and it did nothing to calm him down.

Jase pulled back enough so Chris could lift his knees up and hold himself open.

"Please, I need you," Chris pleaded. To his joy, Jase shifted between his legs.

As Jase positioned himself and started to push in, Chris blew out a long breath knowing that it helped to stop tensing up, he didn't want anything to make this perfect moment awkward. Jase pushed in steadily until his balls hit Chris's ass cheeks, giving them both what they craved. In contrast to the wild ride of two nights ago Jase started rocked gently into him, savouring the experience. Chris started to push up against him, trying to get him to go faster.

Jase stopped moving. "My turn, remember?"

It wasn't until Chris forced himself to relax, that Jase started to move again. Chris was pretty sure that orgasm denial would be an effective interrogation technique, because right now, he'd say or do virtually anything to tip over the edge.

And yet, Jase kept up the same maddening slow pace, his eyes fixed on his. Surely this was affecting Jase as much as it was him, even if he had come earlier? He could feel him hard as a rock inside him and sweat beaded on his forehead. The bugger was faking. The desire to see Jase lose it, bypassed the mental need to climax himself, although he wasn't sure his body would listen to him.

If he let his own passion overwhelm him, he'd probably miss watching Jase come. He tried to think of anything else but the constant, spark inducing strokes against his prostate and the way his dick was rubbing against Jase's belly. As his balls started to tighten, he tried to elicit Jase's help.

"Stop, stop I can't hold it, I want to see you go first," he gasped.

Jase clearly wasn't going to show him any mercy. With a swift change of position, Jase leaned on one elbow and grasped Chris's leaking, rock hard shaft, pumping it in time to his hips as he went from gentle rocking to hard, sharp thrusts which slapped their bodies together.

"You bastard. Ah, fuck yes," Chris gasped as his body exploded as Jase continued to thrust into him and pump him with his fist. The sparks of light behind his eyes and his convulsing body, almost completely blanked out the fact that on his third pulse, Jase grunted and strained against him, emptying himself inside him.

Both were left panting and sweat slicked, with their foreheads touching, but it was only a few moments before Jase pulled out slowly making them both wince. Lowering his legs, Chris was more than happy to lay spread-eagled and boneless to bask in the afterglow of the most intense climax he could remember as he dropped towards sleep.

He had a vague idea that Jase wiped him down before crawling into bed and kissing him gently on the forehead. Cuddling into him, drunk on the lassitude that had claimed him he murmured, "Best sex ever."

As Jase's arms went around him, he felt loved, relaxed and totally, utterly, content.

"That's because that wasn't just sex, that was making love."

CHAPTER 37

Jase

J ase smiled to himself as Chris mumbled incoherently, rubbed his face in his pillow and relaxed back into sleep. He'd gotten up at about eight, made himself a coffee and gone back into the bedroom to watch him. It was odd, worrying even, how obsessed he was. Whenever Chris was out of his sight, hell even out of range of his touch, he worried about how quickly he could get to him if there was trouble.

It irritated him that Nate was probably right about him projecting his own fears onto Chris. It annoyed him even more that he knew he shouldn't go to the club tonight to prove to both of them that Chris could look after himself in such a familiar environment.

He looked so vulnerable sleeping in their bed, but Chris wasn't the innocent he appeared right now, even if he should be. This complicated, infuriating young man had certainly seen more of the ugly side of life than Matt. When he'd been in various war zones, yes he'd seen, heard and smelt hideous things, but apart from those few minutes after the bomb had gone off, he'd been able to keep his mental distance. He'd always known there was somewhere familiar in the world where he was guaranteed to be safe and loved. It'd been like a bullet proof vest between him and the hideous realities he'd faced.

What Chris had lived through would have made most people withdrawn and suspicious, or sent them diving for the bottle, the syringe, or a whole bottle of pills. And yet he still smiled and took joy in virtually everything.

Knowing sleep was a precious commodity for Chris, he wandered into the second bedroom. A smile tickled his lips at Chris's insistence that they keep the kiddie carpet. On the desk were several drawings, part of the college assignment he'd been set. His mood fell by a few notches.

These hadn't all been there when they'd left for the club last night. Despite all his efforts, Chris had been up in the night yet again, but at least he'd come back to bed at some point.

Unlike most of his pencil portraits, these were painfully colourful. One depicted Chris's face at the bottom in monochrome, with coloured and distorted images exploded out of his head. A melting clock, a tearing calendar, the back of a young man dancing so fast he blurred and several comic hero 'bangs' and kapows,'; the variety and movement was frantic and uncomfortable. Another showed Chris as a bottle of lemonade as a giant hand shook him. A third showed a colourful blurred figure, streaking across a grey cityscape like the Flash.

If this was how Chris felt, no wonder he blew up so easily. Keeping himself from exploding as much as he did must take major self-control, not a lack of it as Jase had assumed.

He turned his mind to the coming day and how to keep Chris occupied without exhausting him because he had work tonight. The first item on the agenda was food, then he'd give him the bracelet. Although how Chris would react to it was anyone's guess. The rest of the day would be taken up by a day of fun and painting a mural in Ryan's bedroom before he took him back to work. The question of whether to leave him there alone or stay again was one he didn't want to face yet. It was a sure thing that if he did leave him, he'd be on tenterhooks every second, but next week, he'd have to leave him for at least some of every day as Chris had college, and he had work.

Twenty minutes later, Chris ambled into the living room, looking gloriously relaxed and sleep mussed. Before doing anything else, he walked straight up to Jase, wrapped his arms around him and gave him a soft kiss.

"Mornin', sexy," Chris said and smiled against his lips, not showing any desire to release him.

If this was the way Chris preferred to start his day, it was fine by Jase.

"Scrambled eggs on wholemeal toast alright with you?" Jase asked.

Chris pulled a face as he stepped back. "You been taking lessons from the cook at Dad's home? I've still got all my own teeth and my bowels are fine thank you."

"Eggs are good protein, and wholemeal toast gives you slow sugar release. Stops sugar highs and lows."

"Yes, Dad," Chris said with a grin as he settled himself on a stool.

"Don't think you're sitting there like Little Lord Fauntleroy while I do all the work, there's laundry to be done. Those bedsheets must be humming after last night."

Instead of the expected scowl, Chris smirked. "Yeah, that was, erm, pretty damn good, even if it wasn't what I was expecting." He got up and started to move around the counter towards him again.

"The laundry is that way," Jase indicated the bedroom with a finger in between cracking eggs, even though his dick was twitching at the thought of a little morning glory.

This time, he did get a scowl. "Didn't anyone tell you you're a killjoy?"

Jase gave him a bright smile. "Frequently, but I'd rather have you thinking about me all day. As you found out last night, waiting makes things better. Besides, Ryan is waiting for his dragons."

Chris's face fell. "Oh shit, I forgot about that," he said then trotted out of the room to get the bed linen, his disappointment at the lack of morning glory forgotten.

Jase moved to the side to give him access to the washing/dryer as he brought the bundle back. "Do you know how to use that?" he asked as Chris opened the door of the machine.

Straightening up, Chris frowned. "Could you use a washing machine when you were eighteen?"

"Well, yeah. I joined the army at sixteen; they taught me."

"I learned at seven. Mum had a job doing service washes at the laundrette underneath the flat where we were squatting."

"So you spent time there because there was no one else to look after you?"

"Yeah, that's right," Chris muttered as he squatted down and started to load the machine.

Jase put his hand on his shoulder. "Truth, Chris, always the truth."

Chris glared up at him. "Why? So you can feel even more sorry for me? Didn't you get enough of my sob story over the last couple of days? You're an intelligent guy, work it out. With mum the way she was, who do you think did the washing when no one else was around to see?"

Jase squatted down too, even though it made his ankle twinge. "Yes, I feel sorry for you. I'd be a unfeeling bastard if I didn't. Your childhood sucked to the moon and back compared to mine and there's nothing either of us can do about it. But the more I know, the more I understand you. And I want to understand you more than anything else in the world. So, the laundrette wasn't too bad?"

Chris finished loading the machine and got the detergent out from under the sink. He glanced at Jase, then helped him to his feet by bracing his upper arm underneath his armpit and lifting.

"Ask for help if you need it," he said as he let go and put the detergent and softener in the machine drawer and turned it on. "And yes, the laundrette was good, especially when it was cold outside. There was a kiddie colouring corner with crayons and paper."

"What happened?"

He shrugged. "I overheard a woman saying she was going to call social services because they had a kid doing the work. We left that afternoon, but it was a good couple of months."

"What did you do after that?"

He shrugged. "Went to some other squat, same old, same old. At least they didn't mind me drawing on the walls. After yesterday, you probably think my childhood was all crap, but it wasn't. I played in the park, had McDonalds, went swimming, went to the seaside in the summer. I got birthday and Christmas presents, even if they were probably nicked," he said then smirked. "I also learned how to pick locks and pockets, burgle houses, shoplift and beg like a professional."

"Your records don't say anything about being charged with burglary."

Chris's grin got wider. "Guess you're going to have to decide whether I'm a good liar or a bloody good house breaker then, aren't you?"

Jase didn't return the smile. This wasn't a laughing matter. If Chris carried on with his former life of crime, he couldn't continue to have a relationship with him.

Chris tilted his head to one side. "What's going on in that head of yours?"

"You know what my old job was and what my new job is, right?"

"Yeah, I'm not a goldfish. I can retain information for more than three seconds. You were a military copper and now you're going to be a bailiff. Just like the bastards who used to turf us out of squats."

Jase winced. "Bailiffs aren't bastards, they're just getting back money and property for their rightful owners."

"Tell that to the people that end up out on their arses in the snow," he said, then held up his hands in a 'don't shoot me' gesture. "But as it's going to keep a roof over my head, I'm good with it."

"Do you know how much we charge if we need a locksmith to break in to a property?"

"Nope, and I'm not doing it," Chris said adamantly as Jase dished up eggs.

"That's because you probably couldn't."

"Er hello? Who's the goldfish now? State of the art rich git's penthouse with paperclips? Give me a set of lock picks and I can be in anywhere within ten minutes at the most."

"Illegally," Jase reminded him.

"Yep, and I'd do it again if I had to."

Jase's heart dropped at his matter of fact admission, especially as Chris seemed completely unrepentant.

He poked a finger in Jase's direction. "You've never been hungry or cold without knowing you were going to be able to eat or warm up in the near future have you? I have. And just because I don't agree with the way you earn a living, it doesn't mean that I'm going to be on your back about it," he said and started tucking into his eggs as if he hadn't eaten for days.

Jase started eating too, if significantly slower than Chris. What Chris had just said applied equally the other way around. He'd laid down the law about Chris not dancing at the club, even though Chris clearly enjoyed it, and was bloody good at it.

Growing up, he hadn't thought about the people his father evicted, apart from the fact they were doing something illegal, or not paying their bills. The fact that Chris, a vulnerable child, had been on the receiving end multiple times, and that he might have to do the same to other children, wasn't comfortable. Unfortunately, if he didn't, he wouldn't be able to keep a roof over Chris's head. The thought of being homeless probably bothered him far more than it did Chris, who'd spent his life rolling with the punches.

"You done?" Chris asked. When he nodded, Chris reached for his plate. Seeing his slender wrist reminded him of the GPS cuff.

While Chris started on the washing up, he fetched it. Placing it on the kitchen counter, he announced, "Nate got you a present."

Chris turned around, dried his hands on a tea-towel but didn't pick the leather cuff up. "Why?"

"Peace of mind. It's got a panic button under the bar. You just swivel it, press and it sends an alert with your location to a designated mobile phone." Jase waited for the inevitable explosion.

"Sweet," Chris said and picked it up. After turning it over in his hands and examining it closely, he moved the bar to see the tiny button located on the underside. Unless you knew what you were looking for, you'd never see it.

"So if I'm in the shit, I just press this," he did so, and Jase's phone rang a second later. "And the cavalry comes galloping, wherever I am," he said and immediately started to strap it on his wrist.

"You don't mind?"

Chris looked up from admiring the piece of functional jewellery. "Why should I? We both know I'm not exactly Mr Reliable. The trick will be remembering to press the damn button when I need a hand."

"It also sends a 'soft' alert if your heart rate changes dramatically. Just promise me you'll never take it off when we're not together."

"Duh, I'm not that thick. You might have to remind me to put it on before I go out though. I may not be a goldfish, but I'd give a koi a run for its money if my mind's on something else."

Jase chuckled. "Easy enough. Ready to get creative?"

Chris's bright smile lit up his face. "I'm always ready for that. I'm also always ready for–"

"And I'd appreciate it if you don't say things like that in front of Ryan, my very straight best friend and my parents."

Chris's grin got wider. "So Kate's not out of bounds?"

Shaking his head in despair, Jase went to get ready to go out.

CHAPTER 38

Chris

Jase popped his head around Ryan's bedroom door. "You done?"

It took Chris more than a few moments to work out what he was on about. Glancing over at Ryan's 'Shrek' clock he realised his shift at the club started in less than an hour.

He'd been at this for six hours straight, or he would have been if Kate hadn't appeared every few hours to ply him with sandwiches and diet pop. When they'd arrived and the pleasantries were over, Ryan had managed to concentrate long enough to choose which of the dragon sketches he liked the best. As soon as Chris started sketching on the wall, the little boy got bored and went to play outside.

Matt had been sent out to collect the required paints. He presumed Jase had gone to visit his folks as he heard the lawnmower start up next door. By the time Matt had returned, Chris had been just about ready to paint and he'd dived right in.

Standing back, he assessed his work. The foreleg of the red dragon was slightly skinny, but that was about all he could see to correct. He'd alternated between the red dragon and the blue one, so each had time to dry before he started adding gold and silver embellishments respectively.

"What d'you think?" he asked.

"Bloody–" Jase started only to have Matt cough loudly from behind him as Ryan pushed past his legs.

"Wow, Uncle Chris! That's fantastic." Chris swept the little boy up in his arms as he reached a hand towards the still wet mural.

"No touching till tomorrow, Squirt, or you'll smudge them. You don't want smudgy dragons do you?"

Ryan immediately folded his arms, which made Chris laugh. He remembered being told hundreds of times to fold his in school in order to prevent him fidgeting.

"How much do we owe you?" Matt asked.

The expression on Matt's face a second later told him that his answering glare had been successful. "If you ever say something like that again, I will be..." After a pause and a glance down at Ryan he settled on 'very cross.' "This is a present for my favourite nephew, isn't that right, Ry?" he said as he put the boy back on his feet.

"Yeah, Uncle Chris, you're the best." Chris high-fived him, then crouched down so he was almost at his eye level.

"These grown-ups give you any trouble, you just come and talk to me. I'll sort them out."

Ryan frowned. "You sure? Cos Daddy might smack your bum too."

"Why'd he do that?"

"I hid his keys. I wanted him to play in the garden with me instead of going to work."

"Did it hurt?"

Ryan grinned. "Nope. It wasn't even really my bum. He missed and got the back of my leg instead. Mum smacks harder even though she's littler."

Chris had to work hard to stop smiling, and he heard a strangled groan from behind them.

"Well I don't think your Daddy could catch me to smack my bum even if he wanted to. I'm fast."

"My daddy is fast too," Ryan defended.

"I feel a race coming on," Kate said as she squeezed into the small room.

"Yeah. Race, Race, Race!" Ryan chanted as he bounced up and down.

Chris grinned over at his brother. "You game old man?"

"I caught you the first time we met, I can do it again," Matt said with a smile.

"You wish. Right, where we running to?" Chris asked as he started to work the kinks out of his shoulders.

"It better be in the direction of the flat, or you're going to be late for work," Jase said drily.

Ignoring Jase, he looked over at his brother, with a frown. "Was he a party pooper when you were kids too?"

"That would've been me," Matt replied. "Jase was always the adventurous one. How about a lap of the park next Saturday morning? We'll rope some of the drivers in, make it a company exercise. Loser washes the lorries in the afternoon."

"You're on," Chris said quickly, knowing that Jase would probably think up some excuse to stop it. Besides, he usually washed the trucks on a Saturday anyway, or at least he had done before he'd been taken.

After a lightning quick visit home to shower and put on his game face, he joined Jase back in the car. Unfortunately, Jase didn't look happy. *What the hell's wrong with him now?*

As they pulled out onto the main road, Jase asked, "Do you still have to wear make-up if you're not dancing?"

This was what Nate had been talking about; if he didn't take a stand, Jase would mould him into someone he didn't recognise. That might or might not be a good idea, as he was an almost legendary fuck-up. However, if Jase pushed too hard, too quickly, Chris knew he'd likely implode and do his patented buggering off act and lose it all. Jase had said he wanted the truth, so that was what he was going to get.

"I'm trying, I really am. I've agreed to stop podium dancing, but I can't change overnight. I don't even know if I want to. Besides, it's only a bit of mascara and tinted moisturiser."

Jase kept his eyes on the road, with a maddeningly blank expression on his face.

"I take it you don't like it?"

"You're gorgeous without it, I don't see the point."

The pleasure at the compliment was tempered by the fact that he'd probably be asking him to change the way he dressed next. Would he let Jase throw away all his bright slogan t-shirts and skinny jeans and replace them with camo, combats and polite conversation?

As they pulled into the club car park Chris waved to Cuddles as they headed to the far end. When the car stopped, Chris reached for the door handle and heard the lock clunk shut. Sighing, he turned to Jase, and raised his eyebrows for an explanation.

"I only want you to be the best person you can be. There's more to you than eye candy, and I'd like for you to see that, to see what I see one day." The earnest expression on his face made Chris feel all fuzzy inside, but he also knew Jase's faith was misplaced.

"Yeah well, one day at a time, eh?" he leaned across and gave Jase a sweet, chaste kiss.

Getting down and dirty in the car park would not only make him late, but Jase probably wouldn't appreciate the audience. It didn't bother him in the least, which was useful, considering the number of times he'd done exactly that around the back of the club.

"Do you want me to stay with you tonight?" Jase asked.

The question came completely out of the blue. Chris pulled back and looked towards the club. The distance between the car and the entrance seemed to multiply. This was exactly where Dimitar's car had been that night. Cuddles, Russel and Jase hadn't been able to stop him being taken before, but he'd left the building on his own.

Jase kept his eyes glued to me all of last night, there was no way anyone could have gotten to me, but without Jase? Russel's got a job to do, and a staged fight would distract Cuddles long enough for it to happen again. But I don't have the right to turn Jase into my own permanent security guard. At some point, I have to face life without Jase being only a foot away, but tonight?

"You don't want to come in?" he found himself asking. *Christ, I sound like a fucking wimp. They shot me full of smack, they didn't cut off my balls.*

"That wasn't what I asked," Jase's voice was as controlled as he'd ever been.

"Unlock the door," Chris said through gritted teeth. He might beg in the bedroom, but this wasn't a sex game.

"Is it really that hard to admit you need me?"

Turning back around, he looked Jase straight in the eyes. Green eyes that held understanding and sympathy, not pity. Truth Jase had said, so he gave it to him.

"Yeah, actually it is. And I'll cope in there on my own tonight and every other night."

Jase reached out a hand and cupped his face. It felt so good that he closed his eyes and leaned into it briefly. *It would be so much easier if I could just let him take over and just be what he wants me to be.*

When the warmth left his face a moment later and he opened his eyes, Jase was undoing his own seatbelt.

"I thought you weren't coming?"

Jase shot him a smile. "When did I say that? I just asked if you wanted me in there, because whether you do or not, I'm coming."

Chris hastily shut his mouth when he realised he'd been gaping. "You really are a git sometimes, aren't you?" Chris said, but he couldn't help chuckling. Jase had played him like a bloody violin, rather like he had last night.

"Come on," Jase said opening his door. "You don't want to be late and you've got to get your uniform on yet."

* * *

With Jase sitting on a stool at the bar, Chris relaxed and managed to enjoy his evening, although he did shoot the two new go-go boys some evil looks as they gyrated on the podiums. As usual, Russel came out to help behind the bar as the place filled up.

"What d'you think of the new meat?" he shouted into Chris's ear.

"Stiff as boards and not in a good way," Chris replied in the same manner, knowing he was being bitchy and not giving a damn. He was down here, getting covered in beer slops while Pinky and not so Perky were getting all the attention.

"Want to show them how it's done?" Russel's lips curved into a smile Chris remembered well.

Last time he'd seen it, he'd received the pounding of a lifetime a few seconds later. Being in there with Jase the other day had been more than good, but bloody hell, Russel was a big forceful bugger. Just the thought made his dick twitch.

His eyes flicked to Jase, who as he'd done all night, was watching him intently. "Sorry Boss, I can't."

"Because you don't want to, or because he doesn't want you to?"

Chris frowned. "Don't push it. You're my boss and hopefully a friend; I don't want to piss you off. But Jase is...well, Jase."

Ten minutes later, 'Desire' by Years and Years came on. Watching the two guys up on the podiums, doing what he wanted to do, but badly, with his own groupies leering at them, made him sick to his stomach. He loved this song; it had just the right amount of sensuality and pace to make it an ideal, sexy dance tune. Plus, it was sung a gay dude.

"Go on," Jase's voice made him jump. He hadn't realised the man had changed position. *Must be all that military ninja training.*

"What?"

"Get up there and show them how it's done."

"What?" he shouted again, sure he hadn't heard what he thought he had.

"Go dance on that bloody platform before you explode."

With the message received loud and clear, his face almost split in two as he grinned. Not bothering to manoeuvre around Russel and the other barman to the half door, he vaulted nimbly over the bar.

As he got to the only vacant podium, the central one, he found Jase right behind him. To his amazement, Jase boosted him up with his hands on his waist.

Harry and Steve came over from their position at Pinkie's podium and started chanting 'Tigger', which was taken up by most of the rest of the clubbers. He felt on top of the world.

Looking over to Russel he circled his hand above his head. A few seconds later, 'Desire' restarted, and he began moving his hands over his chest as the sensual rhythm began. He lost himself in the music, dipping, twisting and gyrating.

When it started to fade, he looked down to see Jase with a wry smile on his face. When Jase put his hand in the air and circled it, he couldn't believe his luck. A glance over at the bar showed Russel gesturing for him to continue, so he did.

The music took over his body and mind. When he felt a hand on his leg, he nearly kicked it away before even looking down. When he did, it took his foggy mind a few moments to recognise it was Jase down there.

"Come on, down you get," he called over the music.

"I'm good," he replied.

Jase turned into Sarge before his eyes and it sent a shiver of desire up his spine. "Down. NOW."

With a frown, Chris jumped down, only to stumble as his knees went wobbly. Jase and another unfamiliar man stopped him face planting on the sticky dance floor.

"Whoa, careful there sweetie, I think you need a sugar top up," the middle eastern looking guy with a carefully manicured beard said into his ear. One of his hands was on his upper arm. Fear shot through Chris as the man's other hand stroked the front of his shorts. *Fuck, it's one of them, it's happening again.*

He was pulled swiftly against Jase, as Sarge glared at beardy.

"Mine," he growled.

Beardy straightened up, trying to look down his nose at Jase. "I don't see a label on him."

Chris's heart calmed slightly. This guy had a London accent; all of his kidnappers had possessed foreign ones. This was just a pusher punter and he had a gold and silver BDSM symbol pendant nestled in the chest hair visible because of his open shirt.

Chris held up his wrist. "This enough for you? A collar is a bit restrictive when I'm dancing."

The lust and disappointment in the guy's eyes was obvious, but he let go and backed off a step all the same. He didn't look at Chris again.

"My apologies. I didn't know he had a Master. Perhaps you should mark him more obviously and permanently. I certainly would if he were mine. You're a lucky man. Congratulations," the man said before walking away.

Instead of shouting to make himself heard, Jase presented his watch. Crap, it was two thirty, he'd been dancing for over two hours and the club was due to close. Russel always had a 'cool down' period of about half an hour before kicking out time when he stopped the entertainment and slowed the music. It was time for his patrons to pick partners, go home and enjoy them.

They made their way to the staff area, passed couples kissing, talking and groups getting ready to go home. Jase waited while Chris collected his stuff. As Jase was with him, he didn't bother changing. Exhaustion hit him, making his limbs heavy and his mind slow and he intended to hang on to the sensation as long as possible. Unfortunately, the journey home would probably wake him up.

Not bothering to talk, they left the building and Chris slipped his arm around Jase's waist, cuddling in to his side. An arm went around his shoulders.

"You ok? Did that guy worry you?"

"Bit. S'ok though. BDSM types are sticklers for protocol."

"Protocol?" Jase asked as he unlocked Chris's door and waited until he was seated.

Chris sighed. He really didn't want to explain it all if Jase was completely ignorant. Besides, knowing him, he'd probably think it was a damn good idea, being a confirmed dominant type. He appreciated that, he really did, but he didn't want to live in the lifestyle. Rough and ready, over enthusiastic passion, the occasional bondage game and instructions designed to keep him from boiling over were one thing. Being on his knees all the damn time and 'yes Master's' morning, noon and night were not things he wanted, even if it did do it for his partner.

"Yeah. That bloke was into it. The pendant was a BDSM symbol." To stop further conversation, he curled up on his seat and closed his eyes.

The next thing he knew, Jase was opening his door, gently pulling him out and guiding him up to the flat. Without a word, he led him into the dark bedroom, sat him down on the side of the bed, took his shoes off, pushed his shoulder until he keeled over and tucked him in. A few seconds later, he felt the mattress depress and Jase's arm draped over him.

"Go to sleep, I've got you."

Cocooned by someone who loved him, warts and all, he drifted off easily.

CHAPTER 39

Chris

Jase was still asleep when he woke. Glancing at the clock he was shocked to see he'd slept till nine, which was bloody fantastic. To show his appreciation, in a more restrained way than diving under the covers and giving him a blow-job, he decided a full English was on the cards. After a quick shower, having finally got out of his club clothes, he dressed and headed for the front door.

As he reached for the handle, he had to smile at the photo of the cuff stuck to the door frame. Automatically he checked that it was on his wrist. Jase was looking after him, make that nagging him, even when he was asleep. He'd even used a photo instead of a written note to get around his dyslexia. It felt...nice. Leaving the image exactly where it was, he left the flat.

After breakfast, the rest of Sunday was filled with visiting. They popped over to Nate's, apparently so Jase could do some hydrotherapy. Although Chris wasn't surprised when Nate wanted to talk over a cuppa.

"Do you think about it?" Nate asked.

"Smack?" Chris shrugged. "Sure I do, but no more than once an hour." Nate snorted in laughter as he shook his head.

"But I understand my mum a bit better now."

Nate nodded in understanding. "Do you think you'll ever try it on your own?"

Jase's 'truth' lecture popped into his head. "Haven't got a clue, but I hope not."

The encouraging smile on Nate's face told him he'd said the right thing so he carried on. "I've seen loads of people try to get clean. Motivated, determined people who fall off the wagon after a month, or a year or more. Mum lasted two months once. I know it'll always be there at the back of my mind, a way to make all my troubles disappear, but it just creates more in the long run."

"And that's just the attitude to have," Nate said with a smile.

Chris held up his wrist. "Thanks for this."

To his surprise, Nate looked a little embarrassed. "Yeah well, I hope you never have to use it. You're a good man and you've got a hell of a lot going for you. Don't end up like my brother, that's all the thanks I need."

They spent the afternoon visiting his dad at the nursing home. It was odd how old folks were often more accepting than the younger generations. Ten cheeky sketches of staff and residents in compromising situations later they were on their way to Jase's parents for Sunday dinner. Judging from the smiles on the faces of all three Rosewoods, as he and Jase left for home three hours later, he'd managed to behave himself this time.

The following week was taken up with daily visits to a gym where Jase sweated with weights as Chris became the darling of the exercise classes. They visited Jase's sick aunt Jean on Wednesday. It was clear Jase and his aunt had a close relationship, and he tried not to be jealous as they reminisced about Jase's almost idyllic childhood. But he managed to charm the cancer-ridden lady enough to make both her and Jase smile. Little by little, he was starting to understand what made Sarge tick.

Chris did another shift at the club on Thursday and worked on his college assignment, but the 'race meet' on Saturday was put off due to a rush job at Kemp International Haulage. He spent the day washing the lorries that weren't working and doing gardening chores for his brother and Jase's parents. Playing water pistols in the garden with Ryan was fun, especially when they teamed up and attacked Jase when he was reading the Sunday papers on the patio.

All in all, it was probably the most stable, 'ordinary' week Chris had ever had. Jase had made sure he had at least three meals a day, and as a result, his appetite had kicked in big time. Jase had looked on in amazement as Chris helped himself to a third helping of roast potatoes at his parents' place for Sunday dinner.

He'd just grinned and said, "What? You jealous of my fast metabolism old man?"

The comment had led to an all evening sex session where Jase proved without a shadow of a doubt that there was nothing about him that was remotely 'over the hill'.

Seven hours later, Chris was still roaming their flat, wide awake as Jase slept. He'd finished his small portfolio for Tracey and in a few hours he'd be on his own at college. Jase could be a hundred miles away evicting some poor sod.

He wanted to run, wanted to lose himself in dancing or some other vigorous physical activity. More rampant sex 'Chris style' would be good, but just because he couldn't sleep he didn't have the right to inflict his insomnia on Jase. The poor bloke had done his very best to wear him out tonight and he had to go to work today. The familiar feeling of the walls closing in as he started to buzz caused him to open the front door and go sit at the top of the steps leading down to the parking area. Even with cuff on, he didn't think Jase would appreciate it if he took off for a run without telling him. Besides, it was still dark and that bothered him now.

There were a scattering of lights in the housing estate behind the shops. Had they been left on for a child afraid of the dark or were there other insomniacs out there? Maybe one or two were parents tending to infants. Knowing he wasn't the only one awake as he watched the sun rise made him feel a little less isolated.

Movement from behind him, caused him to turn. Jase stood in his boxers and vest top a few feet away. Despite the frown, or even because of it, he looked seriously sexy. Chris wondered if he'd ever get used to having him in his life, or whether this was just a wonderful interlude he'd remember and cling to for the rest of his life. Whether this was a short or a long-term thing, he was going to enjoy it and try not to let his own stupid behaviour bugger it up. The last two weeks had been pretty much perfect.

"Sorry. I didn't want to disturb you, I got up early, big day."

Jase wordlessly indicated the door to the flat with his head. His mood deflating at the thought of the lecture he was going to get, Chris pulled himself to his feet.

Jase was busy in the kitchen, getting a bowl of cereal and a mug of black coffee.

"Want some?" he asked.

"Yeah, thanks."

Once they were both eating, Jase paused between mouthfuls. "How long did you stay in bed after I dropped off? And don't bother with the 'got up early' line. The bed was cold."

Chris winced. "About an hour. No big deal. I've had a more than a few good nights lately, thanks to you. Besides, I didn't want to disturb you."

Jase put his spoon down. "You don't have to go into college if you don't want to. If you need more time, that's fine. You could go to the gym and hang out with your dad and Kate today."

"I'm good," Chris replied around a mouthful. "Got to be done some time."

* * *

Jase was ready to leave for work half an hour later, dressed in his black bailiff's uniform. It wasn't nearly as appealing as his green military one. Chris kept busy with his sketchpad, not wanting to associate his lover with the people who had put him out on the street again and again.

"Kiss for good luck?" Jase said.

"Don't need it," Chris mumbled keeping his eyes averted.

"I was talking about me."

Knowing he wasn't going to get out of it, he kept his eyes on Jase's face as he pecked him silently on the cheek. Wishing him luck, when he was hoping to take some poor bugger's home or possessions away, didn't seem right.

As he pulled away, Jase held on to his upper arms. "This really bothers you doesn't it?"

He shrugged. "A bit, but it's necessary, like going to the dentist. Doesn't mean I have to be all excited about it, does it?"

"No it doesn't. And we all have to do things we don't like sometimes, like when you went to the police which I am still in awe of by the way. Just so you know, I've always wanted to start my own private investigation agency, but it's this while we get ourselves sorted out financially, ok?"

Chris blinked in surprise. "You're doing a job you don't really want to just because of me?"

Jase smiled and cupped his face. "You do it for me," he said before brushing his lips against his again. "Now, remember to charge your phone, but keep it on silent. You don't want it going off in a lesson. And try not to piss off too many people on your first day."

Chris smirked. "Me? As if. I'll be the definition of a model student."

Jase gave him a pointed stare, but the corner of him lips twitched with amusement. "And I'm Batman. Just behave yourself."

Chris kept the smile on his face until the door shut and then he slumped. *School again, bloody brilliant.* He'd thought he'd left all this behind when he'd left his last foster home. The difference was that now, if he really didn't like it, he could leave without the threat of a truancy officer hunting him down.

Not wanting to sit around the flat on his own, he stuck on his tight red 'I'm a Cunny Funt' shirt and dark blue skinny jeans. Remembering Jase's instructions, he stuck his charged phone, wallet and keys in his pocket, his art in the folder Matt had bought him, and checked that the cuff was on his wrist.

It was only seven thirty when he reached the college, having jogged most of the way in hope of getting rid of some of his fidgets. The college didn't open for another hour, but music drifted out from inside. If he wasn't very much mistaken, that was 'Grease Lightnin'. Curiosity got the better of him and he tried the door. It opened.

Following the sound, he found himself in a new part of the building.

"Tense your abs Chloe, you're never going to get a smooth twist if you don't. Good, Annette, just try to point your toes a little more. Remember, use the energy in the music," a strident female voice called out.

Judging from the noise, this was some sort of dance or exercise session and it was probably a good idea that it wasn't going on when normal classes were happening.

Why the hell didn't they have classes like this at any of the schools I've been in before? Then again, this was a specialist arts college, not one of the dumping ground comprehensives schools he'd be assigned.

Turning a corner, he saw a couple of guys leaning up against the wall, chatting quietly.

The blond one looked over, smirked slightly as he read Chris's shirt. "You waiting for your girlfriend?"

"Nah, just heard the noise. I'm early; it's my first day."

The guy nodded. "It's pretty good here. I'm Artie, that's Jim. We're music majors. My girlfriend is taking performing arts. Jim is just hoping." Artie grinned and rubbed his side where Jim had elbowed him.

"What're you into?" Jim asked.

"Art. What are they doing in there anyway?" Chris nodded towards the door.

Both boys grinned. "Pole dancing," they said at the same time.

Chris returned the smiles. "Hoping to get an eyeful are you?"

"Wouldn't you?" Jim, the one with brown hair, replied.

Chris decided to keep his opinion about ogling girls to himself until he knew them a little more. Jase wasn't just across the corridor today.

"You're not going to see much out here are you?"

"The teacher kicks everyone out that isn't actually in the class once it starts, but we go in for a few minutes while they warm up and then when they cool down at the end," Artie said and waggled his eyebrows.

"Got to love those stretches," Jim added.

"Why don't you just join the class? Poles aren't that different to the rings or a pommel horse."

Jim frowned. "How the hell would you know?"

Giving away what he did for a living probably wasn't the best idea in the world. Although he wasn't particularly proficient at the pole, the Toolbox did have one and he'd practiced quite a bit when the club wasn't open. When he'd first started going there, there had been a girl who had been pretty good. She'd shown him a few things before moving on to a straight club. The Toolbox was heavily male biased and she hadn't been getting the amount of tips she'd expected.

He shrugged. "I've tried it a couple of times. It's definitely a talking point if you're trying to pick someone up."

Artie chuckled. "I bet it is. Bit gay though, isn't it?"

Hiding his preferences had never been part of his personality, and if he pretended to be straight and it came out he wasn't, which it would, it probably wouldn't go down well.

"Depends on who you're trying to pick up. As it has two good looking blokes hanging around with their tongues hanging out, just for a glimpse, I'd say the girls in there have got the right idea."

The boys glanced at each other. "You're erm, gay then?" Jim said hesitantly.

Giving them a friendly smile he said, "Yeah, but I've got a boyfriend, a jealous, ex-military grumpy one, so you're not in any danger." He paused, and looked them up and down a little more carefully. "Although, come to think of it–"

Jim's eyes lit up and he pointed a finger at him. "Your name's not Chris is it?"

Alarm bells started to ring. He'd only been in the building for a few minutes and it was going tits up already. Maybe school wasn't such a good idea. Glancing towards the exit, he wondered how fast these two were. They looked quite fit, but it could be 'skinny teenager' syndrome rather than 'work out' fit.

"Yeah, why?" he asked warily.

Jim punched his friend on the shoulder, a wide smile on his face. "This is the dude who drew that art teacher's brother-in-law sucking dick." He looked at Chris, "Right?"

"In my defence, I didn't know they were related when I did it."

Artie's face was also split by a big grin. "At the cost of sounding American, that was awesome. Everybody's been talking about it. What the whole college wants to know is, was it you in the picture?"

Chris glanced down at his shoes trying to think of a suitable answer that wouldn't have him labelled even more than he already had been.

"Whoever it was, he isn't very proud of it. And as he didn't have much of a choice at the time, I'll keep his identity to myself if you don't mind. I'd better get going," he said and turned to go, not wanting to field any more embarrassing questions.

"Hold on, you don't have to go," Artie said. "Yeah there are still some homophobic arseholes around, but we're not."

"My sister's gay," Jim announced as if it was a badge of honour.

"Good for her?" Chris said hesitantly. Did these 'progressive' youngsters want a round of applause for not being bigots? Nevertheless, he was pleased he didn't have to make a run for it.

The music stopped in the dance studio. The instructor told her pupils to keep up with their daily fitness program.

Artie opened the door and a wave of heated, sweaty air blasted out. "Hey Philippa, I think we have a new recruit for you," he called out as Jim pushed Chris through the door.

"This is THE guy, you know the one that did THAT picture," Jim informed the class.

The universally female students all turned towards him. Some had contempt and disgust written all over their faces, although most just looked interested.

The blonde, pony-tailed thirty-something teacher frowned at the three male invaders to her feminine preserve.

"This is a female only class," the teacher said. It was exactly the right response to remove Chris's reticence.

"It's alright, he's gay," Jim piped up helpfully.

Some of the girls giggled. Chris ignored all of them and plastered a smile on his face.

"Miss? It doesn't say anything about it being female only on the prospectus," a tall, dark-haired girl said.

"That's Annette, my girlfriend," Artie whispered to him proudly.

The teacher turned to her. "This is a class for those serious about learning pole fitness, not larking about."

"Oh, I'm serious," Chris said, although he'd had no intention of joining in until that moment.

Philippa raised an eyebrow. "Well, would you like to show us what you can do?"

"Sure," he said. The look of surprise on her face was very satisfying as he crouched to undo his trainers. "How about you play 'You can leave your hat on,' again?"

She was about to press the button, when he spoke up again. "Erm, Philippa is it?"

She turned around, a smug expression on her face. "Changed your mind?"

"Not on your nelly. I just wanted to check what I'm allowed to do. I learned from an erm, 'professional' pole dancer."

Philippa looked as if she'd sucked on a lemon and Chris had to work hard to keep a smirk off his face.

"This class is pole fitness, not 'exotic' dancing."

"Oh, I'm fit," Chris assured her with a grin, thoroughly enjoying himself now he knew he wasn't going to get lynched. "Go-go dancing every weekend at the Toolbox keeps me in good nick."

The gasp from the enraptured students made him grin. *Fuck, this is fun.*

"I can have a word with the doorman if anyone wants to pop by, as long as you're over eighteen of course," he said to the crowd behind him that seemed to be growing by the second.

The bell for the first lesson of the day was greeted with a collective student groan. Philippa pointed a finger at him. "Lunch time, you are mine Chris Bacon," she announced and a cheer went up.

"How does she know my name?" Chris asked Artie as he started to do up his trainers again.

"Are you kidding? After the near riot you caused, everyone knows you, mate."

CHAPTER 40

Chris

As soon as he had his shoes on, Chris found himself bundled out of the classroom by Artie, Jim and Annette, although some of the other girls looked at him like he was something they'd trodden in.

"Don't worry about them," Annette announced, "they're just jealous."

Chris blinked at her. "Of what?"

"Of them being so boring when you're so interesting," she confided as she hung onto his arm. "I bet you know all about fashion. You'll have to come shopping with me," she gushed.

"Being gay doesn't mean he's Gok Wan," Artie said, eyeing Chris's shirt.

Chris laughed. "If you're into obscene t-shirts, skinny jeans and gay club gear, I'm your man, anything else, you're up the creek without a paddle." He paused, touched his finger to his lips then pointed at Jim in a very limp wristed gesture. "Actually sweetie, I can see you in purple sequins, they'd go fabulously with your eyes," he said and blew him a kiss before dropping the act as he laughed.

Jim punched him on the shoulder. "I knew it; he's trying to infect us. I'll have you know I'm one hundred percent immune to the gay."

"Ah, but who immunised you? Was it Mr Challis, cos I've seen him watching your arse," Artie teased his friend.

The good natured banter carried on till they got to Annette's form room. "See you at lunch?" she asked him.

He held up his art folder. "As long as the head of art likes my stuff, yeah. If not, here's my number." The three grabbed their phones and hastily input his details.

Chris headed to Tracey's office along mostly empty corridors, quite bemused that he seemed to have made a few friends already. These 'arty' types were a lot more accepting than any students he'd met before, as were the staff. He resolved not to give any of the staff a hard time, unless they started on him. As long as Tracey didn't take one look at his work and tell him to sling his hook. Nerves started to bubble again as he neared her office.

Taking a deep breath, he knocked on the door. A minute later, he was sitting in front of her desk, desperately trying to stop his leg bouncing up and down as she looked at his drawings, one after the other.

Putting them down, she fixed him with a searching look. "I think we can help refine your talent, but I think learning how to commercialize it will be the biggest benefit you can get out of being here. Your portraits are exceptional, but these are pretty good too. However, although our courses are hands on and vocational based, they will require note-taking and some written material."

The panic on his face at the word 'written' must have shown as she gave him a reassuring smile. "And we can help you with that. The point is, it won't all be fun. You'll have to explore some things you won't find easy, some things you probably won't enjoy. The courses contain a wide variety of subjects from fashion to web design."

"According to one of your female students, I've already got a distinct advantage on the fashion front, due to the gayness."

She laughed. "Who told you that?"

"Annette. I was about to show her and the rest of her classmates how to pole dance in a 'vocational' setting," he said as did air quotes.

"You like to dance?"

"It's how I made ends meet before I met Jase. I work at the ToolBox."

"The club?"

He noted with surprise that she hadn't prefix the name with 'gay'. "Yep, I worked the podiums, but I mostly tend bar now. Jase got a severe case of the green-eyed monster when he saw where guys stick the tips." He knew he'd gone a step too far when she winced briefly, but if he hadn't been looking for it, he might have missed it.

"You do know you can study dance here?"

"Ballroom and ballet aren't really my thing. Tights and tight trousers," he thought for a moment, then nodded slightly. "Actually, the tight trousers might work, as long as they're stretchy."

"You can specialise in modern and street dance. Some people do manage two courses at a time."

She stood up as Chris blinked in surprise. "It's something to think about. There's only a few weeks left of this term, the new courses start in September. Use this time to find your way around, talk to the other students, although the ones here now are halfway through their courses. Those graduating have already left."

She took a slip of paper out of her desk drawer. "This pass will give you access to any classes you want to sit in on. Just don't disturb the other students or the teacher if you decide a particular class isn't for you. And remember, the students have been at this since September, so their work might be quite advanced. Now, I do believe there's a design class starting in a few minutes. I'll walk you over."

Chris found himself sitting next to Alex at the back of a classroom with large wooden tables rather than individual desks. This time, he was greeted with a shy smile from under the hood.

"Nice to see you back," Alex said. "Although I'm not sure I can take the excitement of another class with you."

Chris grinned. "I can assure you that was a one off. I'm really boring most of the time. What're you doing?"

Alex's raised his eyebrows at the 'boring' claim, but he still shifted the large design portfolio he was working on so Chris could see it.

Chris examined it for a few minutes, noting the progression from a 'mood board' to more fleshed out designs. They were all universally depressing tattoo designs, an angel of death, skulls, a demon coming out of a rip in skin. Alex had some seriously dark shit going on.

"Ink, huh? You want to be a tattoo artist?"

Alex shrugged. "What I want isn't really on the cards. My folks think I'm going to make a mint in graphic design, adverts, websites, that sort of thing."

"Not your bag though?"

Alex's shoulder twitched again. "It's what my dad does for a living, he owns an advertising company. What do your folks do? And are they alright with you having a boyfriend, especially one who's older than you?"

Going into his background wasn't going to happen, not yet anyway. Alex was freaked out about the fact he was out of the closet, let alone any of the many other dinosaur sized skeletons he had stuffed in there. Then again, looking at his portfolio, Mr Middle Class Emo would probably love his dark and twisted tale of woe.

Leaning back slightly, Chris plastered a shocked expression on his face. "Whoa. Three questions at once? Don't know if I can take the pace."

It made Alex smile, so he hit him again.

"You really should do that more often, you're cute when you smile."

Alex's face turned pink as he looked down, breaking eye contact. "You think?"

Chris bumped his shoulder with his. "You got something to tell me, Alex? Coming over to the dark side are you?"

The boy beside him looked like a rabbit caught in the headlights and Chris immediately felt guilty.

"Don't worry, I won't say anything. As for my folks, up until recently I was on my own for quite a while. My mother didn't mind me being gay." The sharp glance from Alex showed he hadn't missed the past tense reference.

"I met my dad and my half-brother for the first time a couple of months ago, they don't care. About me being gay that is," he hastily added. "They care otherwise. Jase is my brother's best friend. It works pretty well."

"You're so lucky," Alex blurted out.

That wasn't something Chris heard every day, if ever. The majority of spontaneous reactions he elicited were poor kid, shut up, suck my dick, or piss off. The last three often came in that order. To his surprise, he realised he actually was lucky. Life, right at this moment, didn't only not suck, it was pretty damn good.

He was saved from saying anything else by the tutor coming over to discuss Alex's work, although she did nearly all the talking. Alex seemed almost crippled by shyness and Chris resolved to do something about that ASAP.

With his plan firmly in mind, Chris dragged Alex along to the dance studio at lunchtime. Not only were Artie, Jim, Annette and the students from the morning session present, there was standing room only in the corridor.

As soon as he walked into the room, Artie and Jim started chanting, 'dance off, dance off' as the teacher rolled her eyes.

She held up her hands. "No dance off, in fact, everyone out."

Grumbling, most of the students left, but Chris asked if his new friends could stay. Philippa grudgingly agreed.

"I only know one routine well," he announced as he toed his shoes off and removed his socks. "It's a bit erm... raunchy."

Phillippa looked over to Annette. "Stand in front of the door so they can't see in." When the tall girl was in position, the pony-tailed teacher looked to Chris. He started to reach for the pole.

"Warm up?" Philippa's disapproval came through loud and clear.

He grinned at her. "I'm always warm, in fact, I'm smoking." To prove it, he swung up into a side spin, before inverting and performing a spinning chopper.

The round of applause he received made him grin as he turned himself the right way up and did the few other moves he knew, including several variations of the splits, and the eye opener, which always went down well at the club. He supposed it was because the clubbers were imagining it was their 'pole' he was sliding down with his legs pointing upwards in a 'v' on either side of the pole.

When he let go, he bowed to his appreciative audience, but although the students were clapping, Philippa was eyeing him speculatively.

"Go on Miss, show him how it's done," Annette called out.

With a smile, Philippa swung up into a complicated routine that made him gape. When she finished, he was the first to congratulate her.

"Well that showed me, but I bet I can still out twerk you any day of the week," he grinned.

"I'll do you a deal. You show me something else, something clean, and you can come to my pole fitness classes."

"Done," he said quickly, mainly because he was going to ask if he could join the class anyway. Burning off a little energy before lessons was probably a bloody good idea. Besides, the pole at the club was now completely vacant.

The 'clean' aspect of his assignment was the problem, then he had a lightbulb moment.

"You got 'Men in Black' on there? It's not my usual style by a long way, but I did this at my brother's wedding a couple of months ago. I didn't want to give the grannies a heart attack. Not that you're a granny," he hastily added as Artie and Jim sniggered.

Two minutes later, his small audience were all clapping in time to the music as he went through a significantly embellished version of the routine he'd done with Ryan. At the end he got a round of applause instead of the tenners in his shorts he got at the Toolbox, but it still felt good.

Philippa carried on clapping, slowly, after the others finished and he started to feel a little nervous; she was a professional after all. The room became quiet and he rubbed a drip of sweat off his forehead. After thirty seconds, he couldn't stand the silence anymore.

"Well?"

"You sure you haven't had any lessons?" she asked as her face broke into a smile. "I'll see you tomorrow, seven o'clock sharp. Now out, all of you, I've got lessons to organise."

Artie came forwards and high-fived him, closely followed by Jim. Annette gave him a hug and whispered 'I need twerking lessons' in his ear.

"Now that I can do," he told her as the bell went for the afternoon session.

His phone tinkled with a text message.

Did u eat lunch? J. XX

"Bugger," he murmured to himself, then looked up. Alex was the only one still in the studio and he looked a little stunned. Walking over, he asked, "Is there anywhere I can get a quick sugar fix?"

"Cafeteria's got some machines. I'll show you," Alex said quietly.

Chris typed **goin now XX**, pressed send and hurried after the Alex who still had his hoodie up. He noticed that although the others had said hi to him, Alex had only nodded in reply, essentially stopping any further conversation.

"You ok?" Chris asked as he caught up.

"Yeah," came the reply but Alex didn't look up.

"Have you got a lesson now?"

"No, study period," Alex murmured.

Chris grabbed his arm, and swung him around towards the entrance to the college. "In that case, we're going for a McDonalds. Jase will have my guts for garters if I don't eat."

As they walked along the pedestrianised precinct a few minutes later, Alex looked as if he had the whole world on his shoulders. Chris wondered if this was just his 'emo' persona or if he actually had something to worry about. To cheer him up, and because he was still buzzing, he started doing dance moves as he walked down the pavement.

Alex looked quickly from side to side. "Would you quit it? Someone might see."

"And we should care why?" Chris said. "Life is about living, Alex my friend. Yeah, sometimes crap happens, but it's better than living under a bush. And as I've done that, I know it ain't nice."

To prove his point, he decided climbing the lamppost outside Cooper's was an epic idea.

He was halfway up and doing a passable spinning chopper, even if the pole was significantly bigger than a usual dance pole, when a male voice called, "Oi you, get down."

He looked down to see a pissed off security guard from Cooper's. He would have told him it was a public place and he could do whatever he wanted but Alex looked mortified. The kid had shrunk so far inside his hoodie, that Chris couldn't see any skin at all. He came down. Maybe he had gone a little far. Small steps with Alex was probably the order of the day.

"What's the problem?" he asked the guard with an overly contrite expression.

"Go play somewhere else, you're lowering the tone of the area."

Now that was just rude. "And how am I doing that?"

The middle-aged, portly guard scowled and leaned in closer. The smell of cigarettes on his breath nearly knocked Chris over.

"I said, piss off, you dirty little faggot, and don't let me catch you round here again."

There was no way this idiot could ever catch him; he looked as if breaking into a jog would give him a heart attack.

Chris blinked in mock horror and put his hand to his mouth. "Why, Mr Security Guard Sir, you're not... homophobic are you?"

Alex tugged on his arm, muttering "Let's go."

The guard literally growled, "I'd just love to show you what I'd do to you and all the other faggot freaks in the world if I had my way."

Chris couldn't help smirking. "Ooh goodie, a guessing game. Do I get a fifty-fifty, or maybe a phone a friend?"

"And what make you think a shit-stabber like you knows anyone that matters?" the guard said, looking him up and down as if he was a turd.

Chris's smile faded. He'd been playing up till now, but this was getting significantly offensive. This was broad daylight on an English street, and he didn't have to put up with it.

"How about your boss?"

"The head of security wouldn't know a cock sucker like you."

"Higher," Chris said.

"There's only the store manager that's higher than him, and he's married with a mistress," the guard sneered.

Chris leaned in and attempted to put his arm around the man but he pulled away as if Chris had a horrible infectious disease.

"Well that's where you're wrong. Again. Have you ever been up to the penthouse, Mr Security Guard? Cos I have. In fact, I have a standing invitation."

"You're a lying little shit, I should call the police and have you charged with slander. Mr Cooper would never have anything to do with the likes of you."

Chris tilted his head to one side, thoroughly enjoying himself. He knew he was perfectly safe, seeing as there was a crowd gathering. He raised his voice a little.

"All I was doing was dancing. Is that a crime these days?" The crowd started to murmur and the guard grabbed him by the arm and started to frogmarch him towards the entrance to the store. Chris pulled his phone out of his pocket and tossed it to a rapidly paling Alex.

"Call favourite three, tell him what's going on," Chris called over his shoulder.

Ten minutes later, Nate appeared in the security office of Cooper's looking dishevelled and particularly pissed off. Alex was with him. The poor sod looked absolutely terrified. For the first time since this little interlude had started, Chris started to wonder if he hadn't taken this a touch too far.

"Hiya, Nate," he said cheerfully as the security guard turned nearly as pale as Alex.

Ignoring both of them, Nate turned to Alex. "Thank you for calling. I would say chose your friends a little more carefully, but since I know Chris, I won't bother. He has a habit of drawing people in. Like a grinning trapdoor spider."

"Hey!" Chris protested but Nate ignored him and carried on talking to Alex.

"Saying that, I don't think he's got a vicious or vindictive bone in his body. He's just been blessed, or cursed, with more energy than any one person has any right to and no 'off' switch. But if you do decide to keep hanging around with him, and I hope you do, please try to keep him from doing anything too ridiculous? I don't have time to bail him out all the time. I was getting ready to go to work." He turned back to Chris, but the security guard butted in.

"I'm sorry Sir, but—"

Nate quelled him with a glare and the man subsided back into his seat.

"Do you need to go back to college?" he asked Chris. Nate's expression said 'shit and fan' so Chris put on his best contrite face.

"Not as far as I know, but I'd like to. I think Alex definitely does. He really didn't have anything to do with this, I was just showing off. Sorry Alex. Sorry Nate." As usual, his quick 'sad puppy' apologies seemed to work their magic.

"I'll talk to you later. Now get back off to college, the pair of you."

Hoping he'd gotten away with it, Chris gave Nate a quick hug, mouthed 'sorry' again and hurried out as Nate turned to the security guard who was almost quaking in his boots.

Chris gave a grim-faced Alex a grin as they left the building. "See? Wasn't too bad. What did you tell Nate on the phone?"

"I told him a security guard was picking on you, using homophobic language. Who is he?"

Chris hooked his arm across Alex's shoulder. "That handsome hunk of eminently edible man-flesh is Nathan Cooper, heir to the Cooper retail fortune, including this place, although he plays at being a paramedic and drugs councillor. I stayed with him for a while." Chris decided buttoning his lips about the reason he'd been at Nate's was an excellent idea.

The blond boy turned wide eyes to him. "You haven't slept with him have you? Cos he's..."

Chris grinned. "Very hot, not to mention loaded? Yes, he is and no, I haven't slept with him. I'm not a complete slut." He grinned. "Well not any more anyway. But if I didn't have Jase it could probably happen, cos he swings our way and he's always at the Toolbox watching me shake my stuff."

Alex pulled away from him. "I'm not, I'm really not–" he stuttered.

"Yeah, and I'm the Queen of Sheba. I said I wouldn't out you and I won't. That's a decision you have to make, but I hope you can see that not everyone's a bigot, especially if you don't wave it in their faces all the time, which is a habit of mine I may have to look into curbing."

Alex glanced at him, then down at his trainers as he shoved his hands into his baggy jeans. "It's never going to happen for me. My dad would throw me out, after beating the crap out of me."

Chris pulled the taller boy in for a one armed hug as the reason why he was so quiet and withdrawn became clear. "I know it probably seems like the be all and end all now, but being on your own isn't as bad as sounds. Sleeping rough isn't fun, but you get by."

Alex looked at him sharply. "That's sounds like personal experience. I thought you were kidding with the sleeping under a bush comment."

Chris shrugged. "I've learned to roll with the punches and come up swinging."

Alex shook his head. "I don't think I could do that."

His new friend was looking at his shoes again.

The thought of how Alex would have coped if those kidnappers had picked him instead didn't bear thinking about. It made those horrible hours he'd spent at the police station even more worth it. Maybe this 'do-gooder' thing had something going for it after all.

"If the shit ever hits the fan at home, or anywhere else, give me a ring. I don't know if you've noticed, but I happen to have my very own personal cavalry ready and waiting to gallop to the rescue. Plus, I have access to several top class sofas."

When Alex didn't reply, he decided to leave the subject alone. Not everyone was ready to be out and proud; he'd had nothing to lose, but it looked as if Alex did.

He certainly wasn't ready to face an angry Jase when he found out he'd made a spectacle of himself yet again. To say he had his fingers crossed that Nate wouldn't tell Jase about his latest indiscretion was an understatement. Then again, Jase loved him, so it would blow over eventually. Maybe after some significant apology sex, if he was lucky. Feeling eminently cheerful, he jogged off to his next class.

After ten minutes, he decided that it was probably one of the ones Tracey referred to as 'less enjoyable'. Online art marketing wasn't the most intriguing subjects, but if he did what Jase suggested and set up a website for custom portraits, he'd need to know about this. He diligently collected the handouts, which looked like Greek to him, to go over with Jase later before making his way out of the building.

As he started to jog home, he began plotting just what he could do to put a smile back on Jase's face. The list was fairly extensive, especially given last night's 'erotic fantasy' confession session. What he did would really depend on how tired Jase was after his first day at work and whether Nate had told him about his little indiscretion.

He was about five minutes from the flat when the sound of car tyres squealing behind him made him start to turn, just before something hit his thigh hard and he flew up into the air.

To be continued....

Thank you dear reader, for finishing this book, I hope you enjoyed reading the first part of Paint. If you did, please consider writing a review on the site where you bought it. Without reviews, independently published books are virtually invisible on retail sites. By letting fellow readers know what you think, you are helping them and supporting the hard work of authors such as myself.

Scroll down for a sneak preview of the next part of the series Paint #2: Blank Slate, which continues Chris and Jase's story.

If you leave a review for this book on Amazon and/or Goodreads, I'd be so grateful. It doesn't have to be lengthy, even if it's just a single word against your star rating, it would mean a lot to me.

Here are the links you'll need:

Amazon: http://amzn.to/2polLfo

Goodreads:https://www.goodreads.com/book/show/31417087-optical-illusion

Follow Emma Jaye via the following platforms for
exclusive teasers, giveaways, and more:
FACEBOOK: https://www.facebook.com/EmmaJayeAuthor
FACEBOOK GROUP: https://www.facebook.com/groups/jayesjezabels
NEWSLETTER: http://eepurl.com/cPlmC1
WEBSITE: emmajayeauthor.com
GOODREADS: https://www.goodreads.com/author/show/7083115.Emma_Jaye

EMMA JAYE BOOKS

Paint: Contemporary m/m romance
Paint 1: Optical Illusion
Paint 2: Blank Canvas
Paint 3: Invisible Ink

Incubus Paranormal m/m
Incubus Seduction
Incubus Possession
Incubus Pain
Incubus Trial
Incubus Freedom

Call Girls: Contemporary erotic romance
Call girls 1: The Beginning
Call Girls 2: Merissa
Call Girls 3: Sasha
Call Girls 4: Lucy
Call Girls 5: Emily
Call Girls 6: Missy
Call Girls 7: Nick (In production)

Hybrid: Sci-fi Reverse Harem

Hybrid 1: Discovery
Hybrid 2: Experiment
Hybrid 3: Flight
Hybrid 4: Fight
Hybrid 5: Silkash
Hybrid 6: Gladiatrix
Hybrid 7: Chimera
Hybrid 8: Reunited
Hybrid 9: Metamorph (In production)

The succubus Trilogy: Paranormal Dark Romance

Seeking the Succubus
Before the Succubus
Winning the Succubus

Naughty or Nice? Xmas fantasy/humor/romance

Holly Berry
Tinsel Time
Jingle Balls (In Production)

BLANK SLATE

CHAPTER 1

Chris

Spinning up out of unconsciousness had never been one of his favourite experiences. As soon as he worked out where his arms and hands were, he tried to check for needles as the recurring nightmare of dying from a drug overdose claimed mind.

His mother hadn't even finished giving herself that last shot. Hours after the fact, he'd found her with the syringe still in her arm and her fingers on the plunger. If she hadn't pushed those last couple of cc's she might have survived, that time anyway. His recent experiences with heroin at the hands of kidnappers had made the nightmare return with a vengeance, and he sure as hell knew he wasn't waking up from a normal sleep.

His left arm felt as if it was encased in treacle so he used his right hand to check it. Something pulled in the back of his left hand when he touched it. *Those bastards have got me on a fucking drip so I can't wake up.* Clawing at the needle, he tried to pull it out even before he'd managed to open his eyes.

A large hand closed around his wrist and panic surged. Someone was making gurgling noises.

"Easy Chris, easy. You're in hospital. It's just a saline IV; you're safe."

Matt, that's Matt. What's he doing back from honeymoon? The question spun in his mind briefly but his first priority was getting the needle out.

"It's all right Chris, I'm taking it out, just hold still," another male voice came from right near his ear. As Matt carried on holding his arms, a sharp pain in the back of his hand let him know the needle had gone.

"Chris? Can you open your eyes for me?" the voice Chris assumed belonged to a medic asked. Now that the needle was out, the brief surge of adrenaline faded and all he wanted to do was sleep. Even though he could vaguely hear Matt and several other voices, angry voices, he fell back into darkness.

The next time he woke, the spinning sensation was slightly diminished. But Christ Almighty, he had the mother of all headaches. Despite the fact that his eyelids felt as if they had anvils attached to them, he managed to crack them open. It was dark in the room apart from a soft light coming from behind and above him.

He was lying almost flat on his back in a hospital bed. Something was wrong with his eyes as everything beyond about a foot was fuzzy. There was a big silver safety bar on either side of him and his left leg was raised in the air with all sorts of metal work around it. The limb didn't look or feel as if it belonged to him and he certainly didn't feel like moving to test anything.

Straining his eyes, he made out a male figure sprawled in a chair next to the bed. It wasn't Matt. He wracked his mind for what seemed like hours before a name solidified in his mind. Jase. Matt's interfering, bloody-minded and incredibly sexy best man. *It's his fault I'm here, I was running to the club from Matt's wedding reception because soldier boy here was being a domineering dick. Or was I running out of the club? Stuart jumped me on the road and bundled me into Matt's pick-up. Why do I remember some Eastern European blokes being there, with needles?*

As his mind shied away from the jumbled memories, he groaned. A spike of pain lanced through his head at the sound. He froze, not wanting to do anything to cause a repeat.

The man's eyes flicked open. In an instant, he was by his side. Jase looked as if he'd been dragged through a hedge backwards, for several days. *Why isn't he limping? Was his hair always that long?*

"Chris? Oh thank God, I thought I lost you. You're going to have to stop doing this or I'm going to be grey before I'm thirty. How's your head?"

Head? What happened to my head? He tried to speak, but no sound came out.

"Don't worry, I'll get someone. It's so good to see you awake," Jase said, then bent, kissed his forehead gently and wiped his own eyes.

What the fuck? He's crying over me? We barely know each other. Just sharing a bed for one night wouldn't... He remembered Jase holding him tenderly as he rocked gently into his body, smiling as they lay on the sofa in Kate's old flat. *That didn't happen did it? Am I confusing him with someone else? Am I tripping? Did someone slip me some acid? There were needles, I remember needles... Fuck, did I OD?*

His focus was taken off his rapidly rising panic as he heard a door open and a good looking, dark-haired man he vaguely recognised, swam into focus.

"Hi Chris, remember me?"

'No, not really,' he tried to say, but nothing came out. *What the hell happened to me?*

The man smiled. "Don't worry if you can't. I'm Nate, we're friends."

Chris started to repeat the name and heard a gurgle. With horror, he realised he was making a noise like a partially block drain. *Why the fuck can't I talk?*

"Chris? Chris look at me. You've had a head injury so don't worry if you can't remember things or speak properly right now. Now, unless you want an IV back in, you're going to have to take at least some fluids by mouth. Do you think you can cope with a drink? Blink once for yes, twice for no."

Mind whirling, he blinked once. As Nate put a straw to the right side of his mouth another man, older and wearing a white coat, started taking his vitals.

"Chrisander? I'm Dr Beckett; I'm the neurologist in charge of your case. You're at the National Neurology Hospital in London. I'm afraid you had a rather nasty accident."

"Accident my arse, and his name's Chris, not Chrisander," Jase growled from somewhere out of his field of vision.

"Can he be moved now?" An elderly woman with an American accent was speaking. She was probably another hospital official; they must want this posh room back. *How is Matt affording all this?* He finished drinking, and was mortified when Nate blotted his chin with a paper towel. *Have I been dribbling like one of the living dead at Dad's nursing home? Why am I so knackered? I've only been awake for what, two minutes?*

Relaxing back on the pillow, he tried to see where Jase was. For some reason, he'd felt better when he'd been able to see him. Unable to keep his eyes open any more, he stretched his fingers, the ones that worked properly anyway, hoping for some human contact. A hand closed around his. Working hard, he opened his eyes. Jase was leaning over him.

"I'm not going anywhere. Even if we end up sharing a tent, I'm sticking right next to you from now on." Chris tried to smile but his eyes were too heavy to keep open. Instead, he squeezed Jase's hand weakly and felt it squeeze back.

The doctor was speaking again. "Yes, he can be moved in a few days as long as he continues to improve and the plane has a full medical team on board. But there's no guarantee he'll do any better with the intensive facilities you mentioned."

Plane?

"Is he guaranteed to regain all his faculties without them? Is he likely to be worse if he has a dedicated rehabilitation team for as long as it takes?" the woman asked.

"Of course not."

"Do you have the expertise, the time and money to devote a team to a single patient here?"

"This is a world class facility, Mrs Baccioni. We—"

Chris's mind stuttered. *Mrs Baccioni?*

"It's a simple, yes or no, answer, Doctor. Do you have the ability to provide the same level of care I do?"

"No, we don't." The doctor sounded as though he was gritting his teeth.

"So we've established I can provide superior medical care for him. Can you guarantee his safety? Will you have round the clock security to prevent whoever did this from trying again?"

"Nobody is going to hurt him again, not while I'm here and I'm not going anywhere," Jase growled.

"And I'm sure Chrisander appreciates your dedication over the last week, Mr Rosewood. But you do have to sleep sometimes, and you're not exactly fully fit yourself."

"We'll take turns, as we have been doing," Matt said.

You tell 'em bruv.

"For how long, Mr Kemp? You're all getting what, five or six hours sleep a night? The police haven't caught whoever deliberately ran him down, or the gang that kidnapped him. They don't even know if the same people are responsible. Do you agree that your half-brother, my grandson, should receive the best possible care available and be safe on the other side of the world from whomever did this? Someone who might very well want to finish the job they so nearly accomplished?"

Don't send me away, please don't send me away, I've just found you, I can't to be on my own again, please.

"Matt? You can't possibly be thinking about letting him go to America with someone he doesn't know, who doesn't know him, even without his injuries?" Jase's voice was strained.

You tell him Jase. Fuck, I'm so tired.

"We all know Chris has some complex issues. He's likely to run the first chance he gets if he's frightened or overly stressed," Jase continued.

He sounds like he's trying to be calm, but he's not. When is Jase not calm? Come on Bacon, stay awake, you need to know. But he could feel the claws of unconsciousness pulling him back down and he couldn't stop it.

"Mr Rosewood, with my resources, I'm sure I can keep one teenage boy with a broken femur and a brain injury from running anywhere." The sneer in the woman's voice was clear.

Although he couldn't make a lot of sense out of what was being said, something about the woman made him anxious. Jase started to pull away a little and he reached out, not wanting him to go, not wanting to be left alone.

"Sleep. I've got you and I'm not going anywhere."

Lips and a stubbly chin brush his forehead as a hand enclosed his. He immediately relaxed and the annoying beeping noise became a little less frantic. *Jase is here.* Even when his face moved away, Jase still held his hand. It was enough to let him slip away into blackness again.

"You didn't do that well with his mother, did you?"

"How dare you–" the indignant voice started but Matt interrupted her.

"Jase, she's his grandmother. Just like us, she's got his best interests at heart; hell, she's been looking for him ever since she found out he existed. Why do you think his mum made him paranoid about using his real name? She knew they'd take him away from her. And judging from what we know about his childhood, don't you think that would've been a good thing? How about you go with him to provide a link with home? I'd do it, but with Kate expecting, I–"

"No, I'll go, you need to stay here."

"I'm not sure that's a good idea, Mr Kemp," the imperious female voice started.

"Security is my business. He was only left unsupervised that day because I had to go to work. If I hadn't left him, this wouldn't have happened. I'll tell you what Mrs Baccioni, if you don't kick up a fuss about me accompanying him, and believe me, that's what's going to happen, Matt will not object to him coming with you. Plus I'll make sure he doesn't run away like his mother did and like he's done many times before. You've seen his care records, keeping him somewhere he doesn't want to be is virtually impossible unless you want to keep him in a prison cell. And with his ADHD, that might as well be a padded cell and a permanent strait jacket because being confined will turn him bat shit crazy."

CHAPTER 2

Jase

"Fine. We leave tomorrow. I hope your passport is up to date, Mr Rosewood."

"It is, but Chris doesn't have a–"

The woman looked at him as if he was missing several marbles. "Stephanie arranged it yesterday at the American embassy."

Jase breathed a sigh of relief as Kathleen Baccioni swept from the room. He'd never thought he'd have sympathy for Chris's mother, but having grown up with that as a parent was starting to change his mind. He would have wanted to escape too.

The first inkling that anything was wrong had occurred nearly three weeks ago when his phone beeped with the tone he'd set for the alert from Chris's GPS cuff. It had been his first day at work with his dad as a bailiff. As the bailiff's van was a manual, his dad had been driving because of Jase's still healing ankle.

So far, his day had gone better than he'd hoped. Although Chris had been nervy this morning, he'd appeared determined to go to his first full day at the local art college. He hadn't received a phone call from Chris or the head of department, a purple-haired woman called Tracey, saying Chris had got himself into trouble. Considering he'd caused a near riot after being in the building for less than an hour when he'd been interviewed, Jase classed this as a major success.

As for himself, they'd only had two jobs and both had been commercial premises. After Chris's childhood experiences with bailiffs, he'd dreaded having to put a family out on the street despite his dad reassuring him that they always helped vulnerable evicted people to find safe, emergency accommodation. However, he didn't think Marie Baccioni or people like her would have availed themselves of council services. When it had happened to Chris, his mother had just moved him to the next drug den.

Adrenaline flooded Jase's system as he pulled his frantically beeping phone out of the pocket of his black stab vest. The readout showed Chris's heart rate had spiked dangerously high and was now plummeting like a stone. He immediately hit the call button. The mechanical voice telling him the phone he was calling was not responding didn't help his own heart rate.

"Everything ok?" his dad asked. They were in North London, over an hour and a half away from home.

"Something's up with Chris; hang on," he murmured as he activated the GPS app.

Chris was near their flat. He wasn't moving and his heart rate was still falling. Not knowing what else to do, he dialled Nate.

"I was wondering when you'd call. It's alright, I already sorted it." The tall medic sounded thoroughly amused.

"Sorted what?"

"Chris and the homophobic security guard my family's store used to employ, he–"

"Chris is on Parson's avenue. He's not moving and the app says his heart rate is 40 bpm and dropping. His phone's off too."

"I'm on duty; I'll be there with an ambulance in three minutes." The way Nate's voice changed from amused to professional paramedic in the blink of an eye was reassuring.

Nevertheless, the next half hour was one of the longest Jase had ever experienced. The van could have been travelling through Narnia for all the attention he paid to the outside world as his eyes stayed glued to the app. His mind went through all kinds of disaster situations to account for Chris's terrifyingly weak heart rate as he willed it to keep going. Second by second, he flipped from calling Nate and then stopping in case it disturbed him from possibly saving Chris's life. At six, the locator started moving again, but it was going horribly fast and it wasn't following roads.

His phone rang, and he nearly dropped the damn thing he jumped so much. Nate's name blinked on the caller ID. It took a deep breath to gather the courage to answer.

"Jase? He's just lifted off in an air ambulance heading for the National Neurological Hospital; it's near Great Ormond Street Children's hospital in London. They'll be landing in Regent's Park and transferring him."

"Is he..." He couldn't complete the question, because it would make it real, but they didn't airlift non-critical patients.

Nate blew out a breath, he sounded sad and stressed. "We won't know till the experts get a better look, but he's had quite a bash to the head. Bastard hit him and just drove off. He's got a broken thigh too, and a lot of bruising but that's not important right now. Don't panic if the cuff stops working, they'll probably take it off, it doesn't necessarily mean the worst. Have you called Matt?"

"Shit, I didn't think, I–"

"I'll do it, just get your arse over there ASAP. Shit, you're not driving are you? Jase? Jase! You still there?"

The question brought him back out of the fog of shock that had descended.

"Yeah, we're on our way. Dad's driving." He didn't even remember ending the call.

"Where to son?" His father's reassuringly calm voice grounded him. Him panicking was the last thing Chris needed right now.

Jase had never hated London traffic so much, but at least they were going against the evening rush hour. His mind couldn't help swirling over the horrible premonition that they were rushing to see a dead man. The unwanted question of how many people Chris's fit young organs could help if he were brain dead flitted through his mind before he rejected the possibility. Those eyes couldn't possibly be blank, that face couldn't have grinned for the last time. The problem was, he knew how a life, even such a vibrant one, could be snuffed out in a fraction of a second.

It was thirty-six minutes before they pulled up outside the hospital. Jase got out while his dad went to find somewhere to park. It was another hour before he experienced the very welcome sight of Matt striding through the double doors of the waiting area of the intensive care unit. The nurses had only given Jase the 'we're doing all we can' speech because he wasn't family. He shied away from the fact that breathing didn't necessarily rule out brain death.

An immaculately dressed old woman, a late thirties blond man and a dark-haired twenty something girl came in behind him. Jase ignored them as he and Matt embraced.

"Any news?" Matt said as he pulled back.

Shaking his head, Jase said, "Nothing, apart from he's still breathing. You might get more information being next of kin but–"

"Chrisander's next of kin would be me, Mr Rosewood."

The woman had carefully coiffured white hair, and although her face was relatively wrinkle-free under the make-up, her neck was heavily lined.

"And who the hell are you?"

"Jason, mind your manners; we're all stressed here," his father said as he stepped up to Jase's shoulder and nodded to Matt.

"I'm Kathleen Baccioni, Chrisander's grandmother and his closest relative. You may go."

"Like fuck I will." His response wasn't professional by any means, but this wasn't a job, it was Chris.

The blond man took a step nearer to him as Mrs Baccioni's perfectly sculpted nose wrinkled as if someone had farted in her vicinity. She turned to Matt.

"Are you sure this is the man my grandson is infatuated with?"

"Look lady, whoever the hell you say you are, we're Chris's fami–"

"Chrisander. His name is Chrisander Baccioni, the fifth bearer of that name. As much as I think you are unsuitable company for my grandson, I have to thank you for bringing him to my attention. I have been looking for him ever since his mother registered his birth at the American Embassy. Unfortunately, because she used various names and had no fixed address, I was unable to track her down. You have no idea how happy I was to find someone had requested her death certificate and Chrisander's birth certificate."

Even as stressed as he was, he found it odd that she hadn't used Marie's name or mentioned that she was her daughter.

Matt interrupted. "Kathleen, Stephanie and their driver arrived at your parents' place an hour and a half before Nate called. That was where the registrar sent the certificates you requested while he was being held. Your mum sent them over to ours and Kate called me home. Twenty minutes later we got the call from Nate. We came up in her limo."

Jase didn't even glance at the Americans as the door to the waiting area opened and a white coated, middle-aged man entered. He looked tired.

"Bacon family?"

"It's Baccioni," Mrs Baccioni said firmly before anyone else could get a word in. "How is my grandson?"

Although Jase wanted to tell this woman to shut the hell up, at least her attitude seemed to be getting information he hadn't been able to. The quiet girl with her didn't look as if she was much older than Chris and he wondered where she fit into this, a cousin or sister perhaps? He dismissed the man with them as a hireling.

The doctor checked the chart in his hand, then looked up at the sea of faces. "I have a Mathew Kemp listed as his next of kin?"

"That's me, Chris is my brother."

"Half-brother. And his name is Chrisander, not Chris," Mrs Baccioni stated firmly.

The doctor pursed his lips. "That can all be sorted out at a later date. Right now, I'm more concerned about my patient's health rather than his legal name. He's suffered a significant brain trauma from coming into contact with a car windscreen at speed. There has been significant swelling and we've induced a medical coma to prevent further damage. He also has a broken femur which we will keep in traction until he's stable enough for surgery, but that isn't a priority right now."

"Is he going to be alright?" Jase asked.

The doctor gave them all a sympathetic expression that made Jase's teeth itch. "The brain is a complicated organ; it's difficult to make definite predictions in cases such as these. But people with similar injuries can and do fully recover and he also has youth on his side."

Jase knew when he was being bullshitted, and it appeared so did Kathleen Baccioni as she voiced exactly what he was thinking.

"But most do not?"

"Chris will," Matt said with determination.

"We'll do everything we can to give him the best chance possible. Now if you'll excuse me?"

"Can we see him?" Jase said quickly. He needed to confirm with his own eyes that Chris was still alive.

"Only two visitors at a time. This way."

Mrs Baccioni immediately pressed ahead.

"You go in first," Matt told Jase. Although he was grateful, Matt's immediate assumption that this woman had priority over either of them pissed him off.

259

"No, we'll go in together. She's a complete stranger to him. This is about Chris, not Mrs High and Mighty. He needs familiarity around him."

"He's my grandson."

Jase was grateful when Matt spoke to her, as he was about to lose it. *Who would have thought that it would be 'stay at home' Matt out of the pair of them who would be keeping it together?*

"I understand that, but you are also a stranger. I'm not placing blame, just stating a fact. Besides, your daughter made him paranoid about his real name and details. It took Jase weeks to track down his full name and age. Chris may not react well if he works out who you are before he's ready."

She favoured Matt with a condescending stare. "He's unconscious Mr Kemp; he won't know who's here or who's not. I've waited eighteen years to see my grandson, so I'm–"

The doctor interrupted her. "Actually, most patients report having memories of when they were in comas. They aren't always accurate, as the brain plays tricks on you, but familiar voices definitely help. Apparently it's like a dream state; outside influences can cross over. He may think he's in a totally different environment to the one he's in, but it's likely that he'll know on some level that you're with him. I suggest a familiar person stays and talks to him as much as possible. To facilitate that, we have a twenty-four hour visiting policy in the ICU."

They followed him to a set of wide blue double doors, much like any of the others in the hospital. The doctor paused at the entrance to use the disinfectant dispenser on the wall.

"There are a lot of machines in there, but they are all there to either help him or to monitor his condition. He's on various monitors, is being artificially ventilated and has a urine catheter in place. His fractured leg is raised and in a traction brace. He also has a bandage around his head, and his hair has been shaved around the impact site. There are various other superficial cuts, and quite a lot of bruises and swelling." He gave them another sympathetic expression.

"I'm afraid it all looks quite dramatic, but even though it doesn't look like it, it's still him. Don't be frightened to talk or touch him, just try to stay positive, because he might pick it up if you're not. We don't know why some people fight and survive injuries like this and why some don't, but positivity can't hurt. If you feel like it's getting too much, leave the room and come back when you've settled yourself. The machines may beep, but the staff are there to readjust anything you might disturb. Ok?"

Matt nodded, pale and determined. Jase guessed that was probably how he looked too.

"Mrs Baccioni? How about I tell you a little about your grandson while we wait? He's quite a character," his dad said and Jase gave him a tight, grateful smile.

Taking a deep breath, Jase used the disinfectant dispenser on the wall beside the doors, before moving into the room.

He didn't look real. In fact, if the doctor hadn't pointed out which bed he was in, he would have had a problem working out which of the six horribly still patients was Chris. Matt's hand on his back brought his focus back to the situation at hand. Pushing his own feelings down, he forced a smile and approached the bed.

Leaning over, he placed a soft kiss onto the half of Chris's forehead that was pale and yellowish rather than swollen and blue/black.

"Can't leave you alone for a minute can I? Don't worry, we'll get through this just like we've got through everything else."

Matt sat down on the one padded chair next to the bed and took Chris's hand; it had a drip in it. "He's not going to like this when he wakes up."

Jase couldn't agree more. The doctor had said to talk to him, but he couldn't think of a thing to say. Chris wouldn't want to hear about his day as a bailiff, he'd made that quite clear this morning. If Chris had been awake, Jase would have been quizzing him about his day, about what Nate had been going on about, about who had nearly killed him a few hours ago.

It was a surreal thought that if the driver of the car was in the room right now, and if he still had a sidearm, he was a hundred percent sure that he would calmly and deliberately shoot the bastard right in the centre of his forehead.

"Perhaps we should tell them about his...issues," Matt looked up at him.

The uncertain plea had the effect of clicking him back into professional mode, which was probably what Matt had intended. If Chris could hear them, on whatever level, he needed them to be strong and confident of a positive outcome.

"I'll deal. You stay here and don't let 'Morticia' at him. I don't buy the 'I'm a perfect parent' routine. One of us is always with him, agreed?"

Matt shifted uncomfortably. "I'll do my best, but with Kate and the business, it's–"

Jase put his hand on his best friend's shoulder. "I get it. I'll stay with him here, but I could do with being spelled every couple of days so I can get a decent sleep. I'm sure my folks, Nate and maybe even Russel will help out too. Stay for the next hour or so then Dad can take you back."

Jase patted Matt's shoulder, leaned over and pecked Chis on the cheek, whispered, "Back in a minute, Tigger," before going to talk to the nurse in charge about what they could expect from Chris when he woke up. Because that was exactly what was going to happen; Chris was going to wake up.

An hour later, Matt swapped places with Kathleen Baccioni.

"Oh my poor baby," she murmured when she stopped by the bed. "What have they done to you?"

She reached out a hand and cupped his face in a touching gesture that had tears prickling at Jase's eyes. "I'm so very sorry I didn't find you sooner."

He was about to sit down and try to get to know her a little more when a nurse came over. "Mr Rosewood? There's a police detective here to see you."

The thought of leaving Chris again made his stomach twist.

"Don't worry, I won't leave his side; he and I have a lot of catching up to do. But before you go, is it true that he has a passion for art?"

The question brought a smile to his lips. "He's obsessive. It helps him control his hyperactivity. Today was his first day at art college. He was so excited that I don't think he slept a wink last night."

"He gets that from me, the art not the hyperactivity. I was a struggling artist when his Nonno swept me off my feet. My husband enjoyed art, but he couldn't draw anything more than stick figures."

"What did he do?"

"The same thing I still do, run the Baccioni Auction House. You might not have heard of it, as you clearly don't run in those sort of circles, but it's the most prestigious auction house in the Americas. Chrisander is heir to it all," she said wistfully as she continued to stare at Chris's immobile form while she stroked a gnarled, age-spotted finger over his hand. "Now go speak to the police and find out who did this to my boy."

When he came back, he found a priest anointing Chris's forehead and speaking in Latin while Mrs Baccioni knelt beside the bed her eyes shut and her hands clasped together.

"What's going on here?" he asked.

The earnest young man in black turned to him after touching Chris's forehead once again. "I am blessing this young man at the request of his grandmother."

"How do you know he's even a catholic?"

"The Lord's love does not discriminate," the priest said, peace radiating from every pore.

"As far as I know, Chris has never expressed an interest in religion, so perhaps we should wait till we can ask him about his preferences?"

Mrs Baccioni sat back in her chair. "Don't you think that my grandson deserves the right to enter the Kingdom of Heaven?"

It was difficult to keep the bland expression on his face. "That's not going to be an issue anytime soon, so how about you stop indoctrinating him into a religion without his consent?"

The priest kept his serene expression. "I understand what a terrible time this must be for you, but Chrisander's grandmother finds comfort in me being here, and prayer has many positive effects. Surely you wouldn't object to that?"

Jase clenched his jaw. "Firstly, he hate's that name. Secondly, how do you know he's not Church of England, Muslim, Buddhist, Pagan or a card carrying atheist? Finding out you've perform a..."

A petite nurse approached them with a face like thunder. "This is not the place for an argument about religion. Please take this outside."

Jase rubbed his hand over his head, as the priest started to put a black covered bible and a bottle of oil back into a small bag. He was being a dick to this man just because Kathleen was winding him up.

"Look, I'm sorry, Father. As I said, I don't know if Chris would appreciate the religion thing or not. I found the services and the padre helpful when I was in the army even though I'm not religious myself. I won't object as long as he doesn't, ok?"

The priest smiled gently. "Bless you my son. The hospital chapel is always open for quiet reflection or if you need a sympathetic ear. Yes, I am a catholic minister, but the chapel is staffed by a rota of clergy from all faiths." He turned to Kathleen. "Would you like me to show you where the chapel is?"

Jase was left alone with a still, silent body that bore little resemblance to the vibrant person he'd left that morning.

CHAPTER 3

Chris

A clatter pulled him out of sleep. Each time he woke it was a little easier, the disorientation disappeared a little faster. His memory was improving although he still couldn't remember anything much about that day or the ones since.

"Good morning, Chrisander," a pretty young nurse announced as she put the tray down on the rolling table and pulled it across his lap.

"Kis, no kisander," he slurred, but his speech was getting better little by little.

"My, aren't we getting bossy?" she said with a smile. "Today, I have toast and Weetabix for you." She reached for the spoon beside the frankly revolting looking beige mess. Not even his dad had to eat slop like this.

"Me," he said and motioned with his right hand for her to put the food within reach. The fact that he had a tippy cup, complete with lid and spout, was both a blessing and a curse. It was bloody humiliating, but at least he could drink without spilling it down himself.

He wondered where Jase was, but maybe the silly sod had finally gone to find a bed. Time was still very much a fluid quantity. Although his room had a window, the long summer days meant it was almost impossible to tell whether it was morning, afternoon or evening, not that it mattered very much. People came in and out at all hours to poke at him and give him pills and his sensitivity to light meant the blinds had to be kept closed. To tell the truth, any stimulation, sound, movement or light made his headache worse. The only thing that didn't was touch.

At least the bang on the head seemed to have killed the hyperactivity demon; he couldn't keep his eyes open for more than about an hour at a time.

They'd got the message about the IV's after he'd taken the third one out. The poor nurse had only just turned her back when he pulled it out, even with Jase and his brand new grandparent in the room. If they'd had half a brain, they would have put it in his good right arm rather than in his left. He would have had far more difficulty in taking it out that way, but he still would've managed it somehow.

Thinking about his brand new grandparent made his headache worse. As a child, he'd learned not to ask questions about family. Every time he asked his mum, she'd said his father didn't want him. Mentioning her childhood or her family elicited a frown, followed by an immediate need for more of her 'medicine'. He'd been around six before he realised that not everyone's mum had to have daily 'medicine' from a syringe that left her staring at the ceiling with heavy eyes and a vacant smile. He'd only been a little older when he learned not to talk to anyone about his mother's medicine, or anything else that happened at home.

The table under the window contained more get well cards than he could count. As well as the family ones, it looked as if his little nephew's class had turned him into a class project, not to mention the people at the college. He didn't recognise the names on the cards from the art college Jase read out, but they all seemed to know him as they mentioned hoping he got back on the pole as soon as possible.

Nonna, which was apparently Italian for grandmother, had asked what the pole comment referred to. He'd pretended to nod off to avoid the question, it didn't take much acting.

Although he didn't know her, he had an idea that most uptight grannies, and Nonna definitely had a rod up her backside, wouldn't be overjoyed to find their longed for grandson made his living as an exotic dancer in a gay club. The fact that she often dragged a priest along with her, didn't give him much hope that she was liberal minded. Nevertheless, the father had a calm, pleasant voice and even though he didn't possess the powers of concentration to actually take in the words as he read from the Bible, it was nice to listen to.

While Nonna treated him like a little boy, she put the wind up everyone else in her vicinity. Even Jase seemed a little intimidated and the doctors were shaking in their lab coats.

He still couldn't get his head around the fact she was here; not that he could get his head around much right now. Even speaking was a major undertaking. Although it wasn't so much that his mouth wasn't obeying him at all anymore, but that making any sort of noise felt like thunder claps going off in his head.

In less than five months, he'd gone from effectively having no family or friends and sleeping rough, to having a brother, a sister-in-law, a nephew, a flat and steady boyfriend. Not to mention a loaded, American grandmother whom his mother had acted as if she was the devil incarnate.

His medical issues were just as difficult to come to terms with. No one would give him a straight answer about his prognosis, not that he could ask many questions.

He'd poked at his face and head briefly before Jase had told him to stop it and he hadn't seen a mirror. Judging from everyone's 'sad' faces when they looked at him, and Nonna's almost constant 'my poor baby's' he probably looked pretty crappy.

Plus, not only could he not move, he didn't want to. It scared the shit out of him. What was if the hyperactivity came back while he was still unable to move, it'd be like a being inside a flesh prison. If that happened he might as well start shooting up, because being completely out of it was the only way he'd cope with that without losing his marbles.

Using the buttons on the side on the bed, he sat himself a little more upright to tackle his unwanted breakfast. As he picked up a piece of cold toast and stared at it suspiciously with his one fully functioning eye, the nurse straightened the bed, checked the blood flow in his busted leg by pressing on his foot and changed his charming catheter bag.

It tasted like cardboard and the noise as he chewed was like a heavy metal concert. He put it down again, sucking it to death wasn't going to happen.

"Not hungry?" she asked as she came back in from the ensuite bathroom he could see, but not use. It might as well have been a hundred miles away, not eight feet from the end of his bed.

He waved at his ear with his good hand. "Too loud," he mouthed rather than said.

"Do you want to try the Weetabix then?"

The face he pulled must have given her the correct idea. The consequences of all that roughage and his inability to leave the bed, didn't bear thinking about. Having a plastic tube in his dick and his pee in a bag hanging from the side of his bed for everyone to see was bad enough; having to use a bedpan would be the living end.

"You do know that if you don't start eating we'll have to put you back on an IV?"

He gave her the finger with his right hand as it was easier than talking.

"Now, if you can do that with both hands, I'll be impressed."

Concentrating so hard it made his head throb, he stared at his disobedient limb laying on the blanket and managed to extend the appropriate digit.

A ripple of applause had him looking up. Jase was standing just inside the door with Dr Beckett. Both had smiles on their faces, but Jase was beaming.

"Maybe you two can get him to eat something because I certainly can't. He says the toast is too loud and the Weetabix prompted the finger."

Jase's smile turned into a frown as he came over. "You've got to eat something; we're going to the states today."

Chris blinked. He vaguely remembered it being mentioned, but he didn't know it'd be today. He couldn't leave the country without saying goodbye to Matt, Kate and Ryan.

"Now?" he mouthed.

"Not till later this afternoon," Dr Beckett said. "We have to do a few last checks, another CAT scan, get an IV set up—"

"No," he said as clearly as he could.

"It's a normal safety measure, just so they can administer any drugs that are needed quickly. You'd still have a cannula in now if you hadn't kept taking it out."

The nurse joined in with the doctor. "If toast is too loud, how noisy do you think an aircraft is going to be?"

He gave them the finger again.

"How about you get those tests done while he thinks about it?" Jase said.

Dr Beckett pointed at Chris. "Ok, but we will be talking about this later. I'll get a porter take you down."

Jase looked at the uneaten breakfast and pulled a face. "Not that appetising is it? Is there anything else you fancy?"

Chris drew an 'M' on the table, followed by a 'P' with his right index finger.

The nurse, who had been leaning over to see what he was doing, frowned. "McDonalds pancakes are not nutritious."

"And that is?" Jase pointed at the dismal display on the tray. "Tell you what, if you behave yourself while the doctors do their stuff, I'll get Matt to bring some in before we leave."

The thought of leaving his newly found family made his eyes prickle. He hadn't seen Ryan since before the attack. He'd promised the five-year-old that he wouldn't disappear without telling Matt where he was going. Although Matt knew, he wanted to tell Ryan he'd be coming back personally.

"Ry comin?"

Jase didn't look happy. "He's got school, besides you do look a little—"

"Peese?"

"I'll tell you what, I'll talk Matt into letting Ryan play hooky and bringing in McDonald's pancakes, if you let the doctor put in an IV for the flight."

He couldn't believe Jase had just delivered such an ultimatum. He wouldn't really stop him seeing Ryan if he didn't agree to have a bloody needle, would he? It was a damn low blow, but Jase wasn't the only one who could play hard ball.

Using his right hand, pushed the rolling table away and he tucked his left arm across his body in an approximation of folding his arms. "Mm not goin'. Stay Ry."

Looking exhausted, Jase walked over to his bed. "As much as I hate to admit it, I can't keep you safe here. The police haven't got any firm leads about who did this, but it's likely it's connected to you giving the statement about the kidnapping. The police are working on the assumption that it was a professional hit to ensure you never got to the witness box. I agree with them. Your grandmother's chauffeur is outside your door as much as he can be, but neither of us can stay awake twenty-four seven.

"It's not fair to expect your friends and family to guard you for what could be months and it's not fair to put Ryan in danger from being near you. What would have happened if he'd been with you when they ran you over?"

"You bastard," he managed as tears prickled his eyes.

Jase gave him a crooked, sympathetic smile. "So, do we have a deal, Tigger? IV for Ryan and pancakes before we head off to the good old U S of A? Cos you know I'll get my way in the end anyway."

He knew when he was beaten, but he also didn't trust these anonymous, almost interchangeable, medics as far as he could throw them. There was only one medical professional he really trusted.

"Nate do?"

Jase shook his head. "Sorry, he can't come, he's got another houseguest who needs him more than you do right now. He said goodbye yesterday, remember?"

Chris didn't, but it didn't mean it hadn't happened. He remembered being told multiple times what his medical issues were but he still hadn't quite got his head around it. Talking of heads, his bloody well hurt. Leaning his head back on the pillow, he closed his eyes to shut out the light that hadn't bothered him at all five minutes ago, but was now stabbing him like a bayonet.

Jase's hand cupped his face on the uninjured side and his thumb rubbed over his cheek. "You ok?"

"Head," he murmured, keeping his eyes closed.

The chair creaking beside him meant Jase was sitting down and he felt his left hand being picked up. A thumb rubbed firmly over the back of it. He might not be able to make the limb obey him properly yet, but he hadn't lost sensation in it. It was reassuring that Jase wasn't scared of the pretty much useless lump of flesh, it certainly freaked him out and he didn't even want to think about his leg.

"Don't worry, we'll be back before you know it, and there's always Skype. You'll be able to keep in touch with everything that's going on here. By the time college starts in the autumn we could be back and there's always next year. The world of education had lived without you this long, I'm sure it can survive a little longer.

"Besides, don't you want to find out where your mum grew up? You know about your dad's side of the family, it only seems fair that you find out about your mum's too. And don't forget that–"

Chris's eyes flew open as his head started to spin. The nurse was withdrawing a needle from the cannula she'd just inserted in his left hand. Jase was holding it for her. As he hadn't felt the needle, Jase must have been rubbing in local anaesthetic cream while he spoke. The shock of the betrayal froze him for a brief second, then pain spiked in his head and leg as he twisted to pull the invading metal in his body.

Jase's large hands closed around both his wrists as he leaned across his body to keep him still.

"It's alright, it'll be easier if you're sleep," Jase said urgently. Lassitude swept over him like a wave and although he tried, he couldn't fight the morphine any more than he'd been able to fight the unwanted heroin a few weeks ago.

"That's it, just relax, it'll be ok..." was the last thing he heard before the darkness closed over him.

It was exactly what the kidnappers had said, but it hadn't been alright then, and it wouldn't be alright now.

Printed in Poland
by Amazon Fulfillment
Poland Sp. z o.o., Wrocław